SISTER MINE

Also by

TAWNI O'DELL

Back Roads

Coal Run

TAWNI O'DELL

SISTER MINE

A Novel

Shaye Areheart Books
NEW YORK

Published in the United States by Shaye Areheart Books, an imprint of the
Crown Publishing Group, a division of Random House, Inc., New York.
www.crownpublishing.com

Shaye Areheart Books is a registered trademark and the Shaye Areheart Books
colophon is a trademark of Random House, Inc.

Library of Congress Cataloging-in-Publication Data
O'Dell, Tawni.
  Sister Mine : a novel / Tawni O'Dell—1st ed.
     p. cm.
1. Taxicab drivers—Fiction. 2. Sisters—Fiction. 3. Coal mines and
mining—Fiction. 4. Pennsylvania—Fiction. I. Title
  PS3565.D428S57   2007
  813'.54—dc22   2006015355

ISBN 978-0-307-35126-5

Printed in the United States of America

Design by Lynne Amft

10 9 8 7 6 5 4 3 2 1

First Edition

To my biggest fan,
from his biggest fan

For my father, Joe O'Dell

SISTER MINE

Chapter One

I DRIVE A CAB in a town where no one needs a cab but plenty of people need rides. I've been paid with casseroles, lip gloss, plumbing advice, beer, prayers for my immortal soul, and promises to mow my yard, but this is the first time I've ever been offered something living.

The girl's around eleven or twelve. About twenty years too soon, she already possesses the self-centered, self-destructive attitude of a survivor of a string of bad relationships, failed diets, a drinking problem, and the realization that life is just a bunch of confusing, painful stuff that fills up the time between your favorite TV shows.

Her outfit looks like it's been picked out by a pedophile with a penchant for banging hillbilly girls, but more than likely her mom bought it for her. She's dressed in a pair of tight denim shorts with eyelet trim, a pair of clear plastic platform sandals encrusted in silver glitter, and a skimpy halter made from red bandanna material. Her exposed midriff sports a unicorn tattoo which I hope is water soluble.

She wants a ride from Jolly Mount to the mall and wants to pay for it with her four-year-old brother.

"I'm not doing this for my health," I explain to her as I put the nozzle back into the gas pump. "This is my job. I have to make a living. I can't pay my mortgage or my heating bill with a toddler."

"You could sell him," she suggests.

"That's against the law."

"The law won't ever find out."

I screw my gas cap back on. She watches me while she stands with all her weight positioned on one skinny leg, one nonexistent hip thrust out with her hand resting on it, the bent angle and sharp point of her elbow making an almost perfect triangle of bony flesh against the yellow custom paint job of my Subaru Outback.

Her other hand holds the hand of her brother, not tightly but not casually either, the way a daisy holds on to its petals.

"Maybe he doesn't want to be sold," I tell her. "Maybe he wants to stay here."

"Then you could keep him. He can't do much now but when he gets older he could be like a slave for you."

I look down at the little guy. The spray of freckles across his nose and the hand-me-down jeans with rips in the knees and the cuffs rolled up several times remind me of my own son, Clay, when he was that age.

He turns twenty-three today. I have to remember to give him a call later. I don't make a big deal over his birthday now that he's grown. I don't let myself get emotional either, since the emotions surrounding his birth have always left me feeling torn up inside. I guess that's what happens when the best thing in your life is the result of the worst mistake of your life.

I wasn't all that much older than this girl standing in front of me now when my dad dropped me off at the entrance of the Centresburg Hospital, already two hours into my contractions, and told me to call him when I was "done."

Shannon was with us, sitting in the cab of the pickup crushed between the enormous globe of her sister's belly and the silent, hulking presence of our coal miner father who'd been pulled out of the damp, black earth midway through his shift in answer to my emergency call. Since he was going right back to work, he hadn't bothered to clean up or change out of his dirty coveralls. His face and hands were coated with rock dust: the crushed limestone sprayed inside mines to control the combustible coal dust. It gave his skin a bluish-white pallor, like someone who'd been frozen solid and dug out of a snowdrift.

Shannon was this girl's age and full of the same sort of generalized contempt and misplaced confidence in her ability to not care about anything as long as she told herself nothing was worth caring about, but I remember she looked worried that day as I climbed down out of the truck wincing and breathing funny and cradling the baby still inside me. I couldn't tell if she was afraid for me or afraid for herself because she was going home with dad alone.

"I don't believe in slavery," I tell the girl. "Besides, maybe he wants to stay with you."

"I don't think so."

"I think he's pretty attached to you."

We both look at the boy this time. He doesn't have the exuberance of most children his age. He hasn't been fidgeting or whining or trying to get away. He stares back at us with the endlessly patient gaze of a sheep waiting at the gate to be let out or let in.

"But he ain't mine. He's my mom's," she says.

"He doesn't belong to you or your mom."

I walk around to the driver's side of my car. They follow me.

"He's not a dog. He's a person. You can't own another person. Although another person can own you. You'll learn about that when you start dating."

"I already date."

"Okay, enough." I hold up my hands in a sign of defeat. "This is more information than I need. If you don't have any money, what else do you have?"

She opens up her grimy purse, pink with a jeweled kitten on it. I would have killed for a purse like that when I was her age although I never would have taken it outside the house for fear E.J. or some of the other guys would have made fun of me for being a sissy.

She pokes through the meager contents with the tips of her fingers, which are polished in chipped purple: a cracked pink plastic Barbie wallet, a lipstick, a comb, a piece of notebook paper folded into a small square, a lighter shaped like a pig, and a handful of what looks like ordinary gravel.

She gestures with her head toward the boy.

"Kenny collects rocks."

I take the lighter and flick it on. The flames come out the pig's nose.

"The lighter," I state.

"No way. I love that lighter. I just stole . . . I just bought it with my own money inside."

"No lighter, no ride."

It's her turn to size me up. She looks me over. I wonder what she thinks about my outfit, if she's being more generous than I was with hers. Ancient scuffed Frye harness boots, long bare legs, a camouflage miniskirt, olive drab tank top, cheap drugstore sunglasses, and a pink Stetson that Clay gave me two years ago as a Mother's Day gag gift that I was never supposed to wear: looks like she was dressed by a Vietnam vet with a penchant for banging middle-aged cowgirls.

Her gaze leaves me and runs over the car. JOLLY MOUNT CAB is written on both sides but about a month ago, someone blacked out JOLLY and CAB on the driver's side door and added the word ME.

It now reads MOUNT ME.

I don't have any idea who the vandal is. I'm sure it was nothing personal. I've even taken my time getting it fixed. I tell myself it's because I don't have the money, but part of the reason is simple admiration and encouragement for the creative thought process behind it.

When E.J. and I were in sixth grade and the Union Hall was still standing and hosting community events, a square dancing club called

The Naughty Pines came to town to put on an exhibition. E.J. and I switched two letters and the next day the marquee read TONIGHT ONLY: THE NAUGHTY PENIS.

We thought we were the two most brilliant people alive.

It was inevitable that we would be caught, since we bragged openly about what we had done. Eventually word spread throughout the school, and we were sent to the principal's office. I never did understand why our teachers were allowed to become involved, since the act didn't occur on school property or during school hours, but I guess they believed that, since I didn't have a mom to teach me right from wrong, they were responsible for disciplining me.

Apparently, I've passed the girl's inspection because she hands me the lighter and opens the back door.

My cell rings.

"Jolly Mount Cab," I answer.

"I need a cab to drive me from Harrisburg to Jolly Mount," a man's voice greets me. "There's not a single cab company here that will do it. One of the drivers I spoke to recommended you."

"What'd he say?"

"He said he thought you'd take the job."

"No, that's not what I mean. What'd he say about me?"

"He said he thought you'd take the job," he repeats.

The girl crawls inside the car and motions for her brother to follow. Once he's seated beside her she makes him fasten his seat belt but doesn't put on her own.

"What'd he really say about me?" I ask him.

A brief silence.

"He said you're attractive, although he didn't use the word 'attractive,' but I think that was the point he was trying to make."

"Does that make you more eager to have me drive you?"

"I doubt I'd be interested in you in that way."

"Why not? Are you gay? Faithful? Celibate? Impotent?"

"Picky."

"Fair enough," I say.

I'm trying to figure him out. His manner of speaking sounds almost rehearsed. There's not the slightest trace of any kind of a regional accent in his voice; he enunciates too well, and he uses very little inflection. He talks rapidly but he's also fond of dramatic pauses. He's sort of a cross between Captain Kirk and the guy who did the English voice-overs for all the old Kung Fu movies.

My guess is he grew up talking one way and puts a lot of effort into not talking that way anymore.

"Where are you exactly?" I ask him.

"I'm here at this ridiculous, godforsaken excuse for an airport."

"Harrisburg International?"

"International? You can't even fly to New York from here."

"That's true, but there's one flight to Canada."

Another silence.

"Can you pick me up or not?"

"Yeah. Sure. I can pick you up. You realize it's a two-hour drive?"

"Yes, I do. The other cab drivers enlightened me. Is it also true that there are no hotels in Jolly Mount?"

"The nearest motel would be in Centresburg, about thirty miles from here."

"Unbelievable."

"What's your name, sir?"

"Why do you need to know?"

"Because I'm about to invest four hours of my life and sixty dollars worth of gas on the assumption that you're going to be there when I show up. The least you can do in return is tell me your name."

He doesn't answer.

"Fine. I'll just call you Sparky."

"Gerald," he says sharply. "Gerald Kozlowski."

He hangs up.

I click my phone shut happily. A fare from the airport. Big bucks.

Then I notice the two little ones in my backseat.

"Sorry, kids," I tell them while opening the door and motioning for them to get out. "There's been a change in plans. I can't take you to the mall after all."

Kenny does what he's told. The girl glares at me.

"Why the hell not?"

"It was a bad idea to begin with, now that I think about it. If I take you to the mall then you're going to be stranded at the mall. How will you get home?"

She gets out and slams the door. She doesn't answer my question.

"Where is home anyway?" I keep after her. "And what are you doing out by yourself in the middle of town on a Saturday morning?"

"It ain't none of your business where our home is and we can be wherever we want to be. It's a free country."

"So I've been told."

She joins Kenny and takes up a stance next to him with her hands jabbed back on her hips. I notice her gaze flicker toward a red Radio Flyer wagon parked next to the front door of the convenience store.

"Well, I guess you can't live too far away if you pulled Kenny in a wagon," I comment. "Where are your parents?"

All I get from her in reply is hostile silence and sharp elbows.

Kenny gives me the sheep stare.

"Who are your parents?"

Nothing.

"Can I at least know your name?"

She thinks about it.

"Fanci."

I know I've heard the name before. It's unusual enough that it sticks out in my mind, although having an adjective or noun for a name that conjures up images of pretty things isn't that strange around here. I went to school with a Taffeta Tate and a Sparkle Wisniewski. Clay briefly dated a girl named Dainty Frost who had a sister named Lacey.

"What about a last name?" I ask.

"Simms."

"Is your dad Choker Simms?"

"Yeah."

"Well, that explains a lot," I say under my breath.

"Do you know him?" she asks me.

"Yes, I do."

"You probably heard bad things about him because he was in jail but none of it's true. He was set up by a lady cop who had the hots for him and decided to ruin his life when he spurned her."

I'm so stunned by this explanation I laugh out loud.

"'Spurned'?" I practically choke on the word.

"You know. Spurned. When somebody tells you they don't love you."

"Your dad . . . ," I start to say, then stop as I look down into their little faces, hers daring me to say anything bad about their father so she can defend him and his full of genuine curiosity.

She holds out her hand, palm up.

"Gimme my lighter back."

I give it to her.

She returns it to her purse, grabs Kenny by the forearm, and stalks off.

IT TAKES ALL of two minutes for me to drive through downtown Jolly Mount. Aside from the Snappy's gas station and convenience store, there's a Subway, three bars, one church, a drive-thru branch of a bank, a red brick post office, and a two-story abandoned corner building that used to house a five-and-dime store, and an insurance agency.

A corridor of tall, thin row homes, identical except for the amount of color and care spent on them, forms the outlying border. There's a house of flaking bubblegum pink, one of pale turquoise, one a fading canary yellow, and two painted a mint green—all the colors of a bucket of sidewalk chalk interspersed between the traditional whites and tans. Some are well tended; others appear to be uninhabited except for the lawn ornaments, and the limp curtains hanging at lopsided angles behind windows smoky with age and grime.

I take the most direct route to the interstate even though I prefer driving the forsaken, twisting side roads where the worn-down, wooded mountains lie on all sides of me like the backs of slumbering giants.

When I was a kid, I used to believe the land was as alive as any fairy tale ogre. I believed it could feel, and I went around filling in potholes with hay and mud with the same care I used when putting sandwich bags full of ice on my own bruises.

The drive is long but I don't mind. It's beautiful countryside where Nature's majesty and Man's shabby attempts to survive in it have blended together over time into a comfortable harmony of abandoned industries and permanent hills.

The mountains rise and fall for as far as the eye can see like a dark, paralyzed sea. Between the waves are valleys peppered with towns. They have different names but they're always the same town: straight rows of small, dilapidated houses; a few cold, rust-streaked smokestacks; a white church steeple; a gutted warehouse or factory or a silent quarry; an occasional jarring splash of color in the form of a Domino's pizza sign, or a Blockbuster Video storefront, or the ubiquitous golden arches.

I take off my hat and roll down my window and enjoy the mild air blowing in my face and through my hair.

It's been unseasonably warm and sunny for late April this past week. Everyone's enjoying the break from our usual cold and dull white skies this time of year, but no one is taking it seriously. It could snow tomorrow. I've been to cookouts in June where I've worn shorts and a parka.

Picking up fares at the new Harrisburg airport is a piece of cake. It's only a few years old, clean, modern, and never crowded. It's true that there aren't many flights to places people want to go. It's more of a have-to airport: I have to go to Detroit on business; I have to go to Cincinnati to visit my sister; I have to go to Birmingham for a college buddy's wedding.

I've never flown in or out of it. I've only been on a plane once in my life and that was when I lived in D.C. and briefly screwed around with a senator. He flew me to a tropical island once in the private jet of some corporate bigwig who I'm willing to bet contributed mightily to his campaign fund.

I was more interested in the pilot and spent most of the long weekend with him while the senator was tied up with conference calls to Washington, assuring various people that he was going to do things he wasn't going to do, and private calls to his wife, assuring her he was someplace he wasn't.

He wasn't a bad guy, though. I wouldn't say he was morally corrupt, just morally inept. Lying was simply a part of his nature, like undertipping.

I don't regret my time with him. He was generous to me and showed me the Caribbean. In return, I taught him how to check his car for cut brake lines for that inevitable day when his wife was going to try and kill him.

I pull up to the curb at arrivals. I know exactly who I'm looking for even though I've never met the man.

Kozlowski's cell phone number on my caller ID had a Manhattan area code, so it's doubtful he'll express any dismay over the amount of money I'm going to charge him for this trip. He wants to hire a cab rather than rent a car, which would probably end up being cheaper in the long run and more convenient for him.

I've gathered from all this that he's a lifelong, non-driving New Yorker who has money but earned it by working for it because the way he speaks isn't natural Snob-ese but something he learned. So I look for a man standing by himself dressed in black and looking casually uncomfortable.

I spot him immediately.

I'd put him in his mid-thirties. Short dark hair parted on the side. Eyes the color of weak tea. His individual features would be considered the ideal shape and size by most people. As a matter of fact, there might be laminated Polaroid snapshots of his nose, lips, eyebrows, ears, and chin in a plastic surgeon's catalog of parts somewhere. The combination of all of them makes for a face no one can criticize or remember, the kind of face a police sketch artist could capture perfectly yet no one would ever be able to identify.

He's wearing glossy black leather loafers, black wrinkle-free pants with sharp pleats down the front of the legs, a braided black leather belt, and a black silk T-shirt. His black suit jacket is hooked to his finger and thrown over his shoulder. The shirt alone probably costs more than my monthly car payment.

I try to make small talk with him during the drive but he won't bite. He spends the two hours perusing papers from his briefcase and talking on his cell. It's obvious from several of the conversations that he's a lawyer who deals predominantly with contracts.

Nothing I do gets a rise out of him. He doesn't comment on any of the music I play: Sonny Rollins followed by AC/DC followed by the

Broadway score from *My Fair Lady*. He doesn't mind the windows open. He doesn't object to my periodic, animated cursing of left-laners, the self-centered, oblivious assholes who get in the passing lane and don't pass. He doesn't respond at all when I ask him if he wants to hit a McDonald's drive-thru and get an Egg McMuffin.

"We're almost there," I tell him when we're about ten miles south of Centresburg. "Do you want me to drop you somewhere in Jolly Mount or do you want me to take you straight to your motel?"

I glance in my rearview mirror. He begins packing away papers in his briefcase.

"What's your name again?" he asks without looking up.

"Shae-Lynn."

"Right. Shae-Lynn. You can take me to my hotel for now, but I was wondering if you'd be available if I need you during the next couple days to drive me around?"

"I might be."

"I'd pay you well."

I make up my mind instantly to do it, not only because I need the money, but because I want to know what this guy is doing here.

"I guess I can make myself available," I tell him.

"Good," he says.

He clicks the briefcase shut and finally looks up, but not at me. When he speaks again, he's looking out the window.

"I imagine you know a lot of people around here," he says.

"You could say that."

"Do you know a Shannon Penrose?"

At the mention of the name, I temporarily forget where I am and what I'm doing and almost drive off the road. I glance in the rearview mirror, and he's giving me a strange look.

"I . . . ," I start to say, "I don't think so. No."

"Do you know any other Penroses? I've checked phone listings for towns in the area, and I couldn't find any. Although a lot of people are unlisted these days."

"Well," I say, quickly, while gathering my wits again, "Penrose is a common name around here."

"I don't think she's lived around here for a long time, but I know Jolly Mount is her hometown."

"Is that why you're here? You're trying to find her?"

"I have something very important to tell her. It's good news, I assure you."

"Sorry."

I don't trust him. That's why I lie, even though the truth wouldn't help him.

I finish the drive to the Comfort Inn with my heart pounding heavily in my chest.

Before he gets out of the car, he asks me if I'll drive him to Jolly Mount tonight, maybe take him to a bar or someplace where he can meet some locals. His word: locals. He lowers his voice when he says it and uses a dramatic courtroom pause as if he were addressing a jury that's nodding off.

I agree. After he gets out of the car, I watch him walk into the Comfort Inn. Then I pull into the parking lot of the Ruby Tuesday next door and sit.

I don't fall apart and begin to cry. I don't get angry. I don't allow myself to feel guilt or pain. I understand that I will have to deal with all of these emotions eventually, but for now I close my eyes and take deep breaths while trying to find the safe place in my soul.

It's a small, cozy room full of plush, overstuffed furniture, with a fire blazing in a fireplace and a velvet-eared puppy asleep on a rug on the floor, twitching in his dreams. On the table is a deep blue china plate the color of a predawn sky as the sun's glow from behind the mountains begins to lighten the black overhead. It's heaped with some of my mom's homemade cookies: chocolate chip, pecan tassies, and peanut butter thumbprints with Hershey's kisses stuck in the middle. Beside it sits a cup of hot chocolate with mounds of whipped cream. Outside a storm rages, but I know it can't touch me. The room is made of stone and has no doors. The more the wind blows and the thunder rumbles and the rain lashes the only window, the happier I am.

It's the place I always went to as a child whenever I missed my mom too much or when my dad's eyes lost their human spark and began to harden into the red-rimmed, black marble stare of a mad dog straining at his chain.

It's the place I still go to during those rare moments when I allow myself to think of Shannon.

My little sister, Shannon. If someone is looking for her, it must mean she's alive.

For the past eighteen years, I've believed my father killed her.

Chapter Two

JOLLY'S IS A BAR located on the edge of town in a three-story, peeling white clapboard house that used to be an inn. The building is unremarkable and probably never looked new even when it was built 150 years ago, but its age and scruffy simplicity give it a wistful, bygone elegance, like an old man wearing a red carnation in the buttonhole of his threadbare suit.

Somewhere during the inn's more recent history, it fell into the hands of Cam Jack—the owner of J&P Coal—just like everything else around town. He had no desire to modernize it or declare it a historic landmark and try and restore it to its original mediocre splendor, since both would require spending money.

Instead, he closed off the two top floors, leaving only the bar and restaurant open. Eventually he closed the dining room, too, not wanting to deal with the hassles and expense of running a restaurant, although he did keep a deep fryer and grill for when the bar patrons got the munchies.

The place is run by a large, friendly woman named Sandy Flock whose age is impossible to guess because of her size, but I think she's getting close to fifty. She has a pretty face with gemstone blue eyes and has spent her entire life hearing how it's such a shame for a girl with such a pretty face to be so fat when it was probably the pretty face that started her eating in the first place. Some women know what to do with beauty; other women are destroyed by it.

The double front doors are propped open. One side has a sign hanging on it that reads COME IN. WE'RE OPEN. The other side has a sign that reads: HOME OF THE JOLLY MOUNT FIVE. I think the sign is supposed to mean that the town of Jolly Mount is home to the Jolly Mount Five, not that the bar is their home, but they all spend enough time here that it could easily mean either.

I push through the screen doors and let my eyes adjust to the perennial dusk. The place is practically empty. On a day like today, even drunks are enticed by the unexpected sunshine and want to do their drinking outside.

Three burly men and one skinny one, all in ball caps and in need of a shave, are staggered about on stools hunched over beers. I recognize two, but not well enough to greet them.

Sandy spies me and calls out, "Hey, Shae-Lynn. What are you doing here on a day like today?"

"I need a drink," I tell her honestly.

I hold up a finger.

"Just one," I add.

I walk quickly past the old, gouged pool table sitting on massive wooden paws with unfurled claws next to the front windows, which are hung with heavy red curtains coated in a soft gray dust. The walls are papered in tiny brown stagecoaches and hostile red Indians and covered with photos, magazine articles, and newspaper clippings about the Jolly Mount Mine Disaster, four nightmarish days two years ago when five miners were trapped inside Josephine, J&P Mine No. 12. The men who work inside her call her Jojo.

The five miners were nicknamed the Jolly Mount Five by the press. E.J.'s one of them.

I can't help pausing by the collection of clippings and photos even though I've seen all of it a thousand times and I lived through it, too.

There's the *Time* magazine cover proclaiming in big red letters, "All Five Alive"; a copy of the congratulatory letter from the White House; the wire service photo of E.J., black-faced and strapped on an ambulance stretcher with his eyes tightly shut, that was seen all over the world; photos of the five of them posing with everyone from Senator Specter and Oprah Winfrey to Faith Hill and Mickey Mouse; and the newspaper article, "Miner's Girlfriend Tells Governor to Shove It," a recounting of the showdown I had with the governor three days into the rescue when I suspected the families weren't being told the truth about what was going on.

E.J. seemed pissed about the reference to us as a couple. I didn't care. I am not now and never have been E.J.'s girlfriend, but I understood that the press had to find a one-word label to slap on me that their readers could comprehend. It was obvious to all the reporters that I was intimately involved with him, but we weren't related and we weren't sleeping together. What did that make me? A friend? A former schoolmate? A longtime acquaintance? My relationship with E.J. could never be summed up in a banner headline.

I take a seat as far away from the others as I can.

One of the men nods at me.

I nod back.

I never know if people acknowledge me out of gratitude and respect, or fear and loathing. It's a hazard of my former profession.

"What'll you have? A beer?"

"I don't suppose you have any champagne?"

She smiles and shakes her head.

I got turned on to champagne when I dated this French professor at Georgetown. I had never had champagne or French wine before I met him. He was a real wine snob and equally picky about cheese. At first I thought he was a pretentious ass, but I was willing to overlook it because his accent alone was better foreplay than the physical stuff I'd had with most other men. He could practically talk me into an orgasm.

It turned out that once I tasted the French wines and cheeses he recommended, I realized he was right. They were incredible. And when he complained about California wines and Kraft singles it wasn't because he was a snob, it was because his culture produced something superior and he missed it. It would have been no different if I had gone to France and was depressed because I couldn't find a big gun.

He lived in this great old fixer-upper of a house with a terrible death trap of a furnace. He asked me to marry him one night when it broke down. We made a fire, dragged his mattress in front of the fireplace, drank champagne, and had sex under tons of blankets. The next day I found him a repairman who specialized in old furnaces, and I installed carbon monoxide detectors for him before I split for good.

My men: I take a small part of each of their hearts and leave them with an important safety tip.

"A beer will be fine," I tell Sandy.

She brings me one.

I notice an empty mug a few stools down from me with no one sitting in front of it. Instead of whisking it away, she refills it.

The men drink mechanically, absorbed by that empty spot in space about two feet ahead of them that they all seem to find so fascinating.

Only one of them is watching the TV mounted in the corner.

All my life I've been surrounded by heavy drinkers, and a few alcoholics, too. In my book, it's not so much the amount they drink that distinguishes the two but the reason. An alcoholic drinks to avoid life; a heavy drinker avoids life by drinking.

I've kept from becoming either by adhering to two basic rules: I only drink when I'm upset or happy and I never drink alone unless I'm surrounded by other people.

My dad drank all the time, but I would have never called him an alcoholic. He didn't try to avoid living. Despite his constant complaining about his bad luck and how fate had dealt him shitty cards, I think he valued his life; drinking gave him a reason to feel sorry for himself, which gave him a reason to be angry, which was the only time I ever saw him come alive.

It was the job that made him drink. I've never known a miner who didn't drink. They work long, grueling, underpaid hours at a difficult, dangerous, thankless profession that only gets attention when somebody dies. If they want to get a load on now and then, who can blame them?

But my dad took it to a different level than the other miners and no matter how much I tried to make excuses for him by telling myself it was the job that made him drink, I couldn't ignore the terrible reality that it must be his life outside the mines, his life with me and Shannon, that made him drink too much.

I pick up my beer and notice my hand shaking.

Ever since Kozlowski said Shannon's name, I can't stop thinking about her and Dad.

In my mind I see him sitting at the kitchen table waiting for me to feed him before his predawn shift. I'd make him a huge plate of eggs, toast, sausage, bacon, and hash browns, and a pot of black coffee. He'd consume all this without uttering a single word to me, then he'd drink three shots of whiskey one right after the other, wipe his mouth on his sleeve, stoop to receive my daily kiss on his cheek, grab his dinner pail, and step outside into darkness to go work in darkness two miles beneath the frozen ground.

He seemed inhuman to me, but I could never figure out if he was more than human or less. Was he a god or a beast?

Either one could be excused for murder.

Shannon was sixteen the last time I saw her. I had just graduated college and been offered a job in Washington, D.C. I was moving away with Clay and wanted her to come with me, but she wouldn't leave Dad.

I did everything possible to convince her to come with us. I even had a few insane moments when I considered throwing away everything I had worked so hard for and staying in this dead-end town for at least a couple more years so she wouldn't have to be alone with Dad while she was still a kid and dependent on him.

But then I would remind myself of what I had gone through to get my degree: the academic scholarship I had earned, which was a feat so rare in my high school that my guidance counselor never did get his facts straight and to this day thinks I went to college on a basketball scholarship; the loans I had to take out on top of my award that I feared I would be paying off for the rest of my life; my exhausting home life as mother to an infant son, sister to a difficult teen, and daughter to a bully, which wasn't exactly conducive to studying for midterms; the hour-long commute to campus that I'd often have to drive at night over winding dark country roads when I was half asleep; the hollow fear that would jerk me awake after I'd fallen asleep over a textbook that I had failed and the only life I was going to be able to offer my son was one of deprivation and limitation.

Ultimately, Shannon made me choose between her and Clay. Whether or not she knew she was doing this and that she did it on purpose as some sort of warped test of my loyalty to her, I'll never know. I accepted that she was old enough to make her own decisions, and as she so often pointed out, I wasn't her mother. Only her sister. I couldn't tell her what to do. I couldn't make her come with me.

He was her father. The only parent she had. His abuse was irrelevant to her, and I was in no position to argue with her. I had lived with my father for twenty-two years. I had been his wife, as well as his daughter, as well as mother to his other daughter. I never complained. I never tried to leave. Up until I had a child of my own to protect, I never tried to stop him. I believed Shannon and I were obligated to endure his beatings because we were his children. It was part of our hereditary lot in life, no different than if we had been born with grotesque physical deformities. Our father's treatment of us was an inoperable birth defect.

For me to tell her she shouldn't stay with him because I was afraid he might start hurting her again would have been as hypocritical as the speeches E.J.'s dad used to give him about how he should go to college and get a job in a clean, safe building somewhere instead of being a coal miner like he was. E.J. was always appalled at these talks but never loved his dad any less because of them. From the time we were kids, he wanted to be a miner. To be anything else would have been a betrayal.

As for my feelings, Shannon was right; she was not my child, but I had raised her and I thought I had done a good job. I thought she loved me. When she disappeared six months after Clay and I moved, it never occurred to me that she could have run away with the intention of never seeing us again, even though that's what my dad claimed and what everyone else believed.

None of it made sense to me. She didn't take any of her belongings with her. I went through her room thoroughly, all her drawers and her closet. None of her clothes were missing or any of her jewelry or makeup. She didn't take Bony, her favorite stuffed dog she'd been sleeping with since she was a baby.

E.J. and his folks argued with me that runaways don't take their stuff with them. It's not like going on a vacation, they said, and if you're going to choose to leave a place, you're probably not going to want to lug around any reminders of it, but I refused to believe this.

She was last seen at the high school but no one saw her get on the afternoon school bus. They argued that if she was going to run away, wouldn't she want to start from town instead of from our house, which was in the middle of nowhere? But I knew Shannon missed the bus a lot. She could have gotten a ride home from a friend or even from Dad.

And then there was the question I never gave them a chance to explain away because I never asked it out loud: if she ran away, why didn't she run to me?

I gulp down half my beer and motion to Sandy that I want a whiskey and Coke. Just one.

There were other explanations besides running away. She could have been abducted. She could have been murdered by some wandering psycho. No one in town had any reason to kill Shannon. But accidents happened. People panicked and tried to hide bodies.

The police searched for her. Nothing turned up.

I never told anyone about the most damning piece of evidence because I would have had to explain things I didn't want them to know. When I was searching her room, I noticed the rag rug we kept between our beds was gone.

I asked Dad about it, and he told me Shannon got a stain on it and threw it away.

I knew this couldn't be true. We loved that rug. My mom had made it out of hundreds of strips of different colored cloth. When Shannon was little, we used to sit on it and play with toys and read books together. We used to examine each individual strip of fabric and pick out our favorite ones. Shannon loved a piece striped in rainbow colors and a satiny shiny piece of regal purple. I loved a soft strip of pastel pink flannel and a scrap of red holiday material covered in tiny green holly leaves.

And regardless of our sentimental attachment to the rug, we were poor. We never threw anything away.

My dad was lying. Why?

A memory gave me the answer: the day a social worker came to visit, the day my sixth-grade teacher reported a suspicious bruise on my face.

The social worker didn't find anything wrong. The house was spotless. Shannon was in perfect health. My dad was gruffly charming in his country-boy way, calling her ma'am, offering her coffee, and regaling her with poignant tales of how tough it was raising two daughters without a wife.

"Shae-Lynn is a bit of a tomboy," my dad explained to her. "Ask anyone around here. She was roughhousing with those boys she hangs out with and things got out of hand. Came home with a shiner."

I agreed that was what happened. Shannon didn't know what had happened but she could vouch that Daddy was always telling Shae-Lynn to be more like a lady.

That night he came to our room after I was in bed. He pulled me out from under my covers, holding my arm so tightly he left a band of purple fingerprints behind. While I tried to find my safe place, he shook me and explained to me if I ever embarrassed him like that again he'd have to punish me.

Then he tossed me across the room as effortlessly as he did empty beer cans at the sink from his post at the head of the kitchen table.

I crashed into the corner of the dresser and lay on the floor for a minute. Shannon pretended to be asleep like she always did, like I had taught her. The next morning when I woke up, I was dizzy and sick to my stomach. While I was picking out my clothes for school, I noticed the dark stain on the floor and found the hard clot of blood stuck to my hair on the back of my head.

There could have been a stain on the rug, but it would have been Shannon's blood and my dad would have been the one who threw it away. I was sure of it in my gut, but I had no way to prove it. No body had been found, and I knew the local cops would take my dad's word over mine. Plus I didn't want to have to explain to them where my suspicions came from. I didn't want anyone looking too closely at my life for fear they might tell me there was something wrong with it.

I finish my beer and take a few sips of my whiskey and Coke.

All those years I thought she was dead. All those years I thought he did it. Or did I? Was I only making myself believe it because in some sick, twisted way it was easier to believe she was dead than to believe she would leave me without a word?

The men's room door swings open and Choker Simms comes plodding out.

He sits four stools away from me in front of the unclaimed beer and takes a drink from it.

Choker only has one ear. He lost the other one in a roof fall ages ago when he worked briefly in the mines. It also left the right side of his face heavily scarred. I'm fortunate enough to be sitting on the side with an ear.

He turns his head slowly to look at me.

"Hey, Choker. How's life on the outside?"

He takes another drink while his eyes crawl from the tips of my boots, up my legs, over my breasts, and come to rest at a place above my head. There's no appreciation or even a detached fondness in his gaze.

His nickname comes from the advice he gives to men having difficulties with women. No matter how small the problem, he tells them to "choke her."

"Do you know where your kids are?" I ask him.

"My kids? They're at home and if they ain't then they're somewhere else and if they figured out how to get there they can figure out how to get back home when they're done."

"The two of them were hanging out in Snappy's parking lot a couple hours ago."

"Something wrong with that?"

"I thought after all those years away from home, you'd want to spend some quality time with them," I say. "Kenny wasn't even born yet when you were convicted. Shouldn't you be teaching him how to throw a football or how to steal people's TV sets while they're at work?"

The other men at the bar glance in Choker's direction.

He adjusts the bill of his Pennzoil ball cap.

"You're a real commodian," he says, taking a long gulp of beer. "Flush, flush," he adds with a belch.

"Oh, wait a minute. That's right."

I pick up my drink and start walking toward him.

"You didn't steal anything. The way I hear it you were framed by a lady cop who had the hots for you but you spurned her advances. At least that's what your kids seem to think."

"Stay away from my kids."

"Oh, so now you care about your kids? Come on, Choker. Tell me."

I set my drink down on the bar and move close enough to smell the sour mix of beer, chewing tobacco, and sweat coming out of his pores.

"Who's this lady cop? Who's the star of this asinine fantasy of yours?"

"You think you can harass me 'cause you used to be a cop?" he replies. "Well, you can't. I know my rights. You ain't shit anymore. You're nothing. I bet you can't even get fucked anymore. Your titties are starting to sag. Pretty soon you're gonna have nothing to do on Friday nights except hang out with fat girls like Sandy."

I try not to look at Sandy, but I can't help myself. She's pretending to busy herself rearranging glasses beneath the bar.

My response is automatic and unthinking. I grab one of his arms and wrench it behind his back and grab a handful of his hair and slam his head into the bar. I've raised and smashed his face against the wood several times before I notice Sandy standing in front of us.

"Please don't wreck the bar, Shae-Lynn," she says.

Choker's drunk and in shock, or he'd be fighting back already. I take advantage of the situation and pull him off his stool, usher him quickly out of the bar, and toss him down the stairs.

He rolls around in the fringe of grass between the bar and the sidewalk. His nose is bleeding and he's clutching his gut while cursing up a storm.

"Spurned? You told them you spurned me?" I shout, while circling around him waiting for him to get up.

"What the hell are you talking about?" he shouts back at me.

He finally manages to get to his feet.

"Come on, you lying worthless pile of shit," I taunt him.

He rushes at me. I easily step aside. His momentum causes him to stumble and fall again.

The bar's other patrons and Sandy have all clustered outside on the porch at this point. A couple Subway customers have also come outside, one of them chewing on her sandwich as she watches. An old man on his way into the post office stops and stares. The sole teller working in the booth dispensing banking services through a tube actually leaves the booth to get a better look. A few cars slow down.

I notice a freshly washed sheriff's department cruiser parked at one of the pumps across the street. I immediately recognize the slim, polished figure of Laurel County's newest deputy pumping the gas. He's the only one I've ever encountered who keeps his boots spotless and his hat on at all times. He's watching everything from behind a pair of mirrored sunglasses that are cleaner than my dinner plates.

He doesn't seem in any hurry to interfere, but I know he will eventually.

The deputy and I are not strangers.

Choker comes at me again. He takes a couple wild swings that I avoid while I connect with a couple punches to his face. They startle the hell out of him and I'm sure they hurt, but they hurt me almost as much.

I shake out my fingers and can already feel my shoulder beginning to throb.

He tackles me this time, and I lose my hat. I manage to pull myself out of his grip far enough that I can knee him hard in the chin. He lets go and cries out.

I jump up and swing a kick at him, but he surprises me by grabbing my boot and pushing me backward with all his might. I hit the ground hard on my ass.

He comes at me, but by now he's blind with rage and the confidence that there's no way I can get up in time to escape him. He's right, so I don't even try. I draw back my legs and let them fly into his chest, and he goes reeling across the sidewalk into a tree.

"Okay. All right. That's enough," I hear a familiar voice coming from above me.

The deputy comes into my line of vision. He's holding my hat in one hand. He reaches out the other one to help me up.

I realize as I'm getting to my feet that my skirt is pushed up around my hips. I'm wearing cotton bikinis with little yellow construction signs on them and the words MEN AT WORK.

I yank my skirt down.

"Are you going to control yourself, ma'am, or am I going to have to cuff you?"

He knows my name, but he won't use it.

"I can control myself," I promise, breathing heavily.

It's an easy promise to make. Now that the adrenaline is gone, the pain is sinking in.

He hands me my hat and leaves to tend to Choker.

"Is there a reason for this altercation?" he asks when he returns with Choker trailing behind him.

The shiny pink scar tissue striping Choker's cheek and the lump of puckered flesh where his ear should be has turned bright red from the exertion of our workout. His face is smeared with blood.

"She attacked me," he screams, poking a finger in the air at me. "Violent bitch! I wasn't doing nothing. She came after me."

"He abandoned his kids in a parking lot." I'm trying to come up with a reasonable excuse.

"I never abandoned my kids," Choker keeps screaming. "She's just mad at me cause I made fun of her tits."

"I have great tits," I yell back at him. "In your dreams do you get your hands on tits like these."

I reach down to pull up my shirt and flash him, but the deputy places his hand on my arm.

"Walk it off, ma'am," he tells me. "And go on home."

"That's it?" Choker cries. "Ain't you gonna arrest her? If I'da been the one who started the fight, you'd damn sure arrest me."

"Sir, you're an ex-con on parole; she's a former police officer. You're a two-hundred-pound man; she's a hundred-and-thirty-pound woman."

"Hundred-and-twenty-six," I correct him.

"Do you see where I'm going with this? Don't you think you've suffered enough humiliation for one day by being beaten up by a girl?" the deputy suggests calmly. "Do you really want to make it worse by pressing charges and having everyone know about it?"

Choker drops his gaze from the unreadable mirrored sunglasses to a spot of blood on one of his own work boots.

"Forget it," he mutters, then he starts wagging his finger at me again.

"She's a fucking menace to society," he shouts.

"Oooh. Big words, Choker," I say back. "Menace to society. Have you been watching *Dragnet* reruns on TV Land?"

"I'm warning you, ma'am," the deputy reminds me.

"I'm going to drive you home, Mr. Simms," he says to Choker, "since you're obviously intoxicated."

"What about my truck?"

"I'm sure you can find someone to give you a lift back here tomorrow to retrieve your vehicle."

"What if I can't?"

"I'm sure you can. But whatever you do, I advise you not to call a cab. Now go back inside and settle your bill. I'll get my car."

Choker spits a brown stream of tobacco flecked with blood into the grass. It comes perilously close to the tip of my boot. I make a move for him, but he steps out of range and heads back into the bar.

The deputy watches me for a moment from behind his shades.

"Apparently all that time spent in law enforcement was the only thing keeping you from becoming a criminal. Or a menace to society at the very least," he comments. "This is the fifth brawl you've been involved in during the past year that I personally know about."

"I . . . ," I start to explain.

"Feel the need to control every situation?" he finishes for me. "Even if it means resorting to violence?"

I can't come up with a better explanation off the top of my head.

He crosses his arms over his chest.

"Did you look into getting some health insurance?" he asks me.

"I can't afford it."

"What are you going to do if you get sick?"

"Get better? Or die?"

He sighs, turns, and begins to walk across the street.

"Hey," I suddenly remember and call after him, "Happy birthday, baby."

He takes off his glasses for a second and glances over his shoulder at me, wearing the same squint of exasperation that's been puckering his forehead since he was a child.

"Thanks, Mom," he says.

Chapter Three

I'M NOT THE TYPE of person who likes to talk about myself. I don't even like to think about myself.

I'm sure that's one of the reasons why I made a good cop and why I was drawn to the profession in the first place: I knew how to step outside my skin, leaving my emotions and my opinions behind, and be nothing but the job. It's what I did throughout my childhood, then I did it for seventeen years as a police officer. Both periods of my life were basically the same: I protected and I served.

Now I'm at the beginning of a new phase of my life where I do neither, where my thoughts and actions are supposed to be motivated solely by what's best for me.

It was my own decision. No one made me quit being a cop, despite some of the rumors.

Maybe my decision was partly due to the jolt of realizing my son was no longer dependent on me at all, not even to help him pay for college.

For the first time in my life I had no financial obligations other than funding my own existence. The major worries of motherhood were behind me. My child had survived to adulthood. He was gainfully employed, maybe too well adjusted, kept a cleaner house than me, and could cook better, too.

I taught him all those things. I was a single mom and a working mom, and he was my right-hand man. We were partners. I didn't raise him; we raised each other, only to find out that the reward for our success was going to be that we wouldn't need each other anymore. It doesn't always feel like such a prize to me, but other than that things have been pretty tolerable this past year until today when a stranger mentioned my sister's name.

Shannon might be alive. I might be able to find her. I should be happy, but I'm not. All I can think about is how sure I was of her death. I'm plagued with the same thoughts I used to have right after she disappeared, when the pain was so powerful it could double me over.

I thought I was going crazy back then. I couldn't stop reliving her final moments, even though I didn't know what they were and it didn't matter. All that mattered was that I knew she would have been afraid, and I wasn't there to save her.

Her life was over. She was gone. She would never grow up. She would never fall in love. She would never own the pair of red cowboy boots she always wanted. She would never come into my room again and touch all my stuff as she circled around my bed giving me her latest list of grievances against the world. She would never let me cheer her up by taking her to Eatn'Park for a piece of coconut cream pie. She would never bundle Clay into his snowsuit and pull him around the front yard on our old sled. She would never even learn to drive.

I wanted so desperately to believe in heaven. I wanted to picture her someplace beautiful with no cares or concerns, a place where she'd finally have Mom to take care of her, a place where that awful final fear would have been erased and replaced with bliss, but my thoughts kept returning to nothingness. An eternal black abyss.

I never talked to a shrink about any of this. A few of my buddies on the Capitol police force suggested I might want to talk to one when she first disappeared. My lieutenant came pretty close to insisting I see one, but since my job performance wasn't suffering he didn't have any right to push it.

I've always believed psychology is bullshit. I can still remember all the questions on the psych exam I had to pass in order to get my badge and gun. I couldn't figure out what the test was supposed to prove other than how well a candidate knew how to give the answers he knew the force wanted whether they were true for him or not.

I lied on a few questions because I knew I had to.

Have you ever been brutalized by a family member or someone close to you? No.

Do you love your father? Yes.

Do you get urges to physically harm others? No.

But everybody lies on a few.

I knew the Neanderthal from Georgia sitting next to me was answering "yes" to "Do you believe in the equality of the sexes?"

And I knew J.T., the ex-Marine sitting on my other side, had to be struggling like hell with the question "Do you like flowers?"

The only one that completely stumped me was "Do you masturbate?"

This was back in the eighties when women were still fairly rare in law enforcement. Especially in the Capitol police. I was the only woman in my rookie class.

We were an elite group. Our job was to protect the nation's government buildings and our illustrious lawmakers, which made us a federal law enforcement agency. Getting in was no easy feat. The background check alone took six months. They interviewed everyone I'd ever known, including my old elementary school principal, who was kind enough not to mention the Naughty Penis incident. There were eight weeks of intense boot camp. The classes and written exams were more difficult than anything I did in college.

I knew the question about masturbation was directed solely at men, since women weren't an issue when the test was designed. It was a simple question to determine truthfulness. Any man who answered no was a liar.

But for women it was different. We're not supposed to masturbate. Fortunately, this part of the exam wasn't standardized. I had a space where I could write my answer instead of filling in a bubble.

I wrote, "Only when I have to."

I passed, so I guess they found me sane.

And I'm still sane but my sanity is wearing a little thin today.

I decide to go talk to E.J. He's much better than any shrink. He doesn't cost anything, he always provides me with beer, he doesn't ask any questions, and he doesn't offer unrealistic advice. His commentary at the end usually consists of "That sucks" and is always dispensed with more beer.

I brush myself off after my tussle with Choker and check my face in the rearview mirror. There's no damage but I'm going to have a honey of a bruise on my thigh. Probably one on my butt too, which is what I sit on all day to do my job.

I'm a couple miles from E.J.'s house when I come around a bend and find him walking down the side of the road.

I pull up behind him and slow down. He looks over his shoulder, startled at first, then cautious, his look no different than the one my dog gives me from underneath the kitchen table each time I return to the room. There's no suspicion in it, just an animal wariness based on the primal knowledge that everyone who is not you could be a potential problem.

His eyes are very blue in his pale face. Once summer arrives, he'll get to see a couple hours of light at the end of each day, but that amount of sun isn't enough to erase the effects of his subterranean existence. In winter, he doesn't see any daylight at all during the workweek.

Right now the sky is shouting summer; it's a flat, bright blue dotted with white clouds whipped into a motionless lather while the land seems to be barely awake.

"Hey," I greet him.

"Hey," he says back.

"What are you doing?"

"Walking."

"I can see that. You walking anyplace in particular?"

I can't help noticing that I found him at the site of his rescue.

"Back home."

"Where are you walking from?"

He stops. I stop my car.

"Home," he says.

"In other words you're out for a walk."

"That's what I said. Where are you going?"

"To see you."

"I'm not home."

"Get in the car," I tell him.

He starts to walk around to the passenger side then stops and watches an SUV coming from the opposite direction. It slows to a stop and parks on the other side of the road about a hundred feet from us.

A woman gets out and closes the door behind her. She smooths out the front of her pleated tan shorts over her pot belly, puts a flattened hand to her eyebrows like a visor, and scans the empty field stretching toward a horizon of low green and gray mountains.

Two children climb slowly out of the backseat and a man gets out from behind the steering wheel, all three of them blinking suspiciously at the sky.

The woman turns and says something to them. The children respond with groans. Their heads loll back on their necks and their arms flop at their sides like they've been simultaneously struck dead. The man responds by spreading out a map on the hood of his car.

They're tourists.

"Shit," I hear E.J. say.

He's been spotted by the woman, and she's identified him as a local. She starts heading toward him, smiling and waving wildly. I know his gut reaction is to run in the opposite direction, but he knows she knows he's seen her and he's not a rude man.

He stands his ground and lifts a hand in greeting but doesn't smile.

It's been awhile since I've seen any strangers out here. The initial swarms of visitors that jammed the road and snapped pictures of each other posing with backhoes and cranes tapered off fairly quickly into a small but steady stream that lasted for a couple months until it became a trickle then dried up to nothing. People no longer come here for the sole purpose of seeing where the rescue took place, but if they're in the area for some other reason, they sometimes stop by.

"Hello," she calls out to him.

Her smile broadens as she gets close enough to read the J&P Coal Company logo stitched on his ball cap. She's definitely a tourist. He watches her approach in amazement. No matter how many he's dealt with, he still has a hard time believing in their existence. Up until a couple years ago, running into a talking dog out here would have been less surprising than running into someone like this woman.

"I was wondering if you could help me?" she asks him.

He sticks his hands into his jeans pockets and shifts his weight uncomfortably from one foot to the other.

"I can try," he replies.

"Are you from around here?" she asks.

"Born and raised."

She looks at his cap again.

Her facial expression changes from being pleased in general to being pleased with him. He has become more than a potential tour guide; he could turn out to be the tour.

"That's great," she gushes.

I look over at her car and notice her family isn't in any hurry to join her.

"Then I'm sure you can help me. I'm looking for the place where the miners were rescued."

"You found it," he says and motions toward the field with a jerk of his head.

She turns her head expectantly, still smiling, and stares out at the field. Two years ago it was turned into a mud pit by tons of earthmoving equipment, drills, and cranes, all of it illuminated twenty-four hours a day by giant spotlights and flash photography, but now there's nothing exciting or frightening or even slightly unusual about it.

The flat, grassy land is bordered on the south by the road, the north by the hills, and the west by forest. To the east it slopes off into acres of gully. It's one of the best places to come at night to spot deer.

She turns back to him, obviously disappointed.

What do these people expect to see? I always wonder. What they want is a re-creation, like the rooms in wax museums that show different forms of medieval torture. They want to see the five miners, starving, wet, and shivering with cold, huddled together in a chamber no bigger than a bathroom and half its height, staring blindly and crazily into the impenetrable darkness.

They think they want to experience what those men experienced, even if only for a few moments, but they're wrong.

"Are you a miner?" she asks him.

"No, ma'am. I just like the cap."

"Were you around when it happened?"

"No, I wasn't anywhere around. I don't know anything more about it than what you saw on TV and read in the newspapers."

"Oh, I followed every minute of it. I still remember everything about them."

She begins ticking off their vital statistics like someone reading from a baseball card. The only things missing are their heights and weights.

"There was Lib, 56, the boss of the crew. Married with two grown sons and four grandchildren. He was a Vietnam veteran and you could tell how much all the others respected him. Then there was Jimmy, 58, the oldest one on the crew. His wife was a lovely lady, a schoolteacher. He had that adorable accent and used all those quaint sayings. I'll always remember him saying to one of the reporters at their first press conference . . ."

Here she breaks into an attempt at an Irish brogue that sounds like a cross between the Lucky Charms leprechaun and Desi Arnaz.

". . . You wouldn't be trying to soft-soap me, now?" She giggles. "Who uses words like that?"

E.J. glances over his shoulder at me through the windshield and we smile at each other, thinking of some of the other words that only Jimmy uses that wouldn't have made it past the network censors.

"Then there was Dusty, the youngest one, early twenties, with the skinny wife with the big doe eyes and the newborn baby and those sweet little twin girls. He'd only been working in the mines for two years.

"And Ray. The talkative, friendly one. Late thirties. Married with two teenaged daughters."

She lowers her voice confidentially.

"His wife was a piece of work. She managed to get herself into every interview. A big lady and always dressed to the nines. My husband said she looked like a drag queen going to a hoedown."

She laughs.

"And last but not least Jimmy's son, E.J. Good-looking. Never been married. Strong, silent type. Hardly said a word."

"Sounds like you collected the entire set of Trapped Miner Trading Cards," E.J. comments.

"I never saw those," she says seriously, then after a moment smiles knowingly at him. "You're joking with me, aren't you?"

He admits that he is with a nod of his head.

She puts her hand back up to her forehead like she did earlier and peers out at the field again.

"Is there a statue near the hole?"

"No."

"A plaque?"

He shakes his head.

"Well, there should be," she says indignantly.

He doesn't bother telling her that everyone around here agrees that there should be something to mark the spot but no one can agree on what it should be or who should pay for it; while everyone else argued, Nature immediately reclaimed it with grass and weeds.

"Can we walk out there?" she asks.

"Sure."

"Is it dangerous?"

"Only during hunting season."

She gives him a questioning tilt of her head.

"You might get shot," he explains.

"Oh," she says.

Before she can ask him anything else, he mutters something about being expected somewhere and jumps into my car.

We leave her in our dust.

E.J. LIVES IN A SMALL white ranch house set back from the road at the top of a steep gravel driveway. Structurally the house is well cared for but the premises lack any decorative touches. No landscaping to speak of. No flowers. No lawn ornaments. No curtains on the windows.

A detached garage invisible from the road sits behind the house.

His old brown Dodge Ram pickup is parked in front of it with the hood open. A few tools are scattered about. He must have been working on it again before he went on his walk.

I park behind the truck.

He gets out and heads straight to the garage.

Before I follow him, I open my glove compartment and take out a bottle of Advil and dry-swallow a couple capsules. I'm starting to hurt after my fight with Choker.

I find him bent over with his head and torso hidden behind an open refrigerator door and one dirty hand clutching the door handle. The mother in me wants to scold him for wasting electricity and letting all the cold air out. I also want to tell him he needs to do a better job of washing his hands, but I don't say anything.

His decision made—the choices are beer, beer, and beer—he steps back, holding a beer in one hand, and closes the door with a slam, leaving a set of motor oil fingerprints behind to mark his territory.

When he remembers me, he reaches back into the fridge and tosses me a can, too.

I snap it open and beer gushes all over my hand. I look around for a roll of paper towels or something to wipe it off with. I don't see anything.

"Use the finger," he says, gesturing toward a giant yellow foam WE ARE NUMBER ONE finger from a Steelers game.

It's covered in fingerprints, too, and dotted with hardened stains and flecks of dried foodstuffs. A few chunks of foam are missing, like someone has taken a couple bites out of it.

"I'll pass," I tell him.

I pull up a lawn chair and take a seat. The garage is his pride and joy and much homier than the house. He built it himself and has pictures of it in various stages of construction tacked to the back of his workbench the same way my dad used to display baby pictures of me and Shannon.

He has an old couch out here and a small TV. His J&P baseball team cap and jersey hang on a nail and a deodorant stick sits on a shelf between a pair of jumper cables and a flashlight. In amongst a couple Ball jars of random nails and screws is a pair of photos in attached frames that close like a book. His mom just gave them to him: one is his parents' original wedding photo and the other was taken at their fortieth anniversary celebration last month.

Reading material consists of copies of *Field & Stream,* a few Victoria's Secret catalogs he's snagged from a girlfriend's place, and a few hardcover novels in cracked, discolored, plastic library dust jackets, which I'm willing to bet are several years overdue.

He has a makeshift kitchen set up on a card table next to the fridge that consists of a few mismatched plates and bowls, a battered coffee maker, and a George Foreman grill I got him for Christmas. He loves the grill so much he named it. He calls it George.

He keeps his dinner bucket and thermos on the table, too, and I can't stop looking at them.

I have no idea how he's been able to go back into the mines after what happened to him, but I guess car crash survivors get back into cars, and injured soldiers go back into battle, and abused women sleep with their abusers.

I know how hard it would be for him to quit. I know how much he loves running the continuous miner, the sixty-ton cutting machine that's replaced the manual jobs of undercutting and blasting that the miners of the past used to do. The machine is a wonder, according to E.J., but like most miners who have been around for awhile, he had mixed feelings about it when the company first started using it because it did the work of at least fifty men, which meant those fifty men lost their jobs.

He's told me there's nothing in life that thrills him as much as the sight and feel of the miner's gigantic steel cutter head ripping into the coal face, its dozens of carbide teeth chewing up the wall of rock with the same ease as an electric knife carving through a rump roast.

Part of the rush comes purely from the power he feels while guiding it, but I'm sure another part comes from pride. He's one of the best operators in the business. With him at the controls, the massive machine moves cleanly and efficiently. No one—including Lib—can match his speed or get as much coal out of a cut with as little movement.

But even knowing how much he loves it, I still don't understand how he went back.

I still have the occasional nightmare where I wake up clammy and cotton-mouthed thinking I'm still standing numbly and helplessly on the hillside overlooking the rescue site wondering if I should be praying that he's still alive or that he died instantly.

I can't imagine what kind of nightmares he has.

I take a gulp of my beer.

"You want George to make you a burger?" he asks as he pulls up his own lawn chair.

"Not right now. Maybe later."

I look around for a diversion. I want to talk to him. I need to talk. But I'm not anxious to begin.

I spot yesterday's newspaper sitting on top of a stack of papers in his bright orange recycle bin.

"So you guys actually went through with it," I comment, referring to the front-page story about the Jolly Mount Five suing J&P Coal. "It's all anybody's talking about."

He glances over at the paper too, and his face puckers like he's just heard a bad joke.

"We filed the papers. Whatever the hell that means. Now we're waiting to see what he does next."

The way he says "he" I know he can only be referring to God or Cam Jack.

My mind flashes to the visit he paid the miners in the hospital the day after their rescue. It was unannounced and a complete surprise since he had never bothered to show up while they were trapped.

He went to their rooms one after the other. Suddenly there he'd be standing in a hospital room doorway: Cam Jack himself in a fine dark suit with a pristine white shirt, a steel-gray tie the same color as his slicked-back hair, and an American flag tie clip, looking hale and hearty despite his own recent hospitalizations and the rumors flying around about his failing health.

He proclaimed that he didn't give a good goddamn about hospital policy and being politically correct and gave them all boxes of cigars and bottles of whiskey.

He called them "my boys" and even though that term would have caused all of them to bristle if he had used it a week earlier or a month later, at the time they didn't seem to mind. There was nothing like a successful rescue mission to soothe the tensions between the foot soldiers and the top brass, especially when the big man himself showed up brimming with praise and bearing gifts.

He pulled up a chair, settled his bulk into it, and talked to them about their grandfathers and their dads and their uncles. How his own dad always said those boys up in Jolly Mount were the toughest, most dependable miners on God's green earth. He used to say he'd give four of his Marvella miners for just one working Josephine.

He knew the old man watched the whole rescue from his seat up there in heaven. He may have even had something to do with them getting out alive. And you can be sure he was damn proud of them. Lesser men would have given up. Lesser men would have gone nuts.

Personally, he never doubted that they were going to come out of it alive, either. He understood them. They were cut from the same cloth. They were from the same place. They were in the same business, and they were proud of what they did. Outsiders didn't always understand.

Hell, he couldn't tell them how many times he had to defend himself and his family to other rich people because the Jacks made their first fortune in coal. Like that made him dirty or something. Like money made from owning hotels or selling wrinkle cream was somehow superior. Money was money and he had enough to live anywhere he wanted to but he lived in Centresburg, PA, goddammit. This was his home, too.

I was visiting E.J. when I heard him coming down the hall to his room. I ran and hid in the john. I hadn't seen Cam Jack in the flesh for over twenty years.

"You don't sound too excited about it," I tell E.J.

"Dusty and Lib and Ray all want to do it," he answers, hoping I won't notice that he's avoiding telling me what he thinks about it. "Dusty's desperate for the money since his restaurant went belly-up. He doesn't care where the hell it comes from or why he's getting it. Ray's got a family. He needs the money too, plus he'll go along with anything Lib says, and Lib says if a jury of our peers thinks we should have some of Cam Jack's billions then why shouldn't we?"

"He's got a point," I reply. "But I don't get how this works. The investigation's been over for almost a year now and J&P's in the clear."

E.J.'s pucker becomes more pucked.

"According to our lawyer," he begins to explain, "the results of the investigation don't matter in civil court. We don't have to prove anything. All that matters is everybody knows what an asshole Cam Jack is. How bad his mines are. How many safety violations have been cited against him. How everybody knows the explosion in Beverly was his fault too, even though nobody could hang it on him. He says we don't need any proof at all. All we need to do is get up on the stand and tell what it was like to be buried alive for four days. All we need is a sympathetic jury."

I nod my understanding.

"I know your dad's against it," I add.

44

He smiles.

"He really got into it the other night with Lib. My dad said"—here he breaks into a perfect impression of Jimmy's brogue—"'You're a grown man, Lib. No one put a gun to your head and chose your job for you. It was your choice, and every day you went to work you knew there was a chance you'd die. So I say it's your fault. Sue your bloody self.'"

"And you agree with him?"

"All I know is miners don't sue coal companies."

"Why not? Everybody sues everybody nowadays. Why shouldn't you?"

"Everybody's looking to get something for nothing."

"This wouldn't be for nothing. The money would be for—"

"For what?" he interrupts me. "Waiting to die? How much is that worth in dollars?"

He gets up from his seat and heads to the fridge for another beer.

"I don't want his money," he says. "I work for my money. Plus I got enough money from the book deal and that idiotic TV movie."

I know he's sincere. I also know he wouldn't get any personal satisfaction from beating Cam Jack in a courtroom. To a guy like E.J., there's something innately cowardly about hiding behind checkbooks and lawyers and legalese. Beating Cam Jack on the ball field or in a game of pool would be appealing, but court means nothing to him.

He realizes a judge and jury can't fix what he considers to be wrong with the man. His stinginess, his carelessness, his lack of appreciation for the company his dad gave him almost led to the destruction of the mine where E.J. worked. I think this bothers E.J. even more than the fact that he almost died. The threats to his physical well-being are a hazard of the profession that he accepted when he took the job, but the treatment of the mine and the equipment he can't forgive. What kind of man doesn't take care of his own stuff?

"What do you want?" I ask him.

I hear the refrigerator door slam behind me and the snap of a beer can being opened.

"I want my old life back."

I glance around his garage. Anyone who didn't know him the way I do would find his comment funny. The surface of his life now compared to his life before the accident is exactly the same. He has the same job. Lives in the same house. Goes to the same bar. He didn't buy a new truck or a bigger TV or a better mower. He didn't get a new wardrobe or a new philosophy on life or start eating new foods and drinking new beer.

He told me it would have been an affront to the life he had prayed so hard to keep if he changed anything about it after he was allowed to keep it. But something did change that was beyond his control. Something inside himself. I know the feeling. Survival is a great thing, but the knowledge of what you survived never goes away; you can't escape from yourself.

"I think Shannon's alive," I blurt out.

"What?" he says and comes walking back to his lawn chair. "Are you serious?"

I nod. I can't say anything more at first and E.J. doesn't pry.

When I feel properly composed, I tell him all about Gerald Kozlowski.

He doesn't say anything at first. He just stares at a grease stain on the cement floor.

"Have you told my mom?" is the first thing he asks.

"No. You're the first one I've told."

"You've got to tell her. Shannon was like her own kid. So were you."

I know he's right. Isabel took care of Shannon during the years before she was old enough for a full day of school. She quit her job teaching and sacrificed a second income that her own family could have used in order to babysit for the child of a man who never showed any gratitude. When I was a child myself, I simply regarded all of this as some more nice stuff these nice people felt compelled to do for us because of a combination of their niceness and our desperate situation.

It wasn't until I became an adult and raised a child of my own that I understood the rareness and the enormity of their generosity, and how niceness had little to do with it. Isabel and Jimmy had been motivated by anger and outrage; they had been on a mission to save us.

But all of this aside, I don't like E.J.'s tone. He's lecturing me.

"What was I supposed to do? Quit school when I was six years old to stay home with my motherless baby sister? I didn't have a choice. I watched her as soon as I got home. I took care of her at night and on weekends."

"Stop it, Shae-Lynn," he says roughly. "Everything in life isn't a competition. I'm not saying you didn't take care of your sister, and I'm not saying my mom took better care of her. I'm just saying my mom and dad should know about this."

"I was planning on telling them when I know more. Nothing's for sure yet."

"What do you mean, nothing's for sure? This lawyer from New York is looking for her in her hometown. He said he knows this is her hometown. That means he knows her. She's alive."

We both fall silent as we let this fact sink in.

"So what are you going to do?" he asks me.

"I don't know. Maybe I should help him find her."

"You sure you want to find her?"

"What kind of question is that?"

He gets up from his chair and starts pacing.

"Personally, I'm pissed as hell at her. My mom almost died from grief when she disappeared. So did you. Have you forgotten all that?

What she put you through? What she put us all through? Here all along she's been fine and she never tried to contact any of us. You're gonna forgive all that?"

"We don't know she's been fine," I tell him. "We don't even know she left on her own. Maybe she was abducted."

"Abducted? In Jolly Mount? And then I suppose she was taken away and tortured and brainwashed?"

"It happens."

"It's been eighteen years. She never tried to contact you once. You're telling me she was tortured and brainwashed for eighteen years?"

He stops in front of me.

"How does this guy know her?"

"I didn't ask him. I was too shocked. I couldn't think straight."

"And you didn't tell him you're her sister and she's been gone all these years?"

"No. I didn't want him to know I knew her. I don't know why. It was a feeling I had. I don't trust him. I'm not sure I want him to find her. I'm not sure it would be good for her if he did."

I stand up, too. Talking is not helping. It's making me feel worse. He's bringing up too many things I don't want to think about.

"I'll get more information out of him later when I see him again tonight," I tell E.J.

"You're seeing him tonight? You planning to screw it out of him?"

I take a step closer until the tips of my breasts are almost brushing against his chest.

"Don't start on me. You're one to talk. You're the biggest slut I know."

"Men can't be sluts."

"Then you're a pig."

"I'm a stud."

"You're an ass.

"It's a disgusting double standard," I think to add.

48

He smiles and takes a swallow of beer.

"It's a great double standard."

We're almost touching. A few inches more and I'd be able to feel the hard denim of his fly push against my belly. The thought makes me think back to when I was first starting to want him. We were still kids and the sight of the newly developing muscles in his arms and back when he'd go shirtless became so magnetic to me that I found myself looking for any opportunity to brush up against him without knowing exactly why, only that any physical contact with him sent a thrill through my body that would lodge between my legs and make me want to get back on my bike, clamp the banana seat tightly between my thighs, and ride down a particularly bumpy hill.

The feeling wasn't mutual, though. At around the same time, he started hanging out less and less with me. He stopped talking to me at school. Eventually, he was never home when I called or stopped by his house.

I couldn't figure out what had happened. The only explanation I could come up with was to blame my breasts. The equation appeared fairly straightforward: We were best friends, then I got breasts, then we weren't friends anymore.

It wasn't that he wasn't interested in breasts. He was definitely interested. Just not in mine.

I used to sit in the bathtub, crying, trying to scrub them off with a washcloth until my skin was almost raw.

I know it didn't make sense. I should have been happy. I had a great figure; I was suddenly pretty, something all girls were supposed to want. But the way I saw it the only thing my new body did was attract a lot of attention from guys I didn't like and cause me to lose the one guy I did.

My cell phone rings.

I pull it out of my pocket and walk away from him.

"Jolly Mount Cab," I answer.

"Hi, Mom. I have a favor to ask. Actually, it's more of a job. I think I can trust you with it."

"Hi, honey. I'm fine. No broken bones. No missing teeth. Thanks for asking."

"Mom," he sighs, "I know you started it. You can't expect sympathy."

"What's the job?" I ask him.

"I need you to drive out to Pine Mills and help a woman change a flat tire. I'm not going to do it. It's beneath me."

"And it's not beneath me?"

"You drive a cab. I'm an officer of the law."

I love this kid. The things that come out of his mouth. When he was six, he wouldn't eat pie a la mode because ice cream and pie were both desserts and he insisted that eating them at the same time would be a conflict of interests.

"Well, yes, of course. No one should expect an officer of the law to change a tire," I reply, doing my best imitation of Inspector Clouseau so "law" comes out sounding like "loo."

"It's not my job. If she was a different kind of person I'd do it regardless, but I think it's important to teach her some respect for the profession. She has a bit of an attitude."

"What kind of attitude?"

"The kind that would lead someone to think having a flat tire merits a 911 call."

"Why didn't the operator tell her to get bent?"

"She was hysterical during the call and said there had been a fatality."

"She lied and said someone was dead in order to get a cop to change her tire?" I ask incredulously.

"Someone is dead. A groundhog. She hit a groundhog."

I can't help laughing.

"You've got to be kidding."

"No, I'm not. Fortunately, I was in the area so I got here fairly quickly and was able to radio back in time to keep the state police and the fire department from wasting their time coming out."

"So why are you calling me? Why not Mack's or some other garage?"

"I thought you could use the money."

"I can charge her?"

"Charge her an arm and a leg."

"You're still thinking about health insurance, aren't you?"

"Gotta go."

I look back at E.J. He's gazing out the open garage door.

The first time I saw him after the rescue was in the hospital corridor. He was wearing a hospital gown and slippers that looked as ridiculous on him as a circus tutu on a bear. His left arm was in a cast, and his left hand was bandaged.

He'd been bathed and shaved and given a haircut, but nothing could be done to get rid of the hollowness in his cheeks or the ghostly pale of his skin. His face was covered with dozens of tiny brown cuts and purple bruises that made him look like he had a strange rash or a bizarre batch of freckles.

He smelled of smoke and it was instantly obvious to me that he had snuck somewhere to have a cigarette and now he was heading back to his room. I couldn't figure out how he had been able to do it with all the nurses checking on him constantly and all the reporters congregated at every exit.

He stared at me. His pupils were still dilated, and his shock and confusion over being alive were still evident in his eyes, making them appear wild and haunted one moment and as depthless and motionless as pools of night water the next.

He still gets that look sometimes. He has it right now.

He catches me watching him and picks up the first available object as a distraction, which happens to be the photos of his folks.

I always loved my own parents' wedding photo. My mom looked ethereal in her white lace and gauze. Dad looked awkward and too big in his rented tux, but he wore the defiance of youth and the triumph of capturing a pretty girl better than anyone else I've ever seen.

I was around ten years old when I got up the nerve to ask him if I could have the picture when he died instead of him giving it to Shannon.

He gave me a suspicious, startled look. I knew it didn't have anything to do with the photo. He just didn't like me figuring out he wasn't going to live forever.

Chapter Four

CLAY DIDN'T GIVE ME detailed directions to the damsel in distress, which meant he knew I wasn't going to need them.

On the back roads between Jolly Mount and Pine Mills, one doesn't encounter a brand-new, champagne-colored Lexus SUV with Connecticut plates very often. The owner is sitting in the front seat. She has set up three small neon orange hazard signs on the road that probably came with the vehicle in a fireproof, waterproof, wild animal–proof emergency kit along with a flashlight and some pepper spray.

I park my car far enough away from hers that she won't get spooked. I leave my hat and sunglasses on the front seat.

I walk right up to the driver's side window without her seeing me. She's staring straight ahead and her lips are moving. At first I think she's talking to herself or praying, then I realize she has one of those headsets that allows her to use her cell phone without using her hands.

I tap on the window and she almost jumps out of her skin.

I instinctively reach for my creds so I can flash my badge before remembering I don't have one anymore.

I take a step back from the car and try to look as harmless as possible.

She gives me a hesitant smile and rolls down her window. Even from a distance, I can feel the blast of air-conditioning.

"Hi, there. Deputy Penrose gave me a call. Says you're having some car trouble."

I reach out my hand for her to shake.

"I'm Shae-Lynn."

She looks at my hand for a moment. It's hard for me to read her eyes because she's wearing a jaunty white ball cap.

She finally takes my hand. Hers is beautiful. It reminds me of some of the hands of high-priced D.C. mistresses who passed through my security screenings on their way upstairs to visit their sugar daddies in the Capitol office buildings after hours.

The hands of the wives were always nice, too, but none of them had the satiny perfection of the girlfriends'. One of the reasons was age. Another was that most of the wives hadn't always been pampered. They had struggled before their husbands were elected and their lifestyles were elevated. Their hands had changed some diapers and washed some dishes and done some gardening. Not so for the mistresses. These girls were in their twenties and had never done anything with their hands except jerk off other women's husbands.

This one is pale, soft, blemish- and wrinkle-free. It's even hard to make out her knuckles. The nails are almond-shaped and painted in a high-gloss burgundy. Not a smudge or a chip or a scratch on them.

"Pamela," she says, then thinks to add, "Jameson."

"Nice to meet you, Miss Jameson."

She smiles. I knew she'd like that. Her lips are painted the same exact color as her nails and they're equally flawless. Remarkable.

"It's Mrs. Jameson," she corrects me.

"I'm sorry. I'm here to change your flat tire if you'd like me to."

"He said he was going to send a mechanic who used to be a police officer so I could trust him."

"That would be me. Except I'm not a him and I'm not a mechanic. I run a cab company."

I hand her one of my business cards.

"But I'm perfectly capable of changing a flat tire," I go on. "And I used to be a police officer so you can trust me."

"Well," she says slowly. "I suppose if the deputy sent you."

She suddenly holds up one index finger to keep me silent as she finishes her phone call. When she's done, she smiles again and tells me, "That was my sister-in-law. My niece just earned her anti-stress badge in Girl Scouts."

"Anti-stress badge?" I wonder. "Are you serious? How do you earn it?"

"Different activities. They keep a feelings diary. They learn how to give foot massages. They visit a spa. They practice breathing exercises."

"How old are these girls?"

"Between ten and twelve. You'd be amazed at the amount of stress they're already under at that age."

"Like the stress of having to earn an anti-stress badge?"

She doesn't say anything.

I continue standing there while she continues to sit in the car.

"It would be easier for me if you get out of the car," I finally explain to her. "And you'll need to turn off the engine."

"Oh," she says.

I watch her crawl down out of her cockpit. She's wearing a sleeveless, silk blend, mock turtleneck, a pair of white Capri pants, and leather flats that match her top exactly. The tunic and shoes are a blue-green, but I'm sure she'd call the color Lagoon or Waterfall. The matching cardigan lies neatly across the backseat.

"How do you know the deputy?" she asks me. "Did you used to work together?"

I'd put her age around mine. She could easily pass for ten years younger if I only look at the skin on her face, but she has a forty-year-old neck and like all women, no matter how well their outsides have been maintained, her true age shows in her eyes and movements.

She seems to know what I'm thinking and she reaches back into her car for a pair of white Ray-Bans and slips them on beneath the bill of her little cap.

"Not exactly. We're old friends," I answer. "We go way back."

"He was attractive. I was surprised."

"Why's that?"

"Oh, you know the stereotype of the country sheriff and his deputies: fat, stupid, bumbling, bad teeth." She tries to scrunch up her face in disgust but amazingly, nothing moves on it except for her lips, which purse slightly, and her nostrils, which flare. "And they chew tobacco."

I nod.

"I suppose where you come from all the cops look like Brad Pitt."

"We do have a fairly good-looking police force."

"Where are you from?"

"A town in Connecticut. I'm sure you've never heard of it."

"I'm flattered that you assume I've heard of Connecticut," I say.

I turn my back on her and start walking toward the flattened groundhog.

I'm really pissed at my son right now.

She follows along behind me, but stops well away from the carcass.

Apparently, removing the dead groundhog from the road was also beneath an officer of the law.

"Why are they called groundhogs?" she asks me. "They don't look like hogs. Are they actually related to hogs?"

"No," I say, heading back to her SUV. "But they do live in the ground."

"Do you think they feel pain?"

"I would imagine so."

"But they're not intelligent?"

I give her a blank look.

"Say as intelligent as a schnauzer, for instance?"

"I've never spent any time around a schnauzer, so I wouldn't know. Can you show me where your spare tire and jack are?"

She gives me a blank look.

"Never mind."

I find what I need and set about changing her tire.

She hovers over me while I jack up the front of her car.

"Did you take a class?" I hear her ask.

"Pardon me?"

"To learn how to change a tire? Did you take a class?"

This is one of those questions where I believe if a person feels compelled to ask it, he or she is not going to understand the answer.

"No," I say.

"Why are you no longer a police officer?"

I lean into the lug wrench with all my weight to loosen the hubcap nuts.

"Mrs. Jameson," I say through gritted teeth, "I'm kind of busy here."

"Oh, I'm sorry. I talk too much when I'm nervous. I've been meaning to discuss it with my doctor. I believe there's a pill on the market now that can get rid of the problem."

"Yeah. Cyanide," I say under my breath.

It's a hot day, and it's been a long time since I've had to change a tire. Plus every inch of my body aches from my brawl with Choker. I can feel sweat beading along my hairline and between my breasts.

The woman continues to prattle on above me despite her earlier apology for doing so. I can tell she's pacing back and forth behind me by watching her shadow move back and forth across the doors of her car.

I decide if I can't beat her, I'll join her, but I'm taking control of the conversation. This is the second wealthy out-of-towner to show up in Jolly Mount today, and I'd like to know why.

"So what brings you to rural Pennsylvania from a town in Connecticut that I've probably never heard of?" I ask when there's a break in her monologue.

"I'm meeting someone in a town called Centresburg. Do you know it?"

"Yes, I do. It's about thirty miles south of here."

I get up from my crouch to get the spare tire.

"Actually, I'm not exactly meeting her. I'm trapping her."

"Trapping her?" I almost laugh. "What did she do?"

"She stole my baby."

The seriousness of the words stop me in my tracks. I lean the tire against the car.

"Someone kidnapped your child?" I ask her.

"Something like that."

"Isn't that something the police should be handling?"

"No, no. It's very important that I don't involve the police. That's why I didn't tell the deputy, even though it occurred to me that he might be helpful since he knows a lot of people around here. You're not going to tell the police, are you?"

"No." I shake my head. "It's none of my business."

I don't know what else to say to her. I can't read her eyes, since they're safely concealed behind sunglasses and I can't read her face, since it's no longer capable of showing any emotion.

"Maybe you could help me?" she says suddenly. "Do you know a woman who lives around here named Jamie Ruddock?"

The name gives me a start. Shannon rode the school bus with a girl named Jamie Ruddock. If I remember correctly, they hated each other. They were both kicked off the bus for awhile after they got into a fight in the middle of the aisle and the driver had to pull over and separate them. Shannon never did give me a good explanation for their animosity.

Only that Jamie Ruddock thought she was better than us, and I understood that reason.

"Jamie Ruddock stole your baby?" I ask her.

"Do you know her?"

"I know a Jamie Ruddock, only she's Jamie Wetzler now. She's married with four kids of her own. Lives in a double-wide near Jolly Mount, and I'm willing to bet she's never been to Connecticut. I doubt she's ever been farther than the mall."

Pamela Jameson considers this information, then walks back to her car and returns with a photograph. She hands it to me.

My heart starts pounding heavily in my chest exactly the way it did when I heard Gerald Kozlowski say Shannon's name.

I haven't seen her since she was sixteen but the face is exactly the same. Maybe a little fuller. The eyes are mine. The smirk is hers. In her teens she wore her shoulder-length hair chopped up in a feathered cut like 90 percent of the other girls and inflicted so many boxed highlights on it, it was difficult to tell its true color. Now it's all one length and a shiny natural chestnut. In the photo she has it skinned back from her face with a headband.

"Is that Jamie Ruddock?" I hear Pamela ask me.

"No." I shake my head. "Do you know this woman?" I ask her.

"I know her very well. Or at least I thought I did."

"You say she's in Centresburg?"

"Maybe. Do you know her?"

Once again, my gut tells me to lie.

"No," I reply.

I stare at the photo again.

Shannon's standing on a city street holding a big Macy's shopping bag. She's wearing a coat, and a pair of red cowboy boots peek out from the cuffs of her jeans.

"This is the woman who stole your baby?" I ask, holding out the photo of my sister.

"Yes."

"When are you trapping her?"

She takes the picture back from me.

"I think maybe I've said too much."

She walks away from me and doesn't return. I finish changing the tire amidst welcome external silence while my brain is filled with the clanging of a hundred unanswered questions about my little sister.

When I'm done, I assume I'm going to be offered some money and I decide to just take whatever she gives me.

I watch her get back in the SUV and turn on the engine, then I realize she's about to leave.

I walk over to her window and stand there like an idiot. She rolls it down. The air-conditioning is already blasting.

"Yes?" she says.

This is one of those situations where I don't like being a woman. A man does a job and he expects to get paid for it; a woman does a job and she feels like she should say thank you for being allowed to do it.

"That took an hour of my time, not to mention the time it took to drive out here." I show her the filth on the palms of my hands. "And it wasn't exactly what I wanted to do on a Saturday afternoon."

"Oh, I see. You expect to get paid? Well, of course. I'm sorry. I thought you were just doing a good deed. I thought country people were friendly."

"We are. That's why I haven't knocked you unconscious and stolen your wallet and your car the way a city person would."

She smiles and reaches into her purse.

"Fifty," I tell her.

She could easily afford two hundred but I know if left to her own discretion, she's going to give me a twenty.

I pull up the bottom of my shirt and wipe the sweat off my face, then tie it up into a knot below my bra.

I look up and find her holding out fifty dollars to me while staring at my midriff.

"Did you get that in the line of duty?" she asks me.

I follow her gaze to the ragged shiny pink scar on my left side.

"Yes," I tell her. "In the line of duty."

I'm not lying. It's the place where my dad hit me with the claw end of a hammer when I told him I was going to keep my baby.

We all have our own definitions of duty.

Chapter Five

MY HOUSE IS A HOMELY HOME. The barn-red paint job is peeling, and the front porch sags alarmingly. It sits about forty feet from the road and is surrounded by so many trees, including two unruly willows that are twice its height, that it's very difficult to see and if somebody does catch a glimpse of it they usually think it's an abandoned outbuilding belonging to a nearby farm.

The interior consists of two bedrooms, one bath, and a large living room area that extends into a roomy eat-in kitchen.

I don't need much square footage, since I'm only one person and don't plan to become more than one, but I do need a lot of space and that's why I love my house. Even though it's relatively small, it has high ceilings and few walls and hardwood floors. Anything that muffles sound makes me claustrophobic.

As I near my driveway, I'm surprised to see Gimp sitting at the end of it. I could've sworn I left him inside with the door closed this morning.

"Hey, boy," I call out my window.

He raises his gray muzzle and fixes his copper eyes on mine while slowly swishing his tail back and forth across the gravel.

I got him from a farm twelve years ago when I started working for the Centresburg police and moved back to Jolly Mount.

I called ahead so the farmer knew I was coming. E.J. came with me. We parked near the barn and sat in the car waiting for him. The next thing we knew a German shepherd mutt—who turned out to be the mother of the litter—came loping toward us on three legs. We'd find out later she'd been hit by a car. A few minutes after that a three-legged black Lab appeared. He'd been caught in a thresher.

E.J. turned to me and said, "If the farmer comes out on one leg, we're getting the hell out of here."

Afterward, Gimp was the only name we could come up with for the puppy.

He doesn't look particularly anxious to get up and walk back down the driveway.

"Give me a break," I tell him but I go ahead and let the lazy mutt in and give him a lift.

There's a car I've never seen before parked in front of my house. It has a New Mexico license plate.

Gimp won't get out of the car. I have to pick him up and set him back on the ground.

"Have I complimented you lately on your guard dog skills?" I ask him.

At that moment, my front door creaks open and a face peers out.

I head toward her, walking at first, then I'm running.

She meets me on the porch.

I kiss her and touch her hair and nuzzle her neck to see if she still smells like my kin.

I try to hold her, but it's not easy to do since she looks to be about nine months pregnant.

Chapter Six

I'M COOKING DINNER. I keep glancing back and forth between the dried beef I'm sizzling in a frying pan with butter, and the extremely pregnant stranger sitting at my table who was my skinny teenaged sister the last time I saw her. Each time I look in her direction, I expect her to be gone.

"I'm really sorry about this," I say, gesturing at the frying pan with my wooden spoon. "I have no food in the house. Nothing. I really need to get to the grocery store."

"It's okay," she says.

I look over at her toying with the stem of her wineglass. She has her feet propped up and her head tilted back with her eyes closed and her hands resting calmly on the hill of her belly.

I've noticed that she's carrying low for a first baby, and she moves fairly carelessly for a first-time mother. No walking on eggshells. No lowering and raising herself in and out of chairs with infinite patience. No cradling or stroking her stomach.

"I haven't had creamed dried beef since we were kids. We practically lived on the stuff. Remember?"

She smiles at the memory. To me it's not a good memory. It reminds me of how poor we were and how the cooking duties in our household fell to me, a child.

I may never have earned an anti-stress badge but by the time I was the age of Pamela Jameson's niece, I could make a dinner for two children and a 200-pound coal miner out of a loaf of Wonder bread, a can of green beans, and some leftover gravy.

"Yeah, I remember," I say.

"What was it Lib said they called it in the army? Shit on a shingle?" she laughs.

I laugh, too, but I'm not feeling merry. I want to remind her how much she used to hate creamed dried beef, but I don't.

Something's not right with Shannon. During the hour or so she's been here she's chatted happily about our childhood, sugarcoating our lives and our relationship with our father in a hyper-sentimental way usually reserved for bad TV movies about country folk produced by people who've never set foot out of L.A. or New York City.

She even makes the occasional comment about someone outside our family who I'm amazed she can remember, like this reference to Lib who worked with our dad in Beverly back before he became boss of his own crew in Jojo. Shannon would only have known him from company picnics and the times he dropped Dad off at the house when he was too drunk to drive.

To hear her talk, hers was a swell life in a swell place that she remembers vividly and fondly, yet she ran away from all of it and stayed away for eighteen years.

I add some flour to the beef mixture, then the milk.

So far we've managed to completely avoid the topics of why she left, why she never came back, and why she never contacted me, but the questions sit in the room with us, taking up more space and more oxygen than either one of our physical bodies.

She did give me a brief account of her most recent life and the circumstances that brought her to my doorstep. According to her, she's been living in a little town in New Mexico, another one of those towns I've probably never heard of. She had a fairly decent job working at a car rental place until they had to cut their staff in half and she was canned. She not only lost her income but also her health insurance.

That was four months ago. She hasn't been able to find another job—who wants to hire a pregnant woman?—and she had to pay her bills with the little savings she had managed to put away to buy things for the baby. She lost her apartment, and she's two months late on her car payments.

The father of the baby isn't in the picture.

The combination of her dire circumstances and the emotional turmoil of being pregnant with her first child reduced her to a desperate, sentimental wreck, and she decided to drive cross-country into the arms of her big sister in her hour of need, in the hopes that I'd let bygones be bygones and take her in.

I haven't told her that I know there's a New York lawyer looking for her because he has something he wants to "give her," and there's also a rich woman from Connecticut here claiming she kidnapped her child, or that I've seen a photo taken of her about a week ago in New York City where she's holding a bulging Macy's shopping bag and wearing a pair of expensive-looking, handmade cowboy boots, or that I realize from all my years watching rich D.C. ladies come and go through my security checkpoints that the cut and texture and perfect copper highlights in her auburn hair come from an elite salon where an appointment probably costs more than a week's paycheck working at a car rental agency, or that I've heard she sometimes goes by an alias, and it's the name of a girl she used to hate.

I have to give her credit. She's done a good job of dressing the part of a poor, out-of-work, unwed mother: maternity jeans, a big tent-sized work shirt in pink denim that looks like it's been washed a hundred times, and a pair of old white gym shoes. But she forgot about her purse; it's a soft, brown leather Coach hobo bag. She left it sitting on the end of my couch.

It's not only the lying that's bothering me. My emotions are twisted up in a way I can't explain. Our reunion should fill me with so much relief and joy that I can't feel anything else. Instead those feelings are taking a backseat to a slowly building anger and resentment.

I suppose it's no different than the way parents feel when a child is late coming home and can't be tracked down and all kinds of terrible, panicked thoughts begin to invade their minds. When the child does finally appear unharmed, an immense love swells up inside them and they're willing to forgive everything, then this is quickly followed by a desire to beat the child senseless for being stupid and selfish and worrying them.

I've never experienced this firsthand. Clay was always home on time even though I wasn't always there waiting for him.

"Do you mind shelling these hardboiled eggs for me?" I ask her.

"No problem."

I hand the bowl to her, pop some bread in the toaster, and go back to stirring the sauce.

While I'm waiting for it to thicken, I listen to the crack of Shannon tapping the eggs against the table and the clink of each tiny piece of shattered shell as she tosses it back into the bowl.

"This is really informal," I apologize again.

Gimp raises his muzzle and his tail slowly thumps against the floor at the sound of my voice and the sight of me walking to the table with food in my hands.

I set the skillet and a plate of toast in front of Shannon.

"I could have had something great for you if I'd have known you were coming."

I look her directly in the eyes as I say it. Our eyes are exactly the same: the same shape and the same shade of golden brown, like butter and brown sugar melting together. It's the only feature we share. We shared it with Mom, too. I used to show Shannon photos of Mom and she'd take them and stand in front of the mirror holding them up next to her, comparing herself.

I hold her stare for a moment, willing her to explain the abruptness and the true reason for her visit after all these lost years, but she doesn't take the bait.

"At least you have wine," she says.

She raises her glass to me, drains it, and reaches for the bottle.

"Are you sure you should do that?" I ask her.

She gives me a smile that borders on patronizing.

"Don't tell me you're going to start lecturing me on prenatal care. Save your breath. I know . . ."

She stops and looks away from me.

"I know all about it. I've read tons of books, and I had a good doctor up until I lost my health insurance," she continues. "Two glasses of wine aren't going to hurt anything."

"This will be your third."

"I didn't realize. I guess I was all caught up in the celebration."

She takes her hand off the bottle.

Instead she reaches for the toast and rips it into bite-sized pieces she drops on her plate, then takes an egg and dices it with a knife while holding it cupped in her hand.

I take the bottle and fill my own glass.

"Aren't you going to ask me about Dad?" I wonder aloud.

She dumps the egg on the toast and starts heaping spoonfuls of dried beef on top of it.

"He's dead. What's to ask?"

The bluntness of her response catches me off guard, not to mention that she knew he was dead.

The shock must be showing on my face because she goes on to explain, "It was on the news. The accident in Beverly. It didn't get the kind of crazy coverage Jojo got, but that was because the Jojo miners survived. The media can't dwell on dead miners for more than a day or two. You can't put corpses on *Jay Leno.*"

Her sudden flippancy makes her sound like an entirely different person than the one who was looking forward to creamed dried beef. She was the same way as a kid; she could be sweet and accommodating, then turn hostile and defensive for reasons I never understood.

"So you knew about Jojo, too?"

"How could I not know? It was on every channel, every magazine, every newspaper."

"So you knew Jimmy was one of the miners who was trapped? And E.J.?"

She nods while she begins shoveling food into her mouth.

I think about her sitting in a nice home somewhere eating a bowl of popcorn, watching the Jolly Mount Mine Disaster unfold on national news along with the rest of the country and never once feeling like she should get in touch with any of us, never once feeling like she should come home.

It's not the life I'd usually imagine for a former teen runaway. Usually when a girl runs away from home she heads for a big city like New York or L.A. She ends up becoming a hooker or a drug addict or both or something equally awful. She ends up dying young or in jail or with some sort of lifestyle that isn't conducive to re-establishing family ties. She spends each day just trying to survive in a world where everyone she meets wants to use and abuse her.

I watch Shannon eat. She's relaxed, clean, sober, healthy, well fed, and carrying a $400 purse.

"Where were you living when you heard about Jojo? New Mexico?" I ask her.

"Yeah, I've been there for awhile. So how's Clay?" she changes the subject.

"He's good. He's here in Jolly Mount, too. He's a Laurel County deputy."

"No kidding? He was just a little kid the last time I saw him."

"I know," I say.

I take a sip of wine and watch her, waiting to see if she has anything more to say on the subject, but the food on her plate holds her attention.

"So I guess it runs in the family," she says between bites. "Is Sheriff Jack still around? He'd have to be a hundred years old by now."

"He died about a year ago, and he was only sixty-five. Heart attack. You'll never believe who's the sheriff now."

"I give up."

"Do you remember Ivan Z, the hotshot football star at Centresburg High who went on to be the hotshot football star at Penn State and got drafted by the Bears?"

"Of course. He was in the local paper all the time. He was hot."

"What would you know? You were only nine when he graduated from high school."

"I was as old as you were when you were mooning over Lib all the time and spending every waking moment doing God knows what with E.J."

"What are you talking about? I never mooned over Lib, and I definitely never did God knows what with E.J. Never."

"Too bad for you. He was cute, too. So Ivan's the sheriff now?"

I nod and drink.

"He left town for a long time after he had that accident at Gertie and smashed up his knee and couldn't play pro ball."

"I remember that. You would have thought the president died. Didn't they even fly the flag at half mast at the high school?"

I nod again and drink some more.

Ivan was definitely a good-looking kid. He had a great body, too, and one of those magnetic personalities that drew people to him whether he wanted the attention or not, yet at the same time there was a kind of tortured haze clouding his baby blues from time to time. It was the same Doomed Adonis quality that JFK Jr. and James Dean had, only instead of being a Rebel Without a Cause, Ivan was more of a Conformist Without a Reason.

Considering our individual promiscuity and our severely limited mating pool, the law of averages predicted we'd end up together one night, and we did.

We had a good romp. Then we drank a few beers and had another one.

Afterward, he said he'd ask me to marry him if he had any intention of ever settling down but he was planning on a lifetime of sleeping with beautiful girls. I told him it was okay: I was hoping for a lifetime of stimulating conversation.

"He came back a couple years ago and Jack gave him a job as a deputy," I finish telling Shannon.

"Let me guess. Sheriff Jack was a Penn State alum."

She reaches for the skillet and helps herself to a second serving.

We eat the rest of our dinner in silence. I easily finish the bottle of wine by myself.

"If you don't mind, I'd like to lie down. I'm really tired," Shannon says to me as we start clearing off the table.

"Sure. There's a pullout bed in the guest room. I'll get some sheets and fix it up for you."

I glance at her. She does look tired.

"We should probably find you a local doctor, too," I add.

"Don't worry. I'll take care of all that stuff," she replies.

I make up the bed for her and return to find her standing in front of one of my bookshelves.

"You still have these stupid books?" she asks me.

She pulls out the National Geographic volume on India and opens it to an aerial photo of a kaleidoscope of women milling around a crowded marketplace in their dazzling saris.

A few years after my mom died, Isabel and Jimmy gave me a membership to the National Geographic Book Club for my birthday, and every month a slim, hardcover volume filled with glossy photos of exotic locales would arrive with the rest of our mail.

Every night after washing the dishes and giving Shannon her bath, I'd sneak the latest book out from its hiding place in my closet and we'd sit on Mom's rag rug and look at the pictures.

I had to hide the books from my dad because he would never have been able to view them as a kind gesture. He would have seen them as an insult: Jimmy implying he was smarter than him.

Jimmy was smarter than him, but Dad was bigger than Jimmy. Jimmy was funnier, too, and could walk on his hands, a feat that never failed to thrill anyone who saw him do it, but my dad could light a match on his teeth and could lift a couch all by himself. In my eyes, it all evened out.

Shannon and I would look at the books and try to imagine what it would be like to live anywhere else, to live in a sophisticated European city, or an African mud hut, or a Japanese house on stilts with paper walls. We'd try to transport ourselves to one of the Mediterranean fishermen's small white houses with green shutters covered in tangles of vines with orange trumpet-shaped blossoms, or to one of the brilliant green Irish hillsides crisscrossed with stone walls and dotted with puffs of black-faced sheep, where even the dust kicked up by an old man pedaling his bicycle down a dirt road looked pink and soft to me like a girl's face powder, not anything like the stubborn black grime that came from the mines and made everything around here gray, even the petals of daisies and the fur on our big white tomcat.

"Don't call them stupid," I tell her. "You used to love those books."

"You used to love them. I was afraid of them. Remember how you had to hide them from Dad? I hated having those books in the house. I was afraid he'd find them."

She closes the book and slides it back on the shelf.

"But you used to love to look at them with me," I remind her.

"Yeah, I guess I used to like to hang out with you sometimes," she says, "but I could've cared less about the stupid books Jimmy gave you."

"Do you remember how we used to sit on Mom's rug?"

She gives me a look of mild annoyance.

"Yeah," she says. "I'm gonna hit the sack."

It's my opportunity to ask her what happened to the rug and what happened to her but something inside me won't let me ask.

I watch her leave the room, hoping she's going to forget to take her purse with her. She does.

I wait until I finish washing the dishes, then I go through it.

There's no wallet, no ID or credit cards, but she has close to $800 in twenties rolled up and held together with a rubber band. I mentally add up the value of the other contents: Sony cell phone, iPod mini, Ray-Ban sunglasses; probably $500 worth of stuff.

I also find a small blue jewelry box. Inside it are a pair of diamond stud earrings, a silver bracelet hung with baby-related charms (a bottle, a rattle, a teddy bear, a stroller, a rocking horse), and a diamond-encrusted heart on a silver chain. The flip side is engraved: *To our angel on earth. Love, Pam.*

I have a feeling this is Jamie Ruddock's jewelry.

In an inside zipped side pocket is a small spray bottle of Guerlain

Paris perfume covered in delicate gold filigree. Very expensive. I take off the lid and spritz some on the underside of my wrist.

It smells like lilacs: our mom's favorite flower.

I think back to the last time I could stand the scent of lilacs. The memory makes me think of the first time I held Shannon. I was scared to death to pick her up, but I had no choice because she wouldn't stop crying.

Mom had come home from the hospital the day before and some ladies from the church had come over to see us in the evening with a box of baby clothes and had effectually terrified me by lecturing endlessly on the proper way to hold Shannon's head. They had me convinced she was as fragile as a snowflake, and I was surprised by her weight and the solid feel of her.

The clothes they had brought were hand-me-downs, but I could tell by the way Mom smiled and praised each item that she was happy with them. She held up pairs of tiny pajamas and sundresses to show me and asked me what I thought while the ladies passed Shannon around, cooing and fussing over her. I thought the clothes were very nice.

Dad came home in the middle of their visit. He made the ladies leave, and he made them take the clothes with them. Then he yelled at Mom and threatened to do terrible things if she ever tried to accept charity again.

If I concentrate hard enough I swear I can still feel the silkiness of Shannon's baby skin on my fingertips. She was the softest thing I had ever touched. Even softer than my mom's velvet Christmas dress.

I held her tiny, writhing body despite my fear. Her face was purple from the exertion of her screams, her eyes angry slits in her head, and her little fists looked like dark pink walnuts thrashing in the air. I took one of them between my fingers and started to talk to her. I brought it to my lips and kissed it and her eyes opened wide and looked into mine. Her crying stopped for the briefest of moments but it was long enough for each of us to establish the other's existence. I see you, her expression seemed to say. I smiled so she'd know I saw her back.

I crawled into Mom and Dad's big bed with her and sat next to Mom.

I didn't know our mother was dead. I didn't know what death looked like. I knew something was terribly wrong because I couldn't wake her up, yet I knew she couldn't be asleep because her eyes were open. I didn't like the way they stared. They reminded me of the black unseeing eyes of the mangled blue jay our cat had left on our back porch as a gift last month.

I also didn't like the cold that was seeping into her skin.

Dad was gone. It was Saturday morning. He had left the night before after his fight with Mom. He was on a bender that would last until Sunday.

During the day and night before he returned I never thought about going to get help or calling someone, even though we had a list of numbers posted next to the kitchen phone including the Bertollis (Lib and Teresa) and the Phyrsts (Jimmy and Isabel) and the fire department, the police, and Mom's doctor.

The phone rang from time to time, but I never thought of answering it.

My dad's rantings about how we didn't need anybody's help, we could do everything ourselves, we didn't need charity kept echoing inside my head.

I only left Shannon to get her a bottle or pick lilacs off the bush outside our kitchen and put them on Mom's body when she started to smell funny.

I was only six years old. I was a child, too, and no one could have blamed me if I let myself be a child, if I chose to sit in a corner and cry, or run out of the house and down the road in hysterics, or get myself a huge bowl of ice cream with chocolate syrup I wouldn't normally be allowed to have and watch tons of TV I wouldn't normally be allowed to watch, or if I chose to ignore my baby sister altogether, if I chose to hate her, if I chose to blame her.

I chose to take care of her and I never regretted my decision, even though I've ended up paying a price for it. But how could I have known that by taking care of someone so early in my life I was going to make it impossible to ever let anyone take care of me?

I go back to the kitchen sink and wash the perfume off my wrist, then I put everything back in the purse and write Shannon a note with my cell number in case she wakes up and needs me.

I don't give her specifics. I don't tell her I'll be out introducing Gerald Kozlowski to some locals.

Chapter Seven

J OLIMONT, PENNSYLVANIA, BEGAN AS a small trading post
where French trappers, Seneca Indians, British merchants, and
enterprising colonists came to indulge in beaver and booze in the shadow
of a rolling range of calm green mountains not far from a small, slowly
snaking river that eventually leads to a branch of the Susquehanna.

The town itself was never much to look at, just a few ramshackle
buildings. No real businesses, not even a general store. No tradesmen
except for a blacksmith and a tanner, who also served as a surgeon and
dentist when needed and when threatened. And only one place to get a
meal or a room or a drink: the Jolimont Inn.

It wasn't the town that people remembered but the surroundings.
There were far more spectacular natural settings to be seen, but this was
a place that called out to a traveler to stop awhile and feel at peace. The
mountains were protective but not intimidating like the daunting
ranges farther west; they were wild but not unruly, lush but not gaudy.

One hill stood out more prominently than all the others. It was a
little broader, a little higher, and because of the large number of elm
trees growing there, whose buds were red-tipped before turning green,
the entire hillside was tinged a hazy, dark pink each spring.

When describing how to get there, the French always ended their
directions by saying the town was "au pied du joli mont."

At the foot of the beautiful mountain.

Over time—after the beaver were trapped and hunted into near-extinction along with the Indians, and the French and British were asked to leave, and the colonists became known as Americans—the town lost its original reason to exist, and may have ceased to exist altogether if it wasn't for the farms surrounding it and the Jolimont Inn, which continued to be a useful stopping-over point for people journeying to and from Pittsburgh and points beyond.

Then an ancient black rock that could be dug and blasted out of its hillsides and sold in vast quantities to factories and steel plants was discovered. The town had its new and final reason to exist.

However, Jolly Mount never thrived the way some coal towns did. It wasn't the site where the area's most powerful coal baron, Stanford Jack, decided to base his operations. He and his partner, Joseph Peppernack, chose a town called Centresburg, farther south, where more of his mines were located.

Jolly Mount never had the shops and the amenities that came along with the mansions belonging to the mine operators and the other men who were successful in businesses related to or dependent on mining. It never had the impressive courthouse and marble-columned bank. It also never had the noisy, grimy backstreets lined with overcrowded, company-built row homes.

It's stayed basically the same, supplying only the most pressing needs of its residents, most of whom prefer to live scattered throughout the countryside rather than along Route 12, the main road through town.

Jojo and her sister mine, Beverly, still provide most of the jobs. Kids still play around the smoldering bony piles despite their mothers' warnings. The beautiful mountain is still here, too, but the French pronunciation of the town's original name is long gone, having been modified over time to fit the American tongue.

The only things French left in town are the way lovers kiss and the fries at Jolly's when the grill is working.

I finish my tour guide version of the town's history just as Gerald Kozlowski and I arrive at Jolly's.

He doesn't comment, but he did listen attentively when he wasn't on his cell phone, which was most of the time. The calls were all from clients, and consisted predominantly of assurances from him to them that everything was under control.

He didn't seem to care if I overheard his side of the conversations, and I understood why since he never said anything that could be useful to someone trying to figure out what he was up to, but I did notice a change in the way he spoke depending on the caller.

For some, his language was formal, aloof, and peppered with big words: a voice that promised success and prosperity yet was laced with an underlying menace and detachment, like a dictator addressing the starving masses below his palace balcony.

With others, he softened his voice, simplified his vocabulary, and sounded almost as if he were trying to console and control a child.

Jolly's parking lot is full. Saturday nights are usually pretty busy and tonight is no exception.

The weather turned cooler after the sun went down but the evening's still warm for this time of year. People have spilled out of the bar onto the porch with their cigarettes and beers to enjoy the clear, mild night, the women in jeans jackets and the men in insulated flannel shirts.

Kozlowski has made an attempt to look more casual and blend in by putting on a pair of jeans, but they don't help much since he's still wearing his Prada loafers and the black T-shirt and blazer. At first I thought the jacket was the same one he wore earlier but now I realize it's a slightly lighter shade of black.

"So what color do you wear when you're feeling really festive and light-hearted?" I ask him as we push through the people gathered on the porch, all of them greeting me and eyeballing him. "Charcoal? Ash gray?"

He glances at me. I'm wearing a pair of jeans, high-heeled, dusty rose suede boots with snakeskin toes, a silver tank top, my Stetson, and the cropped pink leather motorcycle jacket I bought for myself for my fortieth birthday a couple months ago.

"Adults who wear bright colors are either tasteless exhibitionists," he says to me, "or people trying desperately to seem festive and light-hearted when in actuality they wish they were dead."

We start making our way to the bar, but he gets distracted by the Jolly Mount Mine Disaster clippings and photos posted on the wall.

The story from yesterday's newspaper about the Jolly Mount Five suing J&P Coal has been added to the display.

Someone has already written the words, "Fuck you," in pen next to the headline. I don't know if the sentiment is directed at Cam Jack or the miners.

I leave Kozlowski there while I continue on to the bar to get a drink. It's packed. The tables are full, too.

I spot E.J. and Ray down at one end. Ray waves and smiles and calls out to me.

E.J. looks in my direction, then goes right back to looking into his glass of whiskey.

He's sulking because I called him a slut earlier. And a pig. And then I think I called him disgusting, too. But none of that matters because I'm sure he started it. I'm sure he said something insulting to me first; I just can't remember it anymore.

He's always had this uncanny ability to make me feel like I've treated him badly when I haven't. Usually, he's the one who's treated me badly, then when I react to him treating me badly, he acts like my reaction came out of the blue and I'm some kind of crazy, violent, overly emotional, female head case.

"Hey, Champ."

Sandy appears in front of me. She holds up a fist, shakes it, and smiles.

"You really beat the crap out of Choker," she shouts over the barroom din. "How are you feeling?"

"Okay," I tell her. "Let me have a beer."

"On the house," she says.

Kozlowski joins me.

Sandy eyes him appreciatively and blushes profoundly.

"Grey Goose and tonic," he orders. "On crushed ice."

A shadow of panic crosses her face.

"Grey Goose is a brand of vodka." I help her out.

"Oh, sure. I knew I'd heard of it. I've seen ads for it in magazines at my hairdresser. No, we don't have that here. I'm sorry."

"Absolut?" he asks.

She nods.

"I'm absolutely sure."

"Absolut vodka," he states.

"Give him a vodka and tonic," I tell her. "Whatever vodka you have will be fine."

I turn to him.

"Come on, Gerry. Lighten up. Surely there's been a time in your life when you weren't drinking top-shelf liquor."

He studies me for a moment, trying to figure out how to play me. Should he let me into his confidence a little? Should he keep me completely on the outside?

"I prefer Gerald," he says.

"Okay, Gerald. There's a couple friends of mine at the end of the bar. They're also two of the Jolly Mount Five. Come on. I'll introduce them to you."

We walk over to E.J. and Ray, who are leaning with their backs against the bar now, watching a game of pool. I tell them Gerald's visiting from out of town. He's a lawyer from New York. They both look less than enthused.

"Let me guess; you're not crazy about lawyers," Kozlowski says with a far nicer smile than he's ever tried using on me.

E.J. and Ray look at the hand extended toward them.

"Not exactly," Ray replies.

"Well, I'd appreciate it if you'd give me a chance as an individual before you pass judgment on me in regards to my profession. You know what they say, ninety percent of lawyers give the rest a bad name."

"That's a lot," Ray comments.

Kozlowski looks over at me.

I stick my face in my draft and shrug.

"It's a joke," he explains.

Ray pushes his shaggy brown hair out of his eyes and off his forehead, which is prematurely marked with heavy lines that come from the constant pinched expression most people think is a scowl but is actually concentration.

He's wearing a pale yellow shirt pinstriped in blue. The material is so thin, his sleeveless undershirt is visible beneath it. His shorts are cutoffs that come down to his knees. His sneakers are black canvas with matching holes where his big toes have pushed through. He keeps his tube socks pulled up to the middle of his calves.

Growing up, Ray was one of the truly poor kids like me, but unlike me he never learned to stop dressing like one.

No one looks more at home in a scratched hard hat and dirty rain gear with a miner's tool belt strapped around his waist than Ray does, but every time I see him in a social situation his outfits bring back every uncomfortable memory I have of all the hopelessly unfashionable, ill-fitting hand-me-downs I was forced to wear to school: the flood pants; the frayed, discolored collars on the cheap polyester blouses that always had snags running down the sleeves and quarter-sized shadows of permanent mystery stains dotting the front; the scuffs on the shoes and the slapping echo they made walking down the hall when the soles began to fall off; the faded T-shirts with outdated slogans or corny decals that only kids who weren't given a choice would ever have the guts to put on their bodies.

Ray takes Kozlowski's hand and they shake.

I look down at my ensemble. My clothes may be tasteless in the opinion of some, but they were never worn by somebody else first.

E.J. shakes his hand, too.

"We had a guy in school with a name like yours," Ray ventures.

Kozlowski smiles again and tilts his head a little like he's trying to understand.

"You mean Polish?" he asks.

"Well, of course there were lots of kids with Polish names. There's tons of Polacks work in the mines. My own mom's Polish. No, I mean a guy with a name like Gerald."

He elbows E.J.

"You know who I'm talking about? Remember him? What was his name?"

E.J. takes a drag off his cigarette and looks thoughtful.

"You mean that Jonathan kid?"

"Yeah, that was it: Jonathan. Not John or Johnny or Jay."

They fall silent for a moment.

"Jonathan," Ray says, nodding his head.

"Jonathan," E.J. repeats.

Ray smiles. "You remember him?"

E.J. nods.

"Yeah."

Kozlowski looks blankly from one to the other then back at me again.

I pop a few peanuts in my mouth and shrug again.

"You wanted to talk to locals," I say.

"So you two are part of the Jolly Mount Five?" asks Kozlowski, making an attempt at conversation.

This is the wrong subject to pick, but I let him plow on.

Neither E.J. or Ray responds to Kozlowski's question. They continue drinking and watching him.

"You were heroes," he adds.

"We weren't heroes," E.J. counters immediately. "We didn't do anything heroic."

"We were survivors," Ray adds. "There's a big difference."

"I can see the distinction," Kozlowski says, "but still a lot of people feel you have to have a certain amount of strength and courage to survive something like that."

Ray nods.

"A lot of people called us heroes, but we never saw it that way. We even had some guy from a toy company who wanted to make action figures of us. Remember that, E.J.?"

E.J. nods.

"Remember what Jimmy asked him? He asked him if the action figures were going to be part of a series: trapped coal miners, Indians on reservations, starving Africans, paralyzed soldiers in wheelchairs. He said they could call the collection Luckless Bastards."

They both smile broadly at the memory.

"Or maybe Lucky Bastards would be a better name since you're all survivors," Kozlowski suggests.

"Maybe," Ray says but the smile leaves his face and E.J.'s and neither of them look convinced.

"So what do the two of you do for a living now?"

"We work in the mines," Ray replies.

"You went back in the mines after what happened to you?"

"What else are we gonna do?"

"I guess I don't know." Kozlowski looks authentically stunned. "But surely there has to be something else you can do. Wasn't there a book deal and a movie deal? Didn't you make some money from that?"

"Yeah, we made some money from that but not as much as people think. People think we're millionaires now but we're not," Ray starts to explain. "And what people don't understand is when you make a big unexpected chunk of money like we did, there are all kinds of rules and regulations and fine print the IRS comes up with so you end up paying about half of it in taxes, and as if that's not enough, then they use this new money—which you ain't ever gonna make again in your life 'cause you're sure as hell not planning on getting trapped in a mine again—to say now you're in a new tax bracket and that allows them to take more money than usual out of your regular paycheck, which hasn't gone up at all. Then you got to pay an accountant to do your taxes for you 'cause there ain't no way in hell you can figure them out by yourself anymore.

"And in order to get any of this money from these deals in the first place, you have to get an agent to negotiate things for you and a lawyer to make sure everything's on the up-and-up, including what the agent's doing. So by the time you pay all these people and the government and you buy everyone in your family a new dishwasher, there ain't really that much money left. Especially if your wife makes you buy a bigger house and she goes out and buys a sports car along with a bunch of other stuff."

I check on E.J. He has his cap pulled down as far as it can go without interfering with his drinking. It looks like he'd crawl into his glass of whiskey if he could.

I can't tell if he's reacting to Ray's tendency to talk too much or if he's hiding from a woman he jilted.

I scan the patrons and notice a blonde standing by the pool table in a pair of low-rise, acid-washed jeans, with a Tweety Bird tattoo on her shoulder and her tits practically popping out of a too-tight black halter top, shooting daggers at him from between her heavily frosted blue eyelids.

"But, see"—Ray moves closer to Kozlowski, taking him into his confidence—"no one wants to hear this. No one wants to hear us bitch about the fact that some TV company gave us each $100,000 for doing nothing just so they could make some movie about something that happened to us that was beyond our control.

"Everybody wants to think we're millionaires so they can either hate us or be happy for us, but at the very least we give them something to talk about."

E.J. noticeably cringes at the thought of people talking about him.

"What about the other three? Are they still working in the mines, too?"

"Our boss took early retirement. E.J.'s dad, Jimmy, lost his leg, so he's not working anywhere anymore. Dusty took his money and opened a restaurant. It just went out of business a couple weeks ago."

Sandy comes by with a bottle of Jack Daniel's to refill E.J.'s glass.

"You want another beer?" she asks me.

"Is it on the house, too?"

"Sure. One more."

"Why are you getting drinks on the house?" Ray asks.

"I escorted Choker out of the bar earlier today."

"I heard about that," Ray replies. "What was that about? Unfinished police business?"

"I heard he made fun of her tits," E.J. comments.

He winces the moment the words leave his mouth. I can tell he regrets it, but he won't apologize and I'm not going to cut him any slack.

I notice a table opening up near the door, and I tap Kozlowski on the shoulder.

"Let's go sit over there," I shout at him over the noise. "I want to talk to you alone."

I say good-bye to Ray and turn my back on E.J.

"Why did you want to come over here?" Kozlowski asks me before we're even seated. "I didn't get a chance to ask them if they know Shannon."

"You don't need to ask them because they would have told you what I'm about to tell you."

I let the tension build for a moment while a country-western star on the jukebox sings about a flag he's proud of and a life he can hang his hat on.

"Shannon Penrose is my sister," I announce. "She ran away eighteen years ago, and I haven't seen her since. Up until meeting you, I didn't even know if she was dead or alive."

He sits back in his chair and cradles his drink in his crotch.

"Why did you lie to me?" he finally asks.

"I didn't know anything about you. I didn't know if I could trust you. Maybe you wanted to hurt her. But then I thought about it and since I can't tell you where she is, I figured I might as well be honest and see if in return you'll tell me what you know about her."

He thinks about my proposition while swirling the ice in his drink. The bar is loud, but all I hear are the cubes clinking against the glass.

"Shannon and I have known each other for several years," he tells me.

"In New York?"

"In New York."

"Is that where she lives?"

"Yes. During that time we've worked together on several projects. She recently broke one of our business agreements, and that's why I'm trying to find her."

"What kind of business?"

"That's as much as I'm going to tell you."

"You said you had something you wanted to give her? What is it exactly? A bullet in the head?"

"No. Nothing like that. I don't want any harm to come to her. On the contrary, I want her healthy. I don't have anything to give her. I just want to talk to her and try and convince her to come back to New York with me."

I wonder if he's the father of the baby, but if he is, why would he say they have a business arrangement? What could Shannon possibly do that would lead her to get professionally involved with a lawyer? Then again, he could be lying about everything.

"What makes you think she'd be here?"

He doesn't answer for a few minutes. I can tell he's trying to decide how much he should tell me. He doesn't trust me either.

He takes a sip of his drink, then leans over the table so I can hear him better.

"In all the time I've known her, she never told me anything about her past. Nothing about her family or the place where she grew up.

"Then one day a couple of months ago I was visiting her at her apartment, and she had the TV on. An ad from General Electric came on. It was a group of sweaty, half-naked, gorgeous models—male and female—strategically streaked with dirt, pretending to be coal miners. The point of the ad was to say that now there's technology that can make coal a viable energy source again. The catchphrase was something about coal being beautiful.

"She flew into a rage. I've never seen anything like it. Especially from Shannon. She started ranting about how there's no way coal can ever be a clean fuel. There's no technology that can accomplish this. Anyone who's ever lived in a coal town knows this. It's all lies. And the new technology they're talking about is all automated so it's not going to bring back any jobs. It's not going to help any of the people living in coal mining regions, but what it is going to do is continue to ruin the land that's finally begun to heal and contaminate the water and pollute the air. And for what? To make rich people richer. All the coal companies are owned by oil companies now. It's all the same thing. They're all owned by the same men. It's not an alternative to oil. It's not going to give us cheaper energy. It's going to kill us. They're trying to kill us."

He pauses to take another drink.

"I couldn't believe it. Shannon is the least excitable woman I've ever known, not to mention I've never heard her utter anything that could even remotely be construed as political. For the longest time she thought Condoleezza Rice was the name of that little Hispanic actress on *Desperate Housewives*.

"After she calmed down, I was able to get her to talk a little bit about what set her off," he goes on. "That was when she told me her father was killed in a coal mine in Jolly Mount, Pennsylvania, a long time ago."

"Twelve years ago," I supply for him.

"I asked her if that wasn't the same town where the miners had been rescued a couple of years ago. She said it was. She never talked about the town again, but I'll never forget how upset she was and how attached she seemed to be to the place. If I hadn't known any better, I would have thought she'd just left it a couple of months ago instead of years ago and that she was terribly homesick. It was so out of character. Coming here was just a hunch."

His attention swings away from me. He's watching someone walk toward us.

He stands with his handshake at the ready.

"I'm heading out," I hear E.J. say.

"It was nice meeting you," Kozlowski says.

"Same here," E.J. replies.

He looks down at me, says nothing, and walks away, the son of a bitch.

"Excuse me," I say, getting up out of my chair.

"Where are you going?" Kozlowski asks me.

"I'll be right back," I assure him.

I rush out the front door and down the porch steps. E.J.'s already around the side of the building heading for his truck in the parking lot.

"Where are you going?" I shout after him. "Looking for fresh meat? Nothing left for you around here? Pretty soon you're going to have to start crossing state lines to find someone new to plug."

"Look who's talking," he replies over his shoulder. "You had to cross state lines twenty years ago."

"Go to hell!"

He keeps walking toward his truck. I can't believe he's not going to stay and fight.

I run after him.

"So it's okay for you to screw around because you're a man, but it's not okay for me because I'm a woman," I say once I catch up to him.

He takes his packet of Marlboros out of his shirt pocket and taps one into his waiting fingers.

"Don't start this again, Shae-Lynn," he says, looking tired and annoyed. "You know I don't feel that way. You just want to get in a fight. You don't even care what the fight's about."

"And why would I want to get in a fight?"

"Because it's the only thing you're good at."

His words stop me cold. I feel like I'm ten years old again and he's just made fun of my inferior aim with his BB gun, or he's beat me again in our daily race to the top of Union Deposit Road where we used to throw down our bikes and walk to the guard rail, with our lungs bursting and our T-shirts stuck to our backs with sweat, and stare across the valley at the railroad tracks cut into the mountainside waiting for the 4:05 freight train to go by.

He seems to sense how much he's hurt me and once again he looks sorry like he did in the bar, but he doesn't apologize.

He lights up his cigarette, takes a drag from it, and blows a frail stream of smoke into the thick black country night.

"There's nothing wrong with me getting laid now and then. I never use anyone," he tells me.

"Depends on what you consider using someone. I have a feeling acid-washed Blondie in there feels used," I say more to myself than to him.

"I never lie. Women are the ones who lie," he responds, his voice turning unexpectedly harsh. "They're the ones who say they don't mind if it's just for one night, when actually they do mind. They think if they can get you to sleep with them just once, you're going to be under their spell for life, and they can make you do whatever they want. I'm not looking for a wife. I'm not even looking for a girlfriend. I have sex with women because it makes me feel good. And I don't have to justify myself to anybody. Least of all you. Why don't you go back to your date?"

"He's not my date. He's a client."

"You don't have to make up a reason to be with him. You think I care about you hanging out with that guy?"

"She's back," I announce before I can stop myself.

I feel a lump in my throat, and I swallow it quickly.

"Shannon," I further explain. "She's here. She's sleeping in my guest room right now."

"You're kidding. When did this happen?"

"She just showed up at my house today after I talked to you."

"Holy shit. So what's she got to say for herself?"

"Not much. I didn't really push her. I wanted to give her some time."

"What's her tie to this Kozlowski guy?"

"I still don't know. I didn't tell her about him, and I didn't tell him I know where she is."

"Why not?"

"I'm not sure what's best for Shannon. I think she's in some kind of trouble, but I don't know what. I'm pretty sure she's lying to me about everything. And it turns out there's someone else here in town looking for her besides Kozlowski: a woman who's running around with Shannon's photo but knows her by a different name and is accusing her of something criminal."

"For Christ's sake, Shae-Lynn."

We've reached E.J.'s truck. He leans against the hood and smokes for a minute before he offers any more advice.

"You can't let Shannon jerk you around. Tell her what you know. See if her explanation makes sense. If not, get Clay involved."

"Why are you against her?"

"I'm not against her. I just don't want her taking advantage of you."

I can try and convince myself that Shannon never meant much to E.J., that to him she was just my pesky younger sister who I had to let tag along with me a lot since she didn't have a mom at home to watch her. For the most part, I think he regarded her as less interesting than a puppy and more burdensome than a shadow, but he understood she was as devoted to me as the first and as impossible to get rid of as the second, so he tolerated her presence.

Yet at the same time, I know he cared about her, too, in his way. He would have never dreamed of giving her a hug or calling her by her name instead of "midget," but he built a toy box for her in junior high wood shop, and he used to sneak out of his own house on Christmas Eve after we were in bed and stand below our window with a string of sleigh bells pretending to be Santa's reindeer for her, and he was always available any time she had something that needed to be fixed, whether it was a flat tire on her bike or the mysterious inner workings of the Easy-Bake oven I found for her at the Goodwill Store for a dollar and fifty cents.

When she left she hurt him, too, even though he'd never admit it. He's entitled to his opinion of her, good or bad.

"She's a grown woman who hasn't wanted anything to do with you for almost twenty years," he continues. "She's not your responsibility anymore. If she got herself into trouble, let her get herself out of trouble."

"It's not that simple. She's pregnant. She's going to have a baby any day now."

He shakes his head.

"So that's why she came back. For help with the baby."

"I don't think so."

"The baby's not your responsibility either."

"It will be my niece or nephew."

"It will be her son or daughter. She's the mother."

He tosses the butt of his cigarette onto the parking lot blacktop and stubs it out with the toe of his steel-toed boot. He'll wear the same boots—only an older, more broken-in pair—into the mines tomorrow. I'm suddenly seized by a spasm of terror. I want to grab him by his arm and cling to him and beg him not to go back inside.

Instead I watch his hand reach out and grab my arm. He shakes me gently as he speaks.

"You believed your dad killed her. You believed your own father killed your sister. Do you understand what a fucked-up thing that is to have to carry around inside yourself all these years?"

"Do you realize how fucked up things were to begin with in order for me to be able to believe that?"

"Yeah, I do."

I meet his eyes. In the dark they look silver, not blue, like a pair of liquid nickels.

In all our years of friendship, we never discussed details. I never described my home life to him. I blamed my injuries on my clumsiness like I did at school, but this explanation was destined to fail eventually with E.J. because he knew me better than my teachers and he also didn't have any reason to want to believe the lies.

He spent a lot of time with me. He knew I was athletic and coordinated. He knew I couldn't possibly fall down stairs and run into walls as much as I claimed to when he wasn't around.

I don't know exactly when I began to realize that he knew I was lying and that it wasn't necessary for me to do it anymore. This didn't mean I was going to start telling him what was really going on. Somehow I knew he couldn't stand hearing it any more than I could stand saying it. It was simply enough for me to know that there was someone who knew the truth about me and didn't find me repulsive.

We used to talk about running away together without ever stating the reason why. We talked about taking Shannon with us. We made lists of supplies and grand plans for living off the land. But in the end I couldn't let him do it. He had a great mom and dad. We each had to accept that we were prisoners of our own lives: his a good one, mine a bad one. He was powerless to save me from mine, and I was unwilling to lead him away from his.

I never stopped to think what it must have been like for him to accept that there was nothing he could do to help me.

My cell phone rings. I'm tempted not to answer it, but it's my business number and I'm also a mom so I always have to answer.

"Jolly Mount Cab," I say.

"Hello. I'm trying to get in touch with a Shae-Lynn Penrose."

"That's me."

"Hello, Shae-Lynn. This is Pamela Jameson. We met earlier today."

We met—that's a nice way to put it. Sounds like we attended the same tea party.

"I remember," I say. "I changed your tire."

"Yes, you did. We also talked a little bit about why I'm here. Do you remember that?"

"Yes."

"Well, I have a proposition for you. I'm meeting Jamie Ruddock tomorrow at ten A.M. at a place called Eatn'Park."

I smile to myself despite the fact that I've just received further proof that Shannon is continuing to lie to me. She used to love Eatn'Park pies. Especially the coconut cream. I can picture her as a little kid sitting across from me in a booth with dabs of toasted meringue glistening on the end of her nose and the bottom of her chin.

"You said you were going to trap her."

"Yes, something like that. It occurred to me that I might need protection."

"Protection?"

"Yes. I thought since you have a law enforcement background, and you're obviously a woman who can handle herself in unorthodox situations . . ."

I hardly consider changing a tire to be an unorthodox situation, but I don't point this out to her.

". . . I thought maybe you could help me. I'll pay you, of course."

"Okay," I tell her without even thinking about it. "I'll meet you at your hotel about nine-thirty so we can discuss details before you meet with her."

"That sounds fine. Good night."

I put my phone back in my pocket. E.J. has wandered away from his truck toward the street.

I follow him. He's walking aimlessly, breathing heavily through his nose, his fists and jaw clenched, his eyes open but not seeing.

He's having one of his panic attacks.

He described to me what they feel like once. He begins to doubt where he is, then he stops doubting and he's certain that he's having a dream. The sky, the space, the fresh air, the freedom: it isn't real; it's one more cruel illusion his failing brain is playing on him before he suffocates.

The terror grows inside him. He's sure he's back inside Jojo. He's sure he's going to wake up soon inside that horrible backward new world where only sleep brings scenes of life and waking brings nothing but fathomless black. Reality is darkness until death arrives with eternal darkness. Sight is not reality. Sight is insanity.

I put my hand on his arm and talk to him softly, hoping the sound of my voice will cut through his mounting hysteria.

He takes his cap off. Beads of sweat have gathered along his hairline.

He turns his head in my direction. The frantic glitter begins to fade from his eyes and he unclenches the jaw that was holding back the useless screams of a trapped man.

Chapter Eight

I N M Y D R E A M, I come downstairs after hearing my dad's truck drive away and see his dinner pail still sitting on the kitchen counter. The sight fills me with horror, and I blink my eyes hard several times to make sure I'm really seeing what I think I'm seeing.

It's true. He's forgotten his dinner pail.

I quickly recount the morning's events, looking for any way the disaster can be blamed on me. I remember packing his lunch while his coffee was brewing like I do every morning. I left the pail sitting in the exact spot on the counter where I leave it every morning. His breakfast was ready on time. He wasn't in a hurry because he was running late. We didn't have any type of conversation that distracted him. Our only interaction was the kiss I planted on his coarse cheek. It always tickles my lips like they've brushed across sandpaper.

It's not my fault. This knowledge should make me relax but instead my stomach heaves with fear. It's his fault. This is worse. Because my dad doesn't believe anything is ever his fault. If he can't find a way to blame a problem on me or someone else, he blames it on Fate or as he prefers to call it, his "shitty luck," and the rage that grows out of this idea is incredible.

I know he won't notice he's forgotten his lunch until he gets to work. Beverly is only a few miles away, but he won't drive back. To drive back will be finding a solution to the problem, which will be admitting it's his fault and he has control. By going into the mines and working a grueling eight-hour shift with no food, he will be accepting that he is the eternal victim of Fate's cruel whims. He will suffer in silence and when he unleashes his anger later, in his mind it will be justified.

I'm still standing in the kitchen when I hear Shannon at her toddler gate at the top of the stairs.

"Shae," she calls. "Shae. Come get me."

I look back and forth between the silver bucket and my baby sister, back and forth between the fear of what might happen to me if I don't go and the fear of what might happen to her if I do go, back and forth between my duty to him and my duty to her.

I decide I have to take Dad's lunch to him. He needs it. He can't work all day without a meal, but I'm going to have to ride my bike and Shannon can't come with me.

I grab a box of Cheerios so she won't be hungry and I run upstairs with it. I explain to her that I have to take Daddy his lunch and if she stays in our bedroom like a good girl until I get back, we'll do something fun when I get home from school.

I make sure the windows are firmly latched. I make sure she has her blanket and some toys and the Cheerios, and I tell her she has to stay in the room no matter what.

She sits in the middle of Mom's rug and looks up at me with her coppery eyes and nods.

I leave and lock the door behind me. Our house is very old and the two upstairs bedrooms have doors that can be latched from the outside but not from inside. This has always given me the creeps.

I'm halfway down the stairs when she starts to cry and scream for me. I put on my coat, hat, and gloves, grab Dad's dinner pail, and run for my bike.

I'm a strong kid. Tough as wire. A real tomboy. Even with the weight of Dad's dinner pail slipped over my handlebar banging against my knee and the cold burning my lungs and making my eyes tear and turning my fingers to ice inside my thin gloves, I make good time.

When I come over the last hill approaching the complex and see the knot of miners still waiting for the mantrip, I begin to sob with relief.

I drop my bike and start running toward them. My legs and arms instantly turn to jelly once my adrenaline stops pumping, and I can barely carry the heavy pail. I have to use both hands. I take my gloves off to gain more traction. I watch my legs move beneath me, but I don't seem to be making any forward progress.

Beverly is one of J&P's smaller concerns and much younger than Jojo: a simple slope mine that was made by blasting a couple entries into the hillside, laying down some track for the mantrip, and installing a conveyor belt and some cast-off cutting and loading machinery brought in from one of their larger, more lucrative mines in the southern part of the county.

Six years earlier one of those mines had been the site of the second deadliest mine explosion in the history of Pennsylvania. Up until that time the general public considered Stan Jack's mines to be about as safe as they could be, which to a miner's way of thinking was like saying some ponds aren't as wet as others, but after Gertie blew, killing half the male population of the town of Coal Run, even Stan Jack had to be more careful.

I drag the bucket toward my dad.

The sky and the hills are the same shade of pale lead. A weak sun has begun to rise behind a thick layer of dirty clouds, but it isn't giving off enough light yet for the two dozen shivering, yawning miners to be able to make out the features of one another's faces. They stare at the ground, stamping their heavy steel-toed safety shoes and blowing warm air into their cupped hands, while watching the first spits of snow float into the shafts of yellow light given off by their helmets.

One of them notices me, points, and nudges a buddy in the arm.

Soon they're all looking in my direction, all of them smiling except for my dad.

"Would you look at that?" I hear Jimmy's brogue. "Penrose is gettin' room service."

A chorus of low, rumbling laughter floats toward me, and I feel immediately better. I love the deep tones of men's laughter much more than the cackling of women.

"You forgot your dinner, Daddy," I say when I finally arrive in front of him.

Lib and Jimmy are standing next to him. I know they're much older than me—around the same age as my dad—but today they seem young. Even younger than me. Yet they don't look like children, and I know I'm a child.

For the first time ever I notice how smooth and unlined Jimmy's face is and how the fringe of hair sticking out from beneath his miner's helmet is the glossy auburn color of an acorn's bottom. I notice the mischievous way Lib smiles around the toothpick jutting from between his teeth. Even though it's cold, he has the sleeves of his coveralls and the long underwear beneath rolled up to his elbows and his pale, muscular forearms look like they've been carved from hairy marble.

There's another rumble among the men, this one of praise. My dad takes the dinner bucket from me and gives my head a rub.

I don't dare look up at him.

The others begin to trudge to the mantrip, and he follows along.

Lib lags behind. He finishes smoking his last cigarette for the day and tosses it on the ground, where he crushes it with the tip of his steel toe. He kneels down in front of me and takes my small clean pink hands in his big callused ones, sprinkled with blue-gray scars like bits of pencil points broken off beneath the skin. He rubs them to try and get some circulation back in them.

102

He's only been back from Vietnam for a year, and I still thank God in my prayers every night for keeping him safe.

"You're a good kid, Shae-Lynn," he says.

Then why does my dad hate me? my brain screams, but I will never say those words out loud with my voice.

I breathe in the heady smell of him—tobacco and machinery grease and a hint of minty toothpaste almost masking his morning shot of whiskey—and nod.

He stands up and reaches into one of his pockets and hands me a chocolate bar.

"For the ride home," he tells me.

Up until he says these words I've forgotten about the ride home, then I suddenly remember Shannon and I'm afraid again for a whole different reason.

I ride back to the house imagining the worst, but everything turns out to be fine. Isabel's car is parked in our driveway. She babysits Shannon while I'm in school. It never occurred to me to call her for help.

I fly into the house and find her at the kitchen table feeding Shannon her breakfast.

"Shae-Lynn," she gasps. "I was worried. Where were you?"

"I, I . . . ," I gulp.

"You should have left me a note."

"Is Shannon okay?"

"She's fine."

Isabel gets up from the table, wipes her hands on her apron, and comes over to me to give me a hug.

While she holds me I watch Shannon staring at me from her high chair.

I know my dad will give me a good beating tonight because I embarrassed him, but at least he will be in a better mood than if he'd been hungry all day.

What bothers me more than thinking about what awaits me later tonight is the look in Shannon's eyes right now.

She hates me. There's no denying the sentiment burning in their brittle depths.

I WAKE UP with a start, feeling sick and shaky. It takes me a moment to shake off the memory. It wasn't a dream. I remember everything as clearly as if it happened yesterday, except for Shannon's eyes. Was that merely my subconscious embellishing or did she really look at me that way and I didn't notice it? Or I didn't understand it? Or did I notice it and choose to ignore it? Have I been repressing it all these years?

I ran out on her. It was only briefly, but maybe it was enough to make her never fully trust me again.

I look at my alarm clock. It's almost 9:15. I never sleep this late, even on Sundays.

I sit up. My head starts pounding and my whole body aches. I curse my stupidity, like I always do the morning after a fight. During the fight I'm always convinced I'm doing the right thing and I usually thoroughly enjoy myself, then the next day when I'm tending a torn lip or a bruised rib or scraped knuckles, I begin to wonder if maybe I used poor judgment. I suppose it's similar to the way a hungover woman feels when she wakes up in bed with a fat, smelly stranger she thought looked good the night before. Except my battered self is no stranger to me. For me it's like waking up sober with a fat, smelly husband of thirty years I can't get rid of.

Bits and pieces from last night start coming back to me. E.J. continued on his way after our talk in the parking lot. I hung out with Kozlowski a little while longer at Jolly's, but he wanted to go back to his motel early. I didn't get any more useful information out of him.

Shannon was asleep when I got home. I ended up watching *Bonanza* reruns with my arthritic dog.

I get out of bed and check my naked body for marks before I slip on my robe. I have a big purple bruise high on one thigh and another bruise on my forearm near my elbow. I check my face, too, in the mirror on my dresser. No marks there.

My wood floors are cold. Outside my window the sun is shining brightly, but it's about to disappear behind an ominous bank of steel-blue clouds slowly taking over the sky like cigar smoke filling up a room. I vaguely recall people talking last night at Jolly's about the possibility of snow flurries today. The warm spell is over.

I remember there's something I'm supposed to do this morning, but I can't remember what it is.

Gimp is missing from his corner. My bedroom door is open a crack. I walk out into the hallway and hear sounds coming from my kitchen.

Shannon is sitting at my table eating breakfast and looking through a book. She's already dressed in a pair of pink maternity overalls over an even pinker sweater and looks well rested and freshly scrubbed.

Gimp is sitting at attention at her feet with his tail swishing the floor. Occasionally she hands him something off her plate and his tail swishes faster.

I smell bacon. I know I don't have any bacon in the house.

I remember what I'm supposed to do this morning.

I rush back into my room and throw on a gauzy lavender miniskirt sprinkled with violets and a long-sleeved white T-shirt that covers the bruise on my arm. I yank on my Frye boots and grab a bulky, rusty orange sweater coat in case it does turn cold later.

"Hi," Shannon greets me, smiling. "I made some breakfast and coffee. Want some?"

"I'll have some coffee. No time for anything else," I say as I open one of my cupboards and take down my Steelers travel mug. "I'm running late. Gotta get to church."

"You go to church?"

It's the only explanation that came to me, but I regret it instantly. Any mention of church always makes me think back to my mother's funeral. It was the last time I set foot in a church.

I used to go with her when I was very little. I loved putting on a pretty dress, even if it was the same one I'd worn the week before and the week before that. I loved the happy songs we sang in Sunday school about Jesus taking care of all the little children: red and yellow, black and white, we were all precious in his sight. I loved the Bible stories our teacher told us using colorful felt characters on a felt board with emerald green land and a turquoise sky. I loved the macaroni wise men covered in glitter and tied with pieces of red ribbon we made at Christmastime and gave to our families to hang on our trees.

A brain aneurism was the technical medical explanation for Mom's death.

"Complications of childbirth," people whispered around and above me at our house after we buried her in the church cemetery, as they dug into the casseroles and a rainbow assortment of Jell-O salads crowded onto our dining room table.

"The angels have taken your mommy to live in Heaven with Jesus," the ladies who had brought the box of clothes for Shannon several days earlier told me, kneeling down to my level, caressing my cheek, and playing with my curls.

"Screw the angels," I replied, and watched as they drew back from me, stunned and repulsed.

I was always hearing my dad say "screw" this and "screw" that and lately E.J. had started saying it, too, although never around his mother, who would have washed his mouth out with soap. I didn't know the literal meaning of the expression, but I was certain of the sentiment.

Now that I had seen the reaction of the church ladies, I was doubly sure.

"And don't touch me," I thought to add, then went to hide in the big protective shadow of my grieving widowed father. I was finally beginning to understand why he didn't like those ladies. Or the angels.

"Sure," I say now, blithely. "Sometimes. Where'd the bacon come from?"

"I brought it with me."

"It's travel bacon?"

She laughs.

"It's a craving. Remember how you used to crave blueberry Pop-Tarts when you were pregnant with Clay?"

"Yeah, I remember that."

"And remember how you used to hide them in your dresser drawers?"

"That's because if Dad found them, he'd eat them."

"He paid for them," she says, her voice turning defensive.

I watch her curiously.

"I realize that," I reply simply and wait to see if she's going to continue to champion his behavior.

"You couldn't expect him to be sympathetic about stuff like you having cravings. He was never very happy about you being pregnant. You can't blame him for that."

Saying he was not very happy about my pregnancy is a little bit of an understatement, but I don't correct her.

"No, I guess not."

"Especially since you didn't even know who the father was. Although I suppose that was a lot harder on Clay than it was on Dad."

I don't say anything to this.

I'm perfectly happy with the story I made up for Clay about the identity of his father. He thinks he was a truck driver who I allowed to seduce me with a hot meal followed by a night at the Red Roof Inn before he continued trucking on his merry way the next morning.

I chose a truck driver because I wanted the culprit to be someone passing through who Clay could never track down. I chose a one-night stand so I could claim to be ignorant of his full name and background. I chose to explain the act as a consensual, enjoyable, youthful indiscretion with no blame, shame, or regret attached to it by either party. I'd rather have my son think I was a slut than a victim.

I'd also rather have him think his father never knew about him and might have wanted him instead of having him know what really happened. Sometimes a good lie is better than a bad truth.

Shannon seems to think she's hurt my feelings when she hasn't. I'm impervious on this subject.

"I'm sorry," she says, dropping her eyes to the open book on the table.

I realize it's one of the National Geographic books she was making fun of last night. It's the volume on Africa. I recognize the photo of a beautiful, bald, swan-necked girl swathed in scarlet and tangerine fabric whose face looks carved from coal.

She closes the book.

"I guess I have no right to talk, considering my kid isn't going to have a father either," she says, and runs her hands over the impressive mound of her belly.

"I'm sorry he ran out on you."

She shrugs.

"I'm going into Centresburg to pick up a few things." She changes the subject.

"Why don't you wait until I get back and we'll go together?" I suggest.

"No. I don't want to bother you. It's stuff I can do by myself."

"Okay. I'll see you later then."

I give Gimp a pat and call him a traitor, then I place my hand on Shannon's shoulder and kiss the top of her head the way I've done a thousand times in our distant past.

All the love I had for her as my baby sister is still here inside me, but so is the same icy numbing certainty I've had for the past eighteen years that my baby sister was gone. I don't feel any differently since she's returned.

I think about Clay and the way he became his own man without discarding or damaging my little boy. Maybe Shannon hadn't been capable of this. Maybe she wasn't able to evolve. Maybe this grown woman in front of me has the remains of my Shannon inside her and she's been walking around all these years, a tomb.

I back away from her.

She doesn't turn in her chair to watch me leave but goes back to eating.

"Give my regards to God," she calls after me.

Chapter Nine

I FIND PAMELA JAMESON waiting for me at the Holiday Inn, sitting stiffly on a brown- and orange-striped sofa, holding a Styrofoam cup with wisps of coffee steam crawling from its lip, watching hotel workers clean up the remnants of a wedding reception through a pair of propped-open ballroom doors.

The smell of chlorine is so strong, my eyes begin to sting within seconds of walking into the lobby. I hear splashing and shrieking coming from the pool area and the occasional bellow of a parent.

Pamela smiles at my approach, not because she's pleased to see me again or because she feels any further obligation to show signs of politeness now that our employer-employee relationship has been established. It is an expression of pure relief; I am the signal that her escape is imminent.

She stands to greet me.

Today she's wearing jeans that have been strategically, professionally weathered, and a blazer of pale green and white seersucker over a pale green shirt. Her leather shoes are flat and pointed and the same color as the shirt. I fleetingly wonder what would happen to her mental well-being if I were to suddenly force her to put on a pair of bright purple stilettos.

"Good morning," she says.

"Hi," I say back. "How was your evening? How did you sleep?"

"It was terrible," she replies. "There was a wedding going on until all hours, and there's also a bar here in the hotel."

"Yeah, I know. Houlihanigan's." I nod my sympathy. "It gets pretty rowdy on weekends when they have live music."

"I'd hardly call it music." She begins kneading the space between her eyes with the pad of one index finger. "It was this horrible pounding beat and these screeching guitars."

"Well, no one would know to look at you that you had a sleepless night. You look fine."

I have a feeling nothing ever affects her face. I have a vision of her peeling it off at night and laying it flat on a bedside table, then getting up first thing in the morning and ironing it on a low heat before putting it back on again.

"That's nice of you to say," she tells me.

She picks up her purse, a twin to the bag Shannon carries, and begins walking to the revolving door.

I realize that she and Shannon have the same hairstyle, too: straight and shiny, blunt cut, the ends grazing the shoulders. The only difference is the color: Shannon's is a mahogany brown; Pamela's is a metallic blonde that matches her SUV.

I imagine them sitting side by side in a Manhattan hair salon laughing and sipping champagne while a stylist stripes their heads with highlights. Then the two of them shouldering their matching handbags and going shopping for charm bracelets and red cowboy boots and pink maternity clothes.

The problem is I *can't* imagine it. The Shannon I used to know wouldn't have been able to spend five minutes around this woman's condescension. She would never have accepted a single gift or favor from her. To do so, according to our dad, would have been worse than accepting charity; it would have been admitting Pamela Jameson was better than us, and no one was better than us except him.

"Before we head on over to Eatn'Park, you have to be straight with me about what's going on," I tell Pamela once we're outside. "You said something about this woman stealing your child. I need to know what you mean by that."

She avoids my eyes and intently watches the marquee where a workman stands at the top of a ladder dismantling the words: CON-GRATULATIONS, NICOLE AND BRAD.

"The child isn't born yet," she says without looking at me. "She's carrying our child. My husband's and mine."

"You mean the baby's not hers?" I say with a little too much surprise and intimacy in my voice.

"Excuse me?" she says.

"What I meant to say was . . . do you mean she's a surrogate mother?"

"No," she sighs and reaches into her purse for her sunglasses.

Once she has them on and I can't read her eyes, she looks at me while she talks.

"She's the mother, but it's our child. We paid for it."

"What do you mean you paid for it?"

"An adoption," she says, irritation beginning to rise in her voice. "It's all perfectly legal. Everything is being handled through an attorney."

"Gerald Kozlowski?" I ask without thinking.

She studies me and answers slowly, "No, I don't know any Gerald Kozlowski. What would make you think you know the lawyer handling our adoption?"

"Nothing, really," I reply quickly, trying to cover up another error. "It's just that I happen to know a lawyer in New York who handles adoptions, and I thought maybe he was handling yours. You know what they say: It's a small world."

"It's not that small. Do you have any idea how many lawyers there are in New York handling adoptions?"

"Not off the top of my head."

The sun ducks behind the clouds again and I pull my sweater tighter around me. The trees are bare, the grass is brown, and the few cars driving past still wear spatters of mud and a white coating of road salt left over from the recent icy winter.

We begin walking toward Pamela's SUV.

"So how did you end up here?" I urge her to continue.

"A couple of days ago, Jamie simply disappeared," she confides in me. "I was frantic. The baby is due any day now. I had no idea where to look for her. Then I received a call from her telling me that she's beginning to have second thoughts about the adoption. She said she decided to take a trip and visit an old friend who lives in the country and think things over.

"I begged her to come back. I reminded her of everything we've done for her so far, how we've paid for her medical insurance, her apartment, food, clothing, entertainment, anything to keep her happy and healthy. And this is above and beyond the very substantial fee we're paying for the child."

"Wow," I state flatly, letting the reality of Shannon's situation sink in. "That's a pretty sweet arrangement. So you basically pay for her life while she sits around and grows a baby for you?"

"That is a very harsh way of putting it, and I don't appreciate what you're implying," Pamela snaps at me.

I didn't realize I was implying anything, but the more I think about it I guess I was. My gut tells me there's something sickening in all this, but at the same time I can't help but admire Shannon's resourcefulness.

"I thought you said you had a legal agreement with her? Doesn't that prevent her from being able to skip out on you?"

"The adoption isn't final until after the baby is born and she signs the papers."

"She can back out until the very end?"

"In theory, she shouldn't be able to, but for the time being the biological mother always wins in these cases. You can see why we have to stay in her good graces."

"It sounds to me like she's been using you."

"Oh, no. It's been worth every cent to be with her throughout the entire pregnancy and to be able to keep an eye on her lifestyle. If you adopt a child who's already born, you have no idea what kind of problems can develop down the road, since you don't know anything about the mother: if she did drugs during her pregnancy, or if she drank, or if she had some type of disease. Jamie's been tested for everything under the sun and given a clean bill of health. Not to mention that she's an attractive girl. The baby should be attractive."

"How can you know that? What about the father?" I ask her. "What if she slept with an ugly guy? Or a really stupid one?"

She stares at me coldly. Even without being able to see her eyes, I can tell she's appalled that I would ask such a question.

"I'm sorry." I hold up my hands in surrender. "I was just curious. No offense."

A flatbed truck rumbles into the lumberyard across the road from the hotel. Next to the yard is the Mattress Warehouse advertising a half-off sale on waterbeds, and beside it is the triangular A-frame shell of one of the original Arby's restaurants in the area, rising out of the empty parking lot like a small, dirty, orange pyramid that houses the silent cash registers of a dead economy instead of the opulent riches of a dead king. It went out of business about fifteen years ago. The booths can still be seen behind the filthy glass along with a menu behind the front counter promising a roast beef sandwich, medium drink, and fries for a dollar-fifty.

"So maybe she wasn't using you before, but what about now? It sounds like she's blackmailing you."

She doesn't comment.

"What's the plan for today?" I ask, changing the subject.

"I finally convinced Jamie over the phone to tell me where she is and to let me come and talk to her in person," Pamela explains.

"That's what you're about to do right now?"

"Yes."

"And you want me along because you think she could harm you in some way?"

"I really don't know what to think anymore. I thought I knew this girl. I thought I could trust her. And then she does something like this."

We arrive at her car. She opens her purse and begins searching for her keys.

"Maybe she's just having cold feet like she told you. Maybe she just needs a little assurance and everything will be fine," I suggest, still wanting to think the best of my sister. "It's not easy having a baby by yourself, even if someone is paying your expenses for you. She's the one who still has to go through the pregnancy and the birth and then part with her child. And on top of all that, it's her first baby. She's probably scared."

Pamela pulls the keys from her purse and releases the automatic locks with the press of a button and a muted beep.

She opens the driver's side door.

"Should we take one car?"

"Yeah, I think that would be best."

I settle into the creamy leather luxury of her front seat and wait for the car's engine to begin to purr.

She holds the key in front of her as if she's contemplating its purpose, then she turns her head to face me.

"How did you know it's her first baby?"

"I guess I just assumed," I tell her, mentally kicking myself for allowing yet another slipup.

She lowers the hand holding the key and lets it rest against her thigh. She takes off her sunglasses with her other hand and fixes me with a searching stare.

She has pretty blue eyes, but they've been clouded by discontent and doubt like a clear stream that's been muddied by too many feet seeking relief on a hot day.

She's my age. We're both forty-something white American women. To some, we would be considered peers, equals. We seem the same. To others, we couldn't be more different. We represent the ever-deepening divide between the haves and have-nots. We have nothing in common.

"Do you have any children?" she asks me.

"I have a son."

She drops her eyes from mine as she pauses to consider my answer.

We're different. She has money; I don't. I'm a mother; she's not. But we're both thinking the same thing right now: She's lucky, but I'm blessed.

"I assumed that this was Jamie's first baby, too," she goes on, returning to our previous topic, "especially since she told us she had never had a baby before. Then when she disappeared I called her doctor's office to see if they had heard from her. I talked to one of the nurses who always sees Jamie. I explained my concern that she might go into labor and that she would end up in a strange hospital with a strange doctor and no friends around her.

"The nurse laughed and said I shouldn't worry. She said she was sure Jamie would know what to do and would be fine during the delivery no matter where it took place, since this wasn't her first baby. I was stunned. I asked her point-blank: 'Are you certain she's had a baby before?' And the nurse said that she'd guess from the internal exams that she's probably had several."

She looks at me again.

I hope I'm keeping the shock off my face.

"Jamie lied to me. Why would she lie to me? Because she wants to portray herself differently than she really is. Why would she want to do that? Because she doesn't want me to know what she's capable of doing."

Her voice drops to an angry whisper.

"Now is when the blackmail begins."

She slips her glasses back on and starts the engine.

"Do you carry a gun?" she asks me.

Chapter Ten

ONCE WE ESTABLISH that my role is not to protect Pamela Jameson from Jamie Ruddock but to act as a potential persuasive force if Jamie decides not to agree to Pamela's latest offer, I'm able to convince Pamela that I don't need to be present in the restaurant.

I ask her to show me the photo again of Shannon a.k.a. Jamie, and I tell her that the girl looks vaguely familiar to me. Maybe she is originally from this area. Considering that I was a police officer in this town for over ten years, I don't want to run the risk that she might recognize me and get nervous or suspicious.

I also explain that if I sit within plain view of the two of them, Pamela might subconsciously find herself glancing in my direction and ruin the whole setup.

I tell her we'll keep in touch with our cell phones by using them like walkie-talkies. I have her call me, then leave the line open and lay her phone on the very top of the contents of her purse. I tell her to make sure she leaves her purse unzipped so I'll be able to hear what they're saying.

There's no way I'm going to miss hearing a single word of this conversation.

Pamela heads to the ladies' room first. I don't particularly feel the need to hear her take a piss, so I take a little stroll around the parking lot while I wait for her to meet up with Shannon.

I spot Shannon's car. It's parked around the corner from the entrance. I don't know why she chose to park it there since there are plenty of spots near the door for the time being. In another hour the place will be packed with the after-church crowd.

I checked out her car last night after Kozlowski told me at Jolly's that as far as he knew, Shannon had never lived in New Mexico.

The car had a New Mexico license plate but the glove compartment was completely empty—no registration or proof of insurance or owner's manual—and the rest of the interior was suspiciously clean.

Today it has a New York license plate and a Hertz rental brochure sitting on the dashboard. Pamela told me that Jamie doesn't own a car.

I peer in the side windows more closely and notice the dirty corner of a yellow license plate peeking out from under one of the rear floor mats.

She must have switched plates this morning. There's no doubt in my mind anymore that she came here from New York, where she's known as Jamie Ruddock to Pamela Jameson and Shannon Penrose to Gerald Kozlowski. The New Mexico story is a ruse for me.

I wonder where she got the plate. Probably stole it off some poor tourist's car back in New York City.

I'm reserving my opinion about what's going on between her and Pamela and her and Kozlowski until I know more, but I already know I don't like thinking my sister is a liar and a common thief.

I return to Pamela's SUV and crawl in the backseat, where I keep hidden while I watch the parking lot from the rear window.

This is what I used to do during my six years on Capitol Hill: stand guard; watch and wait; somehow remain intently alert while being bored out of my skull; stay in the same position for hours but be able to spring into action at the first sign of danger; show no fatigue or frustration or fear. It wasn't all that different from life in my father's house.

I suppose I was feeling a certain amount of burnout when I decided to leave D.C., even though this wasn't the main reason I quit my job. But it was true that I was getting sick of babysitting politicians and dealing with their rude staffers and constantly being accosted by tourists who ranged from the slightly confused to the incredibly ignorant. I didn't mind the foreigners who sometimes confused the Capitol Building with the White House, but the Americans who approached me on the Mall, laden with giant Slurpees and foot-long chili dogs and demanding to know where the hell Mount Rushmore was, really got on my nerves.

Some nights when I'd get home after working a twelve-hour shift for the sixth straight day in a row, after I'd send the babysitter home, remove the twenty pounds of hardware I carried around on my body all day long, yank off my boots, peel off my hot, heavy uniform, check on my son, and eat some cereal for dinner while trying not to doze off into the bowl, I'd go to my room and stand naked in front of the eight-dollar Wal-Mart mirror I had nailed to the inside of my bedroom door, in the hopes of recognizing myself after a day of being separated from myself. I'd be overcome with a level of exhaustion that went far beyond the physical demands of my job and raising a child on my own. I was only in my twenties but sometimes I feared I was already tired of living.

I didn't understand the feeling. Clay and I had carved out a nice life for ourselves, certainly a better life than I had ever envisioned having when I was growing up in Jolly Mount.

I had a demanding, potentially deadly, often tedious job, but it was a job that commanded respect and I made good money.

I liked the men and the few women I worked with. I slipped easily and instantly into the confines of cop camaraderie. It was no different than the dynamics I'd witnessed my whole life among the Jolly Mount miners: the blind devotion and dependence on one another and the unspoken acceptance that no one outside the job will ever fully understand you, including spouses and children. Sitting in an Irish cop bar after one of my shifts, I finally began to understand why my dad needed to sit in Jolly's every night after his shift in Beverly. The difference between us was that I wanted to go home and be with my kid.

Clay and I lived in a sprawling redbrick apartment complex about thirty miles outside D.C. that was shaped like a comb that's lost most of its teeth. There were over 500 units, only 300 parking spaces, and no elevators. We had a two-bedroom place on the third floor. It was small but the utilities were free, and we had a tiny balcony we both loved even though it looked out over a highway lined with cut-rate motels and car dealerships. We were able to fit two chairs and a small table on it, and we ate dinner there whenever the weather and my schedule allowed it.

Overall, I was satisfied that I had everything under control. I could look at life's ledger and check off all the big concerns: Job. Home. Child. Friends. Love life.

It was the little things that started to get to me. The traffic. The pointless frantic urban pace. The way the nights were never dark and silence was never quiet. The way people wore their rudeness like a crown.

I hated the fact that Clay couldn't get on his bike and ride for miles, that he would never know the childhood independence of journeying alone on a country road and the freedom of cresting a hill and flying down the other side with the wind bringing tears to his eyes. He didn't even own a bike. There was nowhere to ride it where he wouldn't be run over or robbed.

Sometimes when I look back at that time in my life, I wonder if I sabotaged myself, if I was looking for a way to get Clay and me out of there without having to make the decision by myself. Is that why I chose to have an affair with the self-destructive teenaged son of a foreign diplomat, knowing it would have to end in scandal and that I'd be asked to leave my job at the very least?

I was assigned to protect him and his family during one of his father's visits. I got pulled for diplomatic duty a lot because I was a woman, I was easy on the eye, and I was personable. I got along well with the wives, I knew how to entertain the kids, and the men liked to look at me and fantasize that I might have to shield them from an assassin's bullet by throwing myself on top of them as my shirt flew open and my breasts popped out of a black lace push-up bra.

He was nineteen but he explained to me the first time we met that he had been considered a man in his country since the age of thirteen when he made love to his first woman and killed his first lion on a hunting trip to Kenya with his father.

I told him he sounded a lot like the boys I knew back home, only they killed deer not jungle cats and their first romantic conquests were girls, not women.

He was fascinated by the way I talked about home. He knew America was very big, and that it had many different types of terrain and all sizes of communities ranging from one-dog towns (he meant one-horse towns; I never corrected him) to some of the world's largest cities, but he had always believed that all Americans were the same at their core no matter what their skin color, religion, gender, or class, and that we considered the entire country our home. Wasn't Washington, D.C., my home? Didn't I live here? Couldn't I live anywhere in America and still be at home?

I had never really stopped to think about it before he asked me, but once I did I had to admit to him and to myself that there was only one place I considered home, and right now I wasn't living in it.

Almost all our conversations centered on Jolly Mount. He had no interest in trying to impress me with his wealth and his worldliness, which made him more mature in my eyes than most of the grown men I'd been involved with.

He especially loved my description of a neighbor's hound dog howling over the hill at night, how he only cried when he wanted to mate or kill. He said that was exactly the way he felt.

We had a week together. He was charming and intense but easily distracted, and angered, and bored. It was obvious to me that he was a deeply troubled kid, but I seemed to be the only one who noticed and I wasn't in a position to bring it up to anyone. He had a drug habit and a drinking problem that both parents ignored for different reasons. He was reckless in everything he did, from the way he drove his sports car to the way he fell asleep with lit cigarettes between his fingers to the way he insisted on having a TV set sitting perilously close to the edge of his Jacuzzi.

He was hell around water. When I escorted him to the hotel pool he claimed he'd never been around a pool so small. The pools where he lived were as wide and deep as lakes, he told me, then proceeded to do back flips off the sides and missed smashing his skull into the cement by mere inches.

The day before I put in a request to be relieved of my assignment, I taught him how to make a shallow dive.

He died of a drug overdose the next night. There was some brief talk that it might have been suicide, but he didn't leave a note and everyone in his family was certain he had everything to live for.

I was never outwardly accused of anything, but no one could ignore the fact that I had asked to be transferred away from him the day before he died or that when checking the hotel phone records it was discovered that the last two calls he made were to my home number.

I started to apply for jobs all over the country. I applied to a few in Pennsylvania, but I wasn't trying to move back home. Shannon's death and my dad's life still loomed too large for me in Jolly Mount.

I went back a few times to visit. It was nice to see Isabel and Jimmy even though the black cloud of Shannon's disappearance hung over all our conversations.

I saw my dad, too, despite my suspicions over what he might have done to my sister. I was a grown woman now. A police officer. A single mother of a fine son. I made more money than he did. Yet as soon as I was around him I fell into my old role of subservient daughter, apologizing constantly, never venturing my own opinion, praising everything he said, making him meals, cleaning his filthy house, doing his laundry.

It was a comment from Clay that led me to stop seeing him. He asked me during one of our visits, "Why do you act like you're stupid when you're around Grandpa?"

His question stopped me in my tracks. The way he asked it. The phrasing. Not "Why do you act stupid?" which can basically mean anything, but a very specific "Why do you act like you're stupid?"

I couldn't begin to answer him. I also knew I wasn't going to change. Instead I decided it was in my son's best interest not to see me around my father. I finally had a reason to sever our relationship that I could defend.

I hadn't seen him for four years when I got the news that an explosion in Beverly had killed twelve miners. The job on the Centresburg police force was purely a stroke of luck and timing. I heard about the opening when I went home to bury him.

I came back three months later for an interview and to take the borough test along with seventy men who also showed up at the high school cafeteria. I was the only woman. I knew I was more than qualified for the job, but I was still surprised when I beat out the others.

I found out eventually that the reason the chief chose me was because I offered the perfect solution to a family crisis. One of the candidates was his loser son-in-law, and his daughter expected the chief to give him the job. He knew if he gave it to another male candidate his daughter would never forgive him, and if he gave the job to his son-in-law he'd never forgive himself, so he told his daughter that the latest town budget insisted they hire a female officer in accordance with the Equal Opportunity Employment Act and he hired me. She grumbled and pouted for awhile, but got over it.

My next twelve years as a Centresburg police officer were fairly uneventful although a few of my cases made big local headlines.

PANTSLESS MAN ARRESTED: *A man wearing no pants was arrested outside the Golden Pheasant bar in Centresburg. Local authorities confirm intoxication was a contributing factor in the incident.*

MAN FLINGS GRILL: *An Ebensburg man flung a grill at an RV windshield after his wife poured out the contents of a vodka bottle during a domestic dispute at Yellow Creek Campground.*

DOWNSPOUTING RECOVERED: *A two-foot long section of white vinyl downspouting believed to be the weapon in a recent assault on Lowe's general manager, Harold Brink, was recovered by Centresburg police.*

BIBLE-WIELDING BRIDE SMASHES CHURCH WINDOWS MORNING OF NUPTIALS: *Ashley Dawn Hale, 22, of Marion Center, was charged with destruction of private property and attempted assault Saturday morning after destroying four stained-glass windows in the Pine Mills Presbyterian Church and throwing a Bible at the head of a wedding photographer.*

Hale was allowed to stay for the marriage ceremony before being remanded into police custody.

No explanation was given by Hale as to the reason for her actions. Hale's mother claims her daughter has been under a lot of stress planning the wedding.

MAN DRESSED IN GROUNDHOG SUIT ASSAULTED: *A man wearing a groundhog suit was severely beaten after Friday night's high school football game against Punxsutawney. Centresburg defeated the Woodchucks, 28–3. Go Flames!*

Centresburg is not a high crime area. The majority of calls I responded to dealt predominantly with people acting carelessly, selfishly, or cruelly, but rarely criminally. My job was basically to prevent someone from doing something stupid, to clean up after someone who had already done something stupid, or to find the person who had done something stupid and then left.

I also handled a fair amount of domestic abuse.

I answered a 911 call a year ago and found a twelve-year-old girl with severe vaginal bleeding locked in a bathroom. The call had been made by her little sister. Upon examination I found a lightbulb had been inserted inside her and crushed. After I calmed the girl down and assured her an ambulance was on the way, she explained to me that she was pregnant and her mother told her this was a way to get rid of the baby. Her mother made her lie on the floor; she was the one who pushed in the lightbulb then stomped on the girl's belly. The father of the baby was her mother's boyfriend.

Her mother denied everything during my preliminary questioning of her but when her daughter was wheeled by on a paramedics' gurney, her face turned red and ugly and she spat the word "slut" at her.

I grabbed her by the throat with one hand, backed her against a wall, and jammed my gun into her forehead. It was a beautifully pure moment I will always remember and crave and envy. I gave no thought to rules, boundaries, parameters, consequences, laws, excuses, or the Ten Commandments. It wasn't an intellectual decision or an emotional or moral one. My actions came from base animal instinct: I needed to kill her because she threatened the well-being of my species.

The only thing that prevented me from pulling the trigger was her daughter screaming for me to stop.

I left her with a dime-sized indentation in her forehead from the pressure of my gun, a bruised trachea, and her own urine dripping down her leg.

Back at the station I laid my gun and creds on the chief's desk and said, "It's time for me to quit."

The girl lost the baby, changed her story to say that she had tried to hurt herself, and claimed her mother's boyfriend had never touched her, but she wouldn't support her mother's charge of police brutality against me. Neither would the paramedics. The stories circulated anyway.

A voice pipes up over the background noise coming over my phone.

"Testing. One. Two. Three."

"For Christ's sake," I grumble to myself. "Pamela," I say into the phone. "You're not supposed to talk to me. We don't want her to know your phone is on."

"I was just testing . . ."

"There's no need to test. Put the phone in your purse and go sit down with her. Do you see her?"

"Yes, she just looked up and she's waving at me. She looks happy to see me."

I hear the hope in her voice.

"Okay. That's good. But just remember why you're here in the first place. She might be trying to pull something over on you. Don't trust her."

I can't believe what I'm hearing myself say. When did I become someone who cares about protecting this woman's interests? I should be protecting my sister's interests, but I have no idea what they are.

"Hi, Pam."

"Jamie, how are you?"

Silence. I assume they're embracing.

"You look wonderful."

"Thanks."

"A little tired, maybe."

"I am tired. The baby's due in a couple days, you know."

"Of course I know. I haven't been able to think about anything else. I was worried sick about you. Why didn't you tell me you were going away?" Pamela's voice begins to sound a little desperate. "I could have gone with you, or at the very least you could have let me make plans for you. You could have used our summer house."

"I needed to be by myself."

"Did you find your friend?" Pamela asks. "Are you staying with her?"

"Yes. She's been really good to me."

"Better than I've been to you?" Pamela asks with a laugh.

Jamie's voice turns cold, "She hasn't bought me anything if that's what you mean."

"Good morning, ladies," a waitress interrupts their conversation. "Can I get you some coffee?"

"What kind of coffee do you have?" Pamela asks.

"Regular and decaf."

"Oh." A disappointed and bewildered silence follows.

"Do you have iced tea?" she perseveres.

"Yeah."

"What kind?"

"Regular."

I think I hear Shannon snort a laugh.

"You can put sugar in it," the waitress adds helpfully.

"Fine. I'll have an iced tea."

"I'll have coffee," Shannon volunteers eagerly. "And a piece of coconut cream pie."

I smile.

Shannon was around seven years old and I was about thirteen

when the Eatn'Park Restaurant was built in Centresburg. It was an immediate sensation with its big laminated menu full of mouth-watering photographs of every type of comfort food and its fabulous display case of glistening pies.

Shannon and I never got to eat in a restaurant. We also never got to go to Centresburg. But I had heard so much about the Eatn'Park pies, I was determined that we were going to sample one. I took some of my precious allowance money that Isabel had begun to give me because she said I worked harder than most adults who had full-time jobs with steady paychecks, and I arranged a ride with Lib, who was driving into town to pick up a part for his mower, and Shannon and I set out to have some pie.

I can still picture her standing at the case with her hair pulled back in a shiny pigtail like a rope of braided reddish mink and her freckled nose pressed up against the glass.

She made me tell her the name of each pie and when we got to coconut cream, she looked up at me and asked me if it wasn't true that coconuts grew in Africa.

I praised her for remembering that fact and reminded her of the National Geographic book about Africa we looked at and the pages about the Ivory Coast and the photos of palm trees dripping with bunches of the hairy brown fruit.

We both had coconut cream, and as we ate it we congratulated ourselves on being able to taste Africa, and we tried to remember as many things as we could from the book.

Shannon remembered that in some African tribes old people leave their families when they become burdens and they find a tree they like and climb into it and wait to die. We decided to already pick our tree when we got home that afternoon. Even though we were only children. Better safe than sorry.

She also brought up the pictures of the men who worked in the South African diamond mines. They were dark-skinned and slighter than our miners but had the same clamped jaws and the same stoic stubbornness shining in their weary eyes.

There was one other difference between their mines and ours that we both remembered: Their mines were numbered; they didn't have names. All of J&P's mines were named after women.

This made us feel bad for the African miners. The lack of a name would make it impossible for them to talk about their mines with the same familiarity and affection the J&P miners used when talking about theirs; the way they complained about Beverly's gassiness and Lorelei's dampness or praised the height of Marvella's seams and Jojo's roomy cross-cuts; the way the mention of Gertie made the respectful silence due to all deceased loved ones descend over any conversation.

Our miners trusted their mines, but each day as the African miners approached their dark portals, they would have to feel the trepidation of putting their fates in the hands of a stranger.

Shannon and I couldn't imagine any greater honor for a woman than having a mine named after her. While other girls in other places wanted to have beauty pageant crowns placed on their heads or they longed to have their faces splashed all over fashion magazines, we aspired to have our names be synonymous with a much-needed job to scores of tired, filthy men. We knew the mine could be a place of death and danger and degradation, but it was also our source of life.

Shannon was sure someday someone would name a mine after her, and I made her promise when it happened she'd make sure to have a sister mine named after me.

"I'm having doubts about the adoption." Shannon's words intrude on my memories.

"I don't understand," Pamela responds. "Nothing has changed.

Your situation hasn't changed," she stresses. "You know that Dennis and I can give the baby a wonderful home and every advantage. Not to mention all our love."

Silence. The waitress brings the iced tea and pours the coffee. Both women murmur thank-yous.

"If you love your child, you'll want the very best for him or her," Pamela begins again.

"I do want the best for my child. That's why I'm having doubts. I think I may have found a better family."

Another silence.

"Better in what way?" Pamela finally asks, sounding offended.

"Lots of ways. And they're willing to pay more money than you're going to pay. A lot more."

"I could pay a lot more, too, if I hadn't already paid for the last five months of your life."

"What's that supposed to mean? Are you accusing me of something?"

Bad move, Pamela, I think to myself, but she can't possibly know the lines she can't cross with Shannon. She only knows Jamie, and I'm getting the feeling that this might be the first time Shannon is showing glimpses of her true self to her benefactress.

"No, I'm just pointing out that we've done a lot for you already and this other family has done nothing. Plus we had an agreement."

"Agreements don't matter. Biological mothers always get to keep their kids if they want to."

"But you're not talking about keeping your child. You're talking about selling it to someone else for more money."

"So what? I can do whatever I want. It's my kid."

"It's one thing to decide you want to keep the baby for yourself, but it's quite another thing to go back on our agreement because you see an opportunity to make more money. I'm not sure it's legal."

"Are you threatening me?"

"No. Of course not." Pamela quickly backpedals. "What would I be threatening you with?"

"I don't think you want to try and take me to court," Shannon states flatly. "You'll lose."

"Maybe. But at least we can afford a good lawyer."

Shannon laughs.

"Knock yourself out," she says unconcernedly.

I start to wonder again about Kozlowski's involvement in all this. He said he and Shannon had business dealings, and he also knows her by her real name. He's not Pamela's lawyer but maybe he's Shannon's. That would explain why Shannon isn't intimidated by threats of going to court.

"That looks great," I hear Shannon tell the waitress. "Thank you."

I wonder if the sight of the pie makes her think about me.

"What are these other people willing to pay?" Pamela asks her.

"Eighty thousand," she replies with her mouth full.

"Holy shit," I whisper.

"I see," Pamela says simply.

Their conversation ceases. All I hear is the enthusiastic clink of the fork against the plate as Shannon gobbles her pie.

"Will you excuse me, Jamie? I'm going to use the ladies' room."

"Sure. No problem."

I wait. The parking lot is beginning to fill up with Sunday brunchers getting out of their cars in their church clothes.

"Did you hear everything?" a whisper suddenly hisses over the phone accompanied by the echo from a bathroom stall.

"Yes."

"What should I do?"

"Stall for some time. Tell her you need to discuss it with your husband."

"Yes, that's good."

"Tell her you want to meet with her again tomorrow and try and find out where she's planning on having this baby."

"She doesn't seem very concerned about it, does she?"

"At this point, I wouldn't be surprised if she gives birth in the booth while you're gone, then orders another piece of pie."

"Should I bring up the fact that I know she's had another baby?"

"No," I warn her. "Let her think she's in control. Let her think you believe everything she's telling you. Don't put her on the defensive, whatever you do. Stroke her like a cat."

She falls silent when a couple of chattering women walk into the bathroom.

"Don't get freaked out," I tell her. "This family probably doesn't even exist. She's just trying to get more money out of you."

"I'm sure it exists," she shoots back. "You don't know anything about the adoption market."

I only half listen to the rest of the conversation once she returns to the table.

Shannon remains evasive on the question of where she's staying and where she plans to have the baby, other than assuring Pamela that she knows what she's doing.

She agrees to meet with Pamela the following night for dinner.

I can't stop thinking about the amount of money Shannon just mentioned.

What is the market value of a child these days? Apparently a lot more than a Subaru but less than a two-bedroom house with an eat-in kitchen.

I have to admit that for the briefest of moments part of me considered running out and getting pregnant tonight.

I know better, though. I've been through this myself and I know making a baby is not quite the same thing as baking a cake, either to sell at an upscale bakery or charitably donate to someone who can't bake one of her own. For one thing, the cake doesn't have feelings.

I got pregnant when I was sixteen, and the last thing I wanted in the world was to have a baby. I had none of the ridiculous delusions that some girls have about a baby being fun and always being cute, or a baby loving them unconditionally and filling the void in them that their son-of-a-bitch fathers or their heartless mothers or their good-for-nothing boyfriends had failed to do, or that having a child didn't really impact your life too much.

I had already raised a child while I was still a child myself. I knew they were rarely fun, and although they could be extremely cute they could also be monstrous. I knew they were capable of hating your guts as well as loving you, and I knew they took up all your time. Even when you weren't physically with them, you were thinking about them, worrying about them, anticipating their next meal, their next bath, their next tear.

Plus my own mother had died from complications related to childbirth.

I was terrified to have a baby.

But I did it. Not because I was strong or decent or devout. I made the decisions I made because I was afraid and I was ignorant, which only seems appropriate since these are the exact same reasons that I ended up getting pregnant in the first place.

I had no money. I had no one to help me. I wouldn't have had the slightest idea how to go about getting an abortion, just as I had no idea how to go about putting up a baby for adoption. I might have done either if anyone had come forward to help me. But after Clay was born, once I held him and looked into his eyes, I knew nothing would ever keep me from him. There was already a pure and irrefutable knowledge glowing in their dark gray depths that hadn't seen anything of the world yet except bright lights and sterile hospital walls. We connected without words or actions. He was only a few minutes old but he already knew I was his mom, and he already knew what that meant. I was the one person he could count on. I was the first concept he understood.

That night, after I nursed him, I stared at him for the longest time and he stared back at me with his calm, steady, trusting eyes. A kind of perfect peace I can only describe as bliss swept over me, along with a devastating sadness when I thought of how little time my mom and Shannon had together.

Screw the angels.

Pamela comes walking toward the car looking as upset as her seamless face allows.

I'm angry at her and I'm angry for her. I don't know how I feel about Shannon.

Flushing a pinhead's worth of microscopic cells out of a woman's uterus is a sin but a mother giving away her child is not. Standing outside a bar in the middle of the night without any pants on is a crime but selling a child to the highest bidder is not.

I'm angry at the whole human race.

I need to see my boy.

Chapter Eleven

IT ONLY TAKES TEN MINUTES to walk to the sheriff's station
from Eatn'Park. It's a small, square, nondescript building of tan
brick fronted by a concrete courtyard with nowhere to sit and very few
places to lean if a person decided to loiter. The American flag flapping
on a white pole is of average size: slightly bigger than the one at the
post office but much smaller than the one at the Ford car dealership
across the road.

Sheriff Ivan Z is about to get into his cruiser. He hesitates with the
driver's side door open, trying to determine if I'm someone he wants to
greet or speed away from.

He chooses the first option and comes walking toward me as I approach the building holding a white paper bag with two coffees and
two smiley-face cookies inside it.

"Look at you," I call out, smiling. "All dressed up. Full uniform.
Even a hat. Where are you off to? A costume party?"

Ivan has a notorious dislike of uniforms. It was an ongoing dispute
between him and the former sheriff that Ivan usually won simply because Sheriff Jack wasn't going to show up at his house and force him
into polyester pants and a keystone-shaped belt buckle every morning.
Now that Ivan has the top job, he can't get out of dressing the part from
time to time. His public requires it.

He smiles back at me while wagging a warning finger.

"Better be careful or I'll write you up for hurting the sheriff's feelings. That for me?" he asks, glancing at the bag.

"Sorry," I tell him. "For my kid. How have you been? It's been awhile. How's that hot doctor you were dating?"

"She married that asshole lawyer she was dating."

"That's depressing."

"Yeah. Well, we had some fun together but I'm not ready to settle down yet."

"Still have that lifetime of sleeping with beautiful girls ahead of you?"

He nods.

"How about you and your search for stimulating conversations?"

"I know there's one out there."

He continues smiling at me with his mouth, but the expression has left his eyes. They've become troubled. They're still a striking blue, and I'm sure there are plenty of women eager to be seduced by them, but his years of hard drinking have taken their toll on the face they peer from and he looks older than he is.

He stares past me to the road beyond and past that to something I can't see. He always had this habit even when he was at the height of his glory days and shouldn't have had a care in the world. He never seemed able to stay in the moment for long; he was always searching for something, whether it was on the horizon or deep inside himself I could never tell.

Clay has the same look sometimes. I wonder fleetingly if it has something to do with the fact that both of them grew up without fathers.

Ivan lost his dad in the massive explosion that ripped through Gertie, wiping out half the male population of his hometown of Coal Run in a single morning.

I always felt a kinship with the Coal Run kids even though I had lost a mom instead of a dad and our grief was not entirely the same.

A mom takes care of a child in a hands-on way; a dad's care is more abstract. When I lost my mom, it was like being on a camping trip and coming back from a hike and finding all my supplies missing: my food, my warm sleeping bag, the first-aid kit. When all those fathers were taken away, an entire town lost its compass.

The back to the station opens and Clay steps out. His uniform is pressed, his boots and badge rubbed clean, his dark hair cut short and neat, his body trim, his stride purposeful even when he has no purpose, his sunglasses in place so he can watch without giving away his own thoughts. Add to this his impeccable politeness, his unyielding belief in the necessity of rules, and what I call his "deputy voice," and you have what appears to be, on the surface, the ideal cop.

It's what's going on below the surface that causes problems for him. He can't relax. He can't stop worrying. In his baby book under the Baby's First Sentences heading, I have recorded: "I want goose," which was how he pronounced "juice," "I love Mama," and "Don't drive fast."

One of his very first creative writing assignments in school was to describe his dream vacation. Other kids wrote about going to the beach, or Disney World, or the zoo, or even to their grandparents' house. Clay wrote that he wanted to stay on the balcony outside our apartment with a cool drink and keep an eye on his mom's parking space while she was at work.

Even now, on the occasions when I've seen him at his job, I always feel like he's holding his breath the entire time. He reminds me of a balloon that's been filled with too much air, and as soon as the problem is resolved, I expect him to release his tension all at once and go whizzing crazily through the air until he suddenly settles to the ground and there's nothing left of him except an empty brown polyester deputy uniform with a badge pinned to it.

Ivan intercepts Clay and tells him something and Clay nods and nods again before continuing on his way toward me.

"And Penrose," Ivan calls over his shoulder as he climbs into his car. "You have my permission to take the stick out of your butt while you're talking to your mom."

"Okay. Thanks," Clay yells back.

He takes off his shades, slides them in his shirt pocket, and turns to me.

"That's just the usual banter I have with the sheriff."

"Banter with the sheriff? You sound like you just stepped out of an episode of *Gunsmoke*."

I hand him his coffee and cookie.

"You look tired," I tell him. "Did you do something wild and crazy for your birthday?"

"I spent the night babysitting Dusty at the Golden Pheasant."

"Is he getting worse?" I ask, peeling the lid off my own coffee and watching the steam drift away.

"Brandi kicked him out," Clay tells me. "He's living at his restaurant until the end of the month when the bank takes it."

"Wow. That's terrible." I take a sip of my coffee and stare forlornly at the scuffed tips of my boots. "That doesn't sound like Brandi. Especially with three little kids at home. They've been through so much. She even forgave him for the affair he had with that skinny little fake blond publicist. I could've snapped one of her spindly little arms in two as easily as I can break a pencil."

Clay frowns at me.

"You're the only person I know who categorizes people by how easily you think you can cause them bodily harm."

He slowly opens the bag and peers inside it like the cookie might be alive and eager to escape.

"I guess he's become pretty hard to live with," he goes on. "It's hard enough being his friend anymore."

He pulls out one of the cookies and hands it to me. He takes the other one for himself and leans back against the hood of a car after making sure that it's not dirty.

"He's been acting strange since the accident, and I'm not just talking about the post-traumatic stress symptoms they all suffered from: the chronic insomnia, the nightmares when he does sleep, the panic attacks, the mood swings."

I've witnessed more than a few of E.J.'s panic attacks, but he gets them far less than he used to. Isabel says that Jimmy still has a bad nightmare now and then but for the most part the two of them, along with Lib and Ray, seem to be doing okay.

Dusty, on the other hand, always looks drawn and skittish. Every word out of his mouth is a complaint, or tinged with bitterness.

He's become a far cry from the carefree little hell-raiser who used to sit at my kitchen table all innocent grins and dimples, eating a plate full of bacon and eggs after a sleepover with Clay while waiting for me to find the crayfish he put in my coffee mug.

He and Clay complemented each other perfectly back then. I believe Dusty single-handedly kept Clay from becoming a hermit when he moved back to Jolly Mount during the fifth grade. He dragged Clay to pickup baseball games over at the township park, taught him how to ride a bike, and made him go to his first girl-boy party, while, for his part, Clay explained the importance of periodic bathing to Dusty, taught him the joys of wrapping coins and cashing the rolls in at the bank for paper money, and happened to have a tube of Neosporin ointment and a pack of gauze bandages in his windbreaker pocket the day Dusty ripped open the palm of his hand on a rusted screw while playing on an old abandoned tipple.

Dusty had no fear. No hesitation. Everything he encountered was meant to be experienced physically. He never pondered or studied or wondered. A creek was meant to be splashed into. A road was meant to be crossed. A rock was meant to be thrown. A tree was meant to be climbed. A path was meant to be followed.

He had an equally straightforward way of classifying people. Most of the men around here, including his dad, were meant to be coal miners because they were strong and they weren't afraid of the dark. His mom was meant to be a mom because she had a soft lap and made good food. His pediatrician was meant to be a doctor because he knew what every kind of medicine was for and he wasn't scared of blood. Cam Jack was meant to own everything because his dad owned everything before him. I was meant to be a cop because I liked to help people and then tell them what to do.

To Dusty, everything had only one true purpose, and he didn't like it when something was used in a way it wasn't supposed to be used.

It bothered him that Clay put maps on his wall to show him places he might not ever see instead of using them to get to the places right now.

Those times when he saw me going out in a pretty dress and I didn't come back with a husband upset him.

All the problems he encountered in his young life he believed were caused by things and people being used in ways that went against their true natures.

I can't help being struck by the irony that this same boy who came from a family composed of four generations of miners suddenly decided after the rescue that his true calling in life was to run a restaurant.

No one could fault him for no longer wanting to work in the mines after spending four days slowly suffocating to death trapped inside one, but we were all skeptical from the start about an actual sit-down restaurant's chances of survival in a town that could barely support a Subway. Not to mention Dusty's own capabilities as a businessman. But Dusty was pumped up at the time from his newfound celebrity and wealth and was easy prey for the fawning financial advisors who descended upon him when the money was rolling in.

One was a guy from Pittsburgh who had advised Franco Harris and a few other retired Steelers from the glory-day teams of the seventies. He was the man responsible for getting Franco his own line of frozen pizzas.

He told Dusty that a lot of athletes bought restaurants. It was an easy way to make money. They didn't have to do any work. They simply loaned their names to the places and watched their investments triple and quadruple.

He believed owning a restaurant would work for Dusty for the same reason it worked for athletes. He was a star now.

It sounded good in theory, plus it also helped solve the problem of what Dusty was going to do for a living, so he went ahead and invested all his money in the project. But he soon found out there were two very important differences between him and a revered professional athlete when it came to bankrolling a business.

First of all, professional athletes had enough money to hire people who knew how to run a restaurant to run the restaurant for them, and that's why they were able to own a restaurant and not actually work in it. Dusty only had enough money to convince a bank to loan him more money so he would be able to lease a building, buy equipment, and insure the operation. He hired a few waitresses and a cook, but after six months was rarely able to pay them. A liquor license was financially out of the question, which meant none of his buddies ever came by.

And secondly, people wanted to hang out with star athletes and would do just about anything in order to run into one; it turned out not so many people wanted to hang out with a man who had only been in the news for a couple of weeks, especially a man most of them had known since he was in diapers.

To the rest of the world he had become the epitome of a blue-collar hero, but he didn't live with the rest of the world. He lived among coal miners and unemployed coal miners and retired coal miners, and to them he was no different than they were. This didn't mean that they weren't sympathetic toward him and that they weren't glad that he had lived through his ordeal, but they didn't feel that he had done anything that merited plunking down their hard-earned cash for a mediocre meal on the outside chance he might stop by their table for a chat. He hadn't won any Super Bowls; he had merely survived a really bad day at work.

Clay takes a bite from the perimeter of his cookie. He will eat all along the outside, saving the black icing eyeballs and smile in the center of the yellow icing face for the very end.

"I can't explain it. He's changed. He's not himself anymore."

"What do you mean?"

He thinks about what he's going to say next before he says it.

I watch his face. It's hard for me to see myself there, although I've been told many times how much we resemble each other.

He has my mother's smile. He has Shannon's chestnut hair and my father's large powerful hands. He also has a lot of his own father in his face, but Clay will never know this and neither will anyone else.

"Maybe there are some people in this world who can look at his job and look at his little house and look at him already having three kids when he's barely twenty-four years old and think he's stupid or he's a loser. But he's not. He was content with that life. It's what he wanted and that's all that matters."

"I thought he wanted to be an astronaut."

"When we were kids. Sure," he laughs. "I wanted to be a cowboy."

I smile at him.

"Until you realized horses shit wherever they want to."

"Didn't you have a childhood dream?" he asks me.

Surviving my childhood, I think to myself.

"Sure. I wanted to be a rock star," I throw out to appease him.

He concentrates on the careful eating of his cookie.

"All I know is ever since the accident, he's got it in his head that being a miner isn't good enough anymore. That he needs to prove himself to the rest of the world and be somebody."

He scrunches up his nose when he says the word "somebody."

"Before the accident Dusty had never been farther than Centresburg. After the accident he was flown first class to Hollywood to be on *The Tonight Show*. He went to Disney World. He got a letter from the president and had dinner with the governor. He was on TV and the cover of *Time* magazine. He was famous. And then all of a sudden he wasn't."

I don't point out that the same thing happened to Lib and Jimmy and E.J. and Ray and none of them have felt the need to be somebody, but they're all a good deal older than Dusty and I think they're happy just to be alive.

"Before all that happened he never questioned his life. Any part of it," Clay adds.

"Sometimes it can be a good thing to be exposed to more and question your life."

"Sometimes it's not. They ruined him."

"Who is 'they' exactly?"

He gestures with the final remaining bite of his cookie at the car dealership across the road with its American flag the size of a barn undulating in the breeze like a patriotic sea above the seemingly endless rows of gleaming SUVs.

"Everybody who isn't us."

He finishes eating and looks inside the bag for a napkin. I've already anticipated the need and hold one out to him.

"Now all he has to live for is this lawsuit," he says.

"What do you think about the lawsuit?"

"I don't think there's any way to assign blame in something like this. Cam Jack runs unsafe mines and nobody does anything about it. Coal mining is a dangerous profession; the miners know this. What it boils down to is Cam Jack has more money than God. Why shouldn't the Jolly Mount Five have some of it for themselves and their families after what they went through?"

"So it's a noble cause. Sort of like Robin Hood robbing from the rich to give to the poor."

"Except there's no robbing. They'd come by the money honestly. A jury of their peers would award it to them because they earned it."

Did they earn it? I ask myself. And if so, how much did they earn? What is the market value of a man's sanity these days? What is considered reasonable compensation for spending four days entombed on a cold rock shelf a mile beneath the earth's surface in impenetrable darkness and absolute silence, his tongue swollen with dehydration, his stomach hardened into a starving knot, his breath coming in shallow pants, his nose assaulted by the smells of shit, piss, puke, fear, and sweat and the sickly sweet scent of blood and rot coming from the gangrenous leg of his delirious friend? Should it be more or less than the amount of money Cam Jack's investments earn in a day?

I think about Shannon and the bidding war over her unborn child. Eighty thousand dollars from Family X, or will she be able to get ninety thousand from the Jamesons? Is this a ridiculous amount of money to pay for a child when the world is filled with so many unwanted ones or is it ridiculously low? Shouldn't the price tag be millions of dollars? Or is a child worth anything at all if its own mother is willing to sell it?

He finishes wiping the yellow icing from his fingers, crumples the napkin into a ball, and puts it in the empty bag.

I notice him glance at his spit-shined black boots to make sure there are no crumbs on them.

"Did you change that lady's tire yesterday?" he asks me.

"Yeah. She was a piece of work. Thanks for that."

"You made some money, though, didn't you?"

"Sure. Now I can afford four days of health insurance."

"That's not funny, Mom. I've got to get back to work."

"Clay. Wait. I have something to tell you. Your Aunt Shannon's back."

"What? Aunt Shannon? She's back? Here?"

"Yes."

"I don't understand."

"She just showed up yesterday at my house."

"After all these years? She just showed up?"

"Yes."

He opens his mouth to speak again but nothing comes out. He looks genuinely stunned.

I wonder what's going through his head. Clay was only five years old when we moved out of Dad's house and left Shannon behind, but he had been very attached to her by then and used to follow her around full of the blind devotion and intense fascination that all little kids feel for older kids who pay the slightest bit of attention to them.

Shannon had grown fond of him, too, even though she'd been outwardly jealous at first. It took some time but eventually his solemn brown eyes and the serious way he wrinkled his silky-smooth forehead like a troubled puppy whenever she asked him a question won her over. Plus as they both grew older I knew she enjoyed being adored, even if the only reasons for it were because she could ride a two-wheeler and was allowed to stay up past eight o'clock.

Clay's presence in the house changed a lot of things for us, most notably our relationship with Dad. Once I had a baby of my own, I finally stood up to him. Shannon and I never talked about my sudden surge of maternal strength. I always thought she must have been thankful for it because it benefited her, too, but over time, long after she had disappeared from my life, I began to wonder if she might have hated me for not standing up sooner. Did she ever wonder why I didn't stand up for her? Or myself? Or did she already know the reason?

I did my best to protect her. I kept her out of Dad's way as much as possible. I distracted him from her when I could, offering my own body as an alternate punching bag in the same way I might have enticingly waved a juicy piece of raw meat in front of a ravenous dog who was contemplating a bowl of dry kibble.

But it wasn't within my power to tell him to stop. I assumed she understood this. For seventeen years I felt I had no right to tell him he couldn't beat me and my sister because he was our father and I believed we belonged to him as surely as his lunch pail.

My son, on the other hand, belonged to no one but himself. He would be a man someday. No one could own him. Not even me, his mother. But as his mother I had a responsibility to him, and it was to make sure he would never experience any harm or misery that it was in my power to prevent.

I never saw my dad hit my mom, but I heard the fights. My mother's screams and crying; my father's cursing and shouting; the thumps and thuds and sounds of things breaking—they were all part of the sound track of my life that I'd listen to, hiding in my room with my eyes closed against the horrible possibility of what the picture must be.

I think my mother thought I wouldn't be affected by the violence if I didn't see it. Or maybe that I wouldn't hate my father for hurting her if I didn't witness it with my own eyes. She was wrong on both counts.

I knew from my own experience that letting Clay see his mommy or his revered Aunt Shannon, who could pop a wheelie on her blue two-wheeler, get belted across a room by his grandfather would be harmful to him. I also knew that listening to it happen while he sat helpless and mute in another room would be a form of misery so pervasive and permanent he would wear it for the rest of his life like a skin.

I had never been allowed to make any decisions in regard to Shannon and me because our destinies had been set, but once Clay came along I was presented with a choice: a mother's duty or a daughter's sentence.

Clay never knew about the abuse Shannon and I endured when we were younger. Because of this, after we left Shannon with Dad, I couldn't talk to Clay about my fear that the beatings might have started again, and after Shannon's disappearance I couldn't share my awful suspicions with him about what my dad might have done to her.

All I could do was tell him she ran away and then do my best to hide my grief and fear while listening to him ask all the questions I asked myself: Why would she run away? Why wouldn't she come here? How could she leave us?

I didn't have answers for either of us. Eventually, he stopped asking.

Now I brace myself, wondering if he's going to start asking those same questions again, or break out into some sort of difficult emotional reaction I'm not equipped to deal with, or throw a bunch of accusations at me like E.J. did. But what I get is a big smile.

"Mom," he says and gives me a hug, "you must be so happy."

"Well, yes," I say a little uncertainly as I return his embrace.

"Is she okay?"

"She's fine. And she's going to have a baby any day now."

"A baby? That's great."

His smile grows.

"The baby will be my cousin, right?"

His excitement is contagious. I smile back at him, but my thoughts quickly turn bittersweet as I remember him showing the same kind of enthusiasm every time I'd tell him I was going on a date and he'd get his hopes up that this newest man would turn out to be a potential dad.

I also know that there's the possibility his cousin will be sold.

"Can I see her?"

"Of course you can see her. I'll talk to her when I get home. What are you doing tonight?"

"I'm busy tonight. Maybe later this week."

"I assume this means you're not coming to Isabel and Jimmy's."

Clay and I have a standing invitation to Sunday dinner. Clay rarely goes anymore. I plan to go today to tell them about Shannon.

"No. I'm working."

He shakes his head, still smiling.

"Wow. That's unreal. Aunt Shannon just showing up out of the blue."

He thinks about it a moment longer and the smile begins to fade. His happy gaze falters slightly.

He slips his sunglasses back on before I can see any substantial hurt or betrayal in his eyes.

"It's supposed to snow," he tells me in his deputy voice, glancing at my bare legs. "You should put some pants on."

I watch him turn on his heel and begin walking back toward the building.

I have no idea what he does outside his job, and I only know what he does at his job because I used to have one similar to it. It's hard for me to believe sometimes that this is the same person who used to write me two-page, single-spaced, intricately detailed accounts of everything he had done and thought during the day and leave it for me on the coffee table along with a bottle of One-A-Day vitamins and a calcium supplement on the nights I worked a shift that ended past his bedtime.

I've always thought of boys and men as completely separate beings and girls and women as part of the same whole. Looking at a little girl I can always envision the resulting woman, like a cake before it's been frosted, but I'm never able to see a man in a little boy's face.

A boy becomes a man: The expression used to frighten me. I didn't like to think that one day Clay would become a man. I was very attached to the little boy he already was. It sounded like an act of sorcery. A wand would be waved, some smoke would appear, and my sweet, grinning, gangly, doting little boy would disappear forever and in his place would be a big, hairy, serious man who I would continue to love and hopefully understand but who would be a stranger to me.

This was basically what happened, aside from the smoke.

Chapter Twelve

TALKING WITH CLAY does me some good. His attitude toward Shannon's return helps me push aside some of my darker feelings and lets in a little light. I should concentrate on the positive. She's alive and well and that's better than being dead. She's back and that's better than being away. She's going to have a baby she's planning on selling, but that was before she showed up here; maybe I can help her get her act together and with Clay's help we can convince her to keep his cousin.

In order to feel this way I have to basically ignore everything I heard her say to Pamela Jameson, but I'm able to keep my hopes up long enough to stop by the mall and buy a few things for the baby.

On my way back to my car, I notice two Marines in dress uniform getting out of a Honda Civic.

They're impossible to miss: tall, straight, handsome, impeccably clean, perfectly pressed, their chests covered with medals, their gold buttons gleaming, their hats a shade of white I've never seen except on certain brides.

They stand next to their car, exchange a few words, and look around. Their respective heads turn in opposite directions, searching the parking lot.

As I trek across the parking lot watching them, my phone rings. Caller ID shows that it's Lib's mom, Sophia Bertolli.

Sophia is still capable of driving herself around despite being in her eighties, but from time to time her arthritis acts up and the pain in her knees becomes so great she can't even push an accelerator pedal.

"Hi, Sophia."

"Shae-Lynn? Is that you?"

She always sounds surprised when people answer their own phones.

"Yes, it is. How are you?" I shout.

She has terrible hearing.

"Good. What are you up to today?"

"Not much. Do you need a ride?"

"I need a ride," she tells me.

"Okay. When do you need it?"

"Mm Hmm," she says.

"When would you like me to pick you up?" I try again.

"I drove myself to church and back but now my knees hurt and I'm supposed to go to Lib's house for supper."

"Would you like me to give you a ride?"

"That would be nice."

"How about I pick you up in an hour?"

"Mm hmm," she says. "All right then. Good-bye."

I have no idea if this means she thinks I'm coming or not, but regardless I know she'll be there when I arrive.

One of the Marines appears to spot something of interest. He lightly taps his partner's chest with the back of his hand to get his attention and points out two large, unshaven young men in baggy jeans and ball caps: one wearing work boots and a NASCAR T-shirt, the other in gym shoes with rips down the side and a stretched-out red sweatshirt that's been washed so many times it's pink now, but I'm sure he still regards it as red because he doesn't strike me as the kind of guy who'd wear pink.

The Marines begin striding toward the boys, their legs moving in precise tandem, arms stiff at their sides, backs and necks held straight, yet somehow their heads appear pushed forward slightly like they've picked up a scent and their noses are leading them. They suddenly check themselves, slow down, and try to act casual.

They make contact. They're all chatting now. Smiles are being exchanged. They seem to be pulling off the casual act as well as it can be done by someone wearing flashy red and gold epaulettes and a hat like a 1950s milkman's while standing not far from the gutted front of a Sears anchor store with a huge, faded, peeling GOING OUT OF BUSINESS sign plastered across the doors.

I wonder what they're saying. I could make a good guess. I've been the object of recruitment myself, many times, in both my professional and personal lives.

The roads to Sophia's house are weathered, cracked blacktop, their shoulders shattered from decades of heavy coal trucks traveling over them.

Just when I think I have every pothole memorized, a new batch appears each spring. I try to miss as many as possible, jerking my steering wheel this way and that like I'm in the middle of an obstacle course, all the while making sure I stay as close to my side of the road as possible.

The traffic out here is sparse but deadly. When the occasional vehicle does come barreling from the opposite direction, it's usually driving straight down the middle of the road. I'm used to it and I've got good reflexes but the danger's still there.

A moron in a green GMC Yukon that's roomier than the kitchen in my old D.C. apartment comes tearing around a curve, causing me to swerve hard to the right, and I almost end up in a ditch.

I'm so busy swearing a blue streak and giving him the finger as I watch him disappear over a hill in my rearview mirror that I don't see the kids and their wagon until it's almost too late.

I swerve again, this time into the middle of the road to avoid hitting them. If there had been a car coming in the opposite direction, we'd all be dead.

I slow down and drive about a hundred feet before I have to pull off to the side of the road. My heart is beating like crazy.

I crane my neck around and watch them approach me. It's a little girl pulling a little boy in a beat-up red wagon. She's giving me the finger.

I recognize the pale, skinny legs and the glint of something sparkly.

I get out of my car and start stalking toward them.

"What are you doing?" I shout.

"What are you doing?" Fanci shouts back at me.

"Do you know how dangerous it is to be out here on these roads?"

"It's only dangerous when people drive like assholes."

I look down at Kenny. He's sitting calmly in the midst of a bunch of rocks, holding a big thick stick about four feet long across his lap. Fanci's pink kitty purse lies near the front of the wagon.

He's wearing jeans and a coat. I check out Fanci next. She interprets my roving stare to be an appreciation of her outfit and lets the hand holding the wagon handle drop casually to her side, puts the other hand on her hip, and arches her back in what I'm sure she thinks is a pose of devastating sexiness.

She's wearing a pair of tiny bright pink shorts that look like they're made from rain slicker material and a cropped pink tank top with the words "I love Paris" emblazoned across the front in sparkly red stones, half of which no longer sparkle. A few are missing.

The T-shirt's sentiment raises my spirits temporarily, and I'm about to ask her how much she knows about the French capital and if she'd like to go there someday when I realize with a sinking heart that it's not the city the shirt is touting but the Hilton heiress, the latest female celeb to lend her name to pre-teen slutwear.

"It's starting to get cold," I tell her. "It might even snow later. You need to go home and put some clothes on."

Her arms and legs are covered in goose bumps.

She gives me one of her unnerving, unsmiling appraisals.

"So do you."

"What are you doing out here, anyway?" I change the subject. "You're miles from home."

"We weren't at home. We were visiting our cousins but we hate our cousins so we're doing this instead."

"Who are your cousins?"

"None of your business."

"Why are you visiting them if you hate them?"

"Our dad made us go so he could sleep."

"What about your mom?"

She glances at Kenny, who doesn't show any sign of opening his mouth and tells him to shut up.

"What's with the stick?" I try another topic.

"It's a dog-beating stick. There's a lot of dogs around here," she states flatly.

"You got something against dogs?"

"I got something against wild dogs and people's dogs that come running at you when you walk by their house and want to rip your throat out. Dogs are supposed to be nice. They're supposed to like kids like Kenny."

I look down at him.

"Nice rocks, Kenny," I comment.

I pick up a piece of the coal debris and rub my thumb over its dull black glimmer.

"This one's a pretty one," I say.

"You can have it," he tells me.

"Thanks."

I slip it in the pocket of my sweater. It's the first time I've heard him speak.

"Why don't you let me give you a lift back to your cousins' house?"

"You're making the offer so that means we don't have to pay?"

"You don't have to pay."

"Then take us to the mall."

"No way."

She looks at Kenny. They have a silent conversation conducted with their eyes and pulse rates.

"Then take us home," she says.

They don't have to give me directions to their house. I visited it years ago when the Centresburg police searched it after I pulled Choker over for speeding and DWI (Driving While an Idiot) and discovered his van was full of TV sets and stereo systems he'd been stealing for the past month and then had no idea how to hock.

It's a small shoebox-shaped house set in a small clearing off a mile-long stretch of dirt road that used to lead to a bridge that used to cross a creek that used to continue on to a tipple that used to pour coal into the railroad cars waiting on the tracks next to it. The bridge is gone now. The road and railroad tracks are overgrown with weeds. The tipple has collapsed into a heap of cracked timbers and brown rusted metal that's been consumed by the forest. When the trees lose their leaves in winter, its remains can be glimpsed lying on the hillside like the decaying carcass of some huge beast.

The house is surrounded by a sea of junk: old mowers and appliances; two empty rabbit pens; a dented gray metal filing cabinet; bald tires; rusted sheet metal; black Hefty bags filled with beer cans; rolls of pink insulation; a picnic table without benches; a swing set without swings; and a disturbing number of gnome lawn ornaments without heads.

Fanci and Kenny get out of the car and follow me around to the back of my car.

"I lost my mom when I was six," I tell Fanci as I unload their wagon and dog-beating stick.

"So?" she says.

"Did you ever find her?" Kenny asks me.

"She died."

"Oh," he replies, his face falling for an instant, but he brightens up quickly. "We know where our mom is."

"Shut up, Kenny," Fanci snaps at him.

"Where is she?"

"She's taking a break. When dad got out of jail she said it was his turn to take care of us for awhile."

"And how's that going?"

"It ain't none of your business," Fanci says.

"Right. I forgot."

I hold out one of my yellow business cards to Fanci.

"Here. You never know when you'll finally be able to pay for a ride."

She eyes it, then takes it without looking at me and slips it into her pink kitten purse.

Choker opens the front door wearing tube socks and an old green terry cloth robe with two dark patches on the front where the pockets used to be. The matching belt is missing, too. The robe's cinched around his waist with the brown leather belt and American flag belt buckle that he usually uses to hold up his jeans.

He squints against the daylight. I can hear a TV droning inside the house.

"What the hell?" he greets me.

I put a foot on the bottom step and he moves back behind his door.

"I don't want you around here."

I did a real number on his face. I wonder how he explained it to his kids or if they even bothered to ask.

"Get in the house," he tells them and they hurry inside.

"I'd like to call you a retard, Choker, but I realize that's not politically correct so I'm just going to say you're patriotically challenged."

"What are you talking about?"

I gesture at his truck parked in the yard right up against the house. It's covered in bumper stickers: Proud to be American. Born in the U.S.A. God Bless America. Red, White, and Blue: These colors don't run.

"Who are you trying to impress with your Americanness? Other Americans? Why don't you go drive this thing around Baghdad?"

"Fuck you," he says.

"This is a nice little setup you've got here, Choker. You've really been able to spread out."

"I need my space."

"Right. You're one of those free-range rednecks I've been hearing about."

He scratches at his missing ear.

"Hank Penrose's kid calling me a redneck? If that ain't the kettle calling the kettle . . . a kettle."

I smile at his attempt to remember the old adage.

"Don't hurt yourself."

"What do you want?"

"Nothing. I was just dropping off your kids."

"You better stop messing with my kids," he says.

"Where's your wife, Choker? Did she spurn you, too?"

"I mean it. Stay away from my kids. I ain't doing nothing wrong with them. I love them. I'd never beat on them the way your old man did you."

He slams the door on me.

I pound on it with my fists and kick at it a few times and jiggle the handle, but my enthusiasm quickly passes.

My rage is immense, but my rage against him is half-hearted.

I close my eyes and find my safe place. I settle into the soft, plump cushions of the couch. I feel the heat from the fire warm my cold bare feet searching for the comfort of my mom's rag rug next to my bed on a winter's morning. I hear the puppy's faint whines as he twitches in his sleep chasing rabbits in his dreams. I smell the fresh-baked cookies and taste the sweetness of cocoa on my tongue. I look out the window and see raindrops as big as silver dollars splatter against the glass that's lit from behind by flashes of lightning.

I look again and see a face.

The shock is so great I jump up from the couch and spill hot chocolate all over myself.

No one has ever tried to look in or get in.

I want out. I need out. But I don't know how to do it. There's no door. I've never tried to leave before. I've always stayed as long as I could. I've always wished I could stay longer.

I open my eyes. My heart is thudding sickly in my throat. I'm sitting in my car, although I don't remember walking here.

The face is still there behind the glass, and I stifle a scream. It's only Kenny at his father's window waving good-bye.

Chapter Thirteen

SOPHIA IS WAITING FOR ME on her front porch, sitting in a lawn chair with her big tan pocketbook at her feet. She has on a pair of mint green polyester pants, a long-sleeved white blouse, a quilted vest patterned in peach-colored roses, a tan raincoat, plain white canvas tennis shoes with white anklets, and a small gold crucifix around her neck.

She's sitting in her usual upright position with her head and shoulders against the back of the chair, her feet flat on the floor, and an arm on each armrest like a queen about to receive subjects. In all my years of knowing her, I've never seen her slouched in a chair, or with her feet tucked under her, or sprawled out on a couch. She once remarked to me that people nowadays have even forgotten how to sit.

"Hi, Sophia," I call out to her.

Her eyes are open behind her gold-rimmed glasses, but she could be asleep for all the movement and attention she displays. She's wearing the dreamy expression peculiar to the very old and the very young, where they seem fascinated by something everyone else takes for granted. People find the phenomenon adorable in babies. It means they're inquisitive and intrigued by objects in their new world. In old people they usually chalk it up to senility, but I don't think that's the case. For both, it's the ability to see things in their purest sense. All the knowledge that comes from experience doesn't exist for a child and doesn't matter anymore to an old lady. With a life completely in front of you or a life completely behind you, the world looks basically the same.

She gazes past me at my yellow Subaru. It doesn't register in her brain as a means of travel or the source of a loan payment or the way I make my living. She doesn't care about its safety features or what it's doing to the ozone layer. She doesn't find the words MOUNT ME to be amusing or offensive. It's simply a large roaring machine that disturbs the serenity of the day with its unpleasant noise and exhaust smell.

"Do you still need that ride?" I ask her.

Her eyes travel slowly from my car to my face and take a moment to recognize me.

"Hello, Shae-Lynn."

"Hi, Sophia. Do you still need a ride to Lib's house?"

"I could use a ride to Lib's house."

She rises shakily from the chair. I wait for her at the bottom of her porch steps. I know she won't allow me to help her.

She passes by me. The top of her head, crowned in a small cloud of gray hair like silver spun sugar, barely reaches to my chin.

I open the passenger side door for her and wait for the comment she always makes about the color.

"Well at least everyone will be able to see us coming."

We set off to Lib's house driving faded, snaking blacktop that dips and swells and hugs the hills. The air rushing through my partially open window has the wet, earthy smell of an old, shattered tree stump when the sun starts to warm it after a rainstorm. It blends nicely with the faint scent of Sophia's lavender perfume.

We exchange some small talk while Sophia sits perfectly still, strapped snugly into her seat with her gnarled arthritic hands placed primly in her lap, showing all the composure and concentration of a tiny astronaut.

"So what do you think of all this lawsuit talk?" I ask her.

"You don't want my opinion," she laughs. "I'm an old lady."

"That's exactly why I want it."

"Well, I don't understand any of it." She shakes her head at me. "Back in my day a miner would never have sued his company."

"He never could've won," I remind her.

A trace of a frown passes over her lips dabbed in a shade of coral lipstick she's been wearing for as long as I've known her.

"I don't understand why people nowadays are so anxious to go running to lawyers and judges every time they have a problem. In my day the last thing you wanted to do was bring strangers into your life and have them tell you what to do. You figured out how to fix what was wrong on your own or you learned how to live with the hand God dealt you."

She seems pleased with her brief speech and looks like she's nodding off, then I realize she's staring at her gold wedding band with the same detached expression she wore earlier sitting on her porch.

I wonder what she sees when she looks at it. Is it still a symbol of love and commitment? Does it remind her of her wedding in a church filled with flowers and the raucous reception afterwards in the Union Hall? Does it make her think of her husband as a vital, blushing, young man proposing to her with coal dirt under his fingernails or as the frail, wasted shell of a man whose hand she held in a hospital room the morning his black lungs took their final breath?

Or is it simply something shiny that's caught her eye?

Lib is mowing his front yard when we arrive. His wife, Teresa, is standing over her emerald green gazing ball with a cleaning rag in one hand watching him curiously, the way she might watch a turtle trying to climb a tree.

Back and forth he marches, never breaking stride, his pace constant, his eyes fixed on the dead grass ahead of him. In summer he would be cutting perfect diagonal paths through its green lushness, but this time of year it's the color of hay and matted down from old snow.

He's using his lawn mower instead of the tractor his sons bought him for his birthday five years ago. He loves the tractor. He hardly ever uses the lawn mower anymore. From what Teresa has told me, when he brings it out, it's a bad sign. It means he's trying to physically chew up a problem.

"What's he doing?" I ask Teresa when Sophia and I join her. "There's no grass to mow yet."

"He'd mow snow if he could," she replies without taking her eyes off him.

He has on a J&P ball cap and an old pair of jeans with a white ring permanently faded onto one of the back pockets where he keeps his tin of chewing tobacco. He's shirtless and the hair on his chest and arms is damp with sweat.

Both the passage of time and Teresa's cooking has softened his exterior some, but the core underneath remains rock hard. His gut is like a mattress protecting a boulder, and his arms have the consistency of slabs of packed clay.

"He can blow snow," I say.

"It doesn't seem to give him the same satisfaction."

She finally looks my way with a not-altogether-welcoming yet still neighborly enough smile on her lips. Disapproval flashes in the depths of her dark eyes, but she douses it quickly out of respect for the bond that grew up between us two years ago while we waited for four days and nights with Vonda, Isabel, and Brandi to find out if our men were going to live or die.

She thinks I should dress my age. I'm not sure exactly what she means by this, but whenever I've heard her make this comment about other women it's seemed obvious to me that she believes there is a sort of unspoken dress code regarding appropriate attire for women at every age, and we are all under an obligation to memorize and practice it daily.

I don't take her opinion on clothing too seriously. She's only in her mid-fifties but she's been dressing like she's in her mid-seventies since she's been in her mid-thirties. Today she's wearing a pair of elastic-waisted navy blue polyester pants and a blouse in a blue and white check that fits her like a dental hygienist's smock.

Neither piece of apparel is very flattering stretched across her heavy bosom and backside. She's always been busty with ample hips but in her youth she also had an enviably small waist and petite doll's hands she liked to show off in dainty gloves. I remember the pair of soft white ones with little pearl buttons she used to wear to church in spring and a pair of scarlet ones with matching dyed rabbit fur trim she wore at Christmas.

When I was a girl and in the full flush of my longing for Lib and his dark-eyed, Italian good looks, I hated and adored her. I wanted to be just like her yet I wished she'd disappear off the face of the earth.

I used to get out my mom's high school yearbook and stare at Teresa's picture. I was more fascinated by it than my own mother's picture.

In her way, I believed my mother was just as pretty, but it was a completely different kind of beauty, fresh and unrestrained. In her senior picture, my mom looked much younger than the other girls. Part of the reason was the way she wore her hair. It was long and free, tied back with a polka-dot ribbon and falling in waves around her wide, sunburned cheeks. All the other girls wore their hair in teased bobs with meaningless tiny bows lost in the middle of them.

Her smile was different, too—wide and engaging—while the others had closemouthed, beatific Mona Lisa smiles that I'm sure they practiced for hours before a mirror.

Teresa, on the other hand, was a dead ringer for Snow White. Porcelain skin. Ruby red lips pursed in a pouty bow. Her smooth black hair grazing her shoulders and curled at the ends in little flips. Her eyes black and empty like lovely polished stones.

Now her face is lined and careworn and her hands are rough and callused, but her hair is still a young, shiny blue-black that she wears in a thick braid that falls down the middle of her back.

Sophia gives Teresa's arm a squeeze.

"What's he worried about now?"

"Oh, I don't know. He's been upset all week ever since we went and had our will made."

"I guess that makes sense," I say without thinking.

I can tell instantly that Teresa feels I have no right to hold any opinion on this particular highly personal topic.

"All I mean is he's probably been thinking about dying all week if he just made a will." I try to explain myself and end up making things worse.

Sophia nods her agreement.

"We don't have much but I want to make sure what we do have ends up in the right hands," Teresa says, sounding a little defensive.

"She wants to make sure Angie doesn't take any of her jewelry," Sophia tells me.

She's standing next to me, her eyes fixed on the road as she speaks, her purse hanging from the crook of one arm, looking like she's waiting for a bus.

Angie is the daughter-in-law Teresa likes less than the other one.

"That's not true," Teresa protests.

Sophia nods that it is.

"Lib was terrible the whole time," she tells us. "Then the lawyer made the mistake of saying it was lucky Lib had two Purple Hearts because that way he could give one to each son and not have to worry about choosing between them."

"Lib got furious. He said he sure as hell didn't feel lucky at the time he was getting two of them but he sure felt lucky now if it meant it was going to get him out of a goddamned lawyer's office a couple minutes earlier."

168

I laugh.

Sophia frowns at the cursing.

"As far as Lib's concerned, the only thing he owns of any value is his tractor mower," Teresa adds.

"What's he going to do with it? It was a gift from both your boys, wasn't it?"

"Yes, and he thought it wouldn't be fair to choose between them. I didn't have the heart to tell him that neither one of them wants it."

"So who's getting the mower?"

"Jimmy."

"That's perfect," I say.

Sophia nods her approval.

Jimmy will never use it, but he'll park it in a place of honor in his front yard where everyone will see it. He'll keep it waxed and buffed, and talk to it, and drink a toast to it every day.

It's the closest Lib can come to putting the mower out to stud.

"Why don't we go inside and get you some coffee, Mom?" Teresa says to her mother-in-law and begins to guide her toward the house by her elbow.

"Just a minute." Sophia pulls her arm away from Teresa and walks back to me.

"Here, Shae-Lynn."

She hands me a ten-dollar bill and a roll of peppermint Life Savers.

Teresa gives me one more of her disapproving glances, but once again does a good job of keeping it brief.

I know she thinks I should have given Sophia a ride for free, and I'd be happy to give Sophia a ride for free, but Sophia would never call and ask me to give her a ride for free. She would drive herself or call and ask Lib or Teresa to pick her up before she'd do that. She understands that this is what I do for a living.

Teresa hasn't had an easy life by any means and no one could ever look at her immaculate house and yard, or her impressive vegetable garden and the amount of food she cans every fall lining the shelves of her basement, and accuse her of not being a hard worker. She and Lib raised two sons on little money and put them both through college. She knows all about making sacrifices and surviving nightmares, but she doesn't know anything about being on her own.

She went from being one man's daughter to being another man's wife to being the mother of two other men. She moved directly from her father's house into her husband's house and if she outlives Lib, I'm certain she's going to end up living in one of her son's houses even though it may mean the end of his marriage.

She's never had to financially support herself or support others and she thinks women like me choose our lifestyles just to prove a point.

I'm about to leave without interrupting Lib's mad mowing but then I remember Clay's concern about Dusty. I decide to ask Lib what he thinks.

I wave at him. He gestures for me to wait.

I walk back to my car parked in their driveway and lean against the hood while he completes a few more passes at his dead grass.

He lets the engine die and wheels the mower toward me then past me as he heads toward the garage, where he retrieves a pack of Marlboros and a flannel shirt.

I watch him from behind. His bare back is covered with shiny pink patches of new skin from the grafts he had after the explosion because parts of his rubberized rain gear melted through his work clothes into his flesh.

He joins me, smoking a cigarette, and surveys his yard, looking disappointed that he's done. Lib always seems happiest when he has a straightforward task in front of him, whether it's mowing a yard, or eating a barbecued chicken, or playing horseshoes: one thing he can concentrate his full attention upon without having to talk and without having to be talked to.

I assume this mind-set served him well as a soldier. He spent two years in Vietnam, and from what I've heard and seen for myself he didn't come back home depressed or bitter or self-destructive or crazy.

He went right back into the mines upon his return. I imagine that after what he'd been through the world above ground would have lost much of its charm for him. He would always have been tensely waiting for something violent to happen: for silence to be shattered, for the ground beneath his feet to explode, for death to come rushing at him from a line of calm green trees, for a gush of blood to suddenly rupture from a ragged hole in the body of a man standing next to him.

Being deep in the earth, sheltered by mile-thick, cold, black solidity far from the hot, green, unreliable aliveness of a jungle, in his familiar darkness, surrounded by stoic, hardworking men, lulled by the constant sound of the machinery echoing in the tunnels, was probably one of the things that saved his sanity.

I take a deep breath of the mower's gasoline fumes mingled with the smell of mangled earth.

"Good thing you took care of that," I comment on his handiwork. "It was getting a little high."

He gives me a good-natured scowl.

"I'm fifty-eight and I'm retired. Hell, I've got to find something to do."

"Lots of men would love to be retired at fifty-eight."

"The same men who never did shit when they weren't retired," he replies in a growl. "Teresa dragged me off to make a will. Did she tell you that?"

"Yeah, she told me. It's a good thing to have a will."

"All those years I was in the mines. Every day I went to work I could've died and I never had a will. Now she wants me to have a will. You know why? She thinks I'm gonna die from smoking. She thinks I'm gonna die because I'm getting old."

It's obvious from the look on his face that he considers this to be an insult.

"Just because she wanted you to get a will made doesn't mean she thinks you're going to die. People get wills made when they're in their twenties."

"But why now?"

"I don't know. Have you bought her any nice jewelry lately?"

"What's that got to do with anything?"

"Never mind." I smile at him. "She said you weren't very nice to the lawyer."

He takes the cigarette out of his mouth and spits.

"Lawyers," he says, turning his gaze back on his yard again and squinting with disgust. "We had to go to a different lawyer to get a will made from the one who's handling our lawsuit against J&P. And he's a different one from the one who represented us at the investigation. I hate that specialization bullshit. I expected every man on my crew to be able to use a bolter and drive a shuttle car and a scoop."

"Yeah, but you didn't expect everyone to be able to run a miner the way E.J. does it."

He puts the cigarette back in his mouth and nods his agreement.

"Fair enough," he says with the butt jerking up and down between his lips.

"Speaking of your crew, have you seen Dusty lately?"

"Last week. The five of us got together to talk about the lawsuit."

"How'd he seem?"

He slips on his shirt but leaves it unbuttoned.

"Not good."

"Clay's worried about him."

"Yeah, well . . ."

I look away from his face at the cluster of bullet wounds barely visible beneath the hair on his chest like a trio of small puckered pinkish-gray lips.

"I heard about what happened between you and Choker," he comments, making no effort to subtly change the subject; just choosing to avoid it altogether. "What the hell were you thinking? Guy's sitting in a bar trying to have a drink—"

"He abandoned his kids," I interrupt hotly.

"He left two of his kids in town and told them to go play," he counters. "When we were kids, we ran all over the place. Our mothers never knew where we were half the time. And they sure as hell would've never asked our fathers to take care of us because they were too damn tired to do it themselves."

"His wife left him."

"And left the kids? What kind of woman does that?"

"Apparently the kind of woman who marries and reproduces with a man like Choker."

"I'm not defending Choker. I'm just saying it's none of your business how he's raising his kids. They're his kids."

Did Lib used to defend my dad the same way? I wonder. Was he ever heard to say, "Yeah, I know Penrose beats his little girl, but you should see him bolt a roof."

Lib came from a good, solid family and created one of his own and has little tolerance or patience for men who don't do the same. I know he doesn't approve of Choker's kind of family—bullying drunks; weak, long-suffering women; skittish children with haunted eyes—yet he believes it's none of his business to interfere no matter how bad things get. At the same time he distrusts and dislikes all government and law enforcement agencies, so there's no one else to turn to for help.

Ostracism is the only way people around here deal with unsavory family situations, and if it doesn't cause the families to change, everyone washes their hands of them. The men are avoided, the women ignored, and the children are regarded as hapless victims, granted neither sympathy or scorn, because to feel the first implies they should be saved and to feel the second implies they've done something wrong. People wait to see how they turn out as adults before passing final judgment, no different than if the kids were handfuls of unidentified seeds planted in a questionable patch of dirt. Their acceptance is based on what grows there.

I've often wondered what they think I've grown into.

"I suppose you're right. It's none of my business."

I'm suddenly very tired. I feel like I could lie down on his cold matted grass and sleep for days.

I should go home and talk to Shannon and give her the pajamas I got for the baby: yellow with pastel green turtles, since we don't know if it will be a boy or a girl. The blue set had rhinos and the pink set had bunnies. Apparently turtles are harmless to both genders.

"I should get going."

"What did Clay say about Dusty?"

Lib's face rarely shows emotion anymore. When he was a young man he had a ready, hundred-watt smile that was a vital component of his Italian heartthrob good looks, along with his pompadour of black hair and his bedroom eyes.

Now the hair is thinner and shot through with strands of silver, and his face has begun to puff and sag with age and trauma, but I can still see traces of his former self there whenever something rouses his interest or his passion. Teresa has told me it's difficult to do either since the accident.

"Nothing really. Some vague stuff about him not being himself anymore. And I guess you've probably heard about him and Brandi."

He nods and smokes while I watch and wait to see if he has anything helpful to say about Dusty. Instead he begins to tell me about a friend of his getting killed in Vietnam. I give him my full, startled attention. I've never heard Lib talk about the war. I've never even heard any secondhand stories about Lib's experiences.

The only thing I ever remember my dad saying on the subject was even though he knew Lib was glad to get the hell out of Vietnam, he never seemed happy to be home again.

"Sniper fire," I hear him say. "The first shot might not have killed him, but he screamed and gave away his position, and they sprayed him with bullets.

"I watched the whole thing from about ten yards back. I knew I couldn't move or make a sound without giving away my own position so I had to lie there and watch while the bullets tore him up. I saw bits of shit flying up into this blinding blue sky"—he pauses and gestures above him with his cigarette—"bluer than this one—and I knew some of it was mud and leaves but some of it was pieces of him.

"We weren't able to get to his body for almost two days. By the time we did, it was worse than any road kill I'd ever seen back home. Bloated and rancid. His face was unrecognizable; it was this greasy, yellowish black color like a rotten banana peel.

"I remember staring down at him, thinking to myself, Are they really gonna send this thing home to his mother? What did she ever do to deserve that? What about my mom? Was she gonna see me like that someday?"

He's managed to keep his voice emotionless and his stare steady, but there's a slight tremble in his fingers when he brings the cigarette back to his mouth.

"So I'm standing there trying not to puke and I'm thinking about our moms and everyone we know back home and this thought hits me that his hometown and my hometown aren't just different places from where we are right now; they're different planets. I realized even if I made it home again with my body in one piece, I'd never be able to feel right in their world anymore"—he taps the side of his head with an index finger—"up here."

Is he trying to explain himself to me? He gave me rides into town and candy bars and pats on the head. He asked me about school but not about my black eyes or my bruised cheek. I always thought no one could help because no one should help. Is he trying to tell me he didn't help because he understood the futility? Because he understood some things can't be unlearned?

He clears his throat and goes on.

"The loneliest moment of my life was spent in a room full of the happiest people I'd ever seen welcoming me home from a war half of them didn't support and half of them supported for the wrong reasons but a war all of them wanted to pretend never happened. These were people I'd known my whole life. People I loved. All of them clapping and smiling and singing.

"The only thing I could think as I stood there in the doorway watching them with a stupid grin on my face was from now on I'm gonna be a stranger to everyone I've ever known and everyone I'm ever gonna meet."

He takes a deep drag off his cigarette.

"I think that's what happened to Dusty after the rescue. And he can't deal with it. Some people can't."

"Deal with what exactly?"

"Realizing you're alone. Completely alone."

I watch wisps of smoke crowd under the bill of his cap before escaping into the air.

I'm sure he's not talking about Vietnam or Dusty or being trapped in a mine anymore. I'm sure he's talking about my life.

Chapter Fourteen

I STOP BY MY HOUSE expecting to find Shannon, but there's no sign of her.

I had decided to invite her to come along with me to Jimmy and Isabel's house. I played the scene over and over in my mind during the drive. I even stumbled on Bette Midler singing "The Wind Beneath My Wings" on an easy-listening station to use as the sound track.

Instead of telling them about her return, I'd just spring her on them. There'd be a tearful, happy reunion and Shannon would confess all her current sins, repent, and promise to be a good mommy after explaining how she was abducted by aliens after her seventh-period geometry class eighteen years ago, which prevented her from contacting me until now and then apologizing profusely for any worry or grief it may have caused any of us.

Of the entire scenario, I found the existence of aliens to be the most plausible part of the plot.

I wrap the pajamas in some old Christmas wrapping paper since it's the only kind I have and set the package in the middle of the kitchen table with a note that says, "For Junior, from Aunt Shae-Lynn."

E.J.'s truck is parked in his parents' driveway. I'm always initially glad to see it but then I have to stop and remember if I'm mad at him for any reason.

I remember how we left things last night at Jolly's. It wasn't particularly bad or particularly good.

The front door is open. The entire house smells like the rosemary and lemon Isabel stuffs in her chickens.

I walk in and call a hello to her in the kitchen. She's standing at the sink peeling potatoes in a simple blue sheath dress I'm sure she wore to church and a ruffled yellow apron. Her shoes are off but she still has on her pantyhose. She's wearing one of the innumerable pairs of white terrycloth slippers she brought home from the hospital after Jimmy's month-long stay.

Her slightly curling bobbed hair is almost as white as her slippers. She started going seriously gray a few years before the accident and was constantly arguing back and forth with herself over whether she should highlight or lowlight or dye it back to its original strawberry blond.

Within a week after Jimmy's rescue she was completely white and the dilemma was apparently solved for her. She hasn't touched a snowy hair on her head and wears the new shade with the brash boldness of a ship flying its country's colors in enemy waters.

She looks at me over her shoulder, smiling, her complexion a pearly pink from the heat of the kitchen and the exertion of preparing a meal.

"It's a good day," she says.

I nod back at her.

She's referring to Jimmy. Some days he's almost like his old self, full of wit and vigor, joking around about selling all his left shoes to guys who have lost their right legs and calling the shop "Only Foot Forward," or starting a dance studio for left amputees like himself called "No Left Feet."

Other days he's too depressed to even get out of bed and Isabel leaves him upstairs buried under layers of blankets with only the top of his silver head showing, the curtains drawn tight, and the room smelling of stale, cheap whiskey.

I'm relieved to see him sitting in his favorite chair in the family room wearing long johns and an old brown cardigan. A red plaid blanket covers him from the waist down and I can tell from the way it falls flat on one side and the fact that I only see the tip of one scuffed brown slipper sticking out from under it that he isn't wearing his prosthetic today.

I can still remember walking into this room for the first time as a child and not having any idea how I should respond to the shelves and shelves of books. Jimmy and Isabel didn't seem embarrassed by them or act superior because of them, and those were the only two ways I had ever seen people behave around books.

He smiles when he sees me and rubs his hands together.

"Get the Bushmills," he tells me.

We've always liked to play word games together. We started our latest one a couple months ago. Each time I come over for a visit we compete for a sacred shot of Bushmills by seeing who can come up with the best oxymoron.

Isabel has it hidden where he can't find it. Otherwise, the good stuff would disappear as quickly as the bad stuff he drinks the rest of the time.

I know the hiding place. I leave and come back with the bottle and one shot glass.

I'm feeling pretty confident. A good one occurred to me yesterday after my brawl with Choker.

"Small crowd," I say.

He smiles slightly and tilts his head a little to one side.

There are two types of Irish faces: a hard, fierce one and a soft, tender one. Jimmy's is the former but his eyes belong to a shy boy who tends sheep and whistles pointless tunes in a hazy meadow somewhere.

They're hazel: more green on some days, more gray on others, almost blue on rare occasions. When I was a kid I was convinced they operated on the same principle as a mood ring.

They're startling in his suspicious, combative face, like finding a fragile pink flower poking out of spring snow.

"Clearly confused," he counters.

We look at each other over the glass. It's a stalemate.

"A good beating," I say and reach confidently for the glass.

He covers my hand with his own.

"Senate Intelligence Committee."

I smile but shake my head at him.

"Too easy. The day grew shorter."

"Lovely," he says. "A stripper's dressing room."

I reluctantly pull my hand away.

"Yours," I tell him.

He throws back the shot and reaches for the bottle to pour another.

Isabel swoops in from out of nowhere, grabs it, and leaves again promising to return with coffee.

"Bring me something to put in it, would you, dear?" he calls after her.

She returns with three mugs on a small wooden tray painted with brightly colored birds.

"And here are two cubes of sugar and a spoon to put in it."

He takes the cup from her in his scarred, battered hands, trying to conceal their trembling. He just turned sixty but the accident aged him by at least a decade. He almost died from the gangrene in his shattered leg, and his recovery was a slow one.

"That's not what I meant, love, and you know it."

"It's too early for you to start drinking."

"The time of day has no meaning to a man who has no way to spend any of it."

"Your philosophizing doesn't impress me."

"It's past noon."

"Or your ability to tell time."

Isabel takes a seat on the end of the couch just as E.J. comes walking into the room finishing a call on his cell phone.

He hangs up, sets the phone down on an end table, takes one look at the coffee, leaves, and returns with a beer for himself and his dad.

"There's a good lad," Jimmy says.

"Eamon," his mother scolds him.

I smile broadly.

"Yes, Eamon. You're a bad boy."

He starts to say, "Fuck you," then thinks better of it with his mom in the room.

"Go to hell," he tells me.

Thirty years ago he would have knocked me flat on my ass for saying his name out loud. Now he has to content himself with verbal abuse.

He opens his beer and stands in front of a wall of books glaring at me.

"Who were you talking to?" Isabel asks him. "The future mother of my grandchildren?"

"Give it a rest, Mom. There aren't going to be any grandchildren."

Isabel looks genuinely heartsick.

"Why not?"

"Because no woman will have him," I tell her.

"Too many women will have him," Jimmy counters. "That's the problem."

He takes a few gulps from his beer and belches softly.

"What about you, Shae-Lynn?" Isabel asks me. "Do you ever think about Clay getting married and starting a family?"

E.J. snorts a laugh.

"Shae-Lynn a grandmother? I'd love to see that. Instead of baking cookies and knitting sweaters, she'll teach her grandkids how to throw left hooks and pee in a jar while they're on stakeouts."

"Those are very practical skills." Jimmy defends me. "Son, go get me something to warm up this coffee."

"No," Isabel says sternly. "Don't."

"Fine. Make me grovel and beg. Make a legless man crawl on his belly. The breaking of the spirit. No one knows more about it than the Irish."

"Oh, for the love of Pete."

Irritation blazes in Isabel's bright blue eyes.

"No one is trying to break your spirit, but I might break your neck."

Jimmy turns his attention to me.

"Did you know, Shae-Lynn, that long before the Catholic and Protestant churches came to Ireland we worshipped the gods and goddesses of nature?"

"Here we go," E.J. groans as he grabs a copy of *Sports Illustrated* his mother keeps stocked for him and plunks down on the opposite end of the couch from her. "Irish history time."

He sticks his stockinged feet in her lap. She swats them away.

E.J. has always had mixed feelings about his Irishness. He's proud of his heritage but he gets tired of his dad constantly harping on the many virtues of the place and the race.

I remember in third grade we had to make leprechaun traps in school for a St. Patrick's Day project. Kids came up with some truly innovative ideas: devices made from jars and nets and shoeboxes baited with sweets and green foil shamrocks and pieces of counterfeit gold. E.J. came to class with a bottle of his dad's whiskey and a mallet.

"Long before the English put their stranglehold on our country and took our land and our language and our rights all in the name of civilizing us, we governed ourselves just fine with our chieftains."

"When those same chieftains weren't busy slaughtering each other's tribes over cattle and women," E.J. interjects from behind his magazine.

"I won't deny that we had our troubles. There was plenty of blood-shed and squabbling among ourselves. But it was still better."

"You're such a pagan, James," Isabel tells him.

"A pagan who never missed Mass until the good lord saw fit to take my leg."

"So you're a confused pagan."

"Or a confused Catholic," E.J. mutters.

"The English called us barbaric, but they were the ones who hung men and cut off their heads and stuck them on pikes," Jimmy con-tinues.

"While the Irish would just quietly hack them to death with swords and battle-axes," E.J. adds.

"They said we knew nothing about love but they were the ones who regarded unions between men and women to be business con-tracts, loveless and legally binding, unbreakable except by death. While an Irish woman could get rid of a bad husband just by kicking him out and her kinsmen would make sure he didn't bother her anymore."

"By hacking him to death with swords and battle axes."

"You're missing my point."

E.J. puts down the magazine.

"Which is?"

"I need a drink."

E.J. and Isabel exchange familiar exasperated smiles, although I've noticed recently that Isabel's smile is becoming more and more strained.

I don't give it a second thought. I've never paid much attention to what I consider their trivial family malfunctions because I've always been so overwhelmed by how well their family works.

Even now as an adult, every time I visit them I feel the same surreal awe I did as a child, the same sort of out-of-body experience a lowly peasant girl might have had if she had been invited to sup at the king's long table.

It's a combination of feeling happy and privileged to be included but also being full of resentment and shame.

My instinct has always been to hate them, to want to make fun of everything that was good about them so I could feel good about everything bad about me.

Each shared intimacy is like a slap in my face; every laugh, every affectionate touch, every conversation, every meal that isn't spent in stony silence and apprehension is a reminder of my own family's failure and our deprivation.

It wasn't that they had more money. Jimmy made the same salary as my father. They had something far more valuable than material possessions and they didn't even know it. I tried not to blame them. They could never understand how precious it is to be able to sit in a room with your family and not be afraid.

I stare at my hands circling my coffee mug. My knuckles are bruised from my fight with Choker.

"Shae-Lynn," I hear Isabel say. "E.J.'s told us you have some news."

"You told them?" I snap at him.

"What's the big deal?" he snaps back. "You said you were going to tell them."

"It's wonderful news," Isabel gushes, and Jimmy nods his agreement but their cheeriness seems forced.

"It is," I say.

"We should have a toast," Jimmy suggests.

"All those years of worry and grief," Isabel goes on, ignoring her husband, "you can put them behind you now."

"Right," I concur.

"And have your sister back in your life again."

"Right."

"And we hear she's going to have a baby, too."

"Right. She is. Except . . ."

"Except what, dear?"

"I don't think she's planning on keeping the baby."

"You mean she's giving the baby up for adoption?"

"In exchange for a lot of cash."

"She's selling her child?"

"I guess if you're going to give up your kid you might as well make some money from it."

I say the words to defend Shannon but as I hear them come out of my mouth, they sicken me.

"I don't like the sound of that," Jimmy says.

"What do you expect?"

E.J. joins the conversation. He sits up on the couch and addresses me directly.

"She found an easy way to make some money so she's doing it. What does a kid go for on the open market these days?"

"Don't trivialize this," Isabel tells him. "This is her child we're talking about. A woman doesn't easily give up her own child."

"Shannon would."

"What is that supposed to mean?" I ask roughly.

"It means she never cared about anybody. Why would she care about her kid?"

"You don't know what you're talking about," I respond, knowing full well that he does.

I look toward Isabel for some assistance.

"I always worried about her," she says instead of helping me to defend her. "Sometimes I wondered if she had a form of attachment disorder. I had a student once who was diagnosed with it. He reminded me a lot of Shannon. It's when a child can't develop an emotional bond with anyone."

"She was attached to me," I argue.

"Oh, yeah. She was attached all right," E.J. says. "I never said anything at the time because everyone was so torn up, but hell, it's been almost twenty years since she left. She wasn't attached to you, Shae-Lynn. She could've cared less about you."

"How can you say that to me?"

"It's not an insult to you," Isabel tries to defuse the situation.

"Oh, no. Of course not. There's nothing insulting in saying my own sister didn't care about me."

"There isn't."

"Are you going to tell me my dad didn't care about me, too?"

"It's not your fault," E.J. explains. "They were fucked up."

"Eamon, stop it," his mother gasps.

"Shannon was a cold-hearted selfish bitch and your father was a violent prick who got his jollies beating on little girls."

"I said, stop it," Isabel cries.

"Enough. Everyone. Calm yourselves," Jimmy's voice rings out. "Eamon cares about you, Shae-Lynn. It's the only reason he says these things."

People often describe an Irish accent as singsong or lyrical, but I've never thought of it that way. There's more resignation in the cadence than hope. When I listen to Jimmy, I don't hear a melody of optimism but the individual weary notes of survival.

"You've spent your whole life taking care of other people. Why is it so wrong if someone wants to take care of you?" Jimmy asks.

"I don't want anyone to take care of me."

E.J. jumps up from the couch and gestures toward me with his hand.

"See?" he says looking back and forth between his parents like my presence here has suddenly proved some theory they were recently discussing.

I stand up, too.

So does Isabel. She places a hand on my arm.

"Shae-Lynn. Please don't go."

"Stay and have a drink," Jimmy urges.

Isabel whirls on him.

"Enough, James."

"Let him have it, Mom. He's a grown man. He can drink if he wants to."

"It's not good for him."

"His whole life hasn't been good for him."

E.J. leaves the room and comes back with a bottle of Jim Beam and a juice glass.

Isabel rushes to him and grabs at the bottle.

"Mom, let him have it."

They engage in a brief, half-hearted tug-of-war.

"Let him have it," E.J. repeats. "It helps."

Their eyes meet for an instant. They're both thinking about the accident, but from absurdly different emotional angles like a yolk and a hen each contemplating the shell of an egg.

Isabel lets go.

We all watch Jimmy take the bottle and fill the small glass with the amber liquid. He takes a grateful sip and sits in silence, staring out the window at the quiet road and the dark hills beyond lumped up against the white sky like a carelessly tossed coat.

Soon he will be poetically drunk, as E.J. calls it, an inebriated state that occurs only in Irishmen where even the most uneducated and illiterate among them begin to quote Yeats and Joyce and Beckett with an occasional limerick thrown in.

This will be followed by more drinking which will lead to him sitting slumped in a chair for hours staring at nothing while blue antics flash by unnoticed on a TV screen in a dark room before he passes out.

I follow Isabel into the kitchen to help get dinner on the table while E.J. disappears outside. He won't take part in his dad's descent even though he feels he has no right to stop it. I don't blame him for cutting out.

My father was a mean drunk. Jimmy is a pathetic drunk, which is easier to endure but harder to bear.

Chapter Fifteen

SOMETIMES I STAY AND VISIT for awhile, but today I leave right after I help Isabel with the dishes.

On my way home I decide to swing by Dusty's and see how he's doing.

The restaurant sits all alone about two miles west of town in the middle of an unmarked gravel parking lot. Square, squat, devoid of any exterior adornment, painted an almost sinister shade of purple, the building displays all the architectural ambition of a roadside strip club and gives off all the homey warmth of a fire-ravaged garage.

It's only been closed for a month, but the windows are already gray with dirt and neglect. The paint on the exterior walls has begun to flake. The neon sign proclaiming "Dusty's" in cursive script above the front door has been shot out by some kids and all that remains are a few jagged shards of green glass.

He's here. The black Range Rover he bought with some of the money from the movie deal is parked at the side of the restaurant, giving off a glow like a piece of onyx.

Lib bought a new SUV, too, but his fenders are proudly spattered with mud, the windshield dotted with splattered bugs, and it usually has a twig or two sticking out of the grill.

Ray didn't buy a vehicle for himself, but his wife went out and bought a neon-yellow Pontiac Sunfire for herself before there was even a hint that any of them had the potential to make money from what they had gone through. I think she believed that the general populace was going to donate money to her because her husband survived a mining disaster the same way people give money to the parents of children with life-threatening illnesses to help pay their medical bills.

At the last minute I change my mind about stopping. Suddenly I don't feel up to having a heart-to-heart talk with a messed-up kid.

I can't stop thinking about what E.J. said about Shannon and wondering if he could be right, and if he is right how much of it is my fault.

Shannon could be very distant and downright hostile at times but we also had some good times together. Now I'm wondering if those good times were only because she was in the mood for a good time, or because she wanted something from me.

Did she sit on Mom's rug with me and look at books because she didn't have anything better to do? Did she run into my arms only because she wanted protection from Dad? Did she smile at me across a table in Eatn'Park because she was enjoying the moment or only enjoying the pie? Could I have been anybody or nobody at all?

I'm within a couple miles of my house as the crow flies when I spot what appears to be an empty blue Ford with New Jersey plates parked on the side of the road.

I pull up behind it, get out of my car, and walk slowly toward it, keeping a fair distance between myself and its windows until I'm absolutely sure there's no one inside.

The floor is covered in fast-food wrappers and plastic cups with straws sticking out of the lids. A black leather jacket and a black gym bag with "Good Sports Gym" written in gray across one side sits in the backseat, unzipped, with various items of male clothing stuffed inside.

I walk around to the passenger side and try the door. It's unlocked.

I open the glove compartment, and a car rental agreement, a Pennsylvania road map, and a photo of my sister fall out.

Next I go through the gym bag and find nothing but men's clothing: socks, underwear, a couple balled-up T-shirts, and a pair of jeans. I check the pockets of the jacket and only find a lighter and a pack of cigarettes. Nothing incriminating.

The trunk is a different story. It appears to be empty but beneath the spare tire I find a box of bullets.

Pamela Jameson asked me if I carry a gun. I don't. I don't keep one in my car either. I have a Colt .45 auto I've kept since my Capitol police days that I still take to the range once a month for target practice, and I have my Dad's old bolt-action hunting rifle that I keep clean but rarely use.

Right now, I wouldn't mind having my .45 with me. I have a bad feeling about this latest out-of-state plate with a tie to Shannon. Not to mention that things are also starting to get personal. Whoever is renting this car and walking around with a revolver is much too close to my home and my town.

I walk back to my car and write down the name and address and credit card number off the rental agreement and the car's license plate in a small notebook that I use to keep track of my jobs.

My skirt doesn't have any pockets to put my keys in so I take everything off the key ring except my car key and hook it on the side of my bikini underwear. I slip my cell phone inside a leather strap inside my boot that's traditionally used for holding a hunting knife. I put the rest of my keys and the bullets in my glove compartment, lock my car, and start following New Jersey's trail down the side of the road.

It's not hard to do. He's left large, obvious footprints in the mud on the side of the road and the tracks are fairly unique for this area. He's definitely not wearing the kind of shitkickers most men wear around here. I'd say from the point of the toe, the lack of tread, and the deep indentation from the heel that he's either wearing cowboy boots or a slick pair of Jersey ankle boots made for clubbing.

The tracks end suddenly when he decided to sneak off into the woods. He didn't pick a very convenient place to do it. The ground slopes upward, and the undergrowth is thick and brambly. I can see where he slipped and grabbed hold of a branch of mountain laurel that broke off in his hand.

He's not much of a Boy Scout. I wonder what they're teaching Boy Scouts these days if they're giving Girl Scouts anti-stress badges. I suppose they've had to adapt to modern-day concerns as well. Gone is the badge for silently tracking wildlife; it's been replaced by a badge for stalking women across state lines. This guy couldn't have earned either.

But I will give him credit for figuring out how to get from the road to my property through this roundabout, inconvenient, unnecessary way. He could have driven to my front door and parked in my driveway and been less conspicuous to a passerby, but he apparently wants the element of surprise on his side. He wants to ambush Shannon with a gun. What has she got herself into?

I easily follow his trail through the woods. Before I get close enough to see him, I hear him: sticks snapping underfoot, branches swatting against denim, sporadic quiet cursing.

He finally comes into view. He stops next to a bare old oak, stuffs his gun into the back waistband of his jeans, and lights up a cigarette. He's wearing a white T-shirt that makes him stand out against the naked, gray trees like a surrender flag. He's immaculately bald with a bushy, jet-black mustache.

I study him a moment longer, deciding if I can take him. He's not a terrifically big guy—medium height and medium build—but he looks to be in good shape. The muscles in his arms are well defined, and he has the pumped swagger of a guy who lifts weights.

I could try and have a friendly conversation with him, but I doubt if that would get me anywhere. I could head back to my car and probably arrive at my house before he gets there. Then if he makes his presence known, I'll be armed, too.

I could call Clay with the car rental information and have this guy picked up for trespassing and carrying a concealed weapon—which I'm also willing to bet isn't licensed—even though the land isn't posted and a gun charge is meaningless around here, but that would mean letting people find out about Shannon, and I don't want that to happen until I know the whole truth for myself.

I wait until he's done with his smoke and starts moving again, knowing he'll be unsteady and preoccupied.

He takes his gun out from his waistband and holds it casually in front of him at hip height. It's chrome- or nickel-plated and throws off glints of silver as he makes his way through the trees. I don't know what he thinks he's going to run into in these woods. The scariest thing out here, by far, is him.

I get as close to him as possible without him hearing me before I rush him. He starts to twist around just as I'm on top of him, and I hit him full force in his side with my shoulder like I'm trying to take out a linebacker.

The awkward angle of his body and the unexpected force of mine slamming into him makes him lose his balance. He takes a tumble onto his back but still manages to hold on to his gun.

Before he can gather his wits about him, I bring my boot down on his wrist with all my might. He cries out and releases the gun, and I kick it away from him before he grabs my leg with his other hand and tosses me off him.

I'm back up on my feet before he's on his. I call him an ugly prick, wanting to make sure he comes after me instead of going for his lost revolver.

When he does, I duck his swing and stick out my leg while grabbing the front of his shirt with one fist. His speed and weight carry him forward over my hip, and he flips over onto his back again.

He's winded but not down for the count. He goes for my leg again as I make a break for the gun. I feel his grasping hand slide down my calf, trying in vain to get a good grip on me. I yank my foot free, leaving him holding my boot.

"Okay, stand up very slowly," I tell him once I have the gun— a chrome-plated .357 magnum—held two-handed in front of me, pointed at his head.

My heart is beating so loudly, it's hard to hear the sound of my own voice.

"And put the boot down nicely."

He glances at my boot in his hand then whips it as hard as he can off into the woods.

"You son of a bitch," I snarl at him, my attention being briefly averted by the sight of my dearest footwear somersaulting through the air.

He takes advantage of the distraction by making a move toward me, but I recover quickly and train the gun back on him.

"I should make you get on your hands and knees and crawl over there and find it for me."

"It was ugly boot," he says flatly with an accent, possibly Russian. His eyes are as black as his mustache.

"Let's see some ID," I tell him automatically.

I realize instantly how stupid I sound under the circumstances. He does, too, and gives me a slow, mocking smile.

"ID? You sound like cop."

"Ex-cop."

"You? You were cop?"

The smile is a grin now.

"Who did you protect?" he asks me. "Ballerinas?"

"I knocked you on your ass twice. What does that make you? The Sugar Plum Fairy?"

He continues smiling as he reaches into his back pocket.

I lower the gun to his crotch.

He holds his hands up and tries to look harmless. It doesn't work.

"I just want cigarette."

He waits for me to nod my approval.

"I know you're not Mike Kennedy," I tell him, "the name on your car rental agreement."

He shakes a cigarette out of his pack and pops it between his lips.

"I'm very impressed. I see you were famous detective in your day."

He pauses to light up with a lighter behind a cupped hand.

"Why you care who I am? It makes no difference."

I meet his black stare. Short of shooting his balls off I know I'm not going to get him to tell me his name and even then he might not do it. Plus it doesn't matter. He's here at someone else's request; that's the name I want and the reason why.

"I'm willing to give you the benefit of the doubt and say you're out of your element, Boris. Otherwise, you really suck at this."

"Suck at what?"

"Your job. You did a very poor job of tracking this girl. You left your car parked on the side of the road where anyone can see it."

He takes the cigarette out of his mouth and waves it at me unconcerned.

"Nobody drives here."

"But the few people who do are going to notice. You'd have more anonymity parked on the side of the busiest highway in New Jersey.

"You should have rented a car in PA so it would have PA plates," I continue. "You left the car doors unlocked so anyone could go through your stuff and your trunk."

I wait to see if this bit of information ruffles him, but he remains unmoved.

"You left a trail through the woods that would make an elephant proud, and you're wearing a white shirt that makes you visible from a half mile away."

I finish by asking him point-blank, "Why are you stalking her?"

"I'm not stalking nobody. I'm tourist who walks in the woods looking for small furry creatures."

"What do you want?"

"I'm not talking to you."

"Yes, you are."

"You think I'm afraid by you?"

I shoot. The .357 jumps in my palms. The recoil climbs up my forearms while the explosion shatters the silence of the woods and starts my ears ringing. The bullet flies by his head close enough for him to feel the breeze.

His hands leap to his ears, and he falls to his knees.

"Shit!" he shouts.

"How much do you know about her?" I ask him with the gun still pointed at him.

He picks up the cigarette that fell out of his mouth and puts it back in his mouth as he gets slowly to his feet.

"Do you know I'm her sister? Do you know my son is a county deputy? Do you know I used to be a cop around here and I still have a lot of friends in law enforcement who would be more than happy to help make sure no trouble came to me if I decided to shoot some smart-assed Russian in the balls? Do you know anything about me?

About my reputation? About my dislike for balls attached to rude men? Do you know I'm having a bad couple of days?"

I shoot again. This shot is closer than I intended. It grazes his shoulder. A tear appears in the shoulder of his T-shirt, quickly followed by a small red stain.

He makes a noise that sounds like he's coughing. I assume he's swearing in Russian.

The cigarette falls to the ground again.

"Okay! Stop with shooting!"

He touches his shoulder with two fingers and stares incredulously at the blood.

"A friend sent me to talk to her."

"Talk to her?"

"Yes."

"Sneaking up on her through the woods with a gun?"

"She promised them baby. It was all arranged. They pay her lots of money then she leaves. The wife of my friend, she's crazy now. She never leaves house. She takes pills and sits in baby's room all day."

He examines his shoulder more closely. I think he's more upset over the ruined shirt than the damage done to his arm. He doesn't seem to feel much pain.

He stoops down to pick up the cigarette again and returns it to his mouth.

"My friend finds out she's pregnant again, he decides this baby must belong to them. He asks me to convince her to give them baby. I'm here to have persuasive conversation with her."

"You were going to rough up a pregnant woman? Just because she changed her mind and decided to keep her baby?"

Even as I say the part about keeping her baby, I know it's only wishful thinking.

"She doesn't keep her baby," he confirms for me, "which is probably best for baby. She sells it to someone else for more money. This is no ordinary pregnant woman. You say she's your sister? Then maybe you can't see what a monster she is. She sells her babies just like farmer sells his pigs for sausages."

It's hard for me to hear this about my sister, but the more I learn about her, the more prone I am to believe the worst.

"I'm not defending what she did, but I still don't see that it makes her a monster and I sure as hell don't see why it would turn your friend's wife into a fruitcake."

"She did terrible things to this poor woman and for no reason," he tells me. "It wasn't even to get more money."

He smokes and stares confidently into my eyes.

His own eyes remind me of the pieces of bony Shannon and I used to find on the side of the road. I knew what they were but I let Shannon believe they were black jewels in the rough. We polished them and kept them in a jar until one day Dad found us on the front porch with our collection laid out, shining darkly in the sun, and he sent all the pieces flying into the yard with a kick of his boot and told us it was shit coal, bony, slag, worthless.

I picked up as many pieces as I could find after he left. Shannon didn't want to have anything to do with it once she found out it wasn't anything special, but I still thought it was pretty and definitely not worthless.

The Jersey Russian begins to regale me with tales of Shannon's behavior.

"She sent her condolence card on Mother's Day, which says, 'With my deepest sympathy,' and inside she writes it was too bad this lady never could have children herself.

"One time she threatened to have abortion and sends her pictures of dead fetuses, you know, the pro-life propaganda shit? Another time she tells her even if the woman adopts baby she's going to come back someday when baby is older and tell him she's real mother and he was stolen from her. She tortured this woman."

I tighten my grip on the gun. My arms are trembling from the aftermath of the shooting, not from the physical act as much as from the fact that I haven't shot at a person in a very long time.

"Who's your friend?" I ask him.

"It's unimportant."

He takes a step toward me and I tell him to stop. He smiles and shrugs and takes a step backward.

"How did you know where to find her? No one knows she's here. How did you even know she was pregnant again?"

"Kozlowski."

"Kozlowski?" I cry and instantly regret allowing too much emotion and surprise into my voice.

"You know him? That Polish pimp. He arranged everything."

"He told you she was here in Jolly Mount?"

"He told my friend she was here. Kozlowski promised him baby but told him she will need encouragement besides money. Even if he's making my friend pay plenty."

"How much?"

"More than ballerina cop can dream. Maybe you should make babies like your sister. Then you wouldn't have to dress like redneck whore."

I have to use every ounce of my self-restraint not to shoot him. He seems to sense this and bursts out with a deep, hearty laugh.

"You don't look very happy with me anymore. What are you going to do with me now? Is it time to shoot my balls off?"

"You're going to go back to New Jersey and tell your friend he's not going to get this baby either," I tell him icily. "Tell him he has my condolences, too. I can't help it if his wife can't have a baby. Or maybe it's him. Maybe he shoots blanks. Too bad. Some people just aren't meant to have kids."

His black eyes sparkle with what I think is rage. I brace myself in case he decides to try his luck and charge me, but he takes another long drag off his cigarette instead.

"I agree," he says. "And I don't like the wife of my friend, but out of respect for him I won't give him your entire message, only the part about condolences.

"So I can go?" he asks me.

"Yes, but I'm keeping your gun."

"Oh, that's tough for me," he pouts and shakes his head in mock sadness. "I'll never be able to get another one."

I lower the revolver. He doesn't move immediately. He turns his back toward me and looks off through the trees down over the hillside.

A chill passes through me. I'm not sure if it comes from the events of the past fifteen minutes or the ongoing drop in the temperature. I glance above me. The sky is a dirty white and ready to burst with either snow or sleet.

"I feel very bad," the Russian says, turning back around to face me. "I feel like we got off on wrong foot. At least let me go get your boot for you."

"I can get it myself."

"Please."

He starts walking in the direction where he threw my boot.

I don't see any harm in it. I'm going to let him go anyway. What are my options? I'm not going to involve cops. For the time being I don't want anyone to know what Shannon's been doing.

And I'm not going to shoot him. I'm tempted but not tempted enough. I slip his gun into the waistband of my skirt and consider leaving and heading back to my car without him, but I want my boot.

He spends a couple minutes searching for it. I have no trouble keeping track of his white shirt.

He comes walking back toward me, victorious, holding the boot aloft.

I'm usually a good judge of people's characters and intentions, and I also have great reflexes. These are two qualities that served me well as a police officer and as a woman who spent a fair amount of time hanging out in bars.

I've decided that the Russian—although potentially deadly—has currently been rendered harmless by a combination of my defensive skills and feminine charms. Plus he has nothing to gain by trying to harm me at this point.

He gets closer and closer, swinging the boot at his side, until he's standing directly in front of me.

By the time I realize I've misread him, my reflexes can't help me.

My hand leaps to the gun in my waistband, but I'm too late.

The boot catches me full in the face, blinding me, causing my nose to gush with blood, and making me stumble backward.

He tackles me to the ground and easily rips the gun from my hand. He could shoot me or he could stand up and walk away and it would be all over, but he chooses to straddle me and hit me instead. A slap; not a punch. Not too hard. It's meant to make a statement, not to necessarily cause pain in a face that's already burning from being smashed with a boot. I know the difference well between a blow only meant to harm and one meant to show dominance.

I spit at him. Flecks of my own blood appear on his face. He jerks his head away and I take advantage of his momentary discomfort by jamming the heel of my hand into the balls that I should have shot off when I had the chance.

He sucks in a gasp of pain and his face grows pale as he pulls his knees up to his chest and rolls off me onto his back. I crawl on top of him and smack him in the face, but it does little good. When fighting on the ground, it's almost impossible to get any body weight behind a blow with a fist.

I go a different route and stick my little finger up one of his nostrils, pushing it as hard and as deep as I can. It sounds mild enough, but it isn't. It feels like someone is drilling into your brain.

He tries to lift his head back and away from me, but my pinkie goes with him. As his head rears back and his neck stretches I pull my finger free and go for one of the most sensitive areas on the human body.

I drive my thumb into the cluster of nerves in the indentation below his ear and behind his jaw. He screams when I dig into the muscles, separating them so I can squash one of his spinal nerves. But it's not enough. He's stronger than me, and he's fast and experienced.

He palms my face with his hand and snaps my neck back while punching me in the stomach with his fist.

All the air rushes out of me and I see flashes of light against the blackness before my eyes.

"I'm sorry I had to hurt your pretty face," I hear him whisper. His lips are so close, I can feel his hot breath against my ear. "I didn't want to but you gave me no choice."

He grabs my hair and pulls me into a sitting position. I can't catch my breath. I can't breathe at all.

"Tell your sister I'm going to have talk with her soon" is the last thing I hear before he pistol-whips me on the side of the head and I lose consciousness.

The snow wakes me. Cold, wet, soft flakes settling on my exposed skin. I'm chilled to the bone and can't stop shivering. In the distance I hear a muted ringing and have enough sense to realize the sound is coming from my cell phone inside my boot. But I can't move. I feel like I'll never move again.

I close my eyes against the pain and only see shades of purple: Dusty's failed purple restaurant, Lib's Purple Hearts, a froth of purple lilacs on an empty bed, the purple of Jimmy's gangrenous leg, the springtime purple of our hills, the purple of my dad's raging face, the purple of Clay's newborn face, the piece of purple satin Shannon always looked for when we sat down to read on our mother's rag rug.

Chapter Sixteen

MY PHONE WAKES ME. It's Ray's oldest daughter, Autumn. She and a couple of her friends missed the bus. Can I give them a ride to school? And can I promise not to tell her folks?

I say sure, like I always do, and check my clock. It's 7:45 A.M.

It takes me a minute to figure out where I am and how I got here.

I made it home on my own. I made it to bed. I made it through the night.

I have a bad headache and a knot as hard and round as a silver dollar throbbing a couple inches behind my left ear, but the headache could be a lot worse and the lump is easily covered by my hair.

My face could be a lot worse, too, but it's bad enough. I assess the damage in my bathroom mirror. There's a small bright red cut above my eye and reddish-purple bruising on my left cheekbone and jaw. My lower lip is slightly swollen but not unattractive. There are women who pay cosmetic surgeons good money to get lips like this.

I find some old painkillers in my medicine cabinet left over from a previous injury. I take two and stand numbly in my bathroom trying to collect my thoughts and set everything straight in my mind. When I do, I get a sick feeling in my stomach that's unrelated to the goose egg on my head.

The man who did this to me is out there, armed, angry, still in full possession of his balls, and looking for my sister with the intent of having a persuasive conversation with her.

I remember she wasn't here when I got home last night. I tried calling her on the cell phone number Pamela Jameson gave me but got no answer. Shannon told me she doesn't have a cell. She knew I'd be suspicious right away if the number she gave me didn't have a New Mexico area code.

My bathroom window faces the side of my house where I park my car. I glance outside and see my yellow Subaru, covered in a dusting of white, and a car parked next to it. I'm relieved at first until I look closer and see that it isn't Shannon's car. It's the blue rental Boris is driving.

I tiptoe across the hall from the bathroom to my bedroom, take my .45 out of the lockbox in my closet, insert a fresh magazine, ease a round into the chamber, then make my way silently toward the living room and kitchen.

Boris is sitting comfortably at my kitchen table with a cup of coffee in front of him, smoking and reading a newspaper. He's exchanged his white T-shirt for a black one, but other than that he looks exactly the same.

His chrome-plated revolver is lying on the table next to an empty beer bottle he took out of my trash that he's using to put his ashes in. He taps his cigarette against the lip of the bottle, picks up his gun with his other hand, and points it at me as soon as he hears the floor creak. When he looks over and sees my gun pointing at him, he smiles beneath his mustache.

"So what are we doing now? Shooting each other?"

He waves the .357 at me dismissively and sets it down again. He picks up his coffee cup.

"I don't like your bathrobe," he tells me.

It's a short, white terrycloth robe with Pinto patches of brown and black.

"What's wrong with it?"

"If woman is going to wear robe that looks like animal, it should look like leopard or tiger. Not cow."

"It's not cow. It's a pony print."

"There's nothing sexy about ponies either."

"I don't care about being sexy. I care about being comfortable."

"This is your problem."

"I don't have any problems except for you, Boris."

"Stop calling me Boris. I hate this name. I have a cousin Boris. He is pig who owes me money. Call me Vlad."

"Is that your name?"

"No, but this cousin I like better."

He reaches into his pocket and pulls out an open package of Slim Jims. He breaks one in half, feeds it to Gimp, who's been lying beneath the table this entire time, and gives him a pat. The same trick Shannon used.

Gimp wags his tail.

"I want you out now," I tell him with my gun still pointed at him.

"I'm not going anywhere. You want coffee?"

"I'm serious."

"I'm serious, too. Very serious. I thought I made you understand that yesterday."

He fixes me with his black stare.

"If you were going to call police, you would have already called. For some reason you don't want them involved, so this means the question of your sister is only between you and me."

I wrench my gaze away from his.

He gets up from the table and goes to the kitchen counter where he pours a second cup of coffee.

"I think we can come to agreement where I don't have to hurt you again," he says.

"And where I don't have to hurt you again?" I counter.

He walks back to the table and sets the cup down in front of the chair opposite him and takes his seat.

"There will be no trust. We agree on this, right? But we can maybe also agree to keep your pretty face and my balls safe from harm. What you say?"

I don't say anything.

"I realized after we talked yesterday you don't have a clue what's going on with your sister. Your little gift to Junior shows it even more."

We both glance at the package on the table wrapped in Santa Claus paper. Knowing I referred to myself as Aunt Shae-Lynn makes me feel suddenly vulnerable. I'd prefer to be standing here naked in front of him rather than have him know I have feelings for Shannon's unborn baby.

"It's clear for me you don't know shit about this woman, and you don't know where she is. That makes two of us. So I'm going to sit here and wait."

"What if I find her first and make sure she never comes back here?" I ask.

"You still have to come back here."

"So what are you going to do? Hang out in Jolly Mount indefinitely, waiting for me to give up my sister? Aren't you going to a lot of trouble over this? Wouldn't it make a lot more sense for your friend to just buy someone else's baby?"

He shrugs.

"It's not that easy. Besides, this is personal. Like I told you."

He stretches his arms out over his head and sighs.

"This is nice. I don't mind. I like it here. I think I'll make a fire."

My cell phone rings. It's sitting on a side table next to the front door. We both look over at it.

"I checked your voice-mail," he tells me. "There was nothing from your sister."

I don't show any sign that I care one way or the other if he listened to my messages. I answer my phone.

It's Brandi. She needs a ride to the pediatrician and back. Her appointment's in an hour. Her car won't start this morning and Dusty isn't available, she explains awkwardly.

I tell her I'll be there.

I return to my bedroom without saying another word to the thug in my kitchen. I have to get dressed, which isn't going to be an easy process.

I pull on a pair of white leggings and a low-cut pink sweater covered in big white snowflakes. Next comes a quilted silver ski jacket with a white fur-trimmed hood and matching silver fur-trimmed boots with pom-poms on the ends of the laces.

I had a fling once with an ex-professional baseball player from Kansas City who I met while he was testifying on Capitol Hill about his steroid use. He dressed me like a Barbie doll and I taught him math. I've kept some of the outfits he bought for me for those days when I want to pretend I'm not real. I believe this particular one also came with a pink stuffed poodle in booties and a pair of bejeweled silver skis that I've lost somewhere along the way.

I haven't worn the jacket in a long time. I check the pockets and find a pair of mirrored pink sunglasses along with some cotton candy-flavored lip balm.

"Much better," Vlad comments from behind his newspaper when I reappear. "Much better to be snow slut than housewife dressed like pony."

"What do you know about Kozlowski?" I ask him.

He makes his usual shrug.

"Not much. He's pimp. Worse than pimp. He's lawyer who specializes in adoptions between girls in trouble and rich couples who pay anything for healthy white baby. But rumor is he goes even further. He finds girls before they're pregnant and convinces them to get pregnant in order to sell their babies."

This new bit of information is disgusting, but I don't let any emotion show on my face.

"So you know him?" he asks.

"A little."

"He's not as good-looking as me."

"I don't like mustaches."

"I don't like your robe. You took off the robe. I can shave the mustache."

I don't comment. I pick up my keys and start for the door. I'm not going to bother to tell him to leave again. It will only make him stay.

"Oh, Sweetie Pie," he calls out to me, exaggerating his accent and making the American domestic endearment sound all the more ridiculous. "Can you stop at market on your way home and bring me good crusty bread—not that sliced spongy shit—and some vodka, some red wine, and some chicken? I'm going to make a paprikash."

"I thought you were Russian."

"Russian father, Hungarian mother. What about you?"

"No father, no mother."

"Interesting. Usually there is at least a mother and she can plead immaculate conception if she doesn't want to remember the father."

He blows a wreath of smoke around his head and continues to study me.

"So you are like Thumbelina? An old witch gives seed to barren woman. She plants it, and a beautiful flower grows, and when the bud opens there you are asleep in the petals, a tiny ballerina cop."

I stick my gun in my pocket and put on my pink sunglasses.

"Something like that," I tell him.

The snowfall was light but still enough to make the roads slightly treacherous.

210

During the drive I try Shannon's cell phone again and get no answer. I think about calling Kozlowski, but I'm not sure exactly how I want to deal with him yet so I decide to wait.

I think about calling Pamela. She's supposed to have dinner with Jamie tonight. At the time we parted company, she wasn't sure if she wanted me to come along or not. I decide to wait and call her later, too. I don't want to arouse any suspicions.

Part of me feels like I should go back to the house and wait for Shannon to show up in order to keep her away from the Russian. Falling back into the role of protector is instinct for me. But another part of me is feeling used and is more than a little pissed off at her lies and the way she showed up for one day and then disappeared again. I don't want any harm to come to her, but at the same time the problems she's facing right now are of her own making. I also remind myself that she's managed to survive very nicely for the past eighteen years without any help from me.

I decide I'm not going to be her bodyguard or her mommy or her conscience. I'll be her sister, which means I'll worry about her, I'll loan her anything she wants, and I'll lecture her if I get the opportunity, but I won't try to control her and I won't pay her debts.

Ray and Vonda's new house is the size and shape of a barn, constructed of yellow siding, with white shutters on the windows and a completely unnecessary white picket fence surrounding the yard. It sits at the end of a long, winding driveway at the top of a lumpy, bare hill that reminds me of a fat woman's freshly shaved knee.

Behind the house is the beginning of the same forest that stretches for miles all the way to my house, but as for their own property there's not a single tree visible and the new shrubs and bushes Vonda planted are only about a foot high. She adheres to the slash-and-burn school of landscaping.

Their old house was small, but I get the feeling when I talk to Ray that he preferred it. It only had one bathroom and their two daughters had to share a room, but according to Ray, now that each girl has her own room, they fight even more than they used to and more noise comes out of each separate room than ever came out of the one. And now that they have three bathrooms, he can never get into any of them.

I park and toot my horn.

The front door bangs open and sixteen-year-old Autumn comes clunking down the walk in three-inch-high platform sandals that make her sound like a horse and move like a giraffe. She's followed by two of her friends, all of them talking at the same time in a high-speed, high-pitched unintelligible garble. I can occasionally make out the words, "she goes," and, "he was like," and, "you know."

They all wear variations of the same open-toed sandals, the same tight, torn jeans resting low on their hips, and the same tight T-shirts, each with a different profound proclamation written across the front: "Your Future Ex-Girlfriend" and "Blonde" and "Save the Drama for Your Mama." They each have an armload of bangle bracelets and ears bristling with multiple earrings. Their fingernails are painted various shades of red and orange and their toes are painted a matte blue.

Even though it's barely forty degrees, they aren't wearing coats because they're afraid it will make them look fat; meanwhile the rolls and bulges of hip and belly flesh spilling out over their jeans don't seem to bother them. These are not small girls. Each of them has on a skimpy cropped hooded sweatshirt that she wears unzipped.

I know it took at least three hours, two bags of chips, and a two-liter bottle of Mountain Dew for them to arrive at these ensembles last night in one of their bedrooms. The thought makes me sleepy.

"Good morning, ladies," I greet them.

They pile into the backseat.

I watch them in my rearview mirror.

"So I guess I can spare you the lecture on how you need to be more responsible and it's not good to lie to your parents."

"Yeah, we remember it from the last time," Autumn says.

"And the time before that," one of her friends adds and they all laugh.

The girls talk nonstop during the entire drive at a breathless, mumbled speed that makes it impossible for me to understand any part of their conversation even if I wanted to.

When I pull into the parking lot I remind them they each owe me five bucks and they all start digging in their purses and backpacks.

The high school hasn't changed much since I graduated from it back in the '80s. It's a long, low, redbrick, utilitarian, L-shaped building. There's nothing remarkable, interesting, or unique about it. Slap bars on the windows and it could be a prison. Park ambulances in front of it and it could be a hospital. They put desks inside it so it's a school.

The football field, on the other hand, has been through multiple renovations and improvements since my time here: new scoreboard, new bleacher seats, new lights for night games, improved sound system, a bigger sign with bigger letters made up of brighter red lightbulbs that proclaims the field to be HOME OF THE JOLLY MOUNT GIANTS. Even though Ivan Z played for the Centresburg Flames, there's a framed poster-sized photo of him breaking a tackle during a Penn State game. Next to it, hanging behind the counter of the new, much bigger snack bar, is one of him shaking hands with Mike Ditka after he signed his contract to play with the Bears.

I pull up to the curb. The buses have all departed after dropping off their passengers. The last straggling students are wandering inside the building. The courtyard leading to the front doors is almost deserted except for a burly, shaggy-headed kid with a goatee leaning against a wall, dressed entirely in baggy olive drab, and one of the sparkling

Marines I saw at the mall yesterday standing ramrod straight next to the flagpole. They're both talking earnestly to boys with backpacks slung over their shoulders: one selling drugs, the other selling the military.

"The Marines recruit in front of the school?" I ask.

"Yeah. There's usually two of them," Autumn answers me. "They're here before school and when we get out, but they can't come inside."

"Yeah, they even follow kids out to their cars," her one friend volunteers.

"They even talk to girls," the other one says.

"Remember when they came up to us?" Autumn asks then lowers her voice to mimic the Marine. "Girls, do you value your freedom?" she says in a crisp baritone.

"What did you say?" I ask.

"We said no."

They burst into the exaggerated, exclusionary laughter special to teenaged girls that makes everyone else think they're the butt of their jokes.

They hand me money over the backseat, get out of the car, and start to walk away.

"Teddy's signing up," I hear one of them say in a more sober voice.

"So is Tyler."

I give the Marine a final look before I leave. He glances my way, without pausing in his speech to the boy, and our eyes meet for a second.

I notice a patch of purple crocuses near the flagpole. They poke valiantly through the snow, their tips like little floral missiles. He notices them, too, and makes an effort not to step on them.

Chapter Seventeen

TWO PINK TRICYCLES, a plastic play kitchen, an overturned bucket of sidewalk chalk, a few stuffed animals, an inflatable wading pool filled with water now crusted with ice, and a lawn chair draped with a wet beach towel take up most of Brandi and Dusty's driveway.

I park on the side of the road. Before I'm out of my car, I hear someone screaming in the backyard. All of a sudden a tiny female in a glittering green bathing suit and snow boots, with a ponytail sprouting from the top of her head like a small gold fountain, comes tearing across the front yard. She grabs up one of the bicycles and begins her mad getaway, only to arrive at the end of the driveway and realize she's not allowed to go any further.

She drops the bike and contemplates hiding, then she sees me.

"Are you Goldie or Grace?" I ask her. "Do you remember me? I'm Shae-Lynn."

"I'm Grace," she tells me. "Goldie's mad."

"Why's that?"

"I don't know."

"Oh, I bet you do. Does your mom know you're outside in a bathing suit?"

Brandi comes around the corner of the house at that moment with Rose on her hip and a sobbing Goldie holding her hand.

"Grace!" she shouts. "What are you doing? You're supposed to be dressed and ready to go to the doctor with us."

She offers me a weak smile.

"Hi, Shae-Lynn. Sorry about this. We're obviously not ready."

"Grace," she says, turning her attention back to her daughter. "Did you take your sister's princess crown?"

Grace shakes her head. "No."

"Grace," Brandi states firmly.

"I didn't take it. I put it in the dishwasher," she says proudly and watches her sister burst into more tears.

"The dishwasher? You're not allowed near the dishwasher," Brandi growls, her face darkening as she lets go of Goldie's hand and adjusts Rose on her hip.

Rose appears to be the sick one. Her eyes look glassy and her nose is red. Brandi has her overbundled against the cold in a hand-me-down snowsuit.

"Sometimes there are knives in the dishwasher," Brandi scolds Grace, "and the corners on the door are very sharp when it's open. You could fall and hurt yourself."

"Come on." She grabs Grace by the hand and yanks her toward the house with Goldie following along.

I get in line behind them.

We go in the front door, pass through a family room that's in the same condition as the driveway, and end up in the kitchen.

The remains of breakfast are spread over the table: crusts of toast stained with grape jam, a few remaining spoonfuls of milk and soggy pastel-colored flakes in the bottoms of plastic bowls with cartoon characters on them, and two cups sitting in small sticky puddles of juice.

The tray of Rose's high chair is smeared with banana.

Brandi heads straight for the dishwasher and opens the door. A sparkling tiara sits in the middle of the rack. She takes it out and places it on Goldie's head.

"Okay, Princess Goldie," Brandi says to her now-smiling daughter, "why don't you go play in your castle for a few minutes while your sister gets ready?

"Does Grace get a time-out?" Goldie asks, grinning from ear to ear.

"Yes, she does, but she can't have it now because we have to take Rose to the doctor."

"Mommy!" Grace shrieks. "That's not fair. I told you where it was."

"The time-out is for taking it in the first place and for opening the dishwasher. Now go put your clothes back on."

The twins depart, each with a separate assignment, but somehow I get the feeling their paths are going to cross again in the next few minutes.

Brandi grabs a washcloth out of the sink, wipes off the high chair tray, and sets the toddler down behind it in one fluid motion.

Rose lets loose with a couple hacking coughs.

"So what's going on with you?" she asks me as she starts cleaning off the table. "You look like you've been invited on a ski trip with Hef and some of his Bunnies. What happened to your face? Did Choker do that?"

"Choker?" I laugh. "In his dreams."

"I heard about your fight."

"No, it wasn't Choker. I had a little accident. No big deal."

Most of the women around Jolly Mount consider Brandi to be too thin and too opinionated. I've always thought she was striking, both physically and mentally, ever since I first met her as Dusty's senior prom date.

She's boyish with short dark hair and large dark eyes in a pale chiseled face with a long sensuous mouth that droops at the corners, giving her the appearance of being disappointed and seductive at the same time. A mole sits on the top of her right cheekbone like a droplet that's fallen from her chocolate eyes.

In a city like D.C. she could have thrown on some old jeans and a tattered top, adopted an imperious pout, and slouched around clubs and bars easily convincing everyone she met that she was a European supermodel.

Today her face is haggard from lack of sleep and too much worrying and her luminous eyes are ringed with shadows.

She and Dusty had only been married for two years, the twins were a little over a year old, and Rose was a newborn when the accident happened.

During our four-day vigil, I kept waiting for her to fall to pieces. I couldn't believe someone so young with so many little lives dependent on her could hold it together while she was faced with the very real possibility that she was going to be a widow. But she never cracked.

She took care of everyone, not just her children but all the other wives as well.

Teresa was angry. Ray's wife, Vonda, spent the entire time trying to be interviewed by every reporter she could find. Isabel was simply a wreck: Both her son and her husband were trapped in Jojo.

I spent a good deal of that time curled up on my couch in my safe place and on the surface seemed unflappably cool; I was on duty. I only let my true emotions surface once when I confronted the governor over the conflicting reports we were getting from the rescue site, and as luck would have it, a reporter and photographer were there to document the event. From then on I was labeled a hothead *and* E.J.'s girlfriend.

Brandi found a way to calm Teresa's feelings of betrayal, to periodically remind Vonda that her daughters needed her more than the American public did, and to convince Isabel that miracles do happen. She got down on a blanket on the floor and played with her twins, nursed her baby in a quiet corner, and prayed with Dusty's grandparents.

Watching the way she tirelessly tended to the generations and smoothed all the conflicting emotions in that church basement into one long ribbon of hope, I couldn't help thinking about Dusty's childhood belief that everyone should be true to their natures. If he could have seen her during those few days he would have agreed with me that Brandi was meant to be a miner's wife.

"Do you believe this weather? It's probably what's making Rose sick," she says as she flies around the table, putting dishes in the sink, brushing crumbs into her cupped hand, reaching for the washcloth again.

"I can't decide if I should take her in or not. Maybe I'm overreacting. Maybe I should just let her get better by herself. But I worry the girls will get sick, too."

She pauses in the midst of her whirlwind of cleaning and fixes me with a frank stare.

"We don't have health insurance anymore," she offers by way of explanation.

"I know how that feels," I commiserate.

"I know. Clay's told us."

"Of course he has."

"But why should I be worrying about money?" she says with a brittle laugh. "We're going to be filthy rich soon, right? When we win our lawsuit against J&P."

Rose starts coughing again.

Brandi pours some juice into a sippy cup for her and sticks her head into the other room, yelling at Grace to hurry up.

"You never know," I tell her. "You could win."

"We'd have had a much better chance with wrongful death suits."

She glances my way, looking embarrassed.

"I'm sorry. That was a terrible thing to say."

"Don't worry about it. It's true. They know it, too. I think Ray put it best one night at Jolly's when he said if he had died and Vonda had sued Cam Jack for wrongful death, she'd be making millions for sitting on her ass instead of him making next to nothing working his ass off."

She smiles as she walks past me to a closet, where she takes out a broom and dustpan.

"I don't care about the money. I really don't. We always got by on what Dusty made. We made do. And I figured when the girls started school, I'd get a job, too."

She starts sweeping.

"Dusty'd always been so proud of what he did. He loved being a miner. He loved getting dirty and working hard and knowing at the end of the day that he earned the pay in his pocket with his own two hands. But as soon as he got a big chunk of unexpected money, what did he do? He tried to become a big businessman like Cam Jack. He acted just like him. He cut corners. He treated his employees bad. He started alienating everyone he knew because he became this big pompous ass who only wanted to talk about money and how to make more money. He became exactly the kind of man he used to hate. The kind of man who was responsible for him ending up trapped in a mine in the first place.

"Money makes men stupid," she summarizes. "Money and fame."

"That's because they need outside approval. We shouldn't be too hard on them, since we can't completely understand where they're coming from. We're not the same way."

"What do you mean?"

"A man spends his whole life trying to prove his worth to others. A woman spends her life trying to prove her worth to herself."

Brandi thinks about this for a moment.

"Sucks for us, doesn't it?" she says.

"Yeah."

She dumps the dustpan full of crumbs into a garbage can under the sink and puts the broom away.

"The real problem is he can't work in the mines anymore and there's nothing else he wants to do and there aren't any other jobs around here even if he did want to do something else. And the worst thing is he could still work in the mines like E.J. and Ray. Nobody's stopping him. It's his own fear that's keeping him out."

"No one can blame him for that," I say emphatically. "Personally, I think E.J. and Ray are out of their minds for going back."

"Dusty doesn't see it that way. He thinks he's a coward. If they can do it, why can't he? He thinks he's failing us, but instead of trying to deal with that he puts up this stupid front to the outside world. He tells everyone he could still work in the mines if he wanted to, but he's been exposed to bigger things, and he's smart enough to realize he should want more in life than just being a miner."

"Bigger things? You mean he wants to be somebody?" I ask, repeating Clay's description of the situation.

"He's become somebody already. But not somebody I want to be around. He's changed so much. He was always the most easygoing guy. Full of fun. He loved to play with the girls. He'd come home after his shift and plunk right down in the middle of the carpet and start playing with their toys. I can't remember the last time he did that."

She zips Rose's snowsuit, pulls her out of the high chair, and walks back into the family room calling for the twins.

"What exactly is going on with the two of you?" I ask as I trail along behind her. "Have you officially separated?"

"I don't know what's going on," she sighs. "I asked him to move out for a little while. I need to think."

"So this has nothing do with what's her name?"

"Who? That Tina person? No. We worked that out a long time ago. At first he made all these excuses. He said he wasn't right in his head after being trapped for four days. He said he thought he was going crazy. He blamed having an affair on the firedamp. Can you believe that?"

She plops Rose down on the floor and goes to the closet by the front door to get her coat.

"Then one day we were having a wicked fight and he finally admitted the real reason. I knew it all along. I just wanted to hear him say it."

She picks up a diaper bag from the floor and checks the contents before putting it over her shoulder.

"He said to me: You know how you're always being told you should want a certain kind of woman, just like if you got class you're supposed to want to drink fancy French wines instead of beer or you're supposed to choose the caviar over the cocktail weenies."

"Don't tell me he compared her to caviar and called you a cocktail weenie?"

"He said he finally had the opportunity to try the caviar, so he did, and it wasn't all that good. But he loves cocktail weenies."

"And he does love cocktail weenies," I say, smiling happily. "You know he does."

"I know. He meant it as a compliment. See, I understand that about him. I know him. I love him. That's why I forgave him.

"She's the one I hate," Brandi goes on, her voice turning cold. "She used him. She didn't care about him at all. He was like some sort of intriguing sideshow freak to her, an adventure she could tell her friends about.

"Step right up, ladies and gentlemen," she announces in an imitation of a carnival barker's voice, gesturing with her hands. "In this tent for one night only watch a publicist get screwed by a coal miner. Come experience the terror of a prissy New Yorker being pawed by a creature in dirty coveralls. Is he man or is he beast? Judge for yourself as he prowls the streets of the city. Watch as he refuses to take his ball cap off in a theater. Hear his snorts of laughter each time he sees a guy he thinks is gay. See his confusion when he's charged nine dollars for a dollar-fifty beer."

I'm laughing so hard, I'm almost in tears over her performance.

Goldie and Grace join us, both fully dressed, Goldie wearing her crown and Grace wearing a pair of rabbit ears.

"What's so funny, Mommy?"

"Nothing, honey. Get your coats on."

I glance over at her. There are tears in her eyes, too, but I don't think they have anything to do with being amused.

I end up waiting at the pediatrician's office with them. I enjoy talking to Brandi and she appreciates the little bit of help I can give her with the girls.

When I drop them off at home, she asks me if I'd mind taking some leftovers and a clean change of clothes to Dusty at the restaurant.

I agree to do it.

I find him sitting inside, in the dark, slouched down in one of his deserted booths, his ball cap pulled down over his eyes, holding a half-empty bottle of rum, watching a small TV on the tabletop in front of him. He looks like he hasn't slept, eaten, or shaved for a week.

His initial response at seeing me is embarrassment, and he tries to come up with an excuse for his appearance and his whereabouts until he sees the food in my hands.

He recognizes the plate as one from his home, and he recognizes the smell from beneath the tent of foil as Brandi's chicken and gravy over waffles.

"Hey, Miss Penrose," he says dully.

He still can't call me by my first name. I'll always be Clay's mom.

"Hi, Dusty."

"I guess you've talked to Brandi."

Unlike his wife, the exhaustion and dejection on his face makes him appear younger, not older. He looks like a little boy who's spent the day chasing something that finally got away.

I decide not to tell him that his daughter is sick or that his wife just spent a hundred dollars on a doctor's visit in order to be told that his daughter doesn't need a doctor, just a bottle of cough syrup.

"Yes, I have."

"How is she?"

"She's fine."

"And the girls?"

"They're fine, too. Except they miss you."

He shakes his head.

"I doubt it."

He takes a swig off his bottle.

"You want some? I got lots of glasses around here. It's a restaurant."

He finds this particularly funny and has a good laugh over it.

"Women don't send food to men they don't love," I tell him, taking the bottle from him but not drinking from it.

"I know she loves me. She says she'll always love me. She just doesn't want to live with me anymore. She says she doesn't know me anymore. I depress her."

"Clay's smart," he slurs at me. "Not getting married. Not having kids. It's good to not have anyone depend on you."

He starts shaking his head.

"'Cause you never know. You never know."

His voice trails off into a mutter as his head droops lower onto his chest.

I'm beginning to wonder if he's drifted off to sleep when he suddenly jerks up his head and slams his hand on the tabletop.

"I wanted to be a coal miner," he shouts, semi-coherently. "A coal miner! What's so fucking unreasonable about that? It's not like I wanted to be a pro quarterback or a movie star or the president of some big fucking corporation flying around in my own big fucking jet. I just wanted to be a miner. Like my dad. Like Lib and Jimmy."

His energy expended, he lays his head down on the table.

I have to stop myself from reaching out and stroking his hair the way I used to do with Clay when he was little and would get frustrated.

"I remember when you wanted to be an astronaut," I tell him.

He raises his head a little and peeks out over his arm. His eyes beneath his cap are the pale blue of a snake's belly.

"Coal miners and astronauts have a lot in common," he says and lifts his head a little higher. "We kind of do the same thing, only they're in the sky and we're underground. For instance, we're both explorers. We go where no man has gone before."

"That's true."

He raises his head completely and sits up a little straighter.

"Did you know it used to be astronauts and coal miners were the only professions that couldn't get life insurance?"

"I didn't know that."

"We both work in the cold. We both work in the dark. We both leave the surface of the earth," he goes on with his list.

"We know the job's dangerous but we still do it. And astronauts, they aren't just balls-out jocks and pilots; they have to be scientists, too. Coal miners know all about different kinds of damp. We know all about nitrogen and methane and carbon monoxide."

His enthusiasm is contagious.

"You're right," I tell him. "Miners and astronauts do have a lot in common."

"And get this. 'Naut' is short for 'nautical.'" He leans over the table and points at its surface as if I'm supposed to see the word written there. "I know this shit 'cause Clay loaned me tons of books on astronauts when we were kids, 'cause he knew I wanted to be one. 'Nautical' can mean something to do with the sea, but it can also mean something to do with navigation. 'Astro' means 'space.' 'Naut' means navigating like a sailor. So 'astronaut' means 'space sailor.'"

He sits back in the booth and beams at me like he's just brought home a straight-A report card.

"You know what that makes me?"

I shake my head.

"A rock sailor."

I smile back at him. I've heard him make the astronaut–coal miner comparison during interviews after the rescue, but I've never heard him call himself a "rock sailor."

"A rock sailor. That's definitely what you are."

"Except I'm not anymore." His face falls. "I'm nothing now. Nothing.

"What if I live to be eighty?" he suddenly raises his voice to a panicked shout. "What if I keep on living? What am I going to do for all those fucking years?"

I recognize the same glitter in his eyes and the same strain in his voice that E.J. gets when he's about to lose it.

Right after the rescue, all five of them were treated by J&P to a couple sessions with a shrink. The shrink also talked to family members to let them know what to expect. He told them the men could easily suffer from the same kind of post-traumatic stress disorder that soldiers coming back from war experience: panic attacks, nightmares, mood swings, paranoia, insomnia, listlessness, suicidal thoughts.

It's the suicidal thoughts that I'm starting to worry about.

"Hey, I've got a great idea."

I reach out and pat his arm the way I do with E.J. A human touch seems to help bring them back.

"Let's go see Jimmy."

He tries to focus his eyes on my face.

"I don't want him to see me fucked up," he says.

"Are you kidding? He's probably just as fucked up as you are right now."

"Jimmy's fucked up?"

"Almost every day."

"He always seems good when I see him."

"He's good at seeming good. E.J., too."

A look of amazement passes over his face.

"E.J.'s never been fucked up a day in his life," he tells me assuredly. "He's a rock."

"He's got a rock for a head, that's for sure."

I convince him to come with me and to leave the bottle behind.

We find a fork and he brings Brandi's leftovers and the change of clothes with him. As soon as he gets situated in the car, he tears off the foil and starts wolfing down the food.

I get a call on my cell while I'm walking around to the driver's side.

I check the caller ID. It's not a number I know.

"Jolly Mount Cab," I answer.

"Shae-Lynn? That you? How's my girl?"

"Jesus Christ," I breathe out.

It's been over twenty years, but I'd know the voice anywhere.

"Well, hell. I'm flattered you could confuse us," he laughs, "but it's not Jesus Christ, honey. It's just your old pal Cam Jack."

Chapter Eighteen

SHAE-LYNN? YOU THERE, precious?"

My stomach begins to churn. I try to respond, but nothing happens on my first attempt. My lips move but no sound comes out. I clear my throat.

"Don't call me precious," I manage to say.

He laughs again.

"Whoa. Hold on. Don't sue me for sexual harassment. I forgot. You're one of those feminist types running around fixing your own car and being a cop. I suppose you think your gun is bigger than mine."

"I know my brain is bigger and that's good enough for me."

He laughs again. It's a big, hearty, privileged laugh, the kind that brings to mind images of fat fairy-tale kings holding jeweled chalices of wine and golden legs of dripping venison while roaring over the antics of a court jester no one else finds funny.

"I suppose I always knew you'd turn out that way. You were that way when you were a kid, too. Always dressing like a boy. Covering up those great tits and legs of yours. Playing in the dirt. Getting into fights. Honestly. Tell me the truth. You wish you were a man, don't you?"

"No, I don't. Do you?"

This retort is met with silence.

"Well, Shae-Lynn, I have to be honest with you," he begins slowly, the merriment having left his voice. "I was hoping you might be a little happier to hear from me after all this time."

"What could possibly ever make you think that?"

"Because we had some good times together. Times I thought for sure you'd remember with some fondness."

I'm too stunned to reply.

"We didn't part on the best of terms" is all I can come up with as an explanation.

"That was your fault, not mine."

These words cut right through me. The falseness and injustice behind them makes them sharper than any knife, yet I know he believes what he's saying, and trying to convince him otherwise would be a waste of my time.

"That's why I'm calling you," he says.

"Why?"

"I'd say we have a little unfinished business."

"We have no business together, finished or unfinished."

"Yes, we do, sweetheart, and I need something from you and you're going to get it for me."

"What are you talking about?"

"It's not something I want to talk about on the phone. I think it's best if we talk face to face. Meet me at the J&P building tonight at seven."

"No."

"Don't make me go behind your back."

The kind of fear I haven't felt since my childhood when I occupied the same room with my father sweeps through me.

In my mind I'm watching and waiting, afraid to breathe or speak, sweating, every internal organ having turned to stone, every muscle tensed, my mouth filled with a metallic bitterness while he does nothing more remarkable than eat his dinner or watch a ball game on TV.

I never knew when it would happen or if it would happen at all.

I've dealt with many kinds of fear during my life: the fear of facing a dangerous situation on the job; the fear of ending up broke and homeless; the fear all mothers have for the welfare of their children. But no matter how intense the fear, I could always attach an explanation to the source: I'm a police officer doing my job; life is hard and expensive; there are illnesses, and drunk drivers, and an endless list of random accidents that cause the death of children.

The fear my father inspired in me was entirely different. It was the free-falling terror of having been pushed from a cliff by an unseen hand without reason, without anyone to catch me, without any chance of survival.

Each time he hurt me I felt like I was falling, and each time he stopped I felt like I had hit the bottom of a canyon. I would pick myself up and realize I had become a ghost looking at life from another dimension, unable to feel the things the living felt and unable to care about the same things they cared about. The only course left to me that could bring me any peace was to discover what had I done to make my own father want to harm me. I did everything he wanted and gave him everything he asked for. I had been as generous and uncomplaining as the hills he mined.

"Did you hear me?" Cam Jack breaks into my thoughts.

I'm trying to find my safe place, but for the first time in my life I can't get to it. A fear bigger than the fear of what's scaring me on the outside is keeping me from getting inside. It's the memory of the face at the window—pale, blurred, desperate. That it could be someone who knows me or someone who doesn't, that it could be trying to get in or trying to convince me to come out are equally terrifying thoughts to me.

I glance at Dusty through my reflection on the driver's side window. He's scooping the last bites of waffle into his mouth.

I hover on the glass, a specter of myself: colorless, translucent, temporary.

"Yes," I tell Cam.

"Meet me in my office at seven."

"I will."

In Cam Jack's case, I had been as easy to rape as the land he owned.

Chapter Nineteen

J IMMY STANDS AT HIS DOOR leaning heavily on his cane and looks from me in my snow bunny ensemble with my battered face to Dusty, diverting his eyes ashamedly like a penitent little boy swaying slightly and stinking greatly from the alcohol he's consumed over the past few days. Jimmy doesn't look the least bit surprised to see us.

"Well I can't say you're a sight for sore eyes," he says, "but you're welcome to come in for a visit all the same."

He turns and walks slowly into the family room. He's wearing his prosthetic today, which means Isabel is planning on taking him on an outing when she gets home from school.

He lowers himself into his chair and looks exactly the same as he did when I left him yesterday, right down to his silver cowlicks, except for the addition of a second slipper.

"So don't tell me you two have joined forces and have been out terrorizing the countryside," he comments as we take seats on the couch.

"Our paths just crossed this morning and our conditions have nothing to do with each other," I assure him.

He clears his throat and gestures toward the kitchen with a toss of his head.

I realize what he wants. I get up and return with a shot glass and the Bushmills.

Jimmy's in the middle of explaining our greeting ritual and provid-ing Dusty with an example of an oxymoron.

"I get it. Okay. I get it. Can I play?"

Jimmy raises one eyebrow skeptically.

"By all means. The more the merrier."

I pour the shot.

"Student teacher," I begin.

He's unimpressed.

"Light heavyweight," he counters.

"Chocolate milk," Dusty volunteers.

Jimmy and I look at each other. Jimmy smiles and shakes his head.

"A noble effort, son. Wait and try again."

"Minor catastrophe," I say.

He pauses to consider it, seems to like it, then offers, "Still life."

"That's good," I admit.

"Row boat," Dusty says.

Jimmy almost bursts out laughing but catches himself. He bows his head and reaches out to pat Dusty's knee encouragingly.

"You're getting the hang of it."

"She's turned up missing," I say.

He reaches out and pushes the glass in my direction.

I take it and toss down the drink.

The whiskey hits my empty stomach with a hollow splash and spreads slowly like a warm sludge through my veins. I feel sick, but not as sick as I did while I was talking to Cam Jack.

Dusty looks back and forth between us.

"I don't get that one," he says.

Jimmy reaches out and pats his knee a second time. He notices the bag Dusty has with him.

"Are those clean clothes in that bag?" he asks him.

Dusty nods.

"Why don't you go upstairs and take a nice hot shower and change into them. You're a little ripe. And then we'll talk."

After he's gone, Jimmy reaches for the bottle and pours a shot for himself. I start to object but he holds up a hand to silence me.

"How are you?" he asks me.

"I'm fine."

I can feel him staring at the new bruise on my face, willing me to look him in the eyes. I finally do.

"Shae-Lynn, you're not obligated to go through life with bruises and broken bones. This doesn't have to be your father's legacy to you."

I don't know how to respond to this.

"I'm fine," I repeat. "This has nothing to do with my father. It's my sister."

"Shannon beat you?"

"No, nothing like that. I haven't even seen her since yesterday morning. She didn't come home last night. This is from someone who's looking for her."

"Someone looking for her attacked you? What kind of people is she dealing with?"

"I still don't have all the facts."

"Have you told Clay?"

"He knows she's come back and he knows she's pregnant, but I haven't told him anything about her plans for the baby or anybody else's plans for the baby. There's no point in going to the police. She hasn't done anything illegal and as far as I know neither have any of these people who are looking for her."

I stop and think about what I've just said.

If Shannon as a consenting adult in full possession of all her faculties offered to have sex with a man in exchange for fifty bucks she could be arrested and would be considered morally bankrupt. Yet she can get pregnant and hand over her baby in exchange for a suitcase full of cash and everyone's okay with that.

Jimmy seems to read my thoughts.

"What an arse-backwards world we live in," he says. "It's against the law for women to sell a poke at their honey pots, but it's fine for them to sell their children."

He takes a long, thoughtful drink of his whiskey.

"Pardon my French," he apologizes.

"I thought it was very nicely put."

"What's wrong with the lad?" he asks.

"I think he's losing his mind."

"It's about time," he says, looking almost pleased at my disclosure. "The resiliency of youth. I lost mine not long after it happened."

"I remember."

"But I got it back."

"I think he needs to talk about Jojo with someone, but he doesn't realize that's what he needs to talk about."

"And what about you? What do you need to talk about?"

My thoughts go back to Shannon. I've been trying to reach her on her cell phone all morning and I keep calling my house. I get no answer. I wonder if Vlad would answer if he's still there.

She could have the baby any minute. Or maybe she did have the baby. Maybe she's in the hospital. Maybe the delivery didn't go well and she hasn't been able to call me. All this time I've been assuming she's fine and can handle herself. I was even starting to think that she might be staying away from me on purpose to make me worry, that she's playing some kind of spiteful game with me, or even that she left again. I never stopped to consider the most obvious possibility.

I excuse myself and tell Jimmy I have to make a phone call. I take the bottle of Bushmills with me and return it to its hiding place while he creatively curses me.

I have the hospital switchboard's number memorized from my days as a Centresburg cop. I'm put through to the maternity ward.

I ask the nurse if a Shannon Penrose or a Jamie Ruddock has been admitted. She answers no to both names.

I ask her if any single woman, mid-thirties, with dark hair, probably alone and with no health insurance was admitted.

She asks me what's going on. I'm the third person in the past twenty-four hours to ask for either a Shannon Penrose or a Jamie Ruddock and then ask for any random single woman in her mid-thirties with no health insurance when it turned out there was no such patient.

I ask her if one of the callers was a man and one was a woman. She tells me that much but won't tell me if either one of them left a name or phone number.

So Kozlowski hasn't found her yet, and Pamela must have lost her again.

I hang up the phone and I'm overcome with the same wave of exhaustion that hit me in Lib's yard where I wanted to lie down in his grass and sleep forever.

I decide to take a drive home and see what's going on there: if Shannon has shown up or the Russian has left.

On my way out I ask Jimmy if I can borrow his cassette tape of one of the interviews the Jolly Mount Five did after the rescue.

I want to play it before I see Cam Jack tonight. I want to have their memories and my own fresh in my mind.

Chapter Twenty

VLAD'S BLUE FORD IS gone from my driveway and Shannon's car is still missing, too.

Gimp is stretched out on a rug not far from my front door. He raises his head and thumps his tail.

"Those who swap loyalty for meat by-products forfeit scratchies," I tell him.

He wags his tail more vigorously.

A quick search of the house turns up nothing interesting. Shannon's room looks exactly the same as it did last time I checked it. Her bed is unmade. Her suitcase is open and sitting on the floor. There's a hairbrush, a *People* magazine, a crumpled-up candy bar wrapper, an empty Mountain Dew can, and a tube of moisturizer that promises to help reduce the unsightly appearance of stretch marks sitting on the bedside table.

The present to Junior is still sitting on the kitchen table where I originally left it.

Vlad cleaned up meticulously before he left, washing and drying and putting away the cups, rinsing out the coffee pot, disposing of the beer bottle full of his cigarette ashes, and taking his newspaper with him. I could almost convince myself that he was never here and I imagined our whole encounter, except for the knot behind my ear and my throbbing headache.

I look through my cupboards and refrigerator and remind myself again that I have to go grocery shopping, a task I hate. The only people who come close to annoying me as much as left-laners are cart-hogs, shoppers who leave their carts in the middle of the aisle and wander a few feet away, where they stand with their mouths open staring stupefied at the shelves as if they've never seen food before.

I make a peanut butter sandwich and a cup of tea and retire to my couch along with my old Walkman from my college days and the National Geographic volume on Ireland.

I pop the tape in the player, put on my headphones, and start leafing through the familiar pages of the book, past photos of streets lined with brightly painted storefronts like a crayon box, weathered faces of white-haired old men in plaid caps, their trousers tucked into the tops of their wellies, sheep in long creamy coats grazing on green minty hillsides, lonely thatched white cottages, a fantastic splash of bloodred window shutters against gray stone walls where girls in dull school uniforms loiter before first bell, spectacular views of sheer carved coastline and a raging iron-colored surf.

I stop at a picture of a tiny whitewashed house with a slate roof and a red door. It's surrounded by a heathland of broom bushes, fists of yellow gorse, wild rhododendron, and a carpet of small, long-stemmed orange flowers shaped like kisses, but it's a mere dot in the rest of the bleak, broken landscape. Ragged, treeless mountains rise behind it and a foaming sea lies in front of it. There are no other signs of human life anywhere, not even a road.

I've always imagined it must be one of the most isolated houses in the world. I find it beautiful and terrifying. This is where my safe place is, I used to think. If I could look inside its dark forsaken windows I would see the furnished place inside my soul.

The interview begins. It starts off very official sounding and I think back to the days of stiff, awkward testimony the five of them were forced to give at the initial investigation. I attended every day and watched with morbid fascination as E.J. and the others were paraded back and forth to the microphone in their ill-fitting suits and shiny dress shoes bought just for the occasion, nervous and fidgeting, stripped of the protective camouflage of their ball caps and flannel shirts.

These were some of the toughest, most self-possessed men on the planet. They could handle any physical discomfort and endure any abuse. They weren't afraid of anything except losing their jobs. And here they were, wiping their sweaty palms on their suit pants and mumbling apologetically to men they had never met before and had certainly never wronged.

The five of them testified about smelling the burning rubber. Lib testified about seeing the wisp of smoke, but admitted after lengthy questioning that he couldn't be absolutely sure he saw it in the poorly lit conditions of a mine. They explained why the cable had been taped with duct tape instead of being properly repaired, and as expected this became the fault of the miners, not the company.

Other J&P miners testified that sometimes they jury-rigged equipment, too. No, they responded to Cam Jack's lawyers, they had never been officially authorized by the mine operator to do it, but they knew they were supposed to. How did they know? Could they read minds? No, they admitted that they couldn't. Except for Humpy Dunmire who had been able to predict that his wife was going to leave him after her sister paid for her liposuction. She ran off with a computer programmer a month later. No one else had seen that one coming.

For the most part the miners did an admirable job of not incriminating themselves and not making the company look bad either, which isn't always easy but is something they've been trained to do for generations.

Cam Jack's history of ignoring safety violations came up, too, but the inspectors took most of the heat for his failure to comply.

What good was a rule if no one enforced it? his lawyers argued. Historically speaking, the mine owner has always been put in a difficult position when it comes to miner safety, they went on. Yes, there needed to be safety standards, but with or without them, it was a deadly job. How was Cam Jack supposed to react to the inspection process when one side of society's collective face told him to clean up his act while the other side admitted it was impossible to do so?

No one ever got to put the question directly to Cam Jack, since he never put in an appearance during the entire investigation.

From where I sat, it wouldn't have mattered. He would have put the blame on someone else the same way everyone else did.

It was the inspectors' fault for not enforcing the safety violations. It was the miners' fault for not pushing harder to have the equipment repaired. It was the miners' fault for trying to patch cables with duct tape. It was Lib's fault as crew boss for letting his men work around substandard equipment. It was the fault of the manufacturer for making the equipment in the first place.

They were a roomful of men pointing fingers at each other, but there were only so many men and so many fingers, and inevitably each one of them ended up being pointed at as well as doing the pointing.

When it was over, the Jolly Mount Five hung their suits in the backs of their closets to wait for a funeral or a wedding and felt nothing but relief even though—to those who kept track of such things—they had technically lost. But those same people never lived through what they had lived through and didn't understand the time line of emotions that accompanied cheating death. The bitterness and the need to blame would set in much later. For the time being, they were high from the simple fact of their survival. They felt so lucky to be alive and free, it was hard to feel hostility toward anyone or anything even if they knew deep in their hearts it would eventually be necessary.

INTERVIEWER: *I want to thank all of you for agreeing to talk to me so soon after the rescue. Before we begin, can you each state your full name, your age, and how many years you've worked for J&P Coal?*

LIB: *Liborio Joseph Bertolli, fifty-six. I've worked for J&P thirty-four years.*

JIMMY: *James Francis Phyrst. I'm fifty-eight years old, and I've worked for J&P for thirty years.*

RAY: *Raymond Scott Wylie. Thirty-eight. Fifteen years.*

DUSTY: *Dustin Ross Spangler. Twenty-three. Two years.*

(joking comments from the other men about his youth and inexperience)

E.J.: *Thirty-eight. Twenty years.*

INTERVIEWER: *And your full name?*

(snickering)

E.J.: *Eamon James Phyrst.*

(loud laughter)

E.J.: *Fuck off.*

(more laughter; laughter subsides)

INTERVIEWER: *Let's start with that morning when you arrived at the mine to begin your shift. This is J&P Mine Number Twelve, also known as Josephine.*

RAY: *Jojo.*

INTERVIEWER: *Right. Jojo. Is there anything in particular that sticks out about that morning? Anything you remember?*

E.J.: *Lib needed the bonus money.*

(roaring laughter)

INTERVIEWER: *The bonus money?*

DUSTY: *Top loading crew gets a bonus every month.*

JIMMY: *Lib was taking his lovely wife, Teresa, to the Poconos for their wedding anniversary and needed a little extra money.*

DUSTY: *Yeah, she wanted one of those honeymoon suites with a heart-shaped bed.*

RAY: *And a hot tub.*

E.J.: *Lib'd been busting our asses the whole week.*

LIB: *I should've been busting your heads.*

DUSTY: *We were going to get it no problem but that morning Wayne's wife called in sick for him so we were going to be one man short. Usually we were an eight-man crew. The five of us, Wayne, Sam, and Andy.*

INTERVIEWER: *You mean one of your crew actually called in sick that day?*

RAY: *He was really sick, too. He wasn't faking. He would've never had the balls to play hooky on Lib when we were so close to being top loading crew.*

INTERVIEWER: *After the explosion happened, he must have felt like the luckiest man alive.*

LIB: *He felt guilty.*

(silence)

INTERVIEWER: *So this is what you were talking about before you went inside the mine?*

LIB: *The departing shift came out, and we talked about conditions, machinery, the usual stuff. One of the shuttle cars had stopped working, and the other crew boss told me where they'd left it.*

JIMMY: *We got into the mantrip—*

INTERVIEWER: *Mantrip?*

JIMMY: *It's the cart that takes us to the face where we're cutting. It's battery-powered and rides on rails like a train.*

INTERVIEWER: *Describe the trip.*

LIB: *There's not much to describe.*

E.J.: *It's dark.*

(laughter)

LIB: *You enter the tunnel and head into the mains. You pass through them for a little over a mile before you get near Right Four. It's a mile-long corridor leading off the mains with eight entries of its own and dozens of crosscuts between them. We were working pretty deep in Right Four.*

INTERVIEWER: *How deep is pretty deep?*

LIB: *About seven hundred feet below ground. About two miles from the portal.*

INTERVIEWER: *Can you describe the mine?*

LIB: *Describe the mine?*

JIMMY: *Jojo is a room-and-pillar mine. That means the coal is dug from her one section at a time with blocks left behind to keep the roof from collapsing. She's not a web of long dark tunnels. She's more like a black maze and she's larger than the entire town of Jolly Mount but with a height that never reaches more than five feet.*

245

LIB: *She's low seam but high yield.*

INTERVIEWER: *So you never get to stand at your full height the entire time you're working?*

LIB: *No.*

INTERVIEWER: *That's incredible. What does that do to you physically?*

LIB: *It's hard on the body. There's no denying it. A lot of miners get arthritis. E.J.'s shoulder had been bothering him. You got a shot of cortisone the day before, didn't you? But it wasn't helping much. That's why I ran the miner for the first part of the shift.*

INTERVIEWER: *So you take the mantrip to Right Four. How long does that take?*

LIB: *About forty minutes.*

INTERVIEWER: *So you get to the face. What happens next?*

RAY: *Lib made some adjustments to our work assignments since Wayne didn't show up and we were one truck short.*

E.J.: *And my arm was fucked up. Excuse me. My arm was messed up.*

LIB: *Dusty and Jimmy were bolting. Sam and Andy were driving shuttle cars. And Ray was on the scoop.*

INTERVIEWER: *Can you explain some terms for me? What is bolting? And what exactly is a shuttle car and a scoop?*

LIB: *Bolting is securing the ceiling. You drill holes in the roof and throw four-foot-long bolts up into them and tighten them. Shuttles are the electric dump trucks that take the cut coal to the beltway. The scoop is sort of like a low tractor with a bucket in front. You use it to clean up loose coal and debris.*

I was working the miner since E.J.'s arm was bothering him. He was assisting.

INTERVIEWER: *What is the miner?*

LIB: *Continuous miner. It does the cutting. It has a steel cutter head. Carbide teeth.*

INTERVIEWER: *Is this something you drive or carry?*

(laughter)

LIB: *This is a sixty-ton machine. You operate it with a remote control box you hang around your neck. You stand about twenty feet back for your own safety. Even experienced operators can accidentally tear into an old well or a pocket of firedamp, or hit a seam of rock, or cause a roof to collapse.*

INTERVIEWER: *Are you thinking about the danger?*

LIB: *You know there's danger in this job. You're conscious of it but you don't think about it. If you think about it, you can't do your job.*

DUSTY: *There's danger everywhere. You can get killed in your bathtub. You can have a totally safe job and end up dead. You can be a secretary for an insurance company and a terrorist can fly an airplane into your building and you're dead. It's fate. It's your personal fate. You can't pick your job that way.*

RAY: *You know what they say, eagles may soar but groundhogs don't get sucked into jet engines.*

(laughter)

INTERVIEWER: *What do you wear for protection? What kind of gear?*

LIB: *Wear? Well, some guys wear coveralls. Others wear jeans and flannel shirts. Whatever you're comfortable in but you gotta wear long johns cause you're gonna be cold.*

E.J.: *Knee pads, rain gear, rubber boots—steel-toed. Ear protection. Our helmets.*

JIMMY: *Our tool belts.*

DUSTY: *They have our ID tags on them.*

INTERVIEWER: *Let me ask this. Can each of you try and remember one thing you were thinking before you went off to your individual jobs?*

DUSTY: *I remember looking over at Jimmy, who'd already set off toward the bolters, and I saw his shadow against the wall, all stooped over the way we all walk and he was using his hammer as a walking stick and I thought he looked sort of like a gorilla using a little cane.*

(loud laughter)

JIMMY: *Such deep thoughts from one so young.*

RAY: *To tell the truth, I was thinking about the bonus money, too. My oldest daughter, Autumn, was having her birthday in a couple days and my wife, Vonda, was throwing this big party for her and I was worried about what she was spending.*

INTERVIEWER: *Lib, what were you thinking about?*

LIB: *I was thinking about the broken shuttle car. I decided I'd send Sam and Andy to take a look at it during our lunch break. Andy has a knack for electronics and jury-rigging that comes in real handy in a J&P mine, since Cam Jack never pays to have anything properly repaired or replaced.*

(silence)

LIB: *Allegedly.*

INTERVIEWER: *What do you mean?*

LIB: *We're not supposed to talk about what we think caused the explosion.*

INTERVIEWER: *Who told you that?*

E.J.: *Some lawyer.*

LIB: *Ray's wife, Vonda, had a lawyer waiting for us when they brought us out.*

RAY: *She had potato salad waiting for us, too.*

INTERVIEWER: *What about you, Jimmy?*

JIMMY: *Nothing sticks out in my mind about that particular morning. I was probably thinking what I usually think. There's a certain state of mind we all have to reach in order to do this job. Not necessarily because we're afraid but because it's a different world than what we live in. We might not even be conscious that we're doing it. I do it by thinking of Jojo as a lady, someone who will give us what we want if we treat her well.*

(laughter)

DUSTY: *I like to think we're like astronauts.*

LIB: *Astronauts?*

DUSTY: *We're going where no men have gone before us, just like them. We're space explorers, only we're exploring an inside confined space instead of an outside endless space.*

JIMMY: *Now that is deep, Dusty. I like that.*

INTERVIEWER: *That's very interesting. What were you thinking about, E.J.?*

E.J.: *Lunch.*

(laughter)

INTERVIEWER: *So everyone has gone off to do their jobs.*

LIB: *We were about to break for lunch. I handed the controls of the miner over to E.J. and told him to finish one last cut. I wanted one more car full before moving onto the new room. Ray was still on the scoop. Jimmy and Dusty were settling down to eat. I was gonna drive the last load to the belt.*

E.J.: *All of a sudden, the miner shut down.*

LIB: *We went and took a look at the methane monitor in back.*

E.J.: *I'll never forget that. I'd never seen such a high reading. That was a helluva lot of damp.*

INTERVIEWER: *You mentioned firedamp before. Now damp. What are you referring to?*

LIB: *Damp's a term for any gasses found in the mines. There's blackdamp, that's carbon dioxide mostly, nitrogen mixed with it sometimes. It also means any time when there's not enough oxygen to breathe. Afterdamp's what you call all the gasses mixed together after an explosion. The air's highly poisonous then because of the amount of carbon monoxide. That's what our self-rescuers are for. They provide protection from the carbon monoxide.*

JIMMY: *Firedamp is methane mixed with air. It's highly explosive.*

INTERVIEWER: *Where does the methane come from?*

JIMMY: *Everywhere. Methane comes from the decomposition of coal.*

INTERVIEWER: *Is that what caused this explosion?*

RAY: *Probably.*

INTERVIEWER: *So there's no way to eliminate this problem?*

LIB: *If you're going to put men in a coal mine, you're going to have firedamp.*

INTERVIEWER: *What were you thinking when you saw the reading?*

E.J.: *I'm thinking about what would happen if the tiniest spark got ignited. Even a spark from two particles of coal dust colliding. We'd all be dead.*

LIB: *I'm thinking we're going to have to shut down this room, maybe the whole crosscut. I was seriously pissed.*

I called Ray and Jimmy and Dusty over. We checked out the area with our personal monitors. The gas was everywhere. Then I smelled it.

INTERVIEWER: *Smelled what? The gas?*

LIB: *No, firedamp has no smell.*

I didn't know at first. I just knew it was something we weren't supposed to be smelling. The first thing I did was walk over to the mine phone and call Andy and Sam, who were still fixing the broken shuttle car. I explained the situation and told them to get out. I figured better safe than sorry.

RAY: *Lib saved our lives by doing that.*

LIB: *I didn't save our lives. The rescue crew saved our lives.*

JIMMY: *Because he made that call, Andy and Sam got out. They were able to tell the rescue crews our exact location.*

DUSTY: *We all started to smell it.*

RAY: *It kind of smelled like rubber burning, but it was so faint it was hard to tell.*

LIB: *I left them and started checking out the machinery. Then I started checking the dozens of cables all over the floor. Then I saw it, or at least I thought I saw it. I couldn't be sure. From underneath one of the pieces of duct tape we use to patch cables, I thought I saw a wisp of smoke.*

I turned around and screamed, "Get the fuck out! Get the fuck out now!"

(silence)

INTERVIEWER: *What's the next thing you remember?*

DUSTY: *I never heard the explosion. I heard this loud, whistling wind that picked me up and carried me along, bashing me against the walls. I felt like I was burning up and I could feel all these pieces of coal hitting me in the face. Then all of a sudden the noise stopped all at once.*

It kind of reminded me of the way people stop clapping at a concert. When the noise stopped, the wind stopped, too, and dropped me.

RAY: *I saw this blue flame streak past me, followed by millions of little glittering stars. I guess they were coal dust lit on fire. It was the bluest blue I've ever seen. I can't even describe it. It was beautiful. The whole thing was pretty like fireworks except I couldn't enjoy it since I was pretty sure I was dead.*

E.J.: *I got thrown around, too. And dropped. Pretty much the way Dusty described it. The light on my helmet stayed lit, but it didn't help me to see once I stopped moving. The beam couldn't cut through the twister of coal dust.*

RAY: *That's what it was like. A twister.*

E.J.: *The lamp only lit up the haze from the inside like car headlights in a bad fog. I turned it off. I felt better in the dark than I did in the middle of all these glowing gray swirls. I knew it was gas and dust and all of it was poisonous and combustible. I didn't want to see it. I could move better in the dark.*

INTERVIEWER: *Were any of you together when you came to?*

RAY: *Not at first.*

DUSTY: *It takes a couple minutes to realize what happened. Then you panic. I raised my hand up and hit rock and realized the ceiling was only a foot or two from my face. I started to lose it. I thought I'd been buried alive. The gas was real bad but I was able to get my rescuer on my face. Then I just started screaming. Screaming into a gas mask. How stupid is that? It's like being an astronaut who's been ejected from his rocket in deep space and I'm just floating around out there in all that black shit. All alone. I'm dead. I'm dead but I'm not dead yet. I just got to lie here and wait to die. Wait to suffocate. I'm gonna suffocate.*

(silence)

DUSTY: *I was gonna suffocate.*

E.J.: *Hey, it's okay.*

(murmured assurances)

E.J.: *I think Dusty had it worse than any of us. He really thought he'd been buried alive at first. I had some space. Once the wind died down and stopped stirring up the coal dust, I could see around me. I was in the room where we'd all finally end up.*

INTERVIEWER: *What kind of space are we talking about?*

E.J.: *About ten by fifteen feet. Four feet high.*

INTERVIEWER: *That's not much space.*

E.J.: *I was thankful for it. Believe me. I looked around and found Ray. He was buried up to his neck in coal. At first I thought I only found his head.*

DUSTY: *I did only find Jimmy's head.*

(laughter)

INTERVIEWER: *Well, you must have found the rest of him eventually . . .*

DUSTY: *Once I calmed down I decided to see how bad things were. It turned out there was solid rock all around me except there was an opening to my right. Not much bigger than a garbage can lid. I turned over and crawled into it. It started to get a little wider.*

Then I felt something soft brush against my hand, and I freaked. All I could think of was mine rats. I'd never seen one myself but my granddad used to tell stories of him and the other miners and how they used to feed them. I thought, what if I've stumbled on a nest of them? What if they were going to swarm on top of me and eat me alive?

(silence)

DUSTY: *Then I thought, what if I'd just touched the leg of a gigantic spider?*

(laughter)

DUSTY: *Who knows what all lives down there? Just because we've never seen one doesn't mean they can't exist. Maybe they sleep for hundreds of years but the explosion could have woken one up.*

(more laughter then it begins to subside)

DUSTY: *I couldn't stand the tension so I stuck my hand out and touched it again and I realized it was hair. It was a head. Then I started thinking about all the stories I'd ever heard about mine explosions. Men in pieces. Heads and arms and feet blown everywhere.*

So I reached out again, and I closed my eyes. I remember doing that. I closed my eyes even though I'm in the darkest place in the world where you can't see anything. And I grabbed the hair and yanked with all my might.

(he starts to laugh)

DUSTY: *And the head says . . .*

(he laughs harder, the others join in)

DUSTY: *"What are you trying to do, man? Rip my head off my shoulders?"*

And I said, "Jimmy it's you. Are you all right?"

And he said, "Fuck, no."

(laughter)

DUSTY: *It turned out Jimmy was pinned beneath one of the bolters. And it was wedged beneath a pile of coal. It took awhile to get him free.*

JIMMY: *This is where I leave the narrative, gentlemen.*

I don't remember anything after Dusty here tried to rip my head off my shoulders, although they've told me that I drifted in and out of consciousness. I guess that's the mind's way of dealing with an injury like this so you can maintain your sanity if you survive. I don't remember anything.

E.J.: *His leg was bad. We weren't sure he was going to make it. He was burning up with fever by the end.*

RAY: *You could smell the gangrene.*

DUSTY: *The only one of us who could look at his leg was Lib, since he'd been in Vietnam.*

LIB: *It was crushed. The bones were shattered. They pierced the skin in a couple places. His calf was laid open. You could see all the muscles and tendons.*

(silence)

INTERVIEWER: *How did you all end up reunited?*

DUSTY: *I kept going through the tunnel to see if it led anywhere and it came out into the room where E.J. was. He was digging Ray out of some coal.*

INTERVIEWER: *What was going through your mind, Ray?*

RAY: *When I came to, I was sure I was dead. I couldn't feel or move any part of my body. I knew my eyes were open, but I couldn't see anything. There was this heavy, paralyzing weight on top of me, but I couldn't say I was in pain.*

At first, I kind of felt relief. I thought, so I'm dead. That's that. It wasn't so bad to die.

But I was hoping for heaven. I mean, I don't go to church like I should but I think I'm a fairly decent person. I try to be nice to everybody and I take care of my family. I don't steal or kill or covet other men's wives.

JIMMY: *Just their daughters.*

(laughter)

RAY: *I thought I might have a shot at heaven. But if this was death then maybe this means there's no heaven. This is it. Nothingness. But my brain's still working. I'm still me. I can think. I have all my memories. But I have no senses. I can't move, I can't see, I can't hear or smell or taste. I'm like one of those brains in a horror movie that a mad scientist's keeping alive in a dish. And I'm supposed to do this for all eternity. I was really starting to panic. Then I heard E.J. talking to me. And I knew I wasn't dead.*

INTERVIEWER: *Where was the boss during all this?*

E.J.: *Napping.*

(laughter)

E.J.: *We hadn't found Lib yet. While we were digging out Ray, I'd have to stop every once in awhile because I'd feel sick from the gas. I found this puddle of water and I'd put my head down near it to breathe. There's usually fresh air near water.*

While I was doing it this one time, I noticed this shiny object against one of the walls. I crawled closer and I realized it was a hole and there was a light coming from the other side. I looked through it and saw it was a miner's hardhat, still lit.

I couldn't see Lib but we hoped he'd be over there, because if he was we would get to him.

I noticed a long crumpled piece of metal jutting out of the wall. It turned out to be a mangled part of the scoop. So I figured maybe it wasn't a solid wall but some loose coal covering the scoop.

RAY: *We dug through. It was slow going. We didn't have any tools. Our self-rescuers had stopped working, so we were at the mercy of the damp.*

E.J.: *We'd been hoping for two things: to find Lib and to find a passage that might be able to lead to a tunnel we recognized.*

The area was a dead end, a pocket formed behind the wreckage of the scoop. But we found Lib.

RAY: *He was in bad shape but we were able to wake him up pretty easily. We brought him back with us and we were all together.*

INTERVIEWER: *What's going through your minds at this point? Surely by now you're scared.*

RAY: *We've been scared all along but not terrified.*

E.J.: *The terror doesn't set in at first. Not as long as you've got something to keep you busy. Like digging.*

LIB: *We had four helmets between the five of us, three with working lamps. The batteries were beginning to run low and the light was already flickering on and off. We turned them off to conserve power, because once they went out, that was it. We knew we wouldn't ever see again unless we got out.*

E.J.: *The thirst was the worst thing. We'd been sweating like pigs from the gas and from the digging.*

DUSTY: *I was really cold. I couldn't stop my teeth from chattering.*

RAY: *Plus we couldn't breathe. That's the other thing. You have to remember. We were struggling for each breath.*

E.J.: *We'd all heard the stories. We all knew about miners who'd survived for a week or more without starving to death or dying of dehydration, but we knew we wouldn't have that kind of time. There was no ventilation where we were.*

LIB: *We had no idea what was going on above us. We didn't know if anyone knew we were trapped yet. If Andy and Sam got out alive. If a rescue was under way.*

Dusty asked me, "What do we do now?" I said, "We wait."

INTERVIEWER: *So what's going through your minds when you accept that all you can do is wait? Did you put your fate in God's hands?*

LIB: *We all did our fair share of praying. No doubt about it. But for me, I felt more like we were putting our fate in the hands of men. Specifically the miners and engineers up top who weren't going to give up until they got us out.*

(silence)

DUSTY: *I remember us lying there on the rocks and E.J. said, "Man, I'd do anything for a cigarette right now."*

LIB: *And Ray said, "You gotta quit, E.J. Those things'll kill you."*

(laughter)

Chapter Twenty-One

I'VE SLEPT FOR HOURS. I blink in amazement at the time displayed on my cell phone. Normally, I can never sleep during the day.

I check my messages. I missed two calls for jobs that I slept through and one call from Pamela Jameson.

She answers her cell on the first ring.

"Jamie has cancelled our dinner for tonight."

Relief rushes through me. Shannon's alive and well enough to make a phone call, but that still tells me nothing about the baby.

"When did you talk to her?"

"A couple of hours ago. She says there's no reason for us to meet. She's already come to her decision. She says we can have the baby for one hundred thousand dollars. The figure is non-negotiable."

"Wow. What are you going to do?"

"Pay it, of course."

"Wow," I say again. "And your husband is cool with this?"

"My husband wants a child as badly as I do," she answers me with an edge creeping into her voice.

"No offense. It's just a lot of money."

"The money is a problem, but it's not the biggest problem. She's made some requests of me that are making me nervous."

I get up off the couch and walk into my bedroom, where I check my reflection in the mirror on my dresser. My head is feeling a little better, my stomach, too. The cut above my eye is not so glaring now. I examine the bruising. It's on the far side of my face so I can cover most of it with my hair.

"Such as?"

"She says she won't go back to New York. I don't blame her for that. She shouldn't be traveling, which means she's going to have the baby here. She says she's going to have it tomorrow."

"How does she know that?"

"She doesn't. She can't. Her due date isn't for four more days but she insists it will be tomorrow. She won't let me be involved, but she expects me to stay here until the baby is born. Then she says she'll contact me. She wants to have the adoption handled here. She won't go back to New York for any reason."

"What if the baby's late? You could be hanging out at the Holiday Inn for awhile."

I open my closet door and start looking for something more fitting for a meeting with Cam Jack. Something funereal but with a lot of boob and leg action going on so he won't be able to concentrate.

It's been a long time since I've conversed with him, but I doubt he's changed much in that area. I doubt he's changed much in any area.

"She wants to be paid in cash," Pamela tells me.

"Cash? Are you kidding me? She wants you to give her a hundred grand in bills? You don't find this a little suspicious?"

"It's unorthodox."

"Unorthodox? I'll say. How do these deals usually go down?"

"They're not deals, and they don't go down."

"How are the mothers usually paid?"

"By check or wire transfer, of course. Through a lawyer."

"Whose lawyer?"

"In this case, our lawyer is handling it."

"Does Jamie have a lawyer?"

"No."

I choose a plain, long-sleeved black dress, tasteful except for the plunging neckline and the thigh-high hemline.

"Do you mind if I ask how you found her?"

"There are certain discreet ways of advertising for this type of situation."

"Unwed Mother Weekly?"

"I don't appreciate your humor."

"So she basically answered an ad?"

"Something like that."

"So she came to you. No one told you about her?"

"No."

"You told me you provided her with an apartment."

"A lovely loft apartment. Six thousand a month."

I'm struck temporarily speechless by the amount of money she just mentioned.

"Whose name was the lease under?" I'm finally able to ask.

"Hers."

"You didn't rent an apartment and let her live there?"

"No."

"How did you pay her?"

"Deposits into her bank account."

"An account under the name of Jamie Ruddock?"

"Yes. It's all legitimate. I've seen her driver's license."

"Fake ID. Big deal. Basically, you don't know if the money you gave her for the apartment and for food and baby things and incidentals actually went to pay for those things?"

"If they didn't, how did she get them? Who was paying for them?"

I give her a moment to think it over while I pull on a pair of black lace-top stockings and zip up a pair of black faux leather boots with a four-inch stiletto heel.

"You think this other couple she mentioned . . . ?" she says slowly.

"I think she's been playing you like a fiddle. I think she's been letting this other couple support her, and she's been keeping the money you gave her. I wouldn't be surprised if she's going to try and get both of you to pay for a baby only one of you is going to get."

I don't tell her that I also happen to know there might even be a third couple involved who's employed a thug to make sure they get the baby.

"And I'm willing to bet the couple that's not going to get the baby is the one who's going to pay her in cash."

"But surely she has to realize I'm not going to hand her a suitcase full of money without having the baby and legal adoption papers in hand first."

"No, I don't think she does. I think she thinks she has you right where she wants you, and you'll do anything she says and take any risk no matter how stupid. What if she calls you and tells you she's had the baby? Come and see your beautiful new baby, but only if you bring a hundred grand in cash with you. You say no. She doesn't care. Her swindle didn't work, but she hasn't lost anything. She has another couple lined up to adopt. And she already managed to cheat tens of thousands of dollars out of you while she was pregnant. If you say yes, I guarantee she'll take the money and the baby and run. Either way she has no intention of giving you this baby."

"What can I do?"

I hear the first serious note of panic in her voice.

"Walk away."

"Walk away? After all I've been through? After all we've already spent on her? After all the time I've spent planning on this baby?"

"Walk away. She already succeeded at half her game. Don't let her succeed at the other half. She's not going to give you this baby."

"You don't understand what you're saying."

"No, I guess I don't. I can't put myself in your shoes for a lot of reasons."

The main reason being that I think your shoes are really ugly, I add silently.

"Maybe I can reason with her? Maybe I can threaten her? I'll tell her I'm onto her. I'll go to the police."

"She hasn't done anything illegal."

"Maybe she'll take pity on me."

"I think she already has."

This comment is met with silence, followed by the click of a hang-up.

My next call is to Kozlowski.

I think very carefully about how I should play him after what Vlad told me about him. I now know why he wants Shannon. Her baby is worth a lot of money to him. I think Shannon set up the Jameson adoption on her own and he doesn't know anything about it, but he probably arranged the other adoption and has involved Vlad's employer as well.

He's also not above physically threatening or intimidating her in order to get the baby, since he had no qualms about putting Vlad on her trail. And apparently, he's a real slimeball in general. Not that I believe every word out of the Russian's mouth, but Vlad had no reason to lie about Kozlowski, and what he said made some sense.

Kozlowski obviously hasn't found her or he wouldn't have called the hospital looking for her.

In other words, he wants Shannon bad and I know he does. My knowledge of her whereabouts will make an irresistible piece of bait.

But if I've found Shannon, he has to wonder what she would have told me about him. He has to wonder why I would be willing to give up my long-lost sister to the man she's running away from.

I leave messages for him on his cell and at his room at the Comfort

Inn, telling him I know where Shannon is and I'll be willing to lead him to her for a cut of the money.

Once I've taken care of my phone calls and finished dressing, I check the time. I still have about four hours before meeting Cam Jack. I don't have any jobs lined up for the rest of the day, but that can change at a moment's notice.

I think about driving to Centresburg where there's usually more business, but I'm not eager to get any closer to my final destination.

My stomach's upset and my hands are clammy over the thought of seeing him again. I need something to calm my nerves and build my confidence. There's only one thing that works consistently for me; the problem is I can't always find it when I need it, although I constantly come across it when I don't want it.

I rack my brain trying to think of someone to screw. I haven't had a serious relationship in years, and I usually cross county lines if I feel like pursuing a casual one. I don't have time to do that now.

I finally come up with an idea. I check the time again. I'm pretty sure I know where I can find him.

I drive to the high school.

The Marine is alone, like he was this morning, sitting inside the same white Honda Civic I recognize from the mall with a Corps bumper sticker pasted on the trunk lid and a blue lace garter hanging from the rearview mirror.

He's jerking his head around, moving his lips, and hitting the steering wheel with his white-gloved hands in time to some music I can't hear.

I park a few spaces away from him and get out of my car. As soon as he notices me heading toward him, he switches the music off and puts the hat on.

He watches my approach across the blacktop and rolls down his window.

"What can I do for you, ma'am?" he calls out to me.

I don't answer him until I arrive at the side of his car and lean inside the window, giving him a good shot of cleavage.

"You can not call me ma'am for starters, although I understand it's meant as a term of respect. I was a cop for twelve years. I'm familiar with the philosophy. Good manners. It's the only thing that separates us from the animals."

He smiles. It's a good smile. A recruiter's smile. He probably practices it in front of a mirror every morning. He even knows to make eye contact, but he's not good enough yet to fake with his eyes. There's no warmth in them. They're flat and bored: the eyes of a man who spends all his time hustling strangers and already knows before he asks a personal question that he could care less about the answer.

"Where were you a cop?" he asks.

"Here in Centresburg most recently. Before that I was a Capitol police officer."

"What kind of training you do for that?"

"Eight weeks at FLETC."

Some interest rises to the surface of his stagnant eyes, along with a mild admiration.

"So you're a hard-ass?" he asks, smiling.

"Something like that."

The interest grows deeper and he lets his eyes flick up and down my body, lingering on my legs and the boots.

He's young, not much older than Clay. Not bad looking, although I've never been fond of buzz cuts. The body is nice. Broad shoulders. No sign of a paunch.

"What are you doing now?" he asks, looking past me at my car. "Working for some kind of cab company?"

"It's my own company, but it's not much."

"If you don't mind my saying, you don't look like a cop, and you don't look like a cab driver."

"That's part of my charm."

"Why'd you leave the job?"

"Got tired of cleaning up other people's messes."

"I hear that."

"I have a lot of down time at my job." I decide to come right to the point. "I figure you do, too. I saw you this morning, and I'm a sucker for a guy in uniform. I thought maybe we could have a little fun."

"Are you kidding me?"

"No, soldier," I say, smiling. "I'm not."

He looks all around him inside his car as if he might find the answer to my proposition written out for him on a Post-it stuck to the dashboard or the floorboards.

He looks at his watch. He looks over at the empty courtyard in front of the high school that will be milling with hundreds of kids in about ten minutes.

"School's about to let out. I've got to work right now. How about later?"

"I can't later. Besides, I like to have spontaneous encounters. More exciting that way. You ever have any spontaneous encounters?"

"You mean like picking up a girl in a bar . . . ?"

"No. That's a mating ritual."

I lean into his open window and glance down at his crotch. I can see the outline of his erection straining against the fabric of his perfectly pressed pants. He watches me.

"I mean like having a beautiful stranger approach you in a parking lot and offer to fuck your ears off in the backseat of her cab."

"Are you kidding me?" he asks again but this time his voice almost cracks.

He coughs to cover it up.

"Come on," I say and start to move away from his car.

"I gotta work," he says again but with little conviction.

I pretend I suddenly need to bend down and adjust the zipper on my boot, making sure my dress hikes up enough for him to see the lace tops of my stockings.

"There's a back road not far from here where we can park and have some privacy. You can be back as quick as you'd like."

I don't wait for an answer. I start walking to my car, listening for the sound of his car door opening and closing. I don't hear it and I wonder if I'm beginning to lose my appeal when the slam of a door reaches my ears. I don't look behind me.

He joins me in the front seat of my car.

"Shit. I shouldn't do this," he says.

"That's exactly why you should."

It takes about five minutes to drive to the nameless dirt and gravel power company road that leads up a wooded hill to a humming generator enclosed in concrete and surrounded by a chain-link fence.

For as long as I can remember, kids have been coming up here to park in the small clearing.

It's empty now and completely silent except for the occasional far-off rumble of a truck and the insect whine of electricity leaving the generator and traveling up through the cables.

He looks over at me, not sure what he's supposed to do. Should we make small talk? Should he kiss me? Should he wait for me to do something?

I solve the problem for him by getting out of the car and doing a little bump and grind for him.

I pull my dress up to my hips while I gyrate, then slide my black lace thong down over my legs and kick it off the toe of one boot.

"You're crazy," he tells me, grinning. "What if somebody comes up here?"

I crook my finger at him, and he gets out of the car.

"Take your gloves off," I tell him. "And the hat. I don't want to be responsible for getting them dirty."

He does what he's told.

He comes at me, hungrily at first, his hands and eyes roaming my body, then a fleeting expression of embarrassment passes over his face as if he's suddenly remembered something he's obligated to do. He gives me a hard, fast kiss with too much tongue, but I don't mind; it will be our first and last kiss.

I back him up against the car while I unzip his fly. He moans when I take him out of his pants, and his hands grip the hood of my car as I begin to kneel in front of him.

"What are you?" I ask him. "A staff sergeant?"

"Yeah."

The word comes out like a gasp of pain.

"You want to be a general someday?"

I feel the moist ground grinding into my knees too late and realize I'm probably ruining my stockings.

"I'm hoping to be a civilian someday," he manages to tell me before his ability to form complex sentences is temporarily suspended as I take him in my mouth.

I play with him, licking him and taking him deep in my throat, until he starts to get serious. He grabs my head and begins thrusting with a definite rhythm.

I realize he's going to come soon so I pull away and lead him to the backseat of the car, sit him down, pull my dress off over my head, and crawl on top of him, clamping my thighs around his hips. He slides inside me easily.

He starts to fumble with my bra, and I unhook it for him. His style lacks finesse. It's mostly grab and rub. But he gets an A for enthusiasm, and I enjoy his enjoyment.

He cups my breasts and takes one in his mouth. The feel of his tongue against my nipple sends a raw current of pleasure directly to my pussy. My thighs spread wider, and I ride him.

Afterward, I lay my head on his shoulder and my hand against his chest. His heart thuds rapidly beneath the decorations pinned to the heavy material.

I wanted him to strip, too. I wanted to feel flesh on flesh, but I knew that would have been asking a lot. I know what a pain in the ass it is to take a uniform off and put it back on again.

A couple dozen teachers' cars are all that remain in the parking lot by the time we return. The last bus has left, too.

"I'm sorry," I tell him. "Looks like you missed your chance."

"That's okay," he says. "I'll hit the mall later."

I pull up and park beside his Honda. We both glance over at it.

"A friend of yours get married recently?" I ask, looking at the garter hanging on the rearview mirror.

"Yeah. A buddy of mine. Last weekend. Before he shipped out to Iraq."

"And you caught the garter?"

"Yeah, I caught the garter."

"Did you want to catch the garter?"

"I was pretty drunk. All I know is they rounded up all us guys and somebody threw something into the crowd. It was pretty much instinct that made me fight for it."

He puts his hat and gloves and recruiter's smile back on.

"I guess I should get going," he says.

"Yeah. Me too."

He gets out of my car and starts moving away from me in a Marine's smooth, stiff-legged glide.

"Hey," I call after him. "I noticed earlier the tread on your tires is pretty worn. You might think about replacing them. And your rear left one really needs some air."

"Okay. Thanks."

I sit back in my seat and take a deep breath. I feel good. I feel ready to deal with Cam Jack.

The Marine gets in his car and sits alone in the vacant parking lot staring at the empty school.

As I drive away, it crosses my mind that I may have saved someone's son.

Chapter Twenty-Two

A FEW DAYS AFTER Cam Jack screwed me in the plush burgundy backseat of his silver Cadillac when I was sixteen, I became plagued by nightmares of brutal rapes and obsessed with the literal definition of the word.

I didn't know why. I knew I hadn't been raped. I was sure of that. I hadn't put up a fight. I didn't scream and scratch and punch. I didn't call for help or knee him in the groin or spit in his face, even though I thought about doing all those things.

I had told him I didn't want to have sex and even pushed him away the first time he put his hands on me. He responded by flashing his privileged smile and trying to convince me in his oily carnival barker style that the very thing he wanted from me was something I should be embarrassed by and eager to discard.

I had agreed to meet him, he reminded me. I even put on a pretty blouse that gave him a glimpse of my titties. What did I think was going to happen when I got into a big roomy car with a grown man who had a grown man's needs? Did I think we were going to have stimulating conversation? We were going to go for a drive and get an ice cream cone? Did I think it was the chaste beginning of a beautiful relationship, that Stan Jack's son was going to court and marry one of his coal miners' daughters?

What possible reason could he have had for inviting me? What possible reason could I have had for saying yes?

"Cut the bullshit, Shae-Lynn," he said to me with his trademark forthrightness that came from a lack of intellect and a glut of ego, not from any desire to be genuine or honest. "You know why you're here."

I couldn't argue with him. I did know why I was there. I doubted he knew why I was there, but he thought he did and that was all he needed in order for him to feel that he was successfully manipulating me into becoming a willing accomplice in setting my own trap.

Maybe he found these mind games necessary when seducing other girls. Maybe they needed to be persuaded or he needed to do the persuading, but this wasn't the case with me. I was no innocent virgin who could be tricked or badgered, and I wasn't a prude who had to be flattered and vindicated.

I had been screwing around with boys since I was fourteen. My first time had been unintentional. I was hanging out with Teddy Mullen, the sixteen-year-old son of a nearby farmer who also ran a meat market. Teddy had recently earned his driver's license and sometimes gave me rides home from school. That particular day we stopped off at his dad's farm first because his mom had just finished canning some stew meat and gallons of her homemade vegetable soup and wanted to give me a few jars.

It was a warm day in May and we took a walk around the farm after we loaded the jars in his car and ended up in a dark corner of the barn where slats of white sunshine shone through the cracks between the old musty boards and striped his yellow hair.

Teddy produced a crumpled five-dollar bill from his jeans pocket and told me his dad had begun to give him an allowance now that he'd turned sixteen so he could have gas money. He told me he'd be willing to give me the whole thing if I'd take my top off for him.

Up until then I'd never thought of Teddy as a potential boyfriend.

I'd never thought of anyone as a potential boyfriend even though I'd already had plenty of volunteers for the position. Teddy was certainly cute enough to consider, and he had strong, hard arms and a ruddy, sun-kissed glow to his skin in the summer from all the manual labor he did on the farm.

The problem was each time I thought about having a boyfriend and what it would entail, holding hands and French kissing and having a boy touch me everywhere, I thought about E.J. and I instantly hated myself.

Even then, after Teddy made his offer, the first thing that crossed my mind was wondering why E.J. had never tried to purchase a peek at my breasts, or anything else for that matter.

Because he was totally disinterested, I told myself, because he couldn't care less. But someone cared. Teddy cared.

I snatched the bill out of his hands, stuffed it into the back pocket of my jeans, and pulled my shirt up off over my head, silently cursing E.J.'s stupidity, or was it his wisdom? I didn't care. All I knew was I was sick and tired of thinking about him all the time.

More was promised; and more was taken off. Even more was promised; and body parts were touched.

Before I knew it, I was stripped down to my panties and Teddy had me pushed up against a wall promising me his prize calf that won a 4-H blue ribbon at last year's county fair.

It was an enlightening experience and mutually successful. I had always assumed, like all girls did, that when it came to sex the boys were in charge. They were the knowledgeable ones. They were calling the shots, setting the tempo. They had control of the situation. They were fearless.

It came as a great shock to me that first time and many subsequent times to find out that boys didn't know anything about sex. Not only that, they didn't even need to have actual sex in order to get off. Just seeing a girl's bare butt or getting to touch a breast could be enough.

Plus they were squeamish. They thought they wanted to get their dicks inside you but they didn't want to see where they were going and most of them didn't want to touch it and they sure as hell didn't want to get up close and personal with it.

That first time I unzipped a pair of jeans and got my hands on an erection and saw the pained look on Teddy's face that I realized was a sort of pleasure that went beyond the usual physical boundaries, I thought to myself, I can be in charge here, if I choose to be.

I quickly came to regard boys as flesh and blood launch pads, each equipped with his own little heat-seeking missile, and I was the one who controlled the countdown. I enjoyed the power, especially since I suspected it might be the only power I would ever possess.

Did I agree to meet Cam Jack and get into his car with him because I wanted to have power over him?

Yes.

But once I found myself alone with him, I changed my mind. I didn't want to have sex with this unpleasant, sweaty, groping, soft, grown man. When I tried to back out, he treated me like I was attempting to break off a business deal with him; he dropped all pretenses of pretending to woo me and made it clear that he had owned me all along.

"You know what blackballing means, precious?" he asked me while his hands clamped onto my bare breasts and began kneading them like balls of dough. "It means you want to keep me happy, because if you don't I'm going to make sure your daddy never sets foot in a mine again."

I wanted him to hit me then. I was used to being beaten. I could have dealt with that. I would have preferred it. I would have enjoyed it: seeing the look on his face when he started to get physical, expecting me to be scared, to cry and cower, and instead I would have taken it like a man.

Being the cause of my dad losing his job was something I could not bear. His job was the only thing he liked to do, the only thing he was good at doing, the only thing that gave him a sense of worth. Being a miner gave him a place in the world. By doing it every day he earned his position on a bar stool at Jolly's every night and the right to bitch about the unfairness of life.

All of that would have been taken away from him if I hadn't let Cam Jack put his thick slimy tongue in my mouth and his thick fumbling fingers up inside me.

For the next few weeks, the dreams arrived every night as soon as I dropped off to sleep. They were incredibly vivid and horrifically violent. Each night a different woman restrained in a different manner: her raw, skinless wrists bound with barbed wire; her face wrapped in silver duct tape like a bandaged mummy; a dog collar fastened too tightly around her neck and chained to a railroad tie jutting out of a slab of concrete.

They were violated with bottles, wrenches, fists, and knives. Blood spurted from between their legs, covering their thighs and bellies, spattering walls and the rapist's face and arms. I could never see him clearly, and I never knew the women.

The next day in school I'd be so exhausted and shaken I couldn't concentrate on anything.

I began visiting the library during all my study halls. I'd get a dictionary and go sit at a table as far away as possible from everyone else and stare transfixed at the word "rape."

Rape: 1: To seize and take away by force. 2: An outrageous violation. 3: An act or instance of robbing or despoiling or carrying away a person by force. 4: Sexual intercourse with a woman by a man without her consent and chiefly by force, deception, or threat. 5: A European herb of the mustard family grown as a forage crop for sheep and hogs and for its seeds which yield rape oil and are a bird food.

"Force" was the recurring word in most of the definitions but the word that caught my eye was "despoil."

Despoil: to strip of belongings, possessions, or value.

Cam Jack hadn't been the first person to strip me of my value. That distinction belonged to my father. I was surprised to find that it was possible to have your value as a human being stripped away more than once. For some reason I thought of it as finite and singular and irreplaceable, like my mom's rag rug.

This is how I decided to view my night with Cam Jack from then on: not as sex, not as rape, but as an instance of despoiling.

I decide to have a drink before I go see him at his office, but can't stomach the depressing feel of a blue-collar bar so early in the day.

After taking a few jobs—driving an elderly woman whose failing eyesight prevents her from driving herself into Centresburg to do her grocery shopping and ending up doing her grocery shopping for her; driving a guy who lost his license on a DUI charge to visit his girlfriend who no longer has a car because she had to sell it to pay for the lawyer she employed to handle her divorce and fight for the car (the guy told me in confidence he was getting ready to pop the question to her; I told him it seemed to me they were made for each other); and driving a woman with a broken arm home from work after her usual ride got sick in the middle of the day and left early—I end up at the Ruby Tuesday's on the outskirts of Centresburg. It sits at the corner of an intersection between a Ponderosa Steakhouse and a Red Lobster across the road from the Eatn'Park, with a view out the front windows of the county's PennDOT lot parked full of salt trucks and stacked high with neon orange plastic warning cones.

It's getting close to six and the place is full. It will be empty by eight.

Small parties of large people are seated at booths and scattered tables, mechanically shoveling food into their mouths while their eyes flit back and forth from their plates to one of the TVs mounted in each corner of the room.

I'm sitting at the bar with a spectator's view of the salad bar.

A woman walks past me on her way back to her seat carrying a plate heaped with cottage cheese, macaroni, pudding, and four or five lettuce leaves buried beneath a pile of shredded cheddar, bacon bits, and croutons smothered in a creamy white dressing.

I wonder fleetingly what Pamela and Kozlowski have been eating for the past couple days.

The bartender presents me with my second blue margarita in a glass the size of a small beach bucket. I sip at it through a clear straw while perusing the chaotic walls hung with signed photos of movie stars who've never been here and mint condition antique toys no one's ever played with.

My thoughts wander back to the day I met Cam Jack. It was a one-in-a-million encounter, one of the rare times he stopped in at the Beverly office and the only time since the day I rode my bike to the mine to bring my dad his lunch pail that I had gone there.

Shannon was home sick with the chicken pox and Dad had let me drive him to work and drop him off so I could have transportation during the day if I needed it.

I was picking him up after his shift and Cam Jack was on his way out when our paths crossed in the parking area.

He was twelve years my senior and had been managing the Jolly Mount mines for six years. His dad had put him in charge of them after he returned home from barely getting the Ivy League degree demanded of him.

Most people around here never could figure out why Stan Jack bothered to send his son to college. It was fairly obvious that there was about as much chance of having Cam return home from Yale refined and educated as there was of a garden toad taking off and flying just because someone put it in a bird's nest.

Cam believed his dad did it just to humiliate and degrade him, and it would become the largest grudge he would hold against his dad for the rest of his life. He also would never forgive his father for putting him in charge of two of J&P's smaller mines. He saw this as a slap in the face when he expected a great reward for doing what his father had asked of him.

Most of the rest of his father's operators were lazy, scarcely literate mini-tyrants who had no respect or sympathy for the men who worked for them, but they were afraid of Stan Jack's wealth and power so they attempted to run mines that weren't going to cause him any more scandal and put him in the public eye again the way the major disaster at Gertie had done.

Cam hoped to cause problems. He spent as little time as possible managing the mines. He cut corners wherever he could.

At both Beverly and Josephine the exhaust fans barely worked and needed to be replaced. Electrical equipment was poorly maintained by untrained men. Cables were held together by uninsulated splices. Dangerous levels of coal dust were allowed to accumulate. Some areas weren't rock-dusted at all. None of the miners had been given self-rescuers, the small gas masks that filtered out the lethal carbon monoxide left after an explosion.

A little over a decade later, at the time of the explosion that would kill my father, Beverly had eighteen unanswered safety violations cited against her.

It was the beginning of September. School had just started the week before. The county fair had just ended. Autumn was in the air at night, but the days were pure Indian summer.

I had on a pair of cutoffs and a halter top I had made from a couple of bandannas in Home Ec class.

He was wearing a pair of dark blue suit pants and a white dress shirt with the sleeves rolled up and the top buttons undone. A yellow tie was stuffed into one of his pants pockets and fluttered behind him like a tail when he walked. His shoes were shiny black and remarkably clean.

He said hello. I said hi back. We made small talk. Soon we were smiling and laughing and he was telling me I was pretty.

He asked me if I knew who he was and I told him I didn't. I knew he was management by the way he was dressed and the softness of his hands. When he told me he was Cam Jack, I was as excited as if I was meeting foreign royalty or a Pittsburgh Pirate.

He wasn't terribly bad looking then. He was solid, not beefy yet. He had thick unkempt hair that made him look vulnerable despite the bully's smirk he always wore and a big outdoorsy voice that made me think of cowboys and campfires. He had a way of tilting and lowering his head as if he were trying to hear me better when we talked that I found endearing. This was before I knew the word "patronizing."

I told him my name. He pretended to know my father. He praised the Jolly Mount miners, using the same line he'd use over twenty years later in E.J.'s hospital room after the explosion in Jojo. He said his dad always said he'd give four of his Marvella miners for just one working Josephine or Beverly.

I wanted to ask him why, if he valued them so much, he didn't get them a couple new exhaust fans and some self-rescuers, but I had a feeling this would have put a damper on the rest of our conversation and I wanted him to like me.

I don't know why exactly. Physically, he was the opposite of the type of man I was attracted to. He was nothing like Lib or Jimmy or any of the boys I'd been with. They smelled of cigarettes and engine grease and whiskey. They had big callused, scarred, dirty hands that could easily leave bruises or just as easily convince me that nothing could ever harm me if they chose to love me.

They never appeared to be clean-shaven, and even when they were their cheeks always felt like sandpaper.

They didn't talk much but expressed plenty if you knew how to read them. I could tell exactly what my dad thought of someone by the amount of eye contact he made with him, whether he stuck his hands in his pockets, crossed his arms over his chest or held them akimbo, and how often and how strenuously he spit.

Cam wore an aftershave that made him smell like a freshly shampooed dog. There was something damp and animal about his scent that the cologne couldn't cover up completely. His hands were smoother and softer than the hands of most women I knew. His face was the same. He never stopped talking yet I was never sure what he really thought about anything.

The mantrip rumbled up to the mine's entry, and tired, dirty, squinting men in hard hats carrying lunch pails and thermoses began to straggle away from the hill toward the double-wide trailer they used as a bath house.

The sight of them changed Cam's demeanor. He looked uncomfortable and was suddenly in a hurry to leave.

We parted and I never gave him a second thought except to occasionally think back on our meeting the way I might think about meeting anyone who was rich or famous.

He called me one night about a week later, and I met him the next night in his Cadillac about a mile down the road from our house.

I've often wondered since then if he would have been equally bold with any teenaged girl he might have encountered that day among the rows of pickup trucks or if he sensed something in me that made him take a chance. Did I give off a victim's scent like a cat in heat?

We drove around for awhile talking in his car before we finally parked.

We talked about a lot of things. We even talked about the same miners he seemed in such a hurry to avoid the week before.

I got the feeling he was lonely. I don't think he had any true friends. He complained that the rich kids at his college called him a redneck behind his back. The rednecks back home hated him because of his wealth. I guess it never occurred to him people might dislike him simply because he was an asshole.

Before we moved to the backseat and got down to business, he seemed nervous at having me in the car with him. He explained to me that we couldn't be seen together.

He said it was because the world was full of uptight, holier-than-thou Bible-thumpers and titsy feminists. According to him, the women belonging to either of these groups had pussies that were so dry, dust and cobwebs came out of them when they spread their legs. They all hated men and any type of pleasure, particularly men having pleasure. Their goal was to keep men from satisfying their natural urges, thereby keeping them weak and miserable. Since girls like me were the perfect age for satisfying those urges, they especially hated us.

I didn't completely buy into his pleasure-depriving conspiracy theory, but I listened politely while he expounded on the topic. I tended to think our secrecy had more to do with the fact that if my dad or any of the other miners found out what he was doing they would beat him to death with the same bare hands that worked in his mines every day.

He never called me again after that night. I wouldn't have cared. I had no desire to see him again and I wouldn't have called him either except I felt obligated a few months later to tell him I was pregnant with his child.

I signal to the bartender for one more bucket of margarita.

Chapter Twenty-Three

THE J&P BUILDING IS by far the nicest one in downtown Centresburg. Even before the other buildings in town began boarding up their windows and padlocking their front doors as stores and businesses folded one by one in the wake of the mine closings, it stood out as the most spectacular landmark for miles around.

It's a stately redbrick structure with a gleaming gold clock tower and wide marble front steps leading to a set of white columns supporting a two-story-high balcony where they hang red, white, and blue bunting every Fourth of July and display a life-sized Nativity scene every Christmas now that the courthouse is no longer allowed to do it. Most visitors to town think the J&P Building *is* the courthouse and it might as well be. The two men who have owned it have always had more power than any judge.

I push open the heavy brass and glass front doors and step inside. Everyone is gone for the day. The foyer is empty and the size of a barn. The floor is white marble shot through with black and gray streaks and flecks of quartz that glitter softly in the light coming from the enormous wrought-iron chandelier overhead. It's obviously very old and reminds me of the candle-dripping chandeliers hanging in Transylvanian castles in vampire movies. It adds a sinister element to the otherwise Romanesque opulence of the rest of the cavernous entryway.

The ceiling above it is painted in a panoramic Pennsylvanian version of the Sistine Chapel. Various highly selective scenes of Pennsylvania lifestyle and history are represented.

There's the obligatory portrait of William Penn and the depiction of Ben Franklin flying a kite with a key tied to the end of it. Ragged colonists overwhelm British redcoats who turn and run, and Union soldiers slaughter their Confederate brothers at Gettysburg. A hunter in camouflage and neon orange takes aim at a majestic stag, and black-faced miners trudge home from their shift with their backs turned toward a puffing locomotive carrying off carloads of coal. A red covered bridge and a horse-drawn Amish cart sit against a backdrop of rolling green hills. The steel mills of Pittsburgh, Philadelphia's cracked Liberty Bell, a Hershey bar, a bottle of Heinz ketchup, and Punxsutawney Phil leaving the comfort of his burrow in search of his shadow are all accounted for.

There's not a single woman in the entire painting.

I take a few steps toward a curving staircase carpeted in dove gray leading to the second floor. My boots make loud clacking noises on the marble that echo around the room like gunfire.

I stop and I'm suddenly very conscious of my bare knees. I ruined my stockings in the mud with the Marine and threw them away in the ladies' room at Ruby Tuesday's. Now I'm barefoot and bare-legged inside my boots. Normally it wouldn't bother me but right now it makes me feel poor and cheap.

I continue across the marble, setting my heels down even harder. The sound is almost deafening. Once I reach the staircase, my heels sink into the plush carpet like I've stepped into a field of dandelion fluff.

At the top of the stairs is a long ornate hallway dimly lit by gold sconces with frosted glass globes. The walls are paneled in a rich dark wood and hung with portraits of stern board members past and present. A brighter light spills out from behind an office door that's slightly ajar at the end of the corridor. I make my way toward it.

A small gold plaque is mounted on the door engraved with the words: Cameron E. Jack, Chief Executive Officer.

My palms are sweating. If only he'd take a swing at me then I'd know what to do.

I pull the door open and step inside. He's standing behind his desk with his back to me. He looks like he's staring out the window, but the curtains are drawn.

He turns around, even though neither the opening of the door or my footsteps have made any noise.

"Well, well, well." He smiles at me. "Shae-Lynn."

The office is immense. The distance between the door and his colossal desk is enough to make any supplicant truly nervous as he crosses the room while being scrutinized by the man he's come to report to or beg a favor from.

Everything is done in creams and golds except for the dark wood of the desk and his bookshelves, and the brick red leather of his chair.

The shelves are full of leather-bound books which I'm sure he's never read, and the walls are hung with dozens of framed photos of himself with famous people who I'm sure don't display photos of themselves with him.

There's also a fair number of photos of his parents posing at various civic functions. His mom is a gray mouse of a woman who stands beside his father, dutiful and unsmiling, wearing practical polyester skirts and jackets in diluted popsicle colors with blouses that tie at the neck in big bows.

He hasn't aged well. It's the first thing I thought when I spied on him in E.J.'s hospital room two years ago. His face is jowly and lined; his stomach is too big for his pants. He's expanded the way a yeast bread rises and I have the feeling if I were to poke him with my finger, it would sink into his flesh like it would into an underbaked muffin.

His hair is still thick but has turned pewter gray. He wears it moussed and slicked back, completely covering the top of his head like a steel cap.

"Standing over there you look exactly the same as you did when you were sixteen," he tells me. "Maybe better. You got a little more meat on you now. You were such a scrawny little thing."

I don't know how to respond. I can't and won't make polite conversation with him.

I say nothing.

He gestures at the two chairs placed in front of his desk and asks me to sit.

I do as I'm told.

Up close, he doesn't look well. There've been rumors circulating for years about his failing health. Talk about dialysis machines and experimental drugs.

I forget that I don't look so great either.

"What the hell happened to your face?" he asks me with his typical tact. "Don't tell me you got yourself a boyfriend who knocks you around?"

"It's none of your business." I break my silence.

"Oh, I see. You're gonna be all pissy with me. I was hoping after our conversation yesterday you'd take some time to think about things and get yourself in a better mood. You got no reason to be mad at me."

I stare at him incredulously and hope that my jaw isn't hanging open.

"I'm not saying I haven't made some mistakes," he continues, not sounding the least bit humble. "My dad used to say, 'A clear conscience is usually the sign of a bad memory.' I'm just saying there's no reason to be mad at me."

"No," I tell him, crossing my legs and forcing a strained smile. "There's no reason for me to be mad at you. I should let bygones be bygones."

"That's my girl. Can I get you anything? Coffee, soda, bourbon?"

My head is beginning to throb, and I rub at the knot behind my ear.

"How about some health insurance?" I joke.

"You don't have any health insurance?"

"I'm self-employed now. I can't afford it."

"That's your God-given right as an American."

"Not to be able to afford health insurance?" I wonder aloud.

"To be able to buy health insurance if you can afford it."

He walks over to a cabinet, opens it, and takes out two glasses and a bottle of Old Grand-Dad.

He pours two shots of the amber liquor and hands me one.

I notice in the midst of all his photos he only has one of his wife, Rae Ann.

She's about my age. He married her when he was in his early thirties. At the time I suppose she would have been considered a trophy wife: ten years his junior, as blond as they come, daughter of a real estate mogul, a former Miss Florida runner-up who dreamed of becoming a marine biologist and working at Sea World with trick dolphins but who settled for playing a lot of tennis and living on her parents' 200-acre estate near Boca Raton until she met Cam Jack.

He also only has one photo of his three daughters.

He and Rae Ann never had a son.

"So tell me," he says, taking a seat on the corner of his desk nearest me, "you're good friends with some of those boys that were trapped and rescued up in Jolly Mount, aren't you?"

"Yes, I am."

"How's that working out for them?"

"Well, the part about being rescued is working out real well."

"I mean . . . there was a lot of fanfare after they were rescued. They were regular celebrities there for awhile. Book deals and movie deals and things like that. Oprah treating them like heroes, putting them on her show and giving them all a new set of camping equipment and a hunting trip to Wyoming.

"Did you know she never even called me and asked for my side of the story? I would have been happy to give it to her. I think she's damn attractive for a black woman.

"I bet those boys really cleaned up," he finishes.

I'm starting to get pissed over the "boys" reference.

"Two of those boys are older than you," I point out to him.

"One of them still works for me, doesn't he?"

"Two of them still work for you."

I think about E.J. I think about what he survived, about how he still feels like he's losing his mind sometimes, about the amount of composure and willpower it takes for a man to be able to continue to do a job that almost killed him.

"How about now? How're they fixed for money?" Cam disrupts my thoughts.

"I don't know. Why do you want to know?"

"You know about this lawsuit. Hell, everybody does. I'm trying to figure out where they're coming from. What's their motivation? You think they're only in it for the money or is it personal?"

"Is that why you invited me here? To talk about the Jolly Mount Five?"

"The Jolly Mount Five," he scoffs. "What the hell is that? Everybody calls them that. The Jolly Mount Five: sounds like a goddamned backup group for Willie Nelson."

He tosses back his drink in one gulp and gets up to pour himself another one.

"It took them awhile to decide to do it and that means they had

288

some misgivings," he goes on. "I'll give them credit for that. But I knew they'd eventually do it. The working man doesn't have any honor anymore; that's what it boils down to. It makes me sad. Truly. None of the old-timers would have ever sued my dad. Ninety-six men died in Gertie and nobody ever made a peep."

"Who were they going to make a peep to?"

I'm starting to get angry and I've had enough to drink to loosen my tongue.

"Everyone knew the inspectors never really pushed enforcing the safety violations if they wanted to keep their jobs. And every mine commissioner and muckety-muck in the government was a former mine owner and a friend of your dad's.

"The system's not any less corrupt nowadays, it's just things are harder for you because the public gets involved in everything and there's always a lawyer somewhere willing to sue."

"Shae-Lynn. I'm surprised at you. Where did you ever pick up this bullshit?"

"It's public knowledge. You've just always had a public that doesn't want to think about it because they don't know what they can do to change it and they need the jobs so they ignore it."

"If there were still Communists around, I'd say you sound like one."

I finish my drink and hold it out for him to refill.

"There are still Communists around, you ass. It's called China. You know, the place that makes all the things we used to make here in America?"

He pauses with the bottle held over my glass. His face grows dark and I think I might realize my wish for him to hit me, but he lets it pass and produces an expression that doesn't show the least bit of affection or amusement but still manages to look like a smile.

"Cynicism isn't pretty, sweetheart. No wonder you never got married."

He fills my glass and sits back down on the edge of the desk.

"I'm gonna let you in on a secret. I'm getting out of the coal business. Now on the surface it might not make sense. Coal's coming back in a big way. Not that it ever left. Most Americans would be shocked red as a baby's rashy ass if they knew 60 percent of their electricity still comes from coal.

"They want to run their five TVs and their four computers and have every light on in the goddamned house all night long and never think about where the juice is coming from. Well, it sure as hell isn't coming from the Energy Fairy. And it sure as hell isn't coming from the sun and the wind. You ever been to Holland?"

"No," I answer.

"Neither have I. But I've seen pictures and those windmills aren't doing shit. Nuclear power? Who the hell wants to risk having his hair fall out and his pecker shrivel up from radiation when you can use coal and just have a little old-fashioned air pollution?

"Besides, all that clean air nonsense is becoming a thing of the past anyway. Coal has friends in very high places these days. And we got all these Third World countries needing coal because they can't afford oil and hell, none of them care about clean air. People are calling America the Saudi Arabia of coal.

"That's a compliment," he feels compelled to add.

He gets off the desk and begins to pace. I watch the jiggle of his soft, pudgy body underneath his expensive suit and think of E.J. again. Nothing on him jiggles.

"Fact is, I'm tired of coal. More than that. I hate coal. Coal and coal companies and coal miners and coal dirt and coal money."

And one coal baron in particular whose name you inherited, I think to myself.

"I even hate those stupid little pieces of coal they sell in stores now at Christmastime to put in kids' stockings.

"I was in a store in New York City, and the salesgirl saw me looking at some and she started talking to me about how nice it was that we're finding a different use for coal instead of burning it and destroying the environment.

"'A different use?' I said to her. 'You think selling a dozen pieces of bony in an overpriced doodad store is going to take the place of burning millions of tons of coal every day? Little girl, do you know who I am?' She said she didn't. I explained to her and afterward she was very nice and accommodating, if you know what I mean, but I had her fired anyway."

I sip at my drink. When I sit back in my chair and look at the ceiling, the room seems to spin around me. I concentrate on the green and brass banker's lamp on Cam's desk and everything seems to slow down.

"I started selling off pieces of my dad's coal empire as soon as he died ten years ago. I'm fairly well diversified at this point but most of the capital has gone into the family's oil interests.

"Almost all coal companies are owned by oil companies anyway. My dad always used to say, coal and oil are incestuous: They fuck each other from time to time but they're still part of the same big happy family."

He smiles broadly at his father's wit and wisdom. It's not exactly a maxim I expect to see Sophia Bertolli cross-stitch on a pillow.

"Everything's going to be held under one umbrella corporation. I already have the name picked out: Camerica."

I'm beginning to feel genuinely sick.

I put my unfinished drink on the edge of his desk and stand up slowly.

"Why did you ask me to come here? I don't care about the lawsuit. I don't care about Camerica."

"You don't care about this lawsuit?" he asks me, the same humorless smile he used when I mentioned China appearing on his lips again.

"I think you're gonna care. As things stand now, the investigation cleared me of any criminal wrongdoing. Reckless disregard for human life. Depravity and indifference. All that bullshit. But anyone can sue anyone in civil court.

"I'm not going to let that happen. Have those five miners tell a packed courthouse what it was like being trapped. Their teary-eyed wives and mothers on the stand yanking at the jury's heartstrings. Their lawyers bringing up my previous history of unaddressed safety violations and being able to dig into all my business dealings related to J&P. They might even be allowed to dig into my personal life and try and cast aspersions on my personal self. I won't have that."

He comes and stands directly in front of me. He still has the same shampooed dog smell I remember from when he was younger, only tonight I detect the underlying odor of a slow, sweaty decay.

"The Jolly Mount Five found out today from their lawyer that if they go through with this and sue J&P, J&P's going to declare bankruptcy. I'll close the mines I have left. There's at least a half million dollars worth of equipment belongs to the company I'll have to sell and give to them. But the land and the mineral rights are mine. They belong to my family personally, and they're grandfathered airtight.

"If they sue, mining is over in Laurel County. It's over. I'll plant goddamned trees and flowers and turn Jojo and Beverly into wildlife refuges where tofu-eaters can come have picnics and look for Bambi. No hunting either. No hunting. No mining. See how those boys will take to that.

"Now maybe they won't care about the mines. Maybe they're only out for themselves and the money. If that's true, then there's nothing I can do. Let them come after me. I can tie this thing up for years in the courts with my lawyers and my money."

"You can't do that," I tell him, trying to keep my voice steady. "You still employ a couple hundred men in Jolly Mount. You're the only source of employment we have."

"It's not up to me. It's up to them. Let's see what they're made of."

He's standing so close I think he might try and kiss me. I brace myself to smack him as hard as I can.

"But none of that's why I asked you here. I want to talk to Clay."

I knew this was the reason, but hearing him say my son's name as if he knows him or has any right to know him hits me with an unexpected intensity. I feel like I've been told I only have a week to live. Maybe I do.

"No," I say automatically.

"No?" he laughs. "It's not up to you, precious. I can pick up this phone right now and call him and have him over here in ten minutes. I know he's a deputy. Good-looking kid, too. Not surprising."

I suddenly remember my gun in my purse. Nobody knows I'm here. Nobody knows I have any reason to be here. Nobody knows I have a tie to him. He has tons of enemies.

"Why? Why after all these years? You never tried to see him or have anything to do with him. Why now? He's twenty-three years old. He just had his birthday two days ago."

At the mention of his birthday, a sob blocks my throat.

I'm instantly buried beneath memories of other birthdays. His fifth when he wanted a party with his friends where everyone acted like a dog. We made paper ears for all the kids and they ate their cake and ice cream out of little bowls we decorated to look like dog dishes. On his sixth we had just moved to D.C. and he didn't have any friends yet so we spent the day together, just the two of us. We went to the zoo and had spaghetti and meatballs for dinner, his favorite.

It used to make my heart ache seeing how alone he was that first year after we moved, but he persevered in his earnest, uncomplaining way and before long there was a group of boys constantly showing up at our apartment who he made sure were always dressed warmly on cold days and had memorized the map posted in the stairwell showing the nearest emergency exits and fire escapes.

"Stay away from him," I say, my voice breaking on the final word.

I can't cry. I won't cry. I don't cry. Don't cry, I start chanting inside my head. Don't cry. Don't cry in front of him.

He puts his arm around my shoulders.

"There's nothing to get upset about. You never came after me. I respect you for that. That's why I'm doing you a favor. You understand that? I'm not going behind your back. I'm giving you a chance to explain to him before he meets me. I'm even allowing you to come with him and be present when we talk. Tomorrow. Same time, same place."

I need to get out of here. I wonder if this is how E.J. feels when he has one of his panic attacks, when he believes he's back inside his solid black tomb.

"I have to go," I announce and make my getaway without looking at him again and without looking back.

I don't remember running, but I think I must have because I'm winded when I reach the bottom of the stairs. I'm disoriented, too, and I turn away from the front doors instead of toward them and find myself face to face with a larger than life-sized, full-length portrait of Stan Jack.

It must be eight feel tall. I have no idea how I missed it when I came in.

There's a definite family resemblance between the man and his son, but Stan has the fire of ambition and intellect burning in his dark eyes and a firmness in the set of his jaw that Cam lacks.

I never met his dad. My dad worked his whole life for him and never met him either. But I do know that the miners respected Stan more than his son and that was because Stan had some respect for the miners. Cam never understood why this was important.

He knew that his father had given them jobs and built their homes and schools, but he also saw that it was the miners themselves who gave their children and grandchildren a chance at a better life. He didn't know if he should admire or hate them for this.

He asked me about it during our one night together, but I was a kid and didn't have an answer for him. I still don't. I've never been able to figure out for myself if the Jack family is the enemy or some mercenary kin.

Chapter Twenty-Four

I STEP OUTSIDE THE BUILDING and blink up at the black and gray streaked and smudged night sky that looks like it's been wiped with a dirty rag. The clouds are so thick not a single star or the moon is able to shine through them. They make the sky seem heavy and near instead of endless. I feel another wave of suffocation pass over me.

Not much happens in downtown Centresburg these days: shopping, dining, even banking have all moved to the mall and the roadsides leading to and from the Super Wal-Mart. The only activity that remains is drinking.

I tell myself I'll just have one drink at the Golden Pheasant and then I'll drive home and do the rest of my drinking at Jolly's.

I'm within a few blocks of the bar and beginning to doubt my decision to drink in public when a very distinctive couple leaves the establishment. They're both atypical for Pheasant patrons. She's extremely pregnant, and he's clear-eyed, sharply dressed, and carrying what I believe is called a man-purse in some circles. Around here we call it an-invitation-to-get-your-ass-kicked.

She laughs at something he says and they walk off in the opposite direction without seeing me. I realize instantly that it's Shannon and Kozlowski, but the shock of seeing them and seeing them together keeps me from reacting right away.

I recognize Shannon's car parked down the street. I run back to my own car wondering how I'm going to clandestinely tail someone while driving the only yellow Subaru within the tri-state area.

Fortunately it's dark, and as long as I keep a fair distance behind her, she'll only notice a pair of headlights.

I swing around the block and wait in a nearby alley where I have a good view of them.

It's taking a little time for Shannon to ease her bulk behind the steering wheel. My original theory about Kozlowski's lack of a license must be accurate. Otherwise, I can't imagine him not taking over the driving duties.

I follow her out of town, keeping well behind her. It doesn't take me long to realize she's taking Kozlowski back to his motel.

She pulls into the Comfort Inn parking lot, and I pull into the Uni-Mart next door. She doesn't drop him off. She gets out of the car, too, and goes inside with him.

I give them a few minutes to get situated.

I know Kozlowski's room number from when I picked him up on Saturday. He had a few more phone calls to make before we went out, and invited me up while I waited for him.

"Who is it?" he calls out when I knock.

"I want my sister."

There's some hurried, hushed conversation behind the door.

"Now," I say loudly.

Kozlowski opens the door. Shannon is sitting propped up on the bed with a couple pillows behind her and one under her feet.

"Hello, Gerald. Shannon," I greet them. "Isn't this cozy? Maybe I should call Pamela and the Russian and we can all sit around with our guns and checkbooks and wait for the baby to arrive."

"The Russian?" Shannon asks.

I point at Kozlowski.

"He sent him after you."

She pushes herself up off the pillows.

"You sent that crazy motherfucker after me?"

"I didn't send him after you," he replies calmly. "He came to me. He called me and said he was looking for you on Mickey's behalf. Somehow he heard you were pregnant again and was hoping he could buy this baby. I began to think maybe we could get Mickey to offer more money than the Larsons, and we could get a bidding war going. Technically, Mickey does have a vaguely legal claim to one of your babies, since you ran out on the previous contract. I thought we could use that information to scare the Larsons. And since I also needed help finding you, I thought Dmitri's call was a godsend. I knew if anyone could find you, he could. I told him what I knew about Jolly Mount, and by then I also knew about your sister."

Shannon gets off the bed and lumbers toward a chair where her purse is sitting. She starts rummaging through it.

"I didn't run out on anything," she tells him coldly. "I changed my mind. It's a mother's prerogative. Mickey's wife is nuts."

"You're the one who made her nuts," he tells her. "Sending those photos of aborted fetuses was really over the top. Who's Pamela?"

She takes out a pack of cigarettes and starts to light one.

He tells her to put it out.

"Shut up, Gerry," she snaps at him as she tosses her lighter back in her bag. "When have I ever failed to produce a less-than-perfect baby?"

"So Dmitri is the Russian's name?" I ask.

"No, Dmitri is the fucking Chinaman," she snaps at me.

I maintain my cool.

"Do you want to explain Pamela to Gerry?" I counter sweetly.

She narrows her gold-brown eyes at me.

"How do you know Pamela?"

I shrug.

"This is bullshit," she says grabbing her purse and her coat. "I'm leaving."

"No, you're not. I'm going to have a talk with Gerry here, then I'm taking you home with me. You're grounded until the baby's born."

"Like hell I am."

She starts toward the door. I don't move out of her way.

"What are you going to do?" I ask. "Make a break for it? You really think you can out-waddle me?"

"You're not funny."

I reach into my purse and pull out my handcuffs. I always keep a pair with me. Restraining individuals was one aspect of my job I simply could never give up.

"What are you doing?" she cries as I grab her arm and clap one cuff around her wrist. "What the fuck are you doing?"

I drag her into the bathroom and connect the other cuff to the pipes under the sink while she continues to protest.

She has no choice but to lower herself onto the cold tile floor. I don't help her. I pluck the cigarette out of her hand and flush it down the toilet.

Kozlowski smiles upon my return.

"Shannon said she could handle you. I guess she was wrong."

"Listen, Gerry."

"I prefer Gerald."

"I don't care. I'm not in the best of moods this evening. These past few days have not been very pleasant ones for me. I've been very worried about my sister and her unborn baby. And this Russian prick you put on her tail did this to me."

I pull my hair away from my face so he can get a good look.

"He could have done it to her. A pregnant woman," I add.

Kozlowski shakes his head.

"He wouldn't have hurt her. He knows not to hurt her."

"You lied to me."

"I never lied to you," he interrupts. "I may not have been forth-coming with some facts, but I never lied."

I stare at him and wait for an example of his honesty.

"I've represented Shannon in a few adoptions. I get a substantial fee. She ran out on this one. I came after her."

He shrugs and holds out his hands, palms up, as if this is the kind of situation I should be running into every day.

"Do you always take off in person after girls who run out on you?" I ask.

"I've never had it happen before."

"What made you come to Jolly Mount?"

"I told you the truth. She told me this was her hometown. It was a hunch. That's all. Running into you was pure coincidence."

"But how did you find her once you were here?"

"Easy. She has an insane bacon craving. It's a small town. There are only two restaurants that serve breakfast all day: The International House of Pancakes and Eatn'Park. I went to both and showed her picture around to the staffs and promised a cash reward to anyone who called me if she showed up. One of the waitresses at Eatn'Park said she thought she had already seen her there that morning with another woman. I assumed it was you. A few hours later I get a call from the IHOP. Who's Pamela, by the way?"

"You'll have to get Shannon to tell you. Good luck."

I start heading back to the bathroom.

"I don't wish Shannon any harm," he says. "I just want my money."

"I've already figured that out. The part about only caring about money. Once the baby's born she's on her own again," I explain. "I'm not going to interfere with any of her decisions. But for now I'm taking her home with me, and you're going to go back to New York and leave her alone. I'm not going to make you promise because I don't trust you, but I will make sure you've checked out of here tomorrow and that you haven't checked in anywhere else."

"And what if I don't leave?" he asks.

He offers what I'm sure he considers a very persuasive smile but his eyes are hostile. I think about what Vlad, or Dmitri, told me: that he finds girls and convinces them to get pregnant solely in order to sell their babies.

"If you cause any problems for Shannon or try to get in touch with her in any way while she's staying with me, I have friends around here who will be happy to hurt you for me, once I explain who and what you are. I could do it myself, but I wouldn't feel right since you're a customer."

He laughs.

"Shannon told me you used to be a cop. Is that what you're implying? Are you telling me the cops around here are actually stupid enough to think that they can beat up a lawyer from New York City—an officer of the court—as a favor to someone and get away with it?"

"I'm not talking about cops. I'm talking about coal miners."

I turn my back on him and join Shannon in the john, closing the door behind me so we can have some privacy. Shannon looks extremely uncomfortable on the floor, although at her stage of pregnancy I doubt any position is comfortable.

She's sitting against the tile wall between the sink and the toilet with her legs sticking straight out in front of her and spread slightly apart. The mound of her belly forms a ledge for her breasts to lie on. Looking down at her from this angle, I figure it would be easier to pull the baby up through her throat like a rabbit from a top hat than to try the traditional route.

I take a seat on the edge of the bathtub.

She has taken off the small plastic lids from the shampoo and moisturizer samples and is whipping them against the wall opposite her, where they hit with a click and fly back at her.

"What happened to you?" I ask her.

"Spare me," she says dully without looking at me. "Don't think you can give me a lecture because you kept your baby. We all know you're so fucking wonderful."

"What the hell, Shannon?" I respond angrily. "Is that what this is all about? I got pregnant and I kept my baby so you had to get pregnant and not keep yours? What kind of twisted sibling rivalry is that?"

"I assure you nothing I've ever done in my life has anything to do with sibling rivalry. And I'm not twisted."

"And I'm not fucking wonderful."

"Sure you are. Everybody's wonderful in this situation except for me. I'm sure you think people like Pamela who adopt these babies are so wonderful, too, because they want the baby. Oh, they must be such amazing, loving people because they're willing to spend all that money and go to all that worry over this baby, and I'm a monster because I don't want the baby. They spend the money because they have it. Big fucking deal. They don't give any more thought to the baby than they do to buying a yacht or a golden retriever. It's one more thing for them to acquire, one more thing they can buy to fill up their stupid empty lives."

I can't stand the tone of her voice, the complete lack of feeling in it. I think about what Isabel said, how she thought Shannon had some disorder that kept her from loving people. I think about E.J.'s uncharacteristic display of emotion as he insisted she never cared about me or anyone else. I think about Jimmy not saying anything, because he agreed with them but he didn't want to hurt my feelings.

But I also can't stop thinking about my little sister, snuggled up next to me, sitting on Mom's rag rug, looking at books filled with pictures of places we were still young enough to dream about seeing but already weary enough in our souls to know we would never get to. I think about her crying softly in her bed after Dad had finished beating me. Pretend you're asleep, I always told her. And even after he's gone, don't come to me. Don't risk making the floorboards creak. I think about the way I'd find her standing next to my bed the following morning, watching and waiting: the smile and the hug I'd get once she was sure I was still alive.

"So how can you do it?" I ask her. "How can you give your own child to people you hate?"

She winces as she shifts her immense frontal weight.

"Making babies is the only thing I'm good at. It's my profession."

I don't say anything, but I must be making an expression of disapproval because she says, "Don't look at me like that. What's the difference between rich people paying men to work in their coal mines or paying a coal miner's daughter to have a baby for them?"

I don't have an immediate answer for her.

"Miners like Dad ruin their health," she says. "They get killed. They give their blood for a salary. I'm doing the same thing. I do all the work. I take all the risks and face all the danger. In the end I get paid, and it may seem like a lot, but it's not compared to what I'm giving them."

"So what are you saying?" I ask. "You're a baby mine?"

She begins to absentmindedly stroke her belly.

"But it's not the same thing," I insist. "If a man decides to work in a coal mine, he's making a decision about his own life. You're making a decision for someone else. An innocent little person.

"How can you give your child to Pamela Jameson?" I continue. "What if it's a little girl? She'll have to color-coordinate and earn an anti-stress badge."

She smiles a little.

"I guess you have run into Pam. I have to admit I was impressed she followed me here. She has an unnatural fear of anything natural."

"She's not the only one who followed you here. What about this Russian?"

"He's a full-time thug who works as a bodyguard-driver for this small-time New Jersey politician who's mobbed up. Gerry and I tried to work out an adoption with him. I did a couple things to try and bump the price up. Gerry was putting on an act in there trying to seem like he was appalled at what I did. He totally approved.

"But Mickey's wife turned out to be a complete bimbo bitch, and I didn't want her to have the kid. I hear she's crazy now. Sits in the baby's room and cries all the time. Her husband knows plenty of hookers. Why doesn't he just give one fifty grand to have his baby? What's the big deal? People are such hypocrites."

I want to hit her. I want to beat all the callousness and flippancy out of her and start fresh with an empty Shannon skin and stuff it full of goodwill and happiness, but it doesn't work that way. I know first-hand that a beating from a loved one doesn't teach you anything. It doesn't fill you with respect for the beater or, surprisingly, even hatred. It simply makes you afraid of everything. Including love.

"And the Larsons?"

"They're the family who's supposed to get this baby. Gerry set up the adoption. I ran out on him so I could sell the baby to Pamela for more money."

"And you had both families supporting you throughout your pregnancy?"

"Yeah. Pretty smart, huh?"

"I'm speechless with admiration."

She stretches her arms behind her and begins kneading her lower back with her fingertips.

"It's not a big deal. I'm usually scrupulously honest."

"What happened this time?"

"I've decided to retire. I still have more childbearing years left in me, but I'm tired. I wanted to make a real killing with this last one before I quit. That's why I was playing these families against each other and why I didn't want to share any of the money with Gerry."

"Even if this plan works, you can't possibly make more than a couple hundred grand. How are you going to retire on that? You're only thirty-four."

"For one thing I'm not talking about never working again for as long as I live. I'm retiring from the baby game. That's all. And I'm also not talking about retiring in New York City. I hate it there. I only live there because that's where the marketplace is and when I do live there, someone else is paying my bills. I've got other money saved. I have a cheap little town picked out. I've even bought myself a cheap little house."

"Is it in New Mexico?"

"Maybe."

"So you ran away to the big city and sold babies to rich people all these years so you'd be able to afford to live in a town pretty much like the one you left in the first place?"

She doesn't answer me.

"I don't get it."

"People can change their minds about where they want to live." An edge of defensiveness creeps into her voice. "Just because I didn't want to live in a dead-end, bumble-fuck town when I was sixteen doesn't mean I can't decide to live in one when I'm older. You lived in D.C. all those years and look at you now. Right back where you started. I think that house of yours may actually be uglier than the one we grew up in."

"I came back because I wanted to."

"That's what I'm doing, too."

"So why not move back to Jolly Mount instead of some town in New Mexico?"

"Ha!" she barks. "No, thank you."

"Why come back at all? Why are you here right now? I still haven't figured that out."

She doesn't say anything at first. I swear I can hear the gears turning inside her head as she works on concocting her latest lie.

"When I was thinking where I could go to hide out and have the baby without anybody bothering me, I thought of here. I thought of you," she finally answers.

"Did you ever think about me before?"

"I really want a cigarette."

"Did you?"

"Don't try and make me feel bad," she replies.

"You were gone for eighteen years. Didn't you ever think about me? About Clay and Dad? Jimmy and Isabel? Didn't you ever once think about how worried we must be?"

"I didn't care."

"I don't believe you."

"I said, I didn't care," she repeats slowly, staring me straight in the eyes and willing me to look away first.

"Just like you don't care about your babies."

"They're going to good homes. I suppose it's better to have abortions? It's better to kill them?"

"It's not the same thing," I cry out in exasperation. "Women who have abortions are women who get pregnant by accident. You get pregnant with the sole intention of selling your children."

"Pregnant by accident?" she says, her face screwing up in contempt. "There's no such thing. That's such bullshit. Women don't get pregnant by accident. A woman knows how to get pregnant and a woman knows what birth control is. If she has sex and she's not using birth control, she knows she can get pregnant. There's no accident."

"Sometimes there are accidents."

The disdain on her face melts away and is replaced by the bored yet wholly alert gaze of a copper-eyed cat.

"Are you talking about yourself? You weren't dumb. You knew where babies came from. How'd you end up pregnant?"

"Sometimes there are situations where you can't be prepared."

"What are you saying? Were you raped?"

"No," I reply and immediately search for a way to change the subject. "How many babies have you had? Just out of curiosity."

"This will be ten."

"*Ten?*"

Ten: I can't process this number.

I get up from my seat on the edge of the bathtub and begin to pace in the little room.

Suddenly I crave a cigarette, too, and I've never smoked.

"Ten," I say again.

"I had my first when I was seventeen, just like you," she starts to tell me. "And just like you I wasn't dumb about sex. I knew you got pregnant from having it and I knew about condoms. I was there in health class when we learned how to put a rubber on a banana. But when you're out on the streets and the only way you're going to get a meal or maybe a bed to sleep in is to screw some guy who doesn't necessarily have one or want to use one, sometimes you make exceptions."

I start to feel sick to my stomach. I don't want to hear these stories. This is exactly the kind of life I pictured her having during the times I allowed myself to picture her alive.

"Why didn't you come to me? You didn't have to live like that."

"When I found out I was pregnant that first time I didn't know what to do," she continues, ignoring what I said. "I didn't have any money. I couldn't have paid for an abortion even if I wanted one. I ended up at a church, which is kind of weird if you think about it since you and Dad always hated churches."

Screw the angels, I think to myself.

"They directed me to this church-sponsored home for pregnant teens. It was a great place. Clean. Good food. Your own bed. Hot showers. A doctor who came once a month and gave us checkups.

"After I'd been there a little while, ladies started coming to visit me. They were different than the women who worked there. These ladies were always nicely dressed and perfumed. They always came one at a time. At first they said they were just there to give me someone to talk to, that I should think of them as a sort of mother or an older sister. They'd bring me little things. A candy bar. A lip gloss. Then as time passed they started to talk more and more about the baby and what I was going to do with the baby and how they were so concerned about the baby. The gifts got better, too. Soon I was getting clothes, and CDs, and makeup."

She begins to perk up as she tells the story.

"More time passed and they began to tell me how they couldn't have children of their own but how desperately they wanted children and how much love they had to give. How each one of them had a beautiful home and a beautiful husband and could provide a beautiful life for some poor unfortunate child who would otherwise have a hellish life of poverty and neglect with his worthless piece-of-trash biological mother. Of course they didn't put it in exactly those words. Quite the contrary, they were extremely sympathetic to my situation.

"Right before the baby was born, the gifts reached their peak. I got a fake fox jacket, a Walkman, a pair of suede Nine West ankle boots, and a gold tennis bracelet. The diamonds turned out to be fake but I was an amateur back then.

"I ended up giving the baby to the woman who gave me the boots. It had nothing to do with the boots. I laid the four gifts out on my bed and did Eeny Meeny Miney Moe.

"Once the baby was gone, that was the end of the ladies and the gifts and the church's hospitality. I was out on the streets again, and while I was out there it occurred to me if I got pregnant again I'd be invited back. I'd be warm and well fed and taken care of. More ladies would come bearing gifts. Then I did a little more thinking and thought, why do I need some stupid home for knocked-up girls? I bet I could do a lot better on my own. I bet I can do better than a coat. I bet there are women out there who would buy me a car, maybe even a house in exchange for a baby. I bet there are women out there who might even be willing to skip all this 'pretending to care about each other' bullshit and just give me cash."

She finishes her account. By now her enthusiasm has vanished, and she's returned to her earlier dull detachment.

I feel thoroughly nauseated. I don't blame childless women for trying to find children, and I don't blame teenaged girls for making mistakes that lead to making children they're not prepared to care for, but I can't forgive my sister's lack of compassion for anyone, including herself.

Where did it come from? How did I not see it during all those years we spent together?

"I'm sorry," I tell her. "I'm sorry all that happened to you. But you didn't have to run away in the first place. You could have come to me."

I walk over to her and stroke the top of her head the way I used to when she was little.

"Shannon. I need to know. Did Dad start hurting you again after I left with Clay? Is that why you ran away? Did you blame me for that?"

She looks up at me from the floor.

"You still don't get it, do you? I didn't run away from Dad. I didn't run, period. I left. I went looking for something else. The only reason I didn't do it sooner was because you were there."

"What do you mean?"

"I mean, I wouldn't leave you. You left first."

"That's not fair. I wanted you to come with us."

"Not really. You had Clay to take care of. You put him first and that's the way it should have been. He was your son."

"Please don't talk that way. You know I loved you, too."

"You didn't love me."

"How can you say that?" I ask her, trying to keep my voice from sounding panicked. "I took care of you. I cooked your meals and did your laundry. I read you books and helped you with your homework. I tucked you in at night and nursed you when you were sick."

She doesn't look impressed.

"You did the same stuff for Dad. A guy who treated us like shit. That's not love; that's duty. You were a soldier with an assignment. That's the way I always thought of you. Shae-Lynn the soldier. And I was one of your missions."

She falls silent for a moment when I don't respond.

"When I was a kid, I used to wish you'd be a wreck," she goes on. "Just once I wanted to see you break down and cry, or throw something, or tell Dad to go to hell. It never happened until Clay was born. Then all of a sudden you turned into this rabid mother bear. I used to tell myself you couldn't have loved me because how can you love if you can't feel? You didn't start to feel until Clay was born."

"That's not true," I tell her.

"I know we were kids. I know we were helpless," she adds. "But still. You took it for so long. And then one day, you had the power to stop it. I always wondered if you'd always had the power but you just decided not to use it to save me."

I feel completely at a loss. All I can do is deny her accusations, but I can't find the words to explain why she's wrong.

It wasn't about power. I never had any power. It was about the differences between motherhood and sisterhood.

Clay was my child. My responsibility. He is my creation.

Shannon was my sister. My equal. She is my reflection.

I could mold him, but I could only make changes to her surface.

"I did everything I could for you," I tell her quietly.

She glances up at me and nods.

"Yeah. I guess I know that."

She jangles the handcuffs against the sink's pipes.

"What about now? Can you take these off? I gotta pee."

I catch a glimpse of myself in the mirror above her before I stoop to unlock the cuffs, and I realize she might be right: Maybe I am a soldier, but an ordinary one, not a warrior, living with a soldier's fatigue and limitations and very small chance of glory.

Chapter Twenty-Five

S HANNON DOESN'T SAY A WORD to me during the drive back to my house. She tells me good night once we arrive and goes straight to her room.

I feed Gimp, take a shower, and gratefully exchange my thong and short, tight dress for a pair of old faded pink cotton Hanes panties and some Capitol Police sweats, then begin to pace around my house.

I can't get to my safe place anymore. Ever since I saw the face at the window, I can't find the way. I can't blot out either of my conversations with Cam Jack or Shannon. I can't stop thinking about how I've been used and discarded and how I allowed it to happen. I can't escape.

I'm like a superhero whose secret hideout has been exposed, and now I'm forced to fly around endlessly looking for somewhere anonymous to land.

Dmitri could come back at any time. I know I should stay and protect Shannon; it should be part of my ongoing mission. But after all my years of devoted service, I'm finally going AWOL.

I decide to go see E.J.

I swap my baggy gray sweat pants for a denim miniskirt but keep the sweatshirt.

I think about the Russian as I slip on the Frye boot that he smacked me in the face with yesterday and wonder where the hell he could be.

E.J.'s house is dark, but the light's on in the garage and I hear the radio playing. It's safe. He doesn't entertain lady friends there.

I park my Subaru beside his truck.

The door rolls open before I even announce my presence. A gush of yellow light spills onto the gravel.

He's standing at his grill in a grease-stained white T-shirt, grass-stained jeans ripped at the knees, and his J&P ball cap; he looks great.

"What happened to your face?" he greets me.

I go help myself to a beer before I've been offered one.

"Did you have another go at Choker?" he asks me.

"What is it with Choker? One fight with him and everyone thinks he's my new sparring partner."

I plunk down in a lawn chair.

"I don't want to talk about it."

"So this is one of those visits where you come over because you have something you want to talk about and won't talk about it."

"Yeah."

"George and I are making grilled cheese . . ."

He waves his spatula in the air enticingly.

I smile back at him.

"Sure. I'll have one."

"Did you find Shannon? Dad said you came by the house this morning with Dusty and told him she's missing again."

"Yeah, I found her," I reply, opening my beer and taking a grateful gulp. "I found her with that scumbag lawyer. They're partners. He helps her sell her babies. She does it for a living, E.J. A fucking living. She gets pregnant on purpose and sells her kids. She's been doing it all her life. I have ten nieces and nephews out there going to private schools and being raised by nannies named Consuela."

He looks up from taking two more slices of bread out of the bag and buttering them.

"Are you shitting me? Ten?"

"Yeah."

"Why'd she come back here?"

"She says she's decided to retire, so she's trying to pull off this big scam where she's promising the baby to different families and ripping them off. She says she came to me because she thought it would be a safe place to hide out."

"You bought this?"

"I don't know. I can't come up with any other reason for her to be here. She sure didn't come back to see me. You were right. She couldn't care less. I don't think she's ever cared about anyone."

He slaps a couple pieces of cheese between the bread slices and places them on George, who sizzles softly.

"It's not your fault. She never got to bond with your mom. Maybe it ruined her. Maybe after that she could never bond with anyone."

"Is this one of your mom's theories?"

"Yeah. Is it that obvious?"

"It's obvious it's not yours."

The sandwich is finished. He slides it off the grill and onto a plate and hands it to me. It's a thing of beauty: golden brown and dripping bright orange.

I hadn't realized how hungry I was. I take a bite of the buttery toasted bread and taste the warm melted cheese. It's one of the best things I've ever eaten in my life.

"It's kind of ironic if you stop and think about it," I tell him while I happily chew. "My mom died from having a baby, and the baby that killed her turns out to be able to breed as often and as effortlessly as a brood mare."

"Is that the way you think of Shannon?" he asks, his face taking on a look of concern. "That she killed your mom?"

"No," I answer honestly but my chewing slows as I stop and really consider his question. "At least I don't think so."

"Maybe that's the way Shannon thinks of herself," he says.

"That would be awful."

We both fall silent and eat.

He walks over to me when I finish my sandwich and puts a napkin in my hand. He lets his own hand lie on top of mine for a moment and squeezes. Not hard. Not too quick. Just a steady pressure. I feel all the energy that's left in my tired body rush to my palm. The rest of me is insignificant and would blow away in a breeze if I wasn't anchored to him.

"I got some napkins for you. I know you don't like to use the finger," he says, eyeing the greasy foam Steelers mitt leaning against his lawn chair.

My heart swells with gratitude.

"What's wrong?" he asks me. "You look sick. Was the sandwich okay?"

"It was great. It's . . . thank you," I tell him.

"They're just napkins."

I take a deep breath and say it.

"I think I may have done something unforgivable."

"When? Today?"

"No. It's something unforgivable I've been doing for twenty-three years."

He does the math.

"Does it have to do with Clay?"

I lose my nerve.

"Never mind. It's not important. Besides there's no reason why I should talk to you about it. You weren't even around when I got pregnant with Clay."

"What do you mean I wasn't around? I've always been around. I've never been anywhere else but around."

"You weren't involved in my life."

"Involved in your life? What the hell is that supposed to mean?"

"You know what it means. You stopped hanging around with me when we were in seventh grade and you didn't start hanging around with me again until I came back from D.C. My dad's funeral was the first time we'd talked in years. You took me out for a beer. Remember?"

"Yeah, I remember," he says and walks away from me toward the fridge to get himself another beer.

I watch the door open and his head and torso disappear behind it until I'm left staring at his bent-over backside, a view I've always secretly enjoyed.

"You were weird that day," I say to his butt and the hand holding open the refrigerator door. "You kept making these bad jokes. I didn't understand it. I thought you should be a little more upset and a little more respectful of a fellow miner being blown to bits. Do you remember the toast you made when we had our beers?"

He straightens up again, rips the top off a can, and holds it aloft.

"To Hank Penrose. May he rest in pieces."

"Real funny."

"What did you want from me? You wanted me to like him? To respect him?"

"What are you talking about?"

"Maybe I was a little weird that day because, like you said, I knew I should have been upset, but I was happy."

"How can you say that?"

His face clouds over and he slams the door shut.

He walks over to his workbench and taps a cigarette out of a pack of Marlboros.

"Because I hated him. Because he deserved to be dead. Because I should have killed him myself a long time ago."

He looks terribly angry; then for a moment he looks embarrassed by what he just said, but the anger quickly reappears.

He lights the cigarette and smokes thoughtfully. It seems to calm him, but then he suddenly looks over at me and his face is contorted with a mix of emotions I've never seen there before: rage, grief, impotence.

"I was a coward. Don't you understand? I couldn't stand to see what he did to you, but I couldn't do anything about it. I was a little kid. Then I started getting older and all I could think about was how I could hurt him. How I could fight back for you. But I was still a coward. Even though I'd sit in school and daydream about bashing his face in with a two-by-four, I knew I couldn't do it. I didn't have the guts to do it. So I just started staying away from you. It was too hard to see you. If I wasn't man enough to save you, I thought it was better to let you find someone who was."

He finishes his confession. I think it's the most words he's ever said to me at one time in our lives.

I don't know how to respond. I always thought it was my breasts that ruined everything. I thought he couldn't be my friend anymore because I turned into a girl, but I didn't turn into the kind of girl he wanted for a girlfriend.

"I didn't need to be saved," I tell him.

"Stop it!" he shouts at me.

He stubs out his cigarette and crosses the garage to where I'm sitting. He grabs me by my arms and pulls me up, close to him. I feel the fabric of his jeans brush against my bare knees and the damp heat of his breath on my face as he speaks.

"Stop being so tough all the time. Someone should've saved you. I should've saved you."

He was my dad, I think to myself. You never could've saved me. It's always been too late.

"Save me now," I tell him.

"How?"

"Get me through this night."

Our bodies are already touching; our lips are only inches away from each other, yet neither one of us seems capable of doing more or doing less. We're paralyzed by memories of all the times we could have kissed and didn't and trying to figure out why this time should be different.

E.J. makes the decision, and I feel the same rush of loving gratitude that I felt when he handed me the napkin.

He presses his lips against mine and holds them there, testing. Satisfied with the results, he pushes his tongue between them. I still can't respond. I feel his hands push up under my dress and his fingers crawl beneath my panties and start tugging them down.

His kiss becomes more urgent and something inside me shatters. I hear the sound in my mind as clearly as glass breaking.

I grab his T-shirt and yank stupidly at it. He interrupts our kiss long enough to strip it off over his head. His ball cap goes flying. I've crossed a new threshold of importance.

I dig my fingers into his hair. I run my hands over his arms, shoulders, and back. I want to touch every inch of his flesh. I want to feel my bare flesh crushed into his. I want to leave a permanent indentation.

His hands move beneath my skirt, then he pushes them under my sweatshirt and unhooks my bra. He cups my breasts and rubs his callused thumbs across my nipples. His touch sends a jolt of longing through me that lodges in my womb. A spray of heat that I see in my mind as white sparks from red molten steel settles into my blood. It spreads quickly, liquifying my bones, and for the first time in my life I understand the word "swoon."

He pulls off my shirt and I step out of my skirt and I'm left standing in a dark garage in nothing but a pair of harness boots and pink cotton panties.

He smiles at me and for a terrible, panicked moment, my intellect kicks in and starts to recite all the reasons why I shouldn't have sex with him: because I love him; because we can never be friends again after this; because it could never work out between us. We could never be a couple. He could never be happy with just me. He'd never ask me to marry him. I don't want him to ask me to marry him. I don't want to get married. Why don't I want to get married? Why won't he ask me to marry him? I'm going to be just another notch on his bedpost. What about my bedpost? I'm not going to be good enough. I'm going to be too good. Why did he wait this long? Why is he doing it now? Why didn't he do this when I had a twenty-year-old body instead of a forty-year-old body? Thank God he didn't do this when I had a twenty-year-old's brain.

He doesn't give me any time to consider any of my fears. He lays me down on the couch and yanks off my boots while kissing my legs. When he reaches my thighs, I sit up and unfasten his jeans and slip my hands inside them, over his ass, gripping him and pulling him down between my legs.

After a lifetime of trying to get men to caress, stroke, lick, and suck, tonight all I feel is a deep primal ache to be filled.

I take him in my hand and guide him inside me.

I can't help thinking of Shannon's hurtful words: How can I love if I can't feel? But I *do* feel. I am feeling.

I still try to find my way back to my safe place. I can't help it. It's instinct. But this trip is different. For the first time I see what the purpose of my furnished soul has become, no longer to shelter me from monsters but to help me cope with the emptiness of a ransacked heart.

I relax and join in E.J.'s rhythm. I can go back but I choose not to. I don't have to. I can stay here and find the same thing.

I know now it was his face at my window, not trying to get in but telling me it's time to come out.

Chapter Twenty-Six

THE SOUND OF TIRES on gravel wakes me. It wakes E.J., too. We've fallen asleep on the couch. Some time during the night he got up and got a blanket for us. We're wrapped up tight in it. The garage is cold but we have a delicious amount of body heat trapped inside our cocoon.

We both sit up in unison. I can barely see him in the dark, but somehow I can make out the concerned expression on his face.

"That's Lib's truck," he says.

"You know the sound of his truck?"

He gets up and pulls on his jeans.

"What time is it?" I ask him.

"Almost three."

He stops on his way out to give me a quick kiss. I take this as a good sign.

"I'll be right back," he says.

I wait until he's gone out the back door, then I wrap myself in the blanket and go open a window so I can eavesdrop.

Lib's standing next to his truck.

The grass behind him is covered with a silver frosty dew that glimmers softly in the blurred moonlight like metal shavings spilled across the yard.

E.J. picks his way across the gravel drive in his bare feet. He forgot to take a shirt. I pull the blanket tighter. Just looking at him makes me colder.

"What's going on?" E.J. asks.

Lib looks from E.J. shivering in nothing but his jeans to my car sitting in his driveway in the middle of the night but makes no comment.

"I'm sorry about this," he says. "I know you gotta go to work in a couple hours."

Lib's better dressed for the weather. He has on a camouflage hunting jacket and a pair of heavy boots.

"I thought I could wait until tomorrow to tell all of you. That was my plan. I thought we could all get together at Jimmy's place and have a meeting. But it's driving me crazy. I can't sleep. I can't talk to Teresa about it because she's a woman and she can't understand what I've got to say."

He reaches inside his coat pocket and pulls out a pack of cigarettes. He hands one to E.J. and lights it for him before lighting his own.

"The lawyer called. We heard back from Cam Jack today. If we go through with the lawsuit, he's going to declare bankruptcy and close the mines."

They stand in silence. I watch the orange tips of their cigarettes rise and fall away from their mouths.

"I went and talked to him. The lawyer. He kept going on and on about Cam Jack's mines and what he's going to do with his mines and how he's choosing to operate his mines. And I started to get really pissed. I swear I was seeing red. His mines. The man's never set foot in a single one of them. I'm the one who's spent my life inside Jojo. I'm the one who knows her. He may own her, but she's not his."

E.J. smokes and nods.

"And he'd close her. I'm sure he would. He'd close her just like that. He doesn't care. He doesn't care about the men who are gonna lose their jobs and he also doesn't care about her. She doesn't want to sit around useless. Her and Beverly. It's gonna happen one of these days but it's not fair to do it to them already. They've both been through a lot."

Another bout of silence passes between them.

E.J. must be cold but he won't show it in front of Lib. Lib must know E.J.'s cold but he won't embarrass him by asking if he is.

Lib shifts his weight from one foot to the other and looks up at the sky. No stars tonight. No moon. Only a layer of clouds that makes the night seem wrapped in gray gauze.

"The whole time we were trapped down there," he says, "I never had a bad thought about her. I never blamed her. I never hated the mine."

E.J. continues nodding.

"What do you think we should do?" Lib asks.

"Doesn't sound like you want to close your mine," E.J. replies.

"Our mine."

"You have to remember I'm slightly biased here because I'd like to keep my job."

"The lawyer's estimating we could each get a couple hundred grand from the sale of the equipment. That's about six years of your salary right now." *$ 33,333 a yr!*

E.J. finishes his cigarette and tosses it onto the stones.

"I've been doing this job since I graduated high school. I've bitched and moaned about Cam Jack just like everyone else does. How he makes a fortune while we take home a lousy fifteen dollars an hour. How we haven't had a raise in almost ten years now. How our health benefits have been cut and our 401(k)s slashed to hell.

"And it's all true and I suppose it's not fair and maybe there are people out there who got the time to dwell on it. But what it all comes down to for me is this: I love my job, and I figure it's better to get screwed doing a job I love than to get amply rewarded doing something I hate."

"So what's your vote?" Lib asks him.

"Fuck him. I got better ways to spend my time than sitting in lawyers' offices and courtrooms."

"Amen to that."

They shake hands.

E.J. claps Lib on the back.

"Get some sleep, boss."

"I'll do that. And what about you? What are you getting tonight?"

He doesn't answer right away. I can't see his face so I don't know if he's smiling.

"An education," he says.

He remains standing calmly in the middle of the driveway with his hands in his pockets until Lib's taillights wink out of sight around a bend in the road, then he races back inside the garage, cursing the stones tearing at his bare feet.

"Jesus, it's cold," he says, trying to take his jeans off while he hops up and down to get warm.

"You spying on us?" he asks me.

"Yep."

"What do you think?"

I walk over to him and wrap his naked body up in the blanket with me.

"I think Jojo's a lucky girl."

Chapter Twenty-Seven

I WAKE FROM A TERRIBLE DREAM. In it I'm wandering through a field full of flowers as tall as I am with faces of girls and halos of sharp purple petals that cut like knives when I brush against them. Their eyes and mouths are open in frightful expressive pain, but they make no sound and I sense they can't see.

Snuffling, filthy hogs and emaciated, iron-eyed cows are feeding off them, leaving behind bloody scars as they tear leaves from their thick writhing stems ending in ropes of twisted fleshy roots clutching the muddy topsoil.

I try to scare off the cows and pigs but nothing will make them leave. I scream and shout. I clap my hands. I kick at them. I try to drag them away. I find a big stick and beat at them. They're immune to everything I try.

Suddenly I understand that it's too late and the impervious livestock are telling me not to waste my time. The plant-girls are already dead, yet somehow alive and suffering horribly, but no one can help them so no one should care.

The dream leaves me disoriented, and I'm not sure where I am when I wake up.

My head still hurts from being pistol-whipped. I reach behind my ear and gingerly touch the knot there, and notice E.J., fully dressed and whistling, standing not far from me, clamping the lid onto his dinner bucket.

I look up at the faintly lit sky through the window and a small surge of panic passes through me as I realize he could be late for his shift.

"What are you doing?" I ask him.

"Hey. I tried not to wake you."

"You're going to be late."

He shoves a last bite of toast into his mouth and washes it down with a gulp of coffee.

"I'm fine. I think I know by now how much time I need to drive to my job."

"Are you sure you're not going to be late?"

He takes a step toward me.

"What's wrong with you, Shae-Lynn?"

I get up, slip into his T-shirt from last night, and move past him to his dinner bucket. I pick it up in order to hold it out to him. The weight is so familiar, even though I haven't held one for twenty years.

"I could've packed it for you."

"I've been packing it for myself for twenty years. It's okay."

"Are you sure?"

"Hey," he says gently and takes the pail from me. "You don't have to take care of me that way. You want George to make you some bacon?"

"Why? Are you saying I can't cook?"

"For Christ's sake, what is with you?" His voice turns rough. "I know you can't cook. I can't either. That's why we have George."

I like the way he said "we."

"I thought you'd be in a good mood this morning," he goes on. "I thought last night would've settled you down."

"Settled me down? Is that why you did it? It was some kind of public service. Maybe if E.J. bangs Shae-Lynn it'll settle her down."

He slips on his coat and grabs his pail.

"I don't have time for this."

"You mean you don't have time for me. You mean I'm not worth it," I rip into him as I run after him heading for his truck. "Maybe if I was twenty-five and blond maybe then you would've woke up and needed to fuck me instead of jumping up off the couch and running to pack your lunch and leave . . ."

He whirls around on me and silences me with a look.

"Oh, yeah. And maybe if I was a senator or a ball player or some fucked-up teenaged prince you wouldn't have slept through me getting up off the couch and you'd be prancing around in a harem girl costume for me right now serving me beer out of a solid gold pitcher."

"Harem girl? You want a harem girl?"

"No, I don't want a harem girl. I live in the real world. I have a real life and a real life is having a job and having to get there on time. Real life is having your old boss come by at three *a.m.* and wake you up and then going back to bed and getting the daylights fucked out of you by a girl you've loved your whole life and then falling fast asleep and over-sleeping so you're running late and don't have time to wake her up and fuck her again before you leave."

"Are you saying I don't live in the real world?"

He looks frustrated enough to hit me but instead he turns his back on me and stares out at the horizon. Most of the clouds have cleared away. The sun has yet to make an appearance from behind the mountains, but the indigo night is beginning to fade into a predawn pinkish blue. Soon the remaining tatters of clouds will be lit from underneath and the sky will look smeared with peach butter.

"You want to fight," he says flatly. "You love to fight. I don't want to fight."

"You mean you don't want me."

He shakes his head but won't look at me.

"I want you. I don't want your crap."

I watch him walk away from me and drive off into a pink chrome sunrise before I go back inside the garage to get dressed.

I stop at the Snappy's on my way home.

I buy one of every snack cake on their shelves along with a couple bags of chips and a box of Lucky Charms cereal.

I open the cereal while I'm sitting in the car in the parking lot and start picking out the marshmallow pieces and popping them into my mouth between sips of a steaming cup of coffee while I think about E.J.

He's stepping into his coal-stained coveralls and pulling them up over his long underwear right about now. He's putting on his knee pads, pushing his feet inside his steel-toed rubber boots, and slipping on his rain gear and his leather tool belt with his name and social security number inscribed on a brass plate. He's grabbing his battered helmet with a peeling American flag sticker on the back and going outside to have a final smoke before heading into the mine.

It's the same helmet he wore when he was trapped. It made it out with him, and he won't wear another.

I think about my politician, my Frenchman, my prince, my third baseman, my Marine, my farm boy, and all the others. I never knew how any of them spent their days, and I didn't care as long as they stayed safe.

I've followed E.J. down into the cold black depths of Jojo before it sinks in that he said he's loved me all his life.

I close up the box of cereal and rip open a pack of RingDings before I start my car.

Sometimes I can be a real left-laner.

THE DAY PASSES at a snail's pace. I have a fair amount of business but my thoughts don't move at all. They're parked at the foot of two large hills of depression: one formed from regret for the way I treated E.J.

this morning and the other formed from the dread I feel over what's going to happen tonight between Clay and Cam and me.

I think about not going tonight and pretending my conversation with Cam Jack never happened, but I know Cam will make good on his threat and see Clay on his own if I don't bring him. I've thought about packing up my few belongings and Gimp and hitting the road so I never have to face Clay again, but I know I can't do that either. I've thought about sitting down with Clay and calmly discussing the truth about my childhood and the choices I made during my teen years that led to my pregnancy, and my decision to have a baby and keep the identity of his father secret from him, but the thought of doing this is what makes the idea of packing up my car and running away so appealing.

I keep telling myself I shouldn't be upset by the thought of Clay finding out. I have nothing to be embarrassed or ashamed about.

I told Cam Jack I was going to have his baby. I didn't keep this information from him. He was the one who rejected me and his unborn son. He was the one who told me he never wanted to hear from us. He was the one who said he'd deny having been with me. Again he threatened to blackball my dad. He said I was a slut. Said the baby probably wasn't his anyway. Said I was a greedy, lazy little hillbilly who was only after his money.

At the time I didn't care about justice. I knew in a fair world he should have been financially obligated to help support his son and should have been a father to him, but I also knew I didn't live in a fair world.

I didn't care about revenge either. I understood the futility of a poor nobody teenaged girl trying to publicly expose a rich powerful man and cause a scandal. I knew it wouldn't work. I knew that people like Cam Jack always bought their way out of problems, always managed to turn the victim into the culprit.

But I did care that he thought I was lazy.

He showed his true colors to me, and I was convinced Clay and I would be better off without him in our lives. My only interest was protecting Clay. I did what I thought was right. My motives were pure and noble. So why am I afraid?

Because now, with twenty-three more years of life behind me, I'm not so sure I was so selfless. Did I make this decision thinking of Clay's best interest or my bruised pride? Did I deprive my son of the possibility of ever knowing his father simply because his father called me names?

I'm afraid Clay isn't going to understand, because I'm not so sure I understand anymore either. And if he doesn't understand, I don't know what I will do.

A mother's love is not warm and cuddly like a soft blanket as it's popularly portrayed. It's a fierce, rabid love, like having a mad dog living inside you all the time. If it's rejected, it can't be locked away and left to slowly starve to death over time, but has to be yanked out immediately and murdered.

I don't know how any woman survives this.

It's almost four in the afternoon and I still haven't found the nerve to call him when I get a call from him.

"Hi, Mom. Do you have a minute? I could use your help with something."

"Sure," I answer with my heart in my throat.

"I'm out at Meade Mercer's place. He called about this little girl beating the crap out of one of his dogs with a big stick. Fortunately I was in the area so I could take care of it and prevent it from becoming something much bigger than it needs to be."

I laugh.

"You're always in the area, Clay. Do you realize that? We're going to have to put it on your tombstone: Here lies Clayton James Penrose. Beloved son and deputy. Fortunately, he was in the area."

He doesn't respond, and it suddenly occurs to me for the first time since he became a deputy and started always being in the area that maybe he's in the area because of me. Could he be keeping an eye on me?

"When I asked her what her name is and where she lives so I can take her and her brother home she said she didn't have to tell me," he goes on. "She gave me your business card and said to contact you instead. I think she wants you to act as her lawyer."

He pauses.

"Does any of this make sense to you?"

"Yes, I know who she is."

"Great. Who is she?"

"Why don't you let me take care of it? I can be there in ten minutes. I don't want to break cabbie confidentiality."

Meade Mercer has a skinny, crooked, sprawling farm that's been carved out of several hundred wooded acres on either side of Route 12 about ten miles to the east of Jolly Mount proper. His cows are precariously scattered on steep green hillsides along with an occasional gnarled, wind-warped tree and a couple of retired, shaggy workhorses.

The barn and the house are almost completely stripped of their original white paint. A sprinkling of flakes is all that remains, but it clings stubbornly to their gray weathered sides like a bad case of wood dandruff.

Meade is standing with Clay next to the road at the bottom of the driveway leading to his house. He's wearing a blue and gray checked shirt with the sleeves rolled up to his elbows and a pair of gray work pants, shiny at the knees, stained with a half dozen substances ranging from cow's blood to axle grease.

I've known Meade since I was a little girl. I used to bring Shannon over here to play with his barn cats.

He takes off his ball cap when I get out of the car and start walking toward them. He's bald and has a face like a big, pale raisin.

Fanci's leaning against Clay's cruiser with her arms crossed belligerently across her chest. Kenny is sitting inside their red wagon holding the dog-beating stick across his lap.

A big brown mutt with a square jaw and red-rimmed eyes lies in the grass, panting, about twenty feet away from us. He looks more exhausted than injured.

"What happened?" I ask.

Meade takes out a handkerchief from one of his pants pockets, wipes the top of his head with it, and puts his cap back on.

He spits a brown stream of tobacco behind him and enlightens me.

"That little girl over there beat the bejesus out of Roger with a stick, that's what happened."

"I assume Roger's the dog."

"Course."

"I think she might be afraid of dogs," I tell them confidentially.

"A kid who's afraid of dogs might hit a dog once to get him to go away. She beat the bejesus out of him. I had to stop her," Meade explains.

"Who is she?" Clay asks me.

"Her name's Fanci. That's her brother, Kenny. They're Choker Simms' kids."

Both men look at her. Both of their faces remain impassive. I can't see Clay's eyes behind his sunglasses or Meade's eyes hidden in the shadow of the bill of his cap but the way Meade's chewing slows down and the way Clay clears his throat show more sympathy than a flood of words from most men.

I walk over to Fanci.

She has on her glittery plastic shoes and a pair of tight sweatpants in a satiny turquoise material that's been snagged in a lot of places and a matching zip-up jacket with a racing stripe. Her nails are painted silver and she's wearing silver eye shadow, too.

"Kenny's afraid of dogs," she tells me.

"No, I ain't," Kenny pipes up.

"A dog bit him once and now he's afraid of them," she explains.

"A dog bit me once," he confirms, "and now she's afraid of them."

"I'm not afraid of dogs."

"You are, too."

"If I was afraid of dogs would I be able to beat them up?"

"You got a big stick. They got nothing."

"They got teeth."

"You got teeth, too."

She shakes her head in exasperation.

"You see how dumb he is?" she asks me.

"So what happened with the dog, exactly?" I try again.

"He came at us."

"Of course he did," Meade says as he joins us. "That's what he's supposed to do."

"Is Roger on a chain?" I ask.

"He don't need a chain. He knows he's not allowed to go on the road. If she'd've stayed on the road he would've never come at her."

"I *was* on the road," Fanci shouts at Meade. "I told you. He came at us when we were on the road."

"But he would've stopped at the road," Meade tells her.

"How was I supposed to know he was gonna stop? He looked like he was gonna kill us."

"That's what he's supposed to look like."

The two of them lock eyes. Meade breaks the stare first. He turns and spits again.

He's reached the moment when he has to decide if he's going to go easy on her because he knows what kind of man her father is or if he's going to go hard on her because he knows what kind of man her father is.

"You go on home," he tells her, "but I don't want you to come by here no more. He's a good dog. He was doing his job."

"Is that okay with you, Deputy?" I ask Clay.

He nods his assent.

"How about I give you and Kenny a ride?" I say to Fanci.

"We don't want to go home just yet."

I think about the great heap of my sister lying in my guest room like a belligerent whale. I was only home long enough to change my clothes, but she shouted more obscenities at me than I usually hear in a year.

She's ready to blow. I told her to call me if she starts having contractions.

I don't want to go home either. At least not alone.

"How about coming to my house?" I suggest. "We'll make some popcorn and watch a movie?"

"You got anything good?"

"I think I have something you'll like."

Clay puts the wagon in the back of my car.

I take the opportunity to ask him if he can meet me tonight in front of the J&P building at seven. I can't get up the nerve to tell him why.

I tell him it's a surprise. He tells me he has to work until ten but he can take a break at seven.

Fanci is waiting for me at the front of the car looking like she wants to say something. I assume it's going to be a disappointed comment about my ensemble or lack of one: jeans, my Frye boots, a Capitol Police T-shirt, and my dad's old J&P windbreaker with PENROSE written across the back in yellow block letters.

She fixes me with a pair of dark, defiant eyes.

"Truth is maybe the dog would've gone away but Kenny called it," she says finally.

"Here doggie. Here doggie," she calls out suddenly with exaggerated enthusiasm, grinning idiotically, and clapping her hands on her thighs in what I assume is an imitation of her brother.

"Why would he do that?" I ask her. "I thought you said he was bit by a dog once. Shouldn't he be afraid?"

She shakes her head.

"He was real little. He don't remember, but I do. He don't understand about things that can hurt him. He still trusts everything."

"I suppose it's not good to trust everything," I agree, "but it's not good to not trust everything, either."

"It's my job to protect him."

"Yes it is, but it's also your job to teach him how to decide what he should trust and what he shouldn't. It's called having good judgment."

She asks if she can sit up front this time. I'm not sure if she reaches the legal height and weight requirement for a front seat passenger in a vehicle equipped with air bags but I figure the drive can't be fraught with any more danger than every moment of the rest of her life outside my car.

"What's all this?" she asks me, shifting her feet around in the garbage on the floor of my car.

I glance at the snack cake wrappers and empty bags of chips.

"I'm working on my anti-stress badge."

Chapter Twenty-Eight

I'M STANDING IN MY KITCHEN waiting for the microwave pop-corn to finish popping while Kenny and Fanci are arguing in front of my TV over whether they'll watch *Pirates of the Caribbean*, *Naked Gun*, or *Bambi* when the shouting starts. It comes from Shannon's room, where Shannon is supposed to be taking a nap, and is comprised almost entirely of cuss words.

I start heading toward her room but she meets me in the hall with a wild look in her eyes.

"What's going on?"

"My water broke."

"Ah, great. That's just great."

All I can think about is the mess and the expense. I'll have to get a new pullout sofa. Nobody's going to want to sleep on old amniotic fluid.

"Come on. I'll drive you to the hospital."

"No."

"What do you mean, no?"

She leans forward and braces herself against the wall while drawing in a gasp of pain.

"It's too late," she pants.

"What do you mean, it's too late?"

"Once my water breaks, my babies come pretty fast."

She puts one hand under her immense belly and holds on to the guest room doorjamb with the other.

"What are you looking at?" she screams at me. "I told you I was going to have the baby today."

"I thought you were joking. No one knows exactly when they're going to have a baby."

"I do."

"Then why didn't you make plans?"

"These are my plans."

"To have it here?"

"You were a cop. You know how to deliver babies."

"I also know how to do body cavity searches. It doesn't mean I want to do them."

She lets out a shriek.

"Okay. Come on. Let's calm down," I tell her.

"Little girl," she shouts over my shoulder, "get me some blankets."

I turn around and find Fanci standing behind me.

"No," I tell her. "We're not going to ruin my blankets. Go in the shed out back. There's a big blue tarp."

"I'm not having my baby on a tarp," she screams at me.

"Yes, you are," I scream back.

I feel a tug on my jeans. Two big, frightened eyes are staring up at me.

"I want to go home," Kenny says.

"No," Shannon barks at him and starts lumbering toward him. "Nobody's going anywhere."

He ducks behind my legs.

Fanci hasn't moved yet. Shannon pins her against the wall with her belly.

"This is what happens when you have sex, little girl," she snarls at her. "If you have sex this is what's going to happen to you."

Fanci's impressive composure shatters. Her face becomes a mask of pure childish terror. She wriggles free of Shannon's bulk and sprints out of the house toward the shed.

"Oh, God," Shannon moans.

"We have to boil water," I tell Kenny.

"She wants Cup-a-Soup?"

"No, it's to sterilize things."

"What's that?"

I start rummaging through my house looking for anything useful. I get a knife, scissors, salad tongs, clothespins, a bottle of whiskey.

Kenny follows me around like a puppy while Gimp remains firmly entrenched beneath the kitchen table.

"What do you need that for?" he asks about the Jack Daniel's.

"We might have to hit her over the head."

"Why are you smiling?"

"Because this is a happy time," I tell him honestly, even after I push aside the image of knocking Shannon unconscious with a bottle of JD. "This is fun. This is good. When this is all over, we're going to have a baby."

He doesn't look all that convinced, but he trots after me as we take our equipment into Shannon's room.

She's sitting propped up on the bed with every pillow in my house behind her, blowing out air like a stalled locomotive.

"You're going to ruin my pillows," I moan.

"I'll buy you new pillows," she spits at me. "I'll buy you a new bed. I'll buy you a new fucking house."

"Watch your language," I tell her. "There's a little kid here."

"You think I care about a fucking little kid? Why is there a little kid here?"

"Can we hit her yet?" Kenny asks.

"Not yet."

Fanci shows up, almost as out of breath as Shannon. She's holding a bright blue plastic tarp in her outstretched arms.

"No way," Shannon shouts when she sees it. "I'm having a baby, not pitching a freakin' tent."

"Just set it there, Fanci," I tell her. "Can you go get a cold, wet washcloth?"

"Oh, God," Shannon screams.

She grips the comforter until her knuckles turn white.

"Are you okay? Maybe I should call an ambulance. One could be here in a half hour."

"No! I'm fine. There's nothing wrong. What do you expect? It hurts. Don't you remember?"

"How far apart are your contractions?"

"I don't know. Do you see me sitting here with a stopwatch? I guess a couple minutes."

Fanci returns.

"Put it on her forehead," I tell her.

She gives me a look of absolute disbelief.

"Do it," I command her.

She moves hesitatingly toward Shannon's side and gingerly places the washcloth on her forehead the way she might pet a cobra.

"Okay," I tell my sister, "let's see what's going on here."

Fanci and Kenny spend the next twenty minutes standing near the door doing their best not to look at Shannon while the contractions grow closer together. I tell them they can go into another room, but they want to stay. I tell them they can sit down, but they want to stand. Kenny leaves once and comes back with the bag of popcorn. Every time Shannon screams, Fanci turns paler and Kenny plugs his ears with his buttered fingers.

When Shannon starts pushing, her face turns a deep purplish red and a blue vein pops out on her forehead. Amazingly, she still manages to have enough energy to swear and scream despite the effort it takes to expel an eight-pound human being from her uterus.

I try to be as encouraging as I can and I try to keep her focused on the work, not the pain.

"There's the top of his head," I say excitedly.

Kenny shows some interest, but Fanci looks like she's going to faint.

"Wait, Shannon. Wait for the contraction. Bear down with the contraction."

"Go to hell! Are you telling me how to have a baby? You've only had one. Big fucking deal."

"You're going to tear," I tell her. "You want me to cut you?"

I hold up the knife so she can see it.

"I'd be happy to cut you."

"Don't cut me. I don't need to be cut. Just let me push it out. I want it out. I want it out. Out. Out. Out."

"I don't get it," Fanci speaks for the first time since bringing the washcloth. "What are you talking about? Where are you going to cut her? Where is it coming out?"

"You know what you've got between your legs, little girl," Shannon tells her through gritted teeth while her vein pulses ominously on her forehead. "Use your imagination."

Fanci's waxen face takes on a tinge of green.

"That's impossible," she says.

"You're almost there, Shannon. You're almost there. Here's his head. I see his face. Oh my God, there's his little face. A shoulder."

I cradle the tiny head and put my hand out as the rest of the body enters the world. He's perfect. And he's a she.

"It's a girl," I cry.

Kenny comes running over.

"How can you tell?" he asks excitedly.

Fanci stays where she is.

"Congratulations," she says weakly.

Her knees finally give out, and she sits down hard on the floor.

"What's wrong with her?" Kenny's enthusiasm wanes. "She's covered in gunk. Why is she purple? She's all wrinkly and ugly."

"She's not ugly," I defend her as I busy myself cleaning her off and making sure she can breathe.

Her eyes are wide open and staring but she hasn't made a peep yet.

"What is that?" Kenny shouts suddenly.

"The umbilical cord," I explain. "It brought the baby food while she was inside her mom."

Kenny rushes over to his sister, grabs her by the hand, and tries to drag her to her feet.

"Fanci, you gotta see this. It's the grossest thing ever."

She stays on the floor.

"Fanci, come here. I need someone to hold the baby while I cut the umbilical cord."

"Cut?"

"Come on. You don't have to watch if you don't want to."

She gets up reluctantly and walks toward me, making certain not to look at Shannon. I have a towel draped over Shannon's legs. I put one over the placenta, too.

"Sit on the bed. Put this towel on your lap and hold her there," I instruct her.

She does what she's told.

She takes the baby and peers into her face.

"She is wrinkly and ugly. Why is she so skinny? I thought babies were supposed to be pudgy. Kenny was pudgy when he came home from the hospital. And he was a nice color, too. And he smelled good."

"She's going to look that way, too," I tell her.

The baby begins to cry.

344

"She's crying. She hates you," Kenny says gleefully to his sister.

"Shut up," Fanci snaps at him. "Why's she crying?"

"We want her to cry. It's good for her lungs. It's what she's supposed to do."

"What's her name?" Kenny asks.

"Babies aren't born with names, stupid," Fanci responds, a little of her old cockiness returning. "Someone has to name them."

"Can we name her?"

"It's not up to us," I explain.

"Can she see? Can she see us?" Kenny leans over her and waves. "Hi, little baby."

She continues crying, and he looks up at me.

"She wants her mom," he states knowingly.

"Okay. I have a few other things to clean up. Why don't you two go into the other room and I'll be with you in a couple minutes."

I take the baby and swaddle her in a pillowcase. I don't have any baby blankets and a towel seems too rough.

I rock her in my arms and coo at her. She starts to calm down.

"She's going to be hungry," I say to Shannon.

"There's formula and bottles in my car," she replies dully.

I hold out the baby to her.

"I don't want to hold her."

"Come on," I urge her.

Maybe if she holds her, she'll keep her, I think to myself. Maybe she's never held one of her children. Maybe that's been the problem.

She won't even look at her.

"I said, I don't want to hold her."

"She's beautiful."

"Of course, she's beautiful. I always make beautiful babies. Lucky for me."

"Can I get you anything?"

"I've got Tylenol with Codeine in my bag for the after contractions. And I could use a glass of water."

"Why don't you let me call a doctor?"

"Why? I'm fine."

"You don't know that for sure."

The memory of Mom dying in her bed fills my head. A complication of childbirth. The angels taking her to live with Jesus. I nestle the baby tighter against my chest and remember holding Shannon the same way. I remember the terror I felt looking at Mom's dead, staring eyes. I tried to ignore them. I kept talking to her. I sat beside her and kept touching her cold arm. Long after I knew it was hopeless, I kept pretending. Long after I knew in my heart I would never feel safe again, I kept living.

I always believed Shannon was immune to all of it. She was too little. She couldn't possibly have known what was going on. She couldn't have felt what I felt. She never knew Mom. She never knew love. She couldn't miss what she never had.

I never stopped to think that the not-having part could be worse than anything else.

"Don't worry about me," she says, staring out the window yet reading my thoughts. "I'm not going to die like Mom. I'm not a wimp."

Chapter Twenty-Nine

CLAY IS WAITING FOR ME outside the J&P Building when I arrive.

I'm in a pretty good mood all things considered. I left mother and daughter sleeping soundly. I pulled a drawer out of my dresser, emptied it, and made a makeshift crib for the baby.

Shannon still didn't have any interest in holding her or feeding her but she promised me she'd take care of her if she woke up while I was gone. She said the baby needed to be in good shape for when she sold her. It was the only moment during the couple hours after the birth where I felt a twinge of dread.

Fanci agreed to stay and watch over them for a nominal fee. I made her call and clear it with her dad, who wasn't home. I told her to keep all the doors locked and not to open them for anyone and if a bald guy with a big black mustache showed up to call 911 first, then me.

Kenny listened solemnly to my instructions and informed me they'd be fine as long as Fanci had her stick.

Seeing Clay, I'm flooded with memories of him as an infant. He was a good baby. He hardly ever cried. He had the most intense gaze. Whenever I'd talk to him, he'd furrow his silky little brow and clench and unclench his tiny fists while he studied every part of my face.

I thought he was trying to commit it to memory and I'd assure him that I'd always be around. I wouldn't ever leave him. He wouldn't ever have to try and remember me.

I'm feeling so good I can almost even be optimistic about our meeting with Cam Jack. Maybe something positive can come from finally having the truth out in the open. I don't have anything to fear. This is my boy. He will understand.

"I still don't get this. Why all the secrecy? Why are we seeing Cam Jack in the first place?" he asks me again as we're walking up the shadowy, silent, plush staircase.

Despite my mood, I'm still not brimming with enough confidence to tell him the truth, although I know I should and I know I'm going to regret not doing it.

"What's it about? Do you know him?"

"Not exactly."

Cam's office door is wide open tonight.

From the moment we crest the staircase, we can see him at the end of the corridor, sitting behind his massive desk, talking on the phone.

We pause in the doorway and he waves us in.

"I don't get it," he says into the phone. "The poster says, 'How can there be too many children? That's like saying there's too many flowers.' What the hell is that supposed to mean?"

He listens for a moment.

"There sure as hell can be too many flowers. There can be too many kids, too. People in general. You ever been to India?"

He listens again, nodding.

"No. I haven't either but I've seen pictures."

More listening.

"Well, it's not my concern, Bill. Not my concern at all. Just thought I'd give you some feedback long as I had you on the horn. You take care now."

He hangs up and smiles at us.

"Friend of mine," he explains. "Running for Congress. Has these pro-lifers supporting him. Some of the slogans they come up with."

He shakes his head, then gets up from his desk. He's in a pair of navy suit pants, a white shirt with the sleeves rolled up to his elbows, and a gold power tie loose around his neck. He walks toward Clay to shake his hand.

"So here he is. One of Laurel County's finest."

I hold my breath. I don't know what I expect to happen when they make physical contact, if I expect Clay to burst into flames or for a cartoon anvil to fall on Cam's head.

Nothing happens. I let out my breath.

"It's a pleasure to meet you, Mr. Jack," Clay says innocently.

The genuine smile on his face and the sincerity in his voice make me hate myself more than I ever thought possible.

I was so caught up thinking about my own discomfort, my own shame, my own fear, I didn't think about Clay at all.

He's unprepared. I've set him up for the biggest shock of his life and he's going to experience it in front of a total stranger who's also his dad.

"Mr. Jack?" Cam asks and shoots me a questioning glance. "There's no need to be so formal. You can call me Cam."

"Well, thank you."

Clay looks pleased with himself.

I want to die.

"This is really a lucky coincidence for me that it turns out my mom knows you," he continues. "I just came up with the idea a couple days ago about contacting you in the hopes that you'd help find a job for one of your former miners, Dusty Spangler. He was one of the Jolly Mount Five. He has a wife and three young children and has had a hard time getting back on his feet since the accident. He doesn't want to go back into the mines, which is understandable under the circumstances, but he knows so much about the mining profession and he's a hard worker and a quick learner. I thought maybe you could find a position for him elsewhere in your company."

Cam gives him his full undivided attention, watching him with a kind of disbelieving curiosity, almost as if he suspected someone was going to appear with a video camera at the end of Clay's speech and announce it was all a practical joke and they'd be showing the tape at the next board meeting for a good laugh.

"Sure, sure. Why not? Here."

He shuffles through some papers on his desk and hands Clay a notepad and a pen.

"Write down his name and phone number. I'll see what I can do."

He glances at me while Clay's busy writing.

"You didn't tell him, did you?"

"I couldn't do it," I reply, almost in a whisper.

"Well, then."

Cam motions for Clay to take a seat after he takes the pad of paper back from him. He positions his bulk on the corner of his desk.

"There's no easy way to say this so I'm just going to say it: You're my son."

Clay smiles and leans forward like he missed the punch line of a joke.

"You're my son," Cam goes on obliviously. "Your mom and I . . . well, it was a long time ago."

"What did you say?" Clay asks.

"I've said it twice already. You're my son."

"I don't understand. I'm your son?"

He points at himself and looks at me, then back at Cam.

"And you've always known?"

"Unless your mom was lying and someone else knocked her up. She was young. I gave her the benefit of the doubt."

Clay stands up.

"You got my mom pregnant when she was a teenager, and you didn't take any responsibility for it?"

"No one twisted her arm. It was mutual consent."

"You didn't take any responsibility for it?" he repeats.

"Under the circumstances, we decided to be discreet."

"We never decided anything. You decided everything," I interject. "I was seventeen."

Clay takes a step toward Cam. I think he might hit him. Or worse. He's also armed.

Cam doesn't sense any of the tension. He gets up from the corner of his desk and walks over to his liquor cabinet.

"That all happened a long time ago," he says while he pours himself a drink. "It's water under the bridge. No use dwelling on it now. You can dwell on it later if you want. Right now I have a business proposition for you."

He looks over at Clay.

"You a drinking man?"

"No," I answer for him.

"Yes," he says.

He pours Clay a drink, too, and takes it to him.

I don't get offered one.

"I don't know what you've heard about my health," he says as he moves behind his desk and takes a seat, "but the bottom line is, it's not so good. I need a kidney transplant."

He glances expectantly back and forth between Clay and me as if we're supposed to know something we don't.

"Which means I need a kidney," he continues. "I'd be willing to pay you quite a bit. Six figures."

"Are you crazy?" I gasp. "Are you out of your mind?"

He ignores me and speaks directly to Clay.

"What do you say? You only need one kidney."

"There's no way," I cry. "You think you can totally disown a child, deny he's even yours, then invite him over for a drink one night out of the blue and offer to buy a body part?"

"I have to think about it," Clay says.

"What?" I practically shriek. "There's nothing to think about."

Clay looks at me coldly.

"He was talking to me, Mom. Not you."

"Good man." Cam sits back in his big leather chair. "You think about it. I had to think about it, too. I realize I'm putting myself on the line here. Your mom wanted to keep our relationship secret forever and that was to my advantage. Now that you know we're related you can try and get an inheritance out of me and frankly, you can do whatever you want after I'm dead. Good luck fighting Rae Ann and her family."

He holds his drink in both hands against his belly.

"The only other problem is it wasn't exactly something I wanted the general public to know about either, if you get my meaning. I thought about it long and hard. Do I want people around here to know I got myself a bastard son? That I knocked up the teenaged daughter of one of my miners? I really struggled with it. You know, the moral ramifications and all. Finally, I came to my senses. I said to myself, Hell, Cam, that was over twenty years ago. Times have changed. Plus you got more money than you know what to do with. You're as close to a king as these people'll ever see. Why would you give a good goddamn what they think? So that's where I stand on it now. You can tell whoever you want because, frankly, I don't care what people around here think of me."

He moves forward in his chair suddenly and throws back his drink in one gulp. He sets the empty glass down on the desk like a challenge.

Clay gets up from his seat.

"Well, you don't have to worry about me saying anything because, frankly, I do care what people around here think of me."

He puts his untouched drink down on the other side of the desk. "And, frankly, I don't want any of them to know I'm related to you."

I FOLLOW HIM outside. He's walking, but I have to run to stay with him. He won't look at me or talk to me as we head down the street.

He stops suddenly and I end up a couple steps past him before I can correct my own momentum.

"You had no right," he shouts at me.

His voice is angry, but his face is screwed up like he's about to cry.

"You had no right not to tell me. You knew my whole life who my father was and he was right here in the same town and you never told me. How could you do that?"

"I was protecting you," I try to explain.

"It wasn't up to you."

"I'm your mother. It's my job to protect you."

"Not from my own father."

"Yes, sometimes it is."

"No. No. No." He shakes his head as he chants. "Never. No one has the right to keep that information from a child. I don't care what kind of reasons you come up with. He's my father. Don't you understand what that means? You're not more important because you're my mother."

"Are you taking his side?"

"Listen to yourself. Sides? You're always talking about sides. This isn't some kind of competition. Is that what it is to you? Even now? He hurt your ego by dumping you so you decided I'd never know who my dad is."

"No. That's not how it happened."

I grab his arm but he shakes me off.

"He dumped us. Don't you understand? Not just me. Us. He didn't want to have anything to do with you. I didn't care about myself. But he didn't want you. I hated him for that."

He keeps shaking his head.

"You didn't give him a chance to even meet me."

"He didn't want to meet you. He told me if I ever tried to see him . . ."

I stop myself from explaining further. I don't want to hurt him more in order to try and make my actions seem more justified.

"It was up to me to find out what kind of man he was. It wasn't up to you to decide I should never find out," he tells me, then takes a few steps away from me.

"I thought I knew you. Now I have to look at you in a completely different way."

"Don't say that."

"I don't know who you are. You're not strong. A strong woman would have told her son who his father is. That takes strength and courage. You're a coward."

The tears finally burst free. They stream down his face.

"I always thought you were so tough. Look at my mom. She doesn't need anybody. She doesn't even need a man. Even though I wished you needed a man. Even though I prayed about it and had dreams about it. Even though I would have done anything to have a dad even if he was just a stepdad. I would've even settled for a steady boyfriend I could have called Uncle Somebody."

"Clay, I'm sorry."

"You're not strong at all. How could you do it? Did he pay you?"

I slap him.

It's the loudest sound I've ever heard in my life. Louder than gunfire. Louder than a mine siren. Louder than the silence in our house as I lay awake waiting for my dad to come home from the bar.

I've never hit my son.

He turns and runs. It's not the first time I've seen him do it. I've seen him run off to play with his friends, run to catch the school bus, run after a pop fly, but the sight has never made me sick with grief before. He was always running toward something, not away from me.

Chapter Thirty

EVERY LIGHT IS ON in my house. I can see it from the road blazing behind the drooping fringe of the willow trees.

Shannon's car is gone.

The front door opens before I even park my car and Kenny and Fanci come rushing onto the porch with Gimp following arthritically behind them.

"The man with the mustache came here just like you said," Kenny shouts at me.

I rush over to them. I kneel down and touch Kenny all over to make sure he's whole.

Fanci's dark suspicious eyes ringed in silver don't look receptive to the idea of being touched so I settle for giving her arm a quick squeeze.

"Are you okay?" I ask them.

"Yeah," Kenny says.

"I would've called you, but they took the phones and hid them," Fanci adds.

"Who's they?"

"Your sister and the man with the mustache."

"His name was Dimwit," Kenny volunteers.

"Dmitri, you idiot," Fanci turns on him. "It's a foreign name like Jonathan."

"He didn't hurt her, did he? Or the baby?"

"They were friends," Kenny says confidently.

"Not really friends," Fanci corrects him. "They got into a fight, but they definitely knew each other."

Kenny tugs on my J&P jacket to get my attention.

"I wanted to hit her with a bottle like you said, but Fanci wouldn't let me."

"You're too little," she tells him, then glares at me accusingly. "I would've hit them with my stick but you made me keep it outside."

"Thank God for that," I say. "You can't go around hitting men with sticks."

"Why not?"

"Because they hit back."

I usher them both inside my house.

A delicious rich spicy smell that can only be chicken paprikash hits me the moment I open the front door. A big pot is simmering on my stove.

Fanci sees where my eyes land.

"He showed up with a bag of groceries and started cooking," she explains. "He said he was making it for the ballerina cop, whoever that is."

"It smells good," Kenny informs me.

We all walk over to the stove. I raise the lid.

"It sure does," I agree with Kenny. "Maybe we should have some."

I get some bowls and plates down out of the cupboard and direct Fanci to the silverware drawer.

"Why don't you set the table? I'll be right back."

I go check out Shannon's room.

All of her belongings are gone. If I didn't know Shannon I might say the room was hastily abandoned. The bed is a mess; the drawer made into a temporary crib is still sitting on the floor. But I know it would never have occurred to her to clean up after herself just as it

358

would never have occurred to her to leave me a note. Both acts would have required her to think about me.

I walk over to the drawer and pick up the pillow I had stuffed inside it to make a mattress. I bring it to my nose and breathe in deeply. It smells like baby.

I never thought for one minute that she would try to leave so soon. I thought I'd have at least a couple days to talk her into keeping the baby and sticking around for awhile. I could barely walk from my hospital bed to the bathroom during the first twenty-four hours after Clay's birth, let alone get in a car and drive.

I glance around the room and feel the same helpless, hopeless emptiness and failure I felt eighteen years ago after Shannon disappeared the first time. I was hoping for an answer then, just as I'm hoping for one now, but nothing comes to me other than the thought that maybe eighteen years ago wasn't the first time she disappeared. Maybe Shannon disappeared a few days after her birth, or at least an important part of her did, the part that would enable her to survive the loneliness; maybe the furnished part of her soul took wing with the rest of our mother's soul that day as it flew away from us to live with the angels while our mortal selves remained behind taking our naps.

Fanci and Kenny are sitting at the table when I return to the kitchen.

I spoon the chicken into their bowls, and they fall upon it eagerly.

I get some for myself, too. My junk food binge this morning made me feel sick the rest of the day and I haven't eaten since. Now I'm hungry on a purely physical level where my body is telling me I need to eat, but I can't enjoy the taste of the food. Right now I don't feel like I'll ever enjoy anything ever again.

"Did Shannon and the man leave together?" I ask them.

"They left at the same time in different cars," Fanci replies as she reaches across the table and pulls pieces of chicken off the bone for Kenny and drops them into his bowl of peppery red sauce.

"What did they fight about?"

"The baby."

"What about the baby?"

"He said he wanted to help pick out the family she's gonna sell the baby to. He said if she didn't let him help he'd stop any adoption she'd try to do."

"Did he say how he was going to stop her?"

"He said he could do it because he's the mythological father," Kenny interjects.

Fanci flashes him an annoyed look. The broad sweeps of silver around her dark eyes remind me of a raccoon's mask in reverse and give her a slightly sinister, wily appearance.

"Biological father, you moron," she corrects him. "Mythological is a kind of story. Remember? Like the story I read you last night in *People* magazine about Britney Spears having a baby."

"Is she gonna sell her baby, too?" Kenny wonders.

I freeze with my fork halfway to my mouth.

"He said he was the baby's father?"

They both nod.

Fanci continues, "Then your sister said, 'Don't remind me. I can't believe I was stupid enough to get pregnant with someone I know.' What's that supposed to mean?"

"Are they gonna sell the little baby?" Kenny asks suddenly with his mouth full of chicken and red sauce dripping down his chin.

"I thought you said it was against the law," Fanci says. "You said I couldn't give you Kenny to pay for a ride because it was against the law."

"Using your little brother for cab fare and deciding to let someone adopt your baby in exchange for a lot of cash are completely different things."

"How?"

"It's too complicated to explain," I reply, starting to feel a little frustrated, especially because I can't readily explain, even to myself, why they're different. "They're both wrong," I add. "They're both morally wrong, because in order to sell something or trade something you have to own it and a person can't own another person."

"But another person can own you," Fanci quotes me.

"You'll learn more about that when you start dating," Kenny adds sagely.

My cell phone rings.

It's so unexpected, the sound makes me jump.

I hope against all hope that it's Clay calling to say he's thought it over and he forgives me for lying all these years and he doesn't hate me, or it's E.J. calling to say he's thought it over and he forgives me for using him last night and treating him like shit this morning and we can still be friends, or it's Shannon calling to say she's thought it over and she forgives me for failing to make her love me and we can still be sisters.

"Hello? Shae-Lynn? It's Gerald Kozlowski."

I'm too disappointed to say anything.

"Please don't hang up," he adds hurriedly. "Hear me out first."

"Make it quick."

"How is Shannon?"

My first instinct is to lie to protect her and the baby but then I realize there's no point to any of it anymore. Kozlowski isn't the enemy. The only person she needs to be protected from is herself.

"As far as I know, she's fine. She had the baby this afternoon. I went out for an hour and she flew the coop."

This doesn't seem to surprise him.

"What kind of head start does she have?"

"A couple hours."

"I don't suppose I could convince you to go after her? I'd pay quite a bit."

"I'm not interested. Plus she may or may not be traveling with Dmitri. I have no desire to run into him again."

"What do you mean? Has he convinced her to sell the baby to Mickey?"

"I don't know what he's thinking about. I only know he expects to be involved in the adoption decision. Probably so he can get his cut of the profits, too. Apparently, he's the father."

This information silences him for a moment.

"You're kidding me. That doesn't sound like something Shannon would do."

"You mean get pregnant with someone she knows?"

"They met when we were working out the adoption with Dmitri's employer. I had no idea they became involved."

"Well, apparently they did, and he knows it's his baby. I'm assuming the reason he came after her was because he wants his share of the money, too, or he'll contest any adoption she tries."

"What a bastard."

I almost laugh out loud at this statement coming from Kozlowski.

"Do you think we can call a truce long enough for you to drive me to the airport tomorrow? I can't get a ride from anyone else."

"We'll work out something," I tell him.

I let the kids finish their meal, then I drive them home.

The drama of Shannon's flight and Fanci and Kenny's company kept me distracted, but once I return to my empty house I'm powerless to keep the thoughts of Clay and Cam at bay.

I'm so sad, I don't feel any of the things I usually feel when I'm sad. I have no desire to drink or hurt myself or hurt someone else or have sex with someone I know I'm going to leave. I'm numb. After a lifetime of not crying, I think it might be nice to finally cry, but I can't. There's no moisture in my body. My insides have turned to ash.

I go to my bedroom closet and bring out a box of Clay's old school papers and art projects and spread them all over my bed.

I pick through macaroni necklaces and Popsicle-stick picture frames, reports on George Washington and time lines of dinosaurs, Thanksgiving turkeys made from the outline of his hand and Mother's Day poems written on paper doilies sprinkled with gold glitter.

One of his worksheets from second grade catches my eye. I remember it immediately. It's about jobs. The questions list different jobs and ask the children why each one is important.

Policemen are important because:

Clay has written: they help people.

Farmers are important because: they feed people.

Teachers are important because: they teach us things.

Doctors are important because: they make people feel better.

Bus drivers are important because: they take people where they want to go.

I'm reading each of his responses when I hear someone pulling into my driveway. I jump up from my bed and rush to the window.

E.J.'s truck comes to a stop beside my Subaru.

I leave the room and go answer the door with the worksheet still in my hand.

"I figure one of us is going to have to be the adult and I know it's not going to be you," he announces the moment I open the door.

I imagine he rehearsed it and decided he was going to say it fast before I had a chance to say anything stupid first.

"Come on in."

I turn and walk to the couch expecting him to follow. I plunk down on the cushions feeling like my entire body is made of lead.

He takes a seat next to me.

"We had a pretty good thing going," I tell him. "I don't want to screw up our relationship by being in love and having great sex."

"Sure," he says, frowning. "I can understand that. Who'd want to be in love and have great sex when they could just hang out and argue and drink beer instead?"

"Exactly my point."

"So this pretty good relationship you're talking about. What is it exactly? A friendship?"

"I guess."

"Okay. Why is it we can't be in love and have great sex and still have our friendship?"

"What planet are you from? When does that ever work?"

"It works for my mom and dad, although I don't particularly like to think about the great sex part with them."

I don't say anything. I sit and stare at the floor, not even aware that I'm still holding Clay's worksheet.

"Lib and Teresa have been together for a long time. They seem happy," he adds.

"It won't work for us."

"How about we won't be in love but we can still have the sex and the friendship?"

"You have to choose one."

"Oh, no. No, no." He shakes his head and holds out his hands like he's stopping traffic. "I know how this works. There's no right answer. If I choose the friendship you're gonna start ranting about how I don't like having sex with you and if you were twenty-five and blond I would've picked sex. And if I pick the sex then you're gonna call me a macho pig and tell me I don't appreciate you as a human being and I only see you as a piece of ass."

I don't contradict him.

"Why can't I see you as a human being and a piece of ass?"

"It can't work."

"Why not?"

"Because nothing ever works for me."

Except for one thing, I continue silently to myself. There was one thing I thought I had succeeded at, but I was wrong about that.

He puts his arm around my shoulders.

"What's wrong?"

"I think I may have lost Clay," I tell him in a whisper.

"What are you talking about?"

I look down at the very last question on the worksheet.

Who do you think has the most important job?

Through my tears I see Clay's answer written by a careful and determined seven-year-old's pencil: Moms have the most important job because moms make people.

Chapter Thirty-One

THE HORRIBLE GIRL FLOWERS and the animals feeding on them are gone. They're only here in summer and now it's fall.

The field has become a park and the crisp air is full of kaleidoscopic eddies of autumn leaves that break apart and scatter: Some are blown against benches and monuments, some get stuck to the damp pavement, others are forced into piles by men dressed in white uniforms wielding gold rakes, while others hover in the air like butterflies in front of my outstretched hand.

They are a riot of color: pumpkin orange and rain slicker yellow, eggplant purple and mushroom brown, pale ginger and dark crimson, tawny and pink and the red of a warning flag. Some covered in bright green veins or streaks of salmon or tiny yellow spots like a rash.

They're so beautiful, I want to take them home with me and keep them forever. I start collecting them and stuffing them into the pockets of the coat I'm wearing. I can't stop myself even after the pockets are full. I keep pushing them down deeper, crushing them, until I begin to hear muffled screams.

I pull my hands out of my pockets bristling with leaves and all of them have the wailing faces of infants.

I'm startled and frightened and even repulsed. My instinct is to throw them away and I do, flapping my hands to shake them off.

They're swept away by an air current, somersaulting and swirling, all the while screaming. I start to chase after them even though I'm not sure I want them, but the wind picks up and soon all the leaves have been lifted off the ground into a gigantic colorful sobbing swarm.

I WAKE WITH a start. My heart is thudding dully behind my eardrums. It sounds like it resides inside my head now instead of my chest.

My son is gone, is my first thought. It's a completely foreign one: one I've never faced before except in maternal nightmares where he swam out too far in a great gray sea and I couldn't get to him, or he ran out in front of a speeding car and I couldn't get to him, or he went to work in black tunnels of rock miles beneath my feet and I couldn't get to him.

My son is gone. It's true but it can't be.

I push the thought away and try to return to a time before I knew the truth, back to that slice of blissful ignorance between sleeping and waking before anything is clear.

I remember feeling this same brief sweet moment as a child where I wasn't conscious enough yet to know my mom was gone. I'd wake up and lie still in my bed with my eyes closed and know she was going to come to me as soon as I called, and as cold, awful reality began to seep into my thoughts I'd still cling to this hope the same way I'd try to fall back asleep on those rare mornings when I woke up from a good dream.

Nothing is clear anymore. My thoughts become more and more muddled.

My son is gone. My sister is here. My sister is gone. My sister is back. My son is gone. My sister was never gone because my sister was never here. I have a niece. My niece is gone. My son is gone. E.J. was gone. E.J. is back. E.J. is here and different. Cam Jack is back. My son is gone. Cam Jack was never here. Cam Jack has always been every-where. My son is gone.

I open my eyes and roll over and find a warm male body in my bed.

My son is gone. My sister is gone. Her baby is gone. E.J. is here. E.J. is here in my bed.

His eyes fly open suddenly, like my stare is a physical presence that just poked him in the ribs.

We find ourselves staring stupidly at each other in the faint half-light of barely six in the morning. I can only hope I don't look half as goofy as he does.

He gives me a lazy, loyal, bad boy grin, the smile of a man who'd risk robbing a bank for me but could never be convinced to drive out of his way to find me an ATM without a service fee.

"Hey," he says.

"Hey," I say back.

He reaches for me and pulls me on top of him. I stretch out over his body, placing my lips against the wiry roughness of the stubble on his chin, pressing my breasts against the hard flatness of his chest, rock-ing the softness of my belly over the tip of his erection, draping my smooth legs over his hairy ones: I'm a blanket of female.

His hands run up and down the length of me, lingering in the small of my back, sliding over my ass, pulling me up and positioning my hips so he can push inside me.

Afterward, I stay on top of him with my head against his chest lis-tening to his heartbeat and feeling a ticklish solitary drop of juice from our coupling trickle down my inner thigh.

I'm drifting back into sleep when E.J. sits up suddenly.

"Shit. Look at the sky."

I look over my shoulder at the window and see the pale gray sky and know immediately what he means.

I roll off him and he bolts out of bed.

"Are you going to be late?"

"Hell, yeah."

He starts darting around my bedroom looking for his underwear.

"What about your lunch?" I ask him, the familiar panic from my childhood descending over me like a hood.

All my other thoughts are blocked out; I'm blind except for the image of my father's disappointed, disapproving face scowling down at me.

I jump out of bed, too.

"You have to have your lunch. I'll make you something. Don't worry."

"It's okay, I have my dinner pail and my thermos in the truck. They're already packed."

"You brought them with you last night already packed?"

He pauses with one foot in his jeans and smiles.

"Yeah, well, I was hopeful."

I smile back.

"And prepared. You should get some kind of Boy Scout badge for that."

"Which one? The looking-to-score badge?"

I hand him his shirt.

"What are you doing today?" he asks me.

"Working. Hopefully. It's been pretty slow lately."

"I mean about Shannon and about Clay."

"I'm not doing anything about Shannon. At least I know she's alive and well. I guess that's something. I'm not going to chase her. She knows where I am if she ever wants to see me again."

"And Clay?"

I wasn't able to tell him everything about my troubles with Clay. I actually told him very little last night, only that I think I may have done something rotten and harmful all the while believing it was heroic and good.

I wasn't able to tell him about Cam Jack. The reopened wound is too fresh for me to be able to talk about it, plus this new phase of my relationship with E.J.—where I'm a human being and a piece of ass at the same time—is too new and experimental for me to risk jeopardizing it by telling this particular story. If the man were anyone else but Cam Jack, I might be able to do it.

"I'm not going to chase Clay either," I say.

I follow E.J. to the door. We're in such a hurry I don't even take time to put on clothes or grab a robe.

He gives me a kiss in the doorway.

"I like this new phase of our relationship," he says, grinning.

"The love phase?"

"The naked phase."

He slaps my bare butt hard and runs off to his truck, whooping in triumph, the way he used to when we were kids after he'd just knocked me down and pinned me for the heck of it.

I dress quickly, feed Gimp, and head into Centresburg to take care of some unfinished business that has nothing to do with my cab. My night with E.J. aside, my house has a barren, depressing feel to it this morning and I'm eager to leave it. Shannon and the baby were in it for such a brief period of time, but even a few hours of a baby's presence is enough to make a lonely house come alive.

I gave Pamela a call last night to see if she had heard from Shannon, more specifically to find out if she was now the proud new mother of a bouncing baby girl.

I decided it was too exhausting to keep coming up with lies, so I leveled with her and told her Shannon was my sister and explained briefly why I didn't tell her all this in the first place.

She took it better than I thought she would. She was too preoccupied with the news about the baby to care much about anything else.

With Dmitri in the picture, I imagined Shannon would be eager to simply dump the baby for as much cash as possible and to do it as quickly as possible so she could pay him and get rid of him. But then again, I know nothing about her relationship with him and maybe she's not eager to get rid of him.

I also don't know to what extent Dmitri's loyalty to his employer stretches. He may insist Shannon sell the baby to this Mickey character with the crazy bimbo wife.

And I also don't know how far Kozlowski's legal powers extend, if he has some binding contract he can slap Shannon with, if he can only find her, and then the baby will go to the Larsons.

Pamela hadn't heard from her as of last night.

We promised to contact each other if either of us heard from Shannon. Otherwise, we planned to meet for breakfast at Eatn'Park.

I find her sitting alone at a booth by a window staring out at the parking lot.

She's wearing a raw silk blazer in pale orange. She'd probably call it crushed tangerine or maybe melon pearl. A camisole of the same color peeks out from beneath it.

I check under the table before I sit down to make sure her shoes match the jacket. They do.

I'm seated and have already ordered coffee before she bothers to glance my way.

Her face looks amazingly fresh and unlined for someone who should have had a sleepless night. I only detect the slightest lavender shadow of exhaustion beneath her eyes that her concealer was unable to completely cover.

It's the eyes themselves that give away her advancing age and the haggard condition of her inner self. The decisions she's made, the goals she's pursuing, the ongoing struggle to make ends justify means: All of it is reflected in their muddied blue depths and none of it can be quickly and easily erased. There's no Botox for the soul.

"I haven't heard anything from Jamie, I mean Shannon," she tells me. "I'm sorry. I can't get used to calling her that."

She picks up her coffee mug with one hand and lays the other hand flat on the table with her fingers splayed out, her flawless nails like an arc of candied almonds.

"I haven't heard from her either."

"How do I know you're not lying?"

Her question surprises me: the content and her tone.

"Why would I lie? What would my motivation be? I'm only here at all because I feel bad for you."

"You feel bad for me?" she says, offended. "I certainly don't need your pity."

"I mean, I feel bad about what my sister did. Even though I haven't seen her for eighteen years I still feel somewhat responsible."

"Why?"

"I raised her."

"You raised her?"

"Our mother died when Shannon was only a few days old."

"So Shannon didn't have a mother?"

She takes a sip of her coffee and ponders this.

"Maybe that's why she turned out to be so callous and awful."

"I know plenty of people who have mothers who turned out to be callous and awful. I think maybe not having a mother is why she can't be a mother."

"Then why get pregnant?"

"I think in some warped way she thinks it's her duty."

"Her duty? I don't understand."

I don't know what to say to her. I can't explain duty to her. I can't make her understand the way we think. I can't spell out an unwritten code of conduct that is never explained or taught to any of us but is simply lived: Whatever situation is put in front of you, you find a way to endure it; whenever you're told to do something, you try to do it well; wherever you end up, you remember where you began.

I can't make a sensible argument for whatever it is that makes E.J. go back into the mines every day after he almost lost his life there and has been treated so poorly by the man who employs him; or what made Lib go to a jungle halfway around the world to fight in a war he didn't understand instead of moving seven hundred miles north to a country similar to his own where he would have been safe; or what made me incapable of leaving or even hating my abusive father until I had a child of my own to protect.

We live life in a parallel universe to hers. We don't do what we want in order to get the kind of world we want; we do what we should in order to survive in the world we've been given.

I wasn't lying and I wasn't being condescending; I do feel bad for her.

"I guess it doesn't matter why she does it," I say with a finality I hope will put the topic to rest.

The waitress comes back, pours my coffee, and hands me a big laminated menu.

I'm starving this morning and dive into the pages eagerly.

Pamela declines a menu with a wave of her hand and a pursing of her lips.

"What do you think she's going to do?" she asks me after the waitress departs.

I'm busy studying the pictures.

I don't look up as I tell her, "I'm not sure. It turns out I was right. There was another family she promised the baby to besides you. And there's another family that she promised an earlier baby to and backed out on the deal who also thinks they have a right to this baby."

"I can't believe it."

"She still might decide to give you the baby, but it's not going to happen here. I'm sure she's left again for good. The father's involved now, too."

"The father? She told me there was no way the father could ever find out or would even remotely suspect she was pregnant with his child."

"Hard to believe she'd lie. I know."

The waitress returns. I order two scrambled eggs, bacon and sausage, a buttermilk biscuit, and a side of hash browns, then call her back at the last minute and ask for a cinnamon bun to start it all off.

Pamela looks appalled.

"I don't usually eat like this. Great sex this morning. Great sex last night, too. Revs up the appetite. You know how it is."

I can tell by her expression that she doesn't.

"Sorry," I tell her.

"This father. How do you know about him?"

"I met him."

"He was here?"

I start dumping packets of sugar into my coffee.

"Yep."

"Was he attractive?"

"In a dark, menacing, Cold War sort of way, yes. Definitely attractive. I can't say for sure if he has all his toes, though."

She doesn't seem to get my joke.

She falls silent and begins to absentmindedly finger the several braided strands of coral wrapped around her neck.

I imagine she must be sad. Hurt, probably. Regretful, maybe. Disillusioned? Disappointed? Livid? Suicidal? Or preoccupied with thoughts of a spring trip to the Caribbean? I can't tell, since her face shows so little expression and her eyes have gone blank.

I think about Shannon's description of the nice ladies, well dressed and smelling good, who came to visit her at the home for pregnant teens and then abruptly stopped coming once the baby was gone. I wonder if they ever thought about her again.

"Let me ask you something. Just out of curiosity. I know right now you're angry at Shannon and rightfully so—she stole a lot of money from you and broke a promise that broke your heart—but while you were together, did you care about her at all?"

She stops playing with her necklace and folds her hands in front of her on the tabletop.

"Of course I did. I was very fond of her. And I'm sure I'll be fond of the next one, too."

"The next one? After what you've been through, you're going to try again? Aren't you afraid the same thing will happen again, or something worse?"

"Every time I go through this I learn something new. Eventually I'll get it right."

"How many times have you been through it?"

"Let's just say several."

The waitress returns with my cinnamon bun. I start pulling it apart and popping pieces into my mouth.

Pamela can't watch. She turns her attention out the window again but continues talking to me.

"With any adoption, there's always the fear of the knock on the door someday. Maybe the biological mother has found a way to contest the adoption, or she's shown up with the father and he's going to contest it for her, or she has no intention of contesting anything but simply wants to ruin the life you've established with your child by planting an idea in his head that he was stolen from her or some other equally damaging story.

"There are always risks," she finishes, "but if it's something you want badly enough, you're willing to face those risks."

I nod my agreement while I finish chewing and swallowing.

She begins to stand up.

"I hope you don't mind if I don't stay. I really want to get back home. It's a very long drive."

"No, I don't mind at all. But let me ask you one more thing before you go. You said you learn something new every time you go through this. What did you learn from Shannon?"

She picks up her purse off the booth—the one that matches Shannon's—and slips it onto her shoulder.

"The only way to be absolutely sure an adoption is safe is to make sure the biological mother is dead," she answers me.

She holds her hand out to shake mine, sees the sticky condition of it, and thinks better of it.

"It was nice meeting you, Shae-Lynn. Good luck to you and your son. Here. Let me pay for this. I insist."

She leaves twenty dollars on the table, reconsiders, and puts down another twenty.

"Thanks, Pamela," I call after her departing back. "Good luck to you, too."

I pocket the two twenties, smiling to myself. It's a five-dollar breakfast.

Chapter Thirty-Two

KOZLOWSKI IS WAITING FOR ME outside the Comfort Inn when I swing by around noon.

He looks exactly the same to me as he did when I picked him up at the Harrisburg airport a few days ago: same clothes, same bored expression on his featureless features, same stance with his black jacket hooked on a finger and thrown casually over one shoulder.

He comes walking toward the car, and I get out to stop him.

"I'm afraid I'm not going to be able to take you to the airport, Gerald. Something's come up."

"I have a flight to catch."

"I know. I'm a professional. I would never leave a client stranded. I've arranged another ride for you. A friend of mine. You'll be in good hands."

He looks skeptical.

"I admit to not being overly fond of you and what you do, but I'm not a judgmental person. I try to see life from inside everyone else's shoes. I have a feeling your shoes weren't always six-hundred-dollar Prada loafers, and I also have a feeling you used to have an accent you were embarrassed by—Polish, maybe, or maybe it was your dad who had the Polish accent you were embarrassed by and yours was from Brooklyn or the Bronx—regardless I'm going to cut you some slack.

I'm disappointed in how you turned out. You're obviously a smart guy, an ambitious guy, a resourceful guy. I think you should have used your powers for good instead of evil. That's all."

He watches me blankly the entire time I'm speaking. Once I've finished he takes his time perusing my outfit: black Caterpillar work boots with yellow laces, black jeans, a tight black tank top with DUMP HIM written across the front in silver glitter block capital letters, a red satin Kansas City Royals baseball jacket, and my pink Stetson.

"I was just thinking that you dress like my neighbor," he comments. "My gay neighbor. My male gay neighbor."

He checks his watch.

"I'm going to be late."

"You're going to be fine."

"Are you sure Shannon was traveling with Dmitri?" he asks me.

"They left together but in separate cars. Whatever that means."

"I don't understand. It's so out of character for her. Shannon gets pregnant from one-night stands. That way she never sees the father again and he has no way of ever knowing she was pregnant in the first place."

"So not only are you creating innocent little lives for the sole purpose of selling them, but you're also making fathers out of men who will never know they're fathers and will never know their children."

"And would never want to know them. Trust me."

"I'd rather not," I reply disgustedly.

He unzips the outside pocket of his bag and takes out a bottled water.

I reach into my pocket and take out what was left of my Eatn'Park cinnamon roll wrapped in a napkin. I couldn't finish everything at the time, but I'm getting hungry again.

"She met Dmitri over two years ago when she was pregnant with the baby before this one," he explains to me as he unscrews the cap, watching me uncertainly. "It's hard to believe they've had a relationship all this time."

A happy thought occurs to me.

"Maybe she's planning on keeping this baby. Maybe she and Dmitri really are having a relationship and—"

"And what?" he interrupts me with a laugh, the bottle hovering in front of his mouth. "They're going to settle down and buy a house in the suburbs and raise a family?"

My optimism disappears.

He takes a long drink and returns the bottle to his bag.

I finish eating and lick icing off my fingers.

"Didn't you say they had a fight over him wanting his cut of the money?" he asks me.

"It wasn't specifically over the money, but I'm sure that's what he meant. He said he wanted a say in who adopts the baby."

"So she must still be planning on selling the baby, but to whom? The only possible advantage of knowing the identity of the biological father is if he signs the adoption papers. Then the adoption is airtight. Otherwise, as long as he's out there—even if the mother claims she doesn't know who he is—there's always the possibility he can show up and contest it."

"That doesn't make sense either," I say. "She ran out on him before she got his signature."

"Knowing Shannon, she was trying to rip him off, too, and not pay him his share, but she knew if she didn't get away with it she could still pay him off and get his signature and make the adoption fail-safe. But I don't know why she'd want to mess with any of that. It's easier to get pregnant by a stranger you'll never see again."

"I think that's the new motto for the Pennsylvania Domestic Abuse Hotline," I tell him.

An old pickup truck pasted in peeling red, white, and blue bumper stickers and in need of a new muffler comes rumbling into the parking lot.

I smile at Kozlowski.

"Here's your ride now."

Choker pulls up in front of us.

Kozlowski doesn't move.

"Hey, Choker."

I wave at him.

He puts his truck in park, gets out, and comes walking over to us to help Kozlowski with his bag. I told him this was a job and I expected him to act accordingly as a representative of my cab company.

"Sorry I'm a little late," he tells me when he arrives in front of us. "There's a big wreck on Electric Avenue and traffic's all blocked up."

Kozlowski comes out of his self-induced trance of denial and smiles pleasantly, trying to make the best of a bad situation.

"Electric Avenue? What a quaint name for a street. Is that where all the excitement is? The nightlife? Restaurants and clubs?"

Choker watches him suspiciously then spits a brown stream of tobacco juice beside him on the sidewalk.

"It's where the electric company is," he explains.

I step between the two of them and clap one hand on Choker's shoulder and the other on Kozlowski's.

"Choker's an ex-con," I tell him, my smile widening. "And you're a lawyer. How perfect is that? You'll have two hours alone together in the cab of a pickup truck to discuss the inner workings of our fine American judicial system."

Choker narrows his eyes first at me then Kozlowski then back at me.

"You didn't say nothing about him being a lawyer."

"Professionalism, Choker. Remember we talked about that? The customer is always right. Plus he's going to pay you a shitload of money."

Choker appears appeased. He goes to grab up Kozlowski's bag. Kozlowski moves to stop him then changes his mind.

"This is going to be fun for you, Gerald," I whisper to him before I depart. "You get to sit on the side with no ear."

I GET A CALL for a job back in Jolly Mount. On my way there I have to pass Dusty's restaurant. I'm hoping he's not here today. I hope Jimmy was able to convince him to go home and try again with Brandi but even from a distance I can see his black Range Rover parked beside the big purple block. Next to it is another car, a white Honda Civic with a Marine Corps bumper sticker.

My instinct makes me stop even though I'm not immediately sure what's going on. At first all I can think about is my encounter with the Marine in the backseat of my cab. Now he's hanging out with my son's best friend.

I can't get past the personal element to see the professional one.

I park and walk inside the restaurant.

Dusty and the Marine are sitting at one of the booths. The tabletop between them is covered with pamphlets and papers bearing American flags and saluting soldiers.

Dusty looks a little better than he did yesterday. He must have shaved at Jimmy's as well as showered. He doesn't smell like a brewery anymore either, but his eyes are bleary and red, and rimmed with dark circles.

The Marine is immaculate in his uniform. The bright blue, pristine white, and regal red and gold is impossible to look away from and seems to have absorbed all the remaining light and color left in the dingy, forsaken room, leaving it entirely in shades of gray like a grainy black-and-white photograph.

Both men are surprised to see me, to put it mildly.

They both stand up at the same time.

"Hey, Miss Penrose," Dusty fumbles.

"Hi, Dusty," I say. "Hello," I begin to say to the Marine then realize I never got his name. "Sergeant," I finish.

He clears his throat.

"Ma'am," he greets me.

We all look at each other awkwardly.

"Could I talk to you for a moment in private?" I ask the Marine.

We continue to look at each other awkwardly.

The Marine doesn't make a move to do anything but Dusty starts for the door.

"I'll go get some air," he says.

"How are you?" I ask the soldier once Dusty's out of earshot.

"Good," he says and smiles. "Small world."

"Small town," I reply. "Do you mind if I ask who sent you here?"

"What do you mean?"

"Someone obviously told you about Dusty specifically. If this had been his idea, he would have gone to the recruiting office, and I highly doubt you found him in front of the high school. Maybe the mall. Is that what happened? Did you pounce on him in the mall parking lot and came back here to talk further?"

His face turns to stone. He takes a step away from me and stands very stiffly with his hands clasped behind his back.

"I don't pounce."

"I'm sorry. Bad choice of words. I'm just concerned. I've known him his whole life. I'm just looking out for him."

"Which means keeping him out of the Marines?"

"For him? Yes. Yes, it does."

"It might be the best thing that ever happened to him."

"Look, I don't want to argue about the pros and cons of military life or even about what's best for Dusty. I'm not trying to steal a recruit from you. This is about something completely unrelated. This is about someone being a colossal jerk. As a favor to me, please, can you just tell me how you ended up here with him?"

He considers my question. I hope our time in the backseat of my cab was memorable enough to merit a favor.

"I received a call from a man who said he knew of a young man who used to work for him who was in need of employment. He said he could vouch for his character and his work ethic and thought he'd make a fine soldier. He gave me his cell phone number. I called him and we set up an appointment to meet here. No one twisted his arm."

"That son of a bitch," I say under my breath. "He was supposed to give him a job with J&P."

"Pardon me."

"Nothing. It's nothing."

"Is something wrong? Is there something I should know about?"

"There's something wrong, but it doesn't concern you. Excuse me for a minute."

I find Dusty standing at the edge of the parking lot whipping gravel sidearm across the road like he's skipping stones on an invisible pond.

I walk over to him and grab him gently by his arm.

"Dusty, what are you doing talking to this guy? Have you given any real thought to this? Have you talked to Brandi about it?"

"I haven't talked to Brandi in days. Besides, she'd be happy about it."

"I don't think so."

"We need the money. It's good pay."

"Sure it's good pay. And all you have to do to earn it is leave your wife and children and risk getting killed."

He shakes loose from my grip.

"Don't start on me about how dangerous it is. I already had a job where I could get killed any day and I almost did."

"That's true. You could have been killed, but you never had to kill anybody else."

He tries to walk away from me, but I grab him again.

"Do you think you can do that?" I ask him. "Do you think you can kill people? People who haven't done anything to you?"

"Lib did it," he shouts at me.

"Lib didn't have a choice."

"And I have a choice?" he continues shouting.

He throws his hands out to his sides, and his eyes fill with tears.

"Tell me, please, what are my choices?"

"Okay, Dusty. It's okay."

He looks like he's going to collapse. I reach out and give him a hug. He resists at first, then crumples against me and starts shaking.

"I don't know what's happening to me," he cries into my shoulder.

"It's okay," I tell him rubbing his back and rocking him against me. "You need help. We're going to get you some help."

I wait for him to calm down then I pull back and hold him at arms' length, waiting for him to look up from the ground and meet my eyes, the way I used to do with Clay when he was at that in-between age where he was embarrassed to cry in front of his mom but still needed to do it from time to time.

"There's nothing wrong with being a soldier," I tell him, "but it's not right for you. You were supposed to be a rock sailor."

He shakes his head.

"But I can't be one anymore."

"Do you know how many astronauts never actually make it into space, and those who do usually only get to go once or maybe twice if they're lucky?"

"Yeah, I guess I know that. What are you saying?"

"I'm saying you had your mission. And it was a spectacular one that had the entire world on the edge of their seats. You survived. You made it back home. Now maybe you could do something on the ground. Not above it and not below it."

"I already tried that."

"You tried to do something on the ground that had nothing to do with being a rock sailor. You tried to run a restaurant. That's not you either. You're a hero, Dusty. You have so much respect within your industry."

"My industry?" he sniffs, looking a little more interested in what I have to say.

"Yes, your industry. The mining industry. You're a part of it. A valuable, knowledgeable part of it. You still are even if you're not a miner anymore. There are still things you can do."

"Like be part of mission control?"

"Yeah." I smile at him. "Something like that."

I notice the Marine out of the corner of my eye standing in front of the dirty windows. He's a flash of brilliant color inside the drab room like a cardinal flitting through a barren winter forest.

"Is it okay if I tell this guy to split for now?" I ask Dusty.

"Yeah, I guess so."

I go back inside the restaurant. I know the Marine watched the whole scene.

"He's not emotionally able to make this decision right now," I tell him bluntly. "He's having a lot of personal problems. He's desperate. You'd be signing up a man who's at the end of his rope. I'd hate to think you guys would take advantage of something like that."

He doesn't say anything, but he begins to clean up his papers and pamphlets.

I start to help him.

"No, thanks," he tells me.

"I'm sorry."

"No, you're not."

He finishes packing up and pauses to catch sight of his reflection in the window. He repositions his hat and turns to me.

"At least be honest with me and tell me what yesterday was all about."

"Some harmless fun."

He brushes past me but pauses at the door.

"You really think you can change things?" he asks me. "You really think keeping me away from the high school for one afternoon is going to have any effect on the big picture?"

"No," I tell him truthfully. "I don't."

He walks outside and stops to exchange a few words with Dusty. They shake hands and separate. The Marine gets in his car and drives away; Dusty goes back to throwing rocks, but he has a little more zip now as he stoops to refill his cupped palm.

I stopped thinking about the big picture a long time ago. I only think about the individual drops of paint and how to maintain the integrity of each color before it hits the canvas.

Chapter Thirty-Three

I CONVINCE DUSTY TO COME HOME with me and hang out for awhile and then stay for dinner.

When we pull off the road into my driveway, my heart starts to race as I glimpse Dmitri's blue rental car parked next to my front porch.

He's leaning against it, smoking a cigarette, and feeding Gimp potato chips out of a blue foil bag. He's wearing his black T-shirt beneath the black leather jacket he had stashed in his car, and his slick black leather boots, made for dancing in clubs not working in mines. I don't see any sign of Shannon or the baby but I assume they're inside, maybe taking a nap.

Dusty and I get out of my car.

"Darling," Dmitri calls out to me immediately and smiles wickedly beneath his coal-black mustache. "Where you been? I missed you."

Dusty looks back and forth between the two of us.

"Who's this guy?" he asks me.

"It's a long story," I explain. "But don't worry. I'm not his darling."

"How quickly she tosses the men aside," Dmitri observes, peering through a plume of white smoke.

"How about you?" he asks Dusty. "You one of her conquests, too?"

"This is my son's best friend," I tell him abruptly. "He is not a conquest and neither are you.

"Why don't you go in the house, Dusty. Have a beer. Relax. I'll be there in a minute."

Dmitri watches him walk past, and the mirth that was just shining in his ebony eyes shifts to glints of suspicion and combativeness. I'm reminded of how we first met and that even though he may have his charming moments, he's also capable of smashing a woman in the face with her own boot.

He studies the silver glitter words on my shirt as I walk toward him.

"Who is this 'him' you're dumping?" he asks me.

"It's just an expression."

"No. 'Slow down and stop to pick roses' is expression."

"It's stop and smell the roses," I correct him.

" 'Dump him' is command. Not expression."

"It doesn't mean anything."

"Sure, it does. Means you don't like men."

"That is such bullshit."

"Tell me"—he pauses to pop one of the chips in his own mouth before giving another one to Gimp—"do you have boyfriend?"

"No. I mean, yes. Well, sort of."

He laughs.

"He must be some boyfriend if you don't even know he's boyfriend."

He clenches his empty hand into a fist and bends his arm up into a body builder's pose.

"I'm bigger, I bet. And stronger, too."

"You're definitely balder," I tell him.

"I can grow hair," he scoffs. "What do I need with hair?"

"You have it all over your lip."

He strokes his mustache and smiles.

"This is sexy. Hair on head is nuisance."

"Dmitri," I begin. "It *is* Dmitri, right?"

He nods.

"Where's Shannon and the baby?"

"Gone. I don't know."

"What do you mean?"

"I mean what I say. I lost her."

"You lost her?"

"She is very crafty. Like wolf."

"You mean like fox."

"No. Fox is small and frightened."

"But they're crafty."

"No, they are small and frightened."

My frustration gets the better of me. I want to reach out and grab him and physically shake the answers out of him, but I settle for shouting instead.

"What do you mean? Do you mean she's not here with you now?"

"She's not here with me now."

"But how could you lose her? She has a one-day-old infant with her. She just gave birth in my guest room. She can't be in very good shape for traveling."

"It's not important how. I just did."

"And you have no idea where she's going?"

"No. "

"Or who she's selling the baby to?"

He takes a long drag off his cigarette and eyes me skeptically.

"What do you know about me and baby?"

"I know you're the father."

He smiles and nods again.

"This baby is very good looking. She has my eyes."

"Shannon told me so many lies. I don't know what to believe. Did she come here because she was running away from you?"

The smile disappears instantly, replaced with a sneer of anger.

"No. Did she tell you this?"

"I'm guessing."

"No. She had no reason to run from me. That's why I followed her. If she had reason to run from me, I let her run. But she had no reason so I come after her."

"Okay. I'll pretend to understand that."

"I knew baby was mine," he continues, the roughness in his voice gradually fading. "We were in relationship. I'm having personal problem and think I'll have to leave New York and New Jersey—whole East Coast—maybe whole country for awhile. I know this is why she gets pregnant with me. She thinks I'm going to be out of picture like all her other fathers. But this don't happen. I stay. She is pregnant. I . . . how do you say . . . I do the math. I figure out. I confront. She denies. I tell her I'll ask for test when baby is born to prove he's mine. So she admits. Then I tell her I'll stop adoption if she doesn't let me pick the family."

"You didn't want the baby?"

"I have no time for babies. I'm only thinking what's best for baby. I would make great father someday. Not now. I'm too . . ."

"Vain? Self-absorbed? Egotistical? Violent?" I provide for him.

"I keep odd hours."

"So you wanted your cut of the money?"

He grows angry again.

"I don't care shit about money."

"What a lie."

"I'm not lying. I don't want money for selling child. This is disgusting. I wouldn't touch the money. Even if I am starving. I would get job washing cars first. I only want to make sure baby goes to good home with good parents. Not like the people I work for."

"I thought the man you work for is your friend."

"He is my friend. What makes a man good friend doesn't always make him good father."

Gimp finally decides he's had enough chips and it's time to acknowledge my presence. He walks over to me and nudges his head beneath my dangling hand.

"Shannon agrees I can help her pick family," Dmitri goes on with his story. "She tells me about the family Kozlowski wants for her. She tells me about this other woman she finds by herself. She tells me the family is paying her expenses, the woman is paying her expenses, so she is stealing their money. I don't approve but I like she's planning to rip off Kozlowski.

"But she was not supposed to run from me. This was our deal. My opinion about the family is as important as her opinion. But she does run. And I don't know where she is. Not before Kozlowski comes to Mickey and they tell me where to look."

"What did you decide? Who's getting the baby?"

"It's not important."

"How can you say that? You just finished telling me how important it is to you to know where the baby is going and now you're going to tell me it isn't?"

"It's important for me. It means nothing to you."

"That baby is my niece."

"You have lots of nieces and nephews you will never know."

The truth behind this depresses me and I suddenly lose all interest in discussing the baby any further. I realize she's a lost cause, and I need to let her go.

I reach for the bag of chips and help myself to a handful.

"I still don't understand why Shannon finally came home again after all these years," I say to Dmitri as I crunch away. "Why now?"

He shrugs.

"I can tell you only what I know. Whole time I know Shannon she never talks about family or past. Where she comes from. It's not just her life is closed book; it's book that was never written.

"One day I'm at her apartment waiting for her. There's a calendar on her kitchen wall, and I start looking at it. It has mostly appointments on it. No birthdays marked. No brothers' or sisters' birthdays. No aunts or uncles. No friends. Not even her own birthday. Except one. Her mother."

"Her mother's?" I ask, startled.

"Yes. So I ask her about this. I ask her how old is your mother? Where she lives? You see her often?

"She says to me, 'She'll be sixty next month.' Then she gets funny look on her face and says, 'Sixty is pretty old. Don't you think? She could be dead by now.'

"I don't know what to say. I think maybe she didn't see her mother for many years and is wondering if she's dead. I tell her maybe not. Lots of people live to be seventy or eighty. Some even to be ninety.

"She gets mad with me. She argues with me, 'No, she could be dead. She could be dead of natural causes.' Natural causes. These are the words she uses over and over. Natural causes. She could be dead of a heart attack or cancer or something that killed her naturally.

"Again I don't know what to say. She's getting very upset. I think it's her hormones. I want to calm her down so I agree. 'Yes,' I say. 'Natural causes could definitely have killed her.'

"This works. She calms down. She almost looks relaxed and happy. She says, 'I can go home now if I want. She'd be dead anyway. It wouldn't be my fault.'

"Does that make sense to you? Where is your mother?"

I don't respond right away. I have to digest what I've just learned.

"She died two days after Shannon was born," I say numbly. "A blood clot in her brain. Complications of childbirth."

"That's it," Dmitri says, snapping his fingers. "The guilt. She stayed away because of guilt. Now it's been long enough she can believe it wasn't her fault."

"But it wasn't her fault."

"It doesn't matter what's true. It only matters what she thinks. Guilt is the most powerful human emotion, after hunger."

"Hunger is a physical need. It isn't an emotion."

"Maybe you've never been hungry enough."

He finishes his cigarette and tosses it onto the stones of my driveway.

"I should go," he tells me. "Too much country air is not good for me."

He reaches into his car and returns with a box he hands to me.

"Here," he says.

"What's this?"

"Something to remember me."

I think he might kiss me. I almost want him to kiss me. But the moment passes as so many do.

He gets into his car and rolls down his window.

"How did you like paprikash?" he asks as he's about to back out.

"It was great. Fanci and Kenny must have eaten three bowls apiece."

"These are children in your kitchen?"

"Yes."

"She is too skinny, and he is too short."

"He's only four years old."

"Oh, well, maybe not so short."

I watch him drive away. Gimp follows his car for about five feet with his tail waving slowly in the air behind him.

I open the box and pull out a royal blue silk robe, perfect for a ballerina cop.

Chapter Thirty-Four

AFTER SCHOOL I SWING by Choker's place and pick up Fanci and Kenny. Choker doesn't make it down to Harrisburg very often, and he's also not usually driving around with a pocket stuffed full of cash. I assumed the combination of these two phenomena would almost certainly guarantee he wouldn't be home in time to dine with his children so I invited them to my place.

Kenny informs me during the drive that his dad isn't much of a cook. His mom is a much better cook, and he can't wait until she comes back as soon as their dad's turn is over and it's her turn to take care of him and Fanci again.

Fanci remains noticeably silent during Kenny's praise of their mother and plans for her impending return.

I think the topic has been dropped but then as we round the final curve in the road before reaching my house, Fanci suddenly asks me, "What was it like to grow up without a mom?"

I'm caught off guard. I try offering a brave, encouraging smile but it doesn't work, and she's not looking at me anyway. Her wet eyes are fixed straight ahead out the window and her lower lip quivers slightly from the pressure of trying not to cry.

I know her so well. She is my sister, too: a force of nature, a giver of life and nourishment, strong and solid on the outside; and a source of many other precious things buried deep inside her that, once discovered, may lead to her being penetrated, emptied, and left in ruins. Some kinds of damage she won't be able to repair, but she will always have the ability to grow new life over it.

I don't try to explain any of this and settle for telling her it isn't the end of the world. And I'm not lying to her. Growing up without a mom isn't the end of the world; it's the end of one very precious specific world.

E.J. shows up for dinner, too. Uninvited. I like seeing his truck rumble up to my front porch as if it belongs here. Part of me believes that it does, and another part of me wonders if it ever truly will, and yet another part of me knows that these kinds of questions are not for me and E.J. but for people who have the emotional luxury of doubting destiny.

Ours is this: I can't imagine him without his garage, and I can't imagine me without my loneliness, and I can't imagine either one of us without the other one. So we will find a way.

I don't let him know that I'm glad he dropped by without asking if he could drop by. I don't want to scare him off by seeming too eager or scare myself off by becoming too accommodating.

I give him some crap about how he can't just assume he can stop by all the time now, and I'm sure as hell not going to feed him every night. He listens in his usual style of ignoring me while paying attention without seeming to. He puts two six-packs in my fridge, greets Dusty, and cracks open beers for the two of them. He introduces himself to Fanci and Kenny and when he finds out they're Choker's kids he tries to say something nice but can't and settles for offering them beers, too, which sends Kenny into peals of laughter and almost makes Fanci blush. I swear I see a slight pink glow appear on her cheeks.

After I get done setting him straight he corners me in the kitchen, steals a kiss and cops a feel, and utters a less than heartfelt, "Yes, dear."

I think the exchange went better than expected.

He's even complimentary about my dinner at first, even though it's pretty bad, but halfway through it he has a small breakdown and storms out cursing only to return an hour later with George and a grocery bag full of meat.

I'm not offended. I believe this is a relationship milestone for him equivalent to that of a woman showing up at her boyfriend's place and installing her children from a previous marriage.

To have it happen so early is a little overwhelming for me but then I stop and think about the E.J. I've always known. I've always implicitly trusted his judgment. This is why I was so hurt when he stopped wanting to be with me after I grew my breasts; I knew his decision had to be the right one and it was. I just didn't know the real reasons behind it and that was the painful part for me. It had nothing to do with me becoming a woman; it was all about E.J. becoming a man.

We're all enjoying perfectly grilled steaks compliments of E.J. and George when a car pulls into my drive.

Fanci is the first one out of her chair. She gets up with uncharacteristic zeal, hurries to the front door, and opens it a crack.

"It's the sheriff," she tells us over her shoulder.

Kenny rushes over to join her, and they both peer out the door.

I'm gripped by an icy hand of fear that yanks me bodily from my chair. Something has happened to Clay. Something happened to Clay, and Ivan has come to tell me in person but before I can get myself too worked up, the sheriff appears in the doorway and he's smiling.

"Good evening, ladies," he greets Fanci and me, "and gentlemen," he adds when he sees the others.

"Are you really the sheriff?" Kenny asks.

Ivan glances down at him.

"Are you really only two feet tall?"

"I don't know."

Fanci rolls her eyes, then they suddenly grow wide and bright as she moves behind Ivan and out the door.

"It's the baby," I hear her cry.

I rush to the door, too, and see Clay walking up the porch steps carrying a little pink bundle.

"We're here to make a delivery," Ivan announces. "The stork was busy."

Clay hands me the baby. Shannon's baby. I'd know her anywhere.

"Look at her," I gush to the kids and kneel down so they can see her. "Isn't she beautiful? Didn't I tell you she was going to get pudgy and pink and smell good?"

They both lean right up against her face and smile broadly. I imagine this could be terrifying for a newborn, but she takes it in stride and puckers up her tiny, downy face into a yawn.

"Did you see that?" Fanci asks. "That's the cutest thing I ever saw."

"Hi, baby," Kenny starts waving. "Hi, little baby."

I look up at Ivan and Clay.

Clay avoids my eyes.

"What's going on?" I ask.

"Aunt Shannon and the baby's father, a Dmitri Starkov, dropped her off at the sheriff's station," Clay explains, diverting his gaze over my shoulder the way cops are taught to do, "complete with signed, notarized adoption papers."

"You'll still have to go before a judge to finalize things," Ivan adds, "but it's just a formality at this point."

He hands me the documents. I check the signatures. Mother: Shannon Penrose. Father: Dmitri Starkov.

"What are you saying? She's mine?"

"She's yours," Clay says.

"She's not hers," Kenny pipes up. "She's not a dog. You can't own another person but another person can own you."

The men all look down, speechless, at the wise toddler.

"You'll learn more about that when you start dating," he thinks to tell Clay.

Everyone laughs.

"I date," Clay says defensively and jerks a finger at me. "What's she been telling you?"

"Nothing," I explain. "It's a joke. And you're right, Kenny. She's not mine, but I guess I can take care of her for awhile."

"How long?" he asks me.

"As long as she wants and as long as I'm able."

I look at Clay.

He's not quick enough this time and our gazes meet for the briefest of moments.

"Hey, is that a George Foreman grill?" Ivan asks. "I'm thinking about getting one for my mom."

He starts walking into the kitchen. E.J. accompanies him. An infant can't compete with an opportunity to extol the virtues of George. Dusty and Kenny tag along.

Fanci lingers but I jerk my head at her, and she reluctantly walks off.

"So you saw your Aunt Shannon?" I ask Clay.

He nods.

"We had a talk."

"Great," I sigh. "I can only imagine what she had to say about me."

"Do you want to know?"

"Sure. Why not?"

"I told her I'm very upset with you right now because it turns out you've always known who my dad was and you never told me. She asked me if I asked you why you never told me and I said you said it was because you were protecting me, and she stared at me like I was the stupidest person she'd ever met."

The baby stirs in my arms. She looks in Clay's direction and he smiles down at her and strokes her cheek with one of his fingers.

Then he looks back at me and his softened expression returns to his usual serious one.

"Shannon said you're a soldier, and I'm one of your missions. She said a good soldier never questions his orders; that's the definition of a good soldier. But sometimes the orders are bad. So sometimes in order to be a good soldier you have to do bad things even though a soldier's intention is always to do good."

"She said that about me?"

He nods.

"What did you think?" I ask him.

"I'm still mad. I may be mad for awhile. I don't know, Mom. I may be mad forever. This is a big deal for me."

Hearing him say the word, "Mom," in his usual exasperated yet devoted tone, is all I need. I know everything is going to be okay. It may take some time for things to return to normal between us, but it will happen.

I'm so relieved, I want to scream and throw my arms around him but I know better.

"I understand that," I reply. "And you're right. It's a very big deal."

"No, I don't think you do understand completely. But I realize after talking to Aunt Shannon that there are things about you I don't understand completely either. I don't care. I don't care about any of it. It gets way too complicated. The only thing I know for sure about us is you're my mom and I'm your son. One major screwup doesn't change that. I'm not going to stop loving you even if the screwup is a really big one. And it is. A really big one."

"I know."

"And I'm still mad."

"You already told me that."

He falls silent, and I do the same. Our conversation for now is probably over and it went far better than I imagined it could but I can't help pushing my luck. He's my child, my territory, my home; I can't let someone invade him without putting up a fight.

"Do you mind if I ask you if you've come to a decision about what Cam Jack talked to you about?"

"You mean what my dad talked to me about?"

I can tell by the catch in his voice and the expression on his face that he's feeling sentimental. It reminds me far too much of the pathetic eagerness that used to shine in his eyes each time he met one of my dates.

"Yes," I concede, "what your dad wanted."

He studies the floor for a moment. When he looks up at me again, he looks more hurt than angry, more purely sad than frustrated.

"If he had asked me for my kidney, I would have given it to him," he tells me. "But he offered to buy it."

His expression turns sour then becomes one of utter disbelief.

"He didn't even try to deal with me like I was a decent person."

A wealth of comments regarding Cam Jack and decency leap to my lips, but I hold them all back.

"Do you think I'm crazy?" he goes on. "It's a lot of money. An unbelievable amount of money. And we're going to need it."

"What are you talking about? We?"

"She's my cousin," he explains, looking down at the baby in my arms. "She's my responsibility, too. She's going to need health insurance."

I smile at my boy.

"Don't worry. We'll find a way to get by. We always do. And I don't think you're crazy. I think you're the most decent man I know."

He bends his face down toward the baby.

"Can you stay?" I ask him. "I think Dusty would like it if you could hang out for awhile."

"Did he get a call from Cam Jack?" he asks eagerly. "Did he offer him a job?"

"Not exactly. I think Dusty should tell you what happened."

"I'm about to go off duty. Ivan already said I can stay if I want to. I'll just need a ride home later."

The crowd around George breaks up reluctantly.

"See you later, Josephine," Ivan says to the baby on his way past.

"Josephine?"

"It's the name Aunt Shannon put on the birth certificate," Clay explains. "Josephine Beverly Penrose."

"Hey, how about that?" E.J. says, smiling over at Dusty, the other representative from the Jolly Mount Five.

Fanci wrinkles up her nose.

"That's a stupid name. It's a name for an old lady. I'm going to call her Josie."

"Josie," I try it out. "I like it."

"One more thing." Ivan hands me an envelope. "For you. From your sister."

I take it from him and know in my heart it will be the last time I hear from her. I don't hurt as much as I think I should, but I still feel as sad as I've always felt at losing Shannon.

"What do you think, Josie?" I coo to the baby as we all walk into the living room. "Who should hold you? Dusty is a pro with babies. There's no challenge there. And E.J. will probably break out in some kind of commitment rash if he holds you. And Clay already got to hold you today. How about your old pal, Fanci? Remember her?"

Fanci takes a seat on the couch, and I place Josephine gently in her arms.

"Watch her head," Dusty and I say in unison.

I leave them for a moment, with Kenny and E.J. staring intently at the baby's skull, and walk into my well-lit kitchen to read the letter.

Dear Shae-Lynn,

I know you didn't believe my retirement story and you were right but part of it was true. I did come home looking for a safe place to hide, only I wasn't hiding from barren women and blood-sucking lawyers or even from the baby's father. I think I was hiding from the thing I came looking for, my past. I think I can deal with it now.

I'm glad I got to see you and Clay. It's funny but when the two of you moved away all those years ago I always knew in my heart you'd come back to Jolly Mount. I knew you were going to need to live here just like I knew I was going to need to stay away, but I've decided even if I can't stay I should still leave a part of me here.

Thanks for everything.

Your Sister Mine,
Shannon

P.S. I always saved these not to remember Mom since I never knew her but to remember you. I guess that says something. I don't need them anymore. Maybe someday you can show them to Josephine and tell her where they came from . . .

I stare at the mysterious postscript, then notice something bulky at the bottom of the envelope.

I reach inside and pull out four strips of old faded fabric: purple satin, pink flannel, tiny green leaves on scarlet cotton, and a piece of a rainbow. Each piece was once lovingly touched by my mother's hands in the hopes of making something lasting and pretty that would keep my feet warm.

I take the four strands and braid them together before there's any chance one of them can get lost.

Acknowledgments

MANY THANKS to my agent, Liza Dawson, who with her usual calm weathered my bouts of self-doubt and patiently coaxed me into finding the story I always knew was there.

To my editor, Shaye Areheart, thank you for providing *Sister Mine* with a loving, devoted, and very enthusiastic home.

A special thanks to my sister, Molly, and her husband, Shawn, for providing me with firsthand insight into the highs and lows of a life in law enforcement.

As always, thank you, Mom, for your constant love, support, and Bloody Marys at the Autoport.

To my children, Tirzah and Connor, who are my greatest works of art. Thank you for being such good kids.

To Bernard, who I could never thank in a few words, for everything he's done for me as my soul mate, as a fellow artist who understands the life, and as the brilliant translator of my novels into French—so I will thank him for one thing only and that is the confidence his love has given me to follow my instincts and my heart as a woman and a writer.

And finally, I'd like to thank all the coal miners—working, retired, disabled, and unemployed—and all the children and spouses and grandchildren of miners who have contacted me and expressed how much my books have meant to them as honest, heartfelt explanations of what life was like growing up in these communities and being part of the mining culture. Your affirmation means a great deal to me.

Even though I left the mining town where I grew up and lived for many years in the Chicago area, my heart always stayed there. I've recently been able to move back to Pennsylvania, and I've never been happier.

It's good to be home.

About the Author

TAWNI O'DELL is the *New York Times* bestselling author of *Coal Run* and *Back Roads*, which was also an Oprah's Book Club selection. She lives in Pennsylvania with her two children and her husband, literary translator Bernard Cohen.